PRAISE FOR ROBERT BAILEY

"*The Professor* is that rare combination of thrills, chills, and heart. Gripping from the first page to the last."

—Winston Groom, author of *Forrest Gump*

"Legal thrillers shouldn't be this much fun and a new writer shouldn't be this good at crafting a great twisty story. If you enjoy Grisham as much as I do, you're going to love Bob Bailey."

—Brian Haig, author of *The Night Crew*
and the Sean Drummond series

"Robert Bailey is a thriller writer to reckon with. His debut novel has a tight and twisty plot, vivid characters, and a pleasantly down-home sensibility that will remind some readers of adventures in Grisham-land. Luckily, Robert Bailey is an original, and his skill as a writer makes the Alabama setting all his own. *The Professor* marks the beginning of a very promising career."

—Mark Childress, author of *Georgia Bottoms*
and *Crazy in Alabama*

"Taut, page turning, and smart, *The Professor* is a legal thriller that will keep readers up late as the twists and turns keep coming. Set in Alabama, it also includes that state's greatest icon, one Coach Bear Bryant. In fact, the Bear gets things going with the energy of an Alabama kickoff to Auburn. Robert Bailey knows his state and he knows his law. He also knows how to write characters that are real, sympathetic, and surprising. If he keeps writing novels this good, he's got quite a literary career before him."

—Homer Hickam, author of *Rocket Boys/October Sky*,
a *New York Times* number one bestseller

BETWEEN BLACK AND WHITE

ALSO BY ROBERT BAILEY

McMurtrie and Drake Legal Thrillers
The Professor

BETWEEN BLACK AND WHITE

ROBERT BAILEY

THOMAS & MERCER

This is a work of fiction. Names, characters, organizations, places, events, and incidents are either products of the author's imagination or are used fictitiously.

Published by Thomas & Mercer, Seattle

www.apub.com

Amazon, the Amazon logo, and Thomas & Mercer are trademarks of Amazon.com Inc. or its affiliates.

ISBN-13: 9781503953079
ISBN-10: 1503953076

Cover design by Brian Zimmerman

Printed in the United States of America

For my mom and dad, Beth and Randy Bailey

PROLOGUE

Pulaski, Tennessee, August 18, 1966

The boy sat on the floor in the den of the two-bedroom shack, listening to the Cardinals game on the radio and practicing his only vice—chewing a big wad of bubble gum. His mother was still at the Big House, cleaning up after the party, but his father had just gotten home, his job done for the night. The boy lay on his back, blowing bubbles and throwing a baseball up in the air and catching it with his mitt.

The gunshots startled him.

They came from outside the house. Two blasts from a twelve-gauge. The boy was only five years old, but he knew what a shotgun sounded like. His father had taken him hunting several times, and he had fired one himself the last time they went. The boy scrambled to his feet and looked out the window.

He saw a wooden cross. Like the cross behind where the preacher spoke at church. It was on fire. Behind the burning cross were men dressed in costumes. Long white robes covered their bodies, and white hoods masked their faces. Holes had been cut out of the hoods for their eyes. All of them held shotguns across their body. One of the men stood a couple feet in front of the others and wore a darker hood than the rest. In the glow from the burning cross and the half moon above, this man's hood appeared to be red.

With one arm the man with the red hood raised his shotgun and fired twice more in the air. The boy jumped back, then knelt to the floor and crawled closer to the window, peeking over the edge of the sill. As he did, Red Hood spoke.

"Roosevelt Haynes, get your ass out here!"

The voice, rough and deep, sounded familiar to the boy, and he felt the hair on his arms begin to rise.

"Roosevelt, I know you're in there!" Red Hood continued, taking a step forward. "Don't make us tear down that door!" The voice was louder. Closer. And the boy definitely recognized it.

"Daddy?" the boy called out, his heartbeat thudding in his chest. "Daddy, what is Mr. Walton—?"

A large hand clasped around the boy's mouth, drowning out his words. The boy started to scream but then relaxed as he heard his father speaking softly in his ear. "Easy now, Bo, let me see."

Then, slowly removing his hand from the boy's mouth, Franklin Roosevelt Haynes peered out the window.

"Damn."

It was only a whisper, but the boy, who was kneeling just inches away from his father, heard it. "Daddy?" the boy whimpered.

Roosevelt ducked down and brought his index finger to his lips, shaking his head at the boy. Then he peered over the sill again. This time he said nothing, but his shoulders slumped, and a noise escaped his lungs that sounded like the moan of a wounded animal. Barefoot and shirtless, crouching below the window in the red pajama bottoms he wore every night at bedtime, Roosevelt covered his face with his hands and mumbled something that the boy couldn't understand.

For the first time in the boy's life, his father—a stocky, barrel-chested man who could handle cows and other livestock like they were rag dolls—looked small. Fear slithered up the boy's chest and took hold of his heart like a boa constrictor. "Daddy?"

Finally, Roosevelt removed his hands from his face and turned his eyes toward the boy. With their heads almost touching, Roosevelt spoke into the boy's ear. "Bo, I need you to promise me a few things."

The boy started to cry and turned his head away from his father.

"Damnit, Bo, look at me." Roosevelt grabbed the boy's shoulders and shook them, and the boy did as he was told. "Bo, this is goin' be hard on your momma. Promise me that you'll take care of her."

Roosevelt stole a glance out the window, and the boy heard Red Hood's voice again.

"Roosevelt, you got twenty seconds! Then we set fire to the house."

The other men began to chant something in a low hum, but the boy couldn't make out what they were saying. His father faced him again, still holding tight to his shoulders.

"Promise me, son."

The boy's teeth chattered. It was ninety-five degrees outside. Deep in the dog days of August. There was no air conditioning in the shack, but the boy was freezing. His tears had dried.

"I promise, Daddy."

"Promise me that you'll make something of yourself, son, you hear me? Make something of yourself." His father shook him, and the boy nodded.

"All right, nigger!" The voice was even louder. Closer to the house. "Ten seconds!"

His father didn't budge, his eyes focused on the boy. "Bo, you probably goin' hear things about this. About why they done this. Don't believe 'em. Not a word. You promise?"

"Ten!... nine!..." Red Hood began the countdown, but Roosevelt still did not move, waiting for Bo to answer.

"I promise, Daddy."

"One day your momma . . . she'll tell you everything, you understand?"

Bo nodded, and his father hugged him hard—so hard it hurt a little—and kissed the boy on the cheek.

"Six! . . . Five! . . ."

Roosevelt stood and took two steps toward the front door.

Fighting back fresh tears, the boy lunged for his father, grabbing him around the ankles and squeezing as tight as he could. "Don't go, Daddy. Please don't go."

Roosevelt knelt and gently removed the boy's hands, holding them in his own. "Bo . . ."

The boy looked up into his father's eyes.

"I love you, son."

"Three! . . . Two! . . ."

"I . . . I love you too, Daddy." The boy choked the words out as snot began to run out of his nose and his eyes clouded over with tears. "Please . . . don't . . ."

His father grabbed the doorknob and turned it. "All right now, I'm coming out!" Before he shut the door behind him, Roosevelt Haynes looked at the boy one last time.

"Don't watch this, Bocephus. Whatever you do, don't watch this."

If only the boy had listened . . .

PART ONE

1

Pulaski, Tennessee, August 18, 2011

By 10:30 p.m. the front parlor of Kathy's Tavern was almost deserted. The four tables were empty, and there were only two men sitting on opposite ends of the long rectangular bar.

One of the men was Clete Sartain, who had just finished his evening shift as a salesclerk at the Johnson's Foodtown grocery store. At seventy-four years old, Clete had a snow-white beard and weighed close to three hundred pounds. Every year for the past two decades he'd played Santa Claus during the Christmas festival downtown. When he wasn't sacking groceries or playing Kris Kringle, Clete liked to down a few Natural Lights and listen to country music, both of which were readily available at Kathy's on Thursday nights.

In the back, a 1980s country cover band was playing "I Love a Rainy Night" by Eddie Rabbitt, and Clete tapped his foot to the music and took a long swallow of beer. The back room at Kathy's had several tables and a stage in the rear, and based on the squeals and Bo Duke–style yee-haws from the crowd, the song choice was a popular one. Live music always drew a good turnout at Kathy's, and from Clete's perch at the end of the bar closest to the back he counted at least fifteen, maybe twenty folks.

Taking another sip of beer, Clete let his eyes drift toward the man seated at the other end of the bar.

With dark-brown skin and a smoothly shaven head, Bocephus Aurulius Haynes had always reminded Clete of that boxer from the '80s, "Marvelous" Marvin Hagler. Of course, Hagler had been a middleweight, and Bocephus Haynes stood six feet four inches tall and weighed well over two hundred pounds—a heavyweight if there ever was one. And though he'd blown his knee out playing football for Bear Bryant at Alabama, Bo still carried the athletic frame of a middle linebacker. Even now, pushing fifty years old and wearing khaki suit pants with a blue shirt, tie undone, and smoking a cigar, Bo was an intimidating sight.

Seeming to sense that someone was staring at him, Bo shifted in his stool and glared toward the other end of the bar.

"Something on your mind, dog?"

Clete held up his hands and smiled, though his entire body had tensed. "Naw, Bo. Just got tired of looking at my ugly reflection in the mirror. You doing all right? How's the law practice? Did you sue anyone today?" Clete smiled, but his heart had begun to thump harder in his chest under the heat of Bo's gaze.

For a couple seconds Bo said nothing, ignoring the questions and just staring at Clete. Then: "You know what day today is, Clete?"

Clete blinked. "Uh, it's Thursday I think." When Bo didn't answer him, Clete shot a glance at the bartender, a cute brunette named Cassie Dugan. "Right, Cassie?"

Cassie was washing a pint glass with a rag. She met Clete's gaze and gave him a concerned look, shaking her head.

"It's not Thursday?" Clete asked, now confused. How many beers had he drunk?

"It is Thursday," Bo said, his voice reeking with bitterness. "Thursday, *August the eighteenth*." Bo paused, turning in his stool so he could face Clete. "You know what happened forty-five years ago on this very day?"

Clete's eyes narrowed and his stomach tightened. Sweat beads began to break out on his forehead. He got it now.

"You were there, weren't you, Clete?" Bo said, sliding off the stool and walking the fifteen feet down the bar. "You were in the Klan then, weren't you? One of Andy Walton's *boys*?"

Bo leaned close to Clete and blew a cloud of cigar smoke into his face. "Answer me."

Clete pushed back his stool and threw a ten-dollar bill on the counter. "Keep the change, Cassie."

When he tried to leave, Bo stepped in front of him.

"Bo, I . . . didn't . . . mean to cause no trouble," Clete said, his voice shaking.

"Did you see my daddy's neck stretch, Clete?" Bo leaned in close, and Clete smelled the strong scent of bourbon and cigar on his breath. "Could you hear him gasping for breath?"

"That's enough, Bo," Cassie said from behind the bar. "I'm going to have to ask you to leave if you don't stop."

"I could, Clete," Bo said, speaking through clenched teeth. "I was five years old and I saw it all . . . and I heard it all."

Clete lowered his eyes, unable to stand the intensity of Bo's glare anymore. "Bo, I just want to—"

"What's going on up here?" The voice, rough and gravel-like, came from the back, and Clete had to blink his eyes to see who it was. The music had stopped, and a man was walking toward him. When he saw who it was, his bladder almost gave.

Andrew Davis Walton stepped into the front parlor flanked by his wife, Maggie, and his brother-in-law, Dr. George Curtis. Andy was a tall, angular man, much thinner now than he had been in the old days.

"Well, look what the cat drug in," Bo said, firmly shoving Clete to the side. "You must have entered through the back," Bo said, lowering his head so that he was almost nose to nose with Andy. "Ain't no way you would walk in here *on this night* with me sitting at the bar."

Andy's voice and gaze never wavered. He looked directly at Bo as Maggie and George shot nervous glances at each other behind them. Clete wanted to just sneak on out the door, but he found that he couldn't move his feet.

"We've been here a while, Bo. Today is Maggie's birthday, and we came here to celebrate." He paused. "She likes this kind of music."

Bo's eyes moved past Andy to the woman standing behind him. Maggie Curtis Walton, called "Ms. Maggie" by everyone in Pulaski, was a petite woman with an elegant sheen of white hair that fell just above her shoulders. She had crystal-blue eyes, which were focused on Bo now with what looked like pity.

"Today is kind of a *special* day for me too," Bo said, turning his gaze back to Andy. "Remember why?"

Andy said nothing, continuing to look at Bo. He moved his right foot back a step and clenched his fists, assuming a fighter's stance.

Bo laughed, dropped his cigar to the floor, and stomped on it so hard that Maggie Walton jumped back. "I'd like to see you try it, old man."

"We're gonna leave now, Bo," Andy said. "If you don't get out of the way, I'm going to have Cassie call the police." He glanced at the bartender, but Bo kept his eyes fixed on Andy.

"I'll do it too, Bo," Cassie said, her voice high and panicky. "I ought to do it anyway. You're scaring everyone off."

The remaining patrons in the back were beginning to walk around them and heading for the front door, but Clete Sartain's feet remained glued to the floor. If Bo attacked Andy, Clete figured it would take him and George both to get him off.

Ignoring Cassie, Bo leaned forward and spoke directly into Andy's ear. *"But if there is serious injury, you are to take life for life, eye for eye, tooth for tooth, hand for hand, foot for foot, burn for burn, wound for wound, bruise for bruise."* Bo paused, adding, "Exodus chapter twenty-one, verses twenty-one through twenty-three." Bo turned to Clete, who had heard every word and was chilled to the bone. "You know your Old Testament, Clete?"

Clete said nothing, and Bo returned his gaze to Andy. "How about you, dog? Do you understand the message?"

Andy also remained quiet, and the bar was stone silent.

"Then let me break it down for you, twenty-first-century style," Bo said, pausing and sticking his index finger hard into Andy's chest. "You're gonna bleed, motherfucker. If it's the last thing I do on this earth, I'm going to make you pay for your sins—*eye for eye, tooth for tooth."*

"Bo, damnit," Cassie started, but Bo took a step back, looking them all in the eye one last time. Then he turned away and slowly walked back to his place at the bar.

For a moment the four remaining patrons just stood there, not knowing what to do next. Then, finally able to move again, Clete Sartain nodded at Andy and walked briskly out of the bar. Andy returned the gesture and took his wife by the hand. "Let's go."

A few seconds later Bocephus Haynes was the only customer left at Kathy's Tavern.

———

Bo gazed into his empty whiskey glass, feeling adrenaline rage through his body. He hadn't seen Andy Walton out in public in almost a year. He had heard that Andy was basically a recluse these days, occasionally dropping in on one of his businesses but mostly just holed up on his farm. The last time Bo had seen him was at a gala the previous September to raise money for Martin College's theater program. They had shared a glare from across the auditorium, but that was it. It seemed almost surreal to see Andy at a normal place like Kathy's.

Of all the nights to run into that bastard, Bo thought. Shaking his head, he looked into the glass, not seeing the ice cubes beginning to melt from the heat of the Jim Beam he'd just consumed. Instead, he saw images of his father as Bo remembered him best, wearing a faded St. Louis Cardinals cap and pitching ball with Bo in the front yard of the two-bedroom shack.

The same yard where the men had come to take him. Andy's *boys.*

Forty-five years, Bo thought. Forty-five years . . .

Bo sighed and looked up from his glass, intending to ask Cassie for another drink, but the bartender wasn't there. He started to look around but then saw another woman's reflection in the glass mirror above the bar. He blinked his eyes, not trusting them for a moment as the woman approached and put a hand on his shoulder.

Over the years Maggie Walton's flowing blond hair had turned a regal white, but otherwise she seemed not to age—her eyes still crystal blue, her posture erect, and her demeanor always perfectly composed. Even now it was easy to see how she had been Ms. Tennessee runner-up in 1964.

"I think Cassie went to the restroom," Maggie said. "Bo—"

"I'm not in the mood for a lecture, Ms. Maggie. Now go on and leave me be." Bo's shoulders had tensed, and he grabbed his whiskey glass, rattling the cubes.

"I don't care what you're in the mood for, Bo. I'm going to say what I have to say and then I'm going to leave."

Bo said nothing, waiting. Since he had moved back to Pulaski after law school in 1985, Maggie Walton had approached him on numerous occasions, asking him to leave her family alone, and he figured this would be no different. He would be respectful and polite, but he would not grant her request. He would never leave Andy Walton alone.

"He's dying, Bo," Maggie said, her voice solemn.

The words hit him like a bolt of lightning. He raised his eyes and met Maggie's gaze through the reflection in the glass.

"That was the real reason why we came here tonight—not my birthday. I wanted him to be around some of his friends. Do something normal. He . . . doesn't have long." She choked back a sob. "He has pancreatic cancer. Stage four. The oncologist says he's probably got about a month, but it could be less." She paused, and Bo saw her grit her teeth in the mirror. "I want you to let him die in peace, Bo. Do you hear me?"

Bo said nothing, still shocked by the news.

"You've spent every day of your life trying to make Andy's miserable, and it's time to let it go." She paused and crossed her arms. When Bo remained silent, she slammed her right fist onto the bar next to him and spoke through clenched teeth. "Hasn't this crusade cost you enough, Bo? Jasmine and the kids couldn't take it anymore, could they?"

Bo wheeled off his stool, his body shaking with anger. "Leave me alone, Ms. Maggie."

Maggie Walton had taken two steps back, but her eyes remained locked on Bo. "Could they?"

When Bo didn't answer, Maggie spoke in a calm, pitying voice. "You've lost your whole family, Bo. Has it been worth it?" She turned and walked to the door. Grabbing the knob, she spoke without looking at him. "I want my husband to die in peace."

2

Birthplace of the Ku Klux Klan . . .

It is the first thing anyone thinks of when Pulaski, Tennessee is mentioned. Google "Pulaski" on your computer, and the initial hits will show images of white-robed and hooded Klansmen marching on the Giles County Courthouse Square and carrying Confederate battle flags. Within the first few paragraphs of any newspaper article written on or about the town, you will see the words "birthplace of the Ku Klux Klan." It is an inescapable and unavoidable part of Pulaski's past.

On Christmas Eve, 1865, just eight months after General Robert E. Lee surrendered at Appomattox, six Confederate veterans met at a building on West Madison Street in downtown Pulaski and formed what they called a "social club." Diversion and amusement were intended to be the club's aims—not vigilante justice and terrorism. "Ku Klux Klan" was chosen as the name, because it came from the Greek word *kyklos*, meaning circle of brothers.

Most white citizens of current-day Pulaski avoid talking about the Klan. However, if pressed, the standard reply is that the Ku Klux Klan of the 1950s and '60s, which used violence and terrorism to fight the civil rights movement, was not the group envisioned by the Pulaski founding fathers.

Bo chuckled bitterly as he peered at the commemorative plaque attached to the building on West Madison. After finally being cut off by Cassie, he'd left Kathy's Tavern and walked down First Street to his office, got a pint of Jim Beam out of the bottom drawer of his desk, and headed back into the night. He was shaken by the conversation with Ms. Maggie. Andy Walton had a month to live. *Maybe less . . .*

Bo needed to think, and his brain worked best on the move. He hadn't really planned on walking anywhere specific, but his legs had taken him here.

The road to hell is paved with good intentions, he thought, taking a sip of bourbon from the pint and spitting it on the plaque. Historians could spin the past however they wished. Bo had seen the Ku Klux Klan up close and personal through five-year-old eyes as they murdered his father.

And he'd spent a lifetime trying to put the men who did it in jail.

———

Bo had opened his law practice in September 1985, just a few months after graduating from the University of Alabama School of Law, and three weeks after his marriage to the lovely Jasmine Desiree Henderson. He'd done well in school, graduating in the top 10 percent of his class. Due to that success and his notoriety from being an Alabama football player with Coach Paul "Bear" Bryant's 1978 and '79 national champions, Bo had offers from numerous Birmingham, Huntsville, and Nashville law firms. Jazz had all but begged Bo to accept an offer in Huntsville, where she had grown up and where her parents still lived.

But Bo would have none of it. From the moment he was accepted to law school, he'd known where he would practice.

Home.

Reluctantly, Jazz had agreed. Pulaski was only forty-five minutes from Huntsville, and despite being the birthplace of the KKK it was also the home of Martin Methodist College, an outstanding liberal arts school, where Jazz eventually accepted a position as an art history professor.

Bo had never lied to his wife about his motives for going home. "I have to bring the men that killed my father to justice."

Jazz said she understood and, at least in the early years, grew to embrace Pulaski.

The 1980s were a tumultuous time in Giles County, and Bo and Jazz moved back right when things were heating up. In 1985 the United States government declared that the third Monday in January would be celebrated as Martin Luther King Jr. Day. In the South the same day had historically been known as Robert E. Lee Day or Lee–Jackson Day in honor of the two famous Confederate generals.

The uproar was immediate, and Pulaski became a battleground. The Ku Klux Klan staged rallies in January of 1986, 1987, and 1988 on the Giles County Courthouse Square, and other Klan groups held additional rallies throughout the year in Pulaski. These groups of Klansmen would stand in line to kiss the commemorative plaque that Bo gazed at now, literally bowing down to it like they were visiting a shrine.

That is, they did until August 1989, when Donald Massey, the owner of the building, removed the plaque and welded it back on backwards. Bo ran his hand along the blank back side of the plaque, which was colored in green and black. Over the two decades since Massey's grand gesture, Bo had seen tourists come and look for the plaque, ambling around downtown like zombies, unable to find it without it being pointed out to them. Bo had always lauded

Massey's reversal of the plaque as the perfect response. A figurative way for the town to turn its back on its unsavory past. Pulaski couldn't disclaim the fact that the Ku Klux Klan breathed its first air downtown. But the town could fight back.

That sense of fight was never more evident than in October 1989, when just a couple months after Donald Massey reversed the commemorative plaque, the entire town of Pulaski shut down in response to the Ku Klux Klan's decision to host a rally with the Aryan Nation on the courthouse square. On the day of the march, over 180 businesses, including Bo's law office, closed in protest of the rally. Wreaths colored in orange, the international color of brotherhood, covered the town. Outside of one lone gas station that remained open, Pulaski, Tennessee had turned into a ghost town—at least for one day.

Jazz, whose parents had both marched with Dr. King in Selma, rallied behind the town's struggle for separation from its Klan past. She and Bo became charter members of Giles County United, a group formed to counter the Klan's rallies and which spearheaded the 1989 boycott.

When he looked back on it, Bo knew that those early days were probably the happiest of their marriage. He also knew that, while Jazz's motives in participating in the town's pushback against the Klan rallies of the late '80s were pure, his own were selfish. He wanted the town to also embrace his own personal quest for justice against Andy Walton and the other members of the KKK that lynched his father on this very night forty-five years earlier.

But he could never garner any support for his cause. The excuses that each sheriff and district attorney that came into office gave were always the same. Bo had only been five years old when he "allegedly" saw his father lynched; Bo was the only eyewitness who had ever come forward; Bo could not see any of the men's faces; Bo's father's body was found in the pond by the clearing, and it was an undisputed fact that Roosevelt Haynes couldn't swim.

All they had to go on was the word of a five-year-old boy that he recognized Andy Walton's voice, and that wasn't enough.

Bo knew they were right—he knew he needed more evidence—but he also knew that the town had an ulterior motive in keeping the truth behind his father's murder buried. Pulaski already had enough bad publicity as the birthplace of the Ku Klux Klan. It didn't need to add a Klan lynching to its résumé. Unless Bo could bring forward conclusive evidence, the town was content to let sleeping dogs lie.

Sighing, Bo lit a cigar and trudged aimlessly up Madison Street.

———

Ten minutes later he stood in the grass in front of his home on Flower Street. Stomping out the cigar on the curb, he took a belt of whiskey and gazed gloomily at the "For Sale" sign that had gone up thirty days earlier. He knew they were asking too much, but his pride wouldn't let him go lower. He didn't need the money from a sale, so . . .

. . . it sat here. Like a monument to his failure at marriage and fatherhood. Bo closed his eyes, and he immediately became dizzy, the alcohol finally working its magic. He staggered forward and almost fell, catching himself with his left hand on the grass, while his right hand brought the pint bottle to his lips again. He heard Ms. Maggie's sharp voice play in his mind over and over again. *"Hasn't this crusade cost you enough, Bo?"*

A minute later he was ambling through the empty house. They had bought it when T. J. was two and Lila was just a baby—a response to needing more space. And from the second they walked in the door, it had been Jazz's pride and joy. For almost two years she had directed a remodeling project, the goal of which was to preserve the historic nature of the home while doubling the square footage.

Mission accomplished, Bo thought, as he admired the hardwood floors, high ceilings, and oversized kitchen. And though the house had always given Bo a great sense of satisfaction—who woulda thunk that a dirt-poor black kid, the son of a murdered father and a mother who abandoned him, could grow up to own one of the nicest homes in all of Giles County?—it had never given him any joy. Truth was he was hardly ever here, and even when he was his mind was always elsewhere. Bo worked his cases daylight to dark, and during the evening hours he investigated his father's murder. Since 1985 Bo had tried forty-five cases to a jury's verdict, winning every trial but one. Initially, he cracked his teeth on workers' compensation and pissant criminal defense matters, but things changed in 1993 when he hit Walton Chevrolet for one point five million in an SUV rollover case. In the blink of an eye, Bo was catapulted into the world of big-time personal injury plaintiffs' cases, and the victory was extra sweet because it came at the expense of Andy Walton's dealership. During this same time frame, Bo figured that he had spoken with over one hundred current and former members of the Tennessee Knights of the Ku Klux Klan, which, at the time of his father's death, had over two thousand members. Bo knew if he could just get one former Klansman to roll on Andy, the floodgates would open.

But despite his dogged efforts, he had failed. In fact, the only thing his investigation had done was bring danger to his family. Bo had lost count of how many times bricks had been thrown into windows of his home or he'd woken up in the morning to see the tires on his vehicle slashed. For the most part these actions were a mere annoyance, causing frustration and tension in his marriage and family life but nothing more.

But things changed last spring when Ferriday Montaigne, a local bricklayer whom Bo had long suspected was present for his daddy's hanging, asked Bo to visit him in the hospital. Ferriday had lung cancer and was dying. Bo had gone to the hospital, sensing that he was about to finally learn the truth, but Ferriday's wife, on the advice of her husband's physician, Dr. George Curtis, wouldn't let Bo inside the room.

Frustrated, Bo had gone home that night and was greeted by a crying Jazz, who pushed a manila envelope into his chest and stormed back to their bedroom, slamming the door. Inside the package were two photographs, one of T. J. stepping out of his car at Giles County High, the other of Lila walking out the side door of their home. In each of the pictures T. J.'s and Lila's faces were in the crosshairs of a rifle scope. There was no cover letter included with the photographs, but the message came through loud and clear.

Jazz was inconsolable. "Bo, your quest for vengeance may cost you your life. I can deal with that. I signed up for that when we married. But I will not, *can not*, let you subject our children to danger. Will you give it up? Tell me you will give it up right now."

When Bo didn't answer, Jazz started packing. She was gone the next day, taking the kids to her parents' home in Huntsville and telling Bo to sell the house. And though she hadn't officially filed the papers yet, Bo knew it was only a matter of time before he was greeted by a process server. Jazz had already accepted a professorial position at Alabama A&M in Huntsville and enrolled the kids in the Huntsville city schools. *She's moving on . . .*

Bo took a long, slow sip of Jim Beam and did one last sweep of the house, remembering T. J.'s and Lila's rooms as they had once been. A fish tank over the dresser next to his daughter's bed. Posters of the Pirates' right fielder Andrew McCutchen and the Saints' running back, Mark Ingram, on the walls in T. J.'s room. Now the walls were completely bare, save a strand of leftover Scotch tape.

Bo stopped when he made it to the kitchen. Through the double glass doors that led out to the backyard, he saw the only remaining holdover of his former life. A swing set, rusted from years of rain and use. Bo wished he could say he remembered pushing his daughter and son on that set, but he couldn't. His only memory was staring at it through the empty kitchen as he did now. The only difference between that memory and tonight was that his wife and kids weren't asleep in their rooms.

They were gone, and Bocephus Haynes was alone in the world. Again . . .

Bo took another sip of whiskey and felt the alcohol burn his throat while the words of Maggie Walton torched his soul.

Then he locked up and stumbled outside, the reality of his predicament closing in around him like a solar eclipse. He had run out of time.

Andy Walton was going to die before Bo could bring him to justice.

3

The stripper's real name was Darla Ford. "Nikita" was her stage name, but it didn't suit her. "Nikita" made Andy Walton think of a tall, thin Russian woman with a sexy foreign accent. A Bond girl.

Darla Ford was none of those things. Five foot three with heels on, bleached blond hair, a voluptuous, almost-plump body, and a syrupy Tennessee accent, Darla was not 007's type. Truth be known, she was a little wide in the hips to usually fit the bill for Andy, but Andy Walton had long since understood that you couldn't typecast sex appeal. When Andy was around Darla Ford, he wanted her. She had "it," whatever "it" was.

"Closing time, Mr. Walton," Darla said.

He had been watching her put her clothes back on, which consisted of a black T-shirt strategically torn down the middle to show her cleavage, and blue jean Daisy Duke cutoffs. One of Darla's many charms was that she still called him Mr. Walton, despite the fact that he had been a regular customer of hers for almost a year. He asked her about it once, and she just said it didn't feel right calling him Andy. She was twenty-five, and he was over seventy. It would be "disrespectful" to call him by his first name.

Andy smiled at the memory. People called him Mr. Walton all day long, but when the words came out of Darla Ford's mouth, they made him hard. Even now, after having enjoyed Darla's talents for over an hour, he still felt the tingle. Seventy-three years old, and he could feel the beginning of an erection thirty minutes after his last one.

Darla Ford was a goddamn miracle.

Two minutes later Andy stepped out the front door of the Sundowners Club and breathed in the humid August air. Even at just past one in the morning, the temperature must have still been in the low nineties. Andy took a long drink from a tall Styrofoam cup and closed his eyes, hoping for the slightest hint of a breeze. The bartender, whom Darla and the other dancers called Saint Peter, had fixed him a Long Island Iced Tea for the road. Even on top of the three bourbons he'd had earlier in the night at Kathy's Tavern and the two beers he'd consumed inside the Sundowners, the drink tasted good and strong.

"You sure you're OK to drive, Mr. Walton?" Darla's voice came from behind him, and Andy opened his eyes. She and Saint Peter were coming out of the door, a set of keys in the bartender's hands.

"I'm fine, darlin'," he said, smiling down on her.

Darla stood on her tiptoes and gave him a soft peck on the cheek. "Be careful," she whispered. Their eyes held for just a moment, and Andy knew her admonition had nothing to do with drinking and driving. She licked her thumb and dabbed his cheek where her lipstick had left a mark. "Promise?"

"Promise," Andy said, squeezing her hand and taking another sip of the Long Island tea.

"He doesn't have far to go," Saint Peter said after locking the door. He winked at Andy, and Andy nodded.

When Peter Burns had been a teenager, he had worked three summers on Andy's farm, doing odd jobs and fixer-upper projects. Live and work in a place for five decades, and you touch a lot of folks. Some in a good way. Some bad. Andy figured his impact on Peter was positive, but who the hell knew? The boy had grown up to pour whiskey at a strip club on the edge of town. He probably wouldn't be giving many speeches in his life thanking those that made it all possible. And what of Darla? She was a twenty-five-year-old stripper making a few extra bucks by sucking Andy's seventy-three-year-old dick in the upstairs VIP room of the same place.

Just give me the Nobel Peace Prize, Andy thought, watching as the cars driven by the bartender and the stripper pulled out of the gravel parking lot. The only vehicle left was Andy's rusty, gray Chevy Silverado truck, and he trudged toward it, feeling old and depressed.

He hadn't planned on visiting Darla tonight, but the confrontation with Bo Haynes had put him on edge. He had told Maggie that he needed to "go out for a while," and she had surprisingly not fussed over him, even though it was her birthday. He figured she probably knew where he went on nights like this—he had never made much effort to hide his nocturnal adventures—but since the death sentence had been handed down by his oncologist last fall, Maggie had finally and mercifully decided to look the other way.

The neon lights of the Sundowners Club flickered off, and Andy blinked to adjust to the darkness. The lot was now almost pitch dark, the only light coming from the half moon above. He fumbled for the keys in his pocket, finally finding them and clicking the unlock button on the keyless entry.

When he climbed into the front seat of the truck, he immediately noticed it. The smell . . . He turned quickly, but there was no one in the truck. But there had been, he knew. The smell was unmistakable. And vaguely familiar. Like a stale cigar . . .

His heartbeat now racing, he placed the key in the ignition but hesitated before turning it. *Be careful,* he thought, hearing Darla's soft voice in his mind.

Andy Walton had made a lot of enemies in his seventy-three years. Funny thing, when you were once the Imperial Wizard of the Tennessee Knights of the Ku Klux Klan, people tended to hold a grudge. Didn't matter what a man had done since. That he had donated hundreds of thousands of dollars to the local college, that the farm was now leased by a black man who utilized black laborers, or that his businesses employed over 10 percent of the people of Giles County.

None of that made one tinker's damn. He had once worn the robe and hood. People had a long memory when it came to the Klan.

Andy tapped his fingers on the steering wheel, thinking again about the run-in with Bo Haynes at Kathy's Tavern. The hate he had seen in Bo's eyes.

Forty-five years ago, Andy and nine other members of the Tennessee Knights had lynched a black field hand named Roosevelt Haynes on Walton Farm. Roosevelt was a meddler and had to be dealt with. Andy knew that he would have eventually been able to forgive himself for the killing.

If only the boy hadn't seen. If only Bo . . .

Andy closed his eyes and turned the key. The truck didn't explode, and truth be known, Andy hadn't thought it would. But he had enemies, and he was about to make a few more.

Andy Walton was an old man. A man who had put down the robe and hood of the Ku Klux Klan in 1976 and made millions in the stock market. So much so that *Newsweek* did an article on him in 1987. "The Warren Buffett of the South" it had been entitled. The article hadn't left out Andy's Klan history but focused on how he had reinvented himself as a financial wizard. The theme was that money didn't care what a man's social beliefs had been. Money had no conscience.

Unfortunately, Andy Walton did have a conscience. And for forty-five years, it had eaten at him. Ever since he had looked through the holes of the hood and into the terrified eyes of the boy. And heard his screams.

He could still hear them at night. They came to him in his dreams.

Andy also had stage four pancreatic cancer. He was going to die in a month, and he wanted the screams to stop before he did. He wanted . . . what did the shrinks call it? Closure.

He knew he would probably still end up in hell—he had done too many bad things in his life. But maybe he wouldn't have a front row seat.

Andy put the truck in reverse, feeling a deep resolve come over him. Now was the time, he knew. *Right now.* If he delayed much longer, it might be too late.

Gazing through the windshield, he saw that Highway 64 was deserted. The ride to the sheriff's office would take no more than ten minutes. The story he would tell would take longer, but he doubted Ennis would mind. Andy eased his foot off the brake and started to back out.

He stopped when he saw the figure in the rearview mirror, blocking his path.

Andy slammed the gear back in park and reached under the seat for his pistol. He usually kept it . . .

It wasn't there. *Damnit*, he thought, remembering the familiar scent he had inhaled when he had first opened the truck.

He looked in the rearview mirror again, but the figure was gone. He spun around, blinking his eyes and trying to focus them in the darkness, seeing nothing. "Where—?"

Four loud knocks came from the driver's-side window.

Andy spun toward the sound, his heart pounding in his chest. Then as his sight adjusted, recognition slowly set in. "Jesus Christ," he said. Sighing, he rubbed his eyes and clicked the automatic button for the window to lower.

It was halfway down when he saw the shotgun pointed at his head.

Andy chuckled bitterly. "So you're gonna shoot me, huh?" He started to say more, but then he saw the thumb click the safety of the gun off.

His question had just been answered. Andy looked into the cold eyes. "Well . . . fuck you then," Andy said.

Funny thing what a man does when he knows he's about to die. Andy Walton didn't try to open the door or fight, and he didn't duck. Instead, he slowly turned his head and looked out the windshield toward Highway 64.

Into the darkness.

The gun fired, but Andy didn't hear the sound of the blast before the shot entered his brain and killed him.

He only heard the screams of the boy . . .

4

The 911 call was made at 2:30 a.m.

"Emergency Services," a monotone female voice answered. "What is your emergency?"

"Yeah, I'm a long-haul trucker and I just passed a brush fire off Highway 64 about a half mile west of the Sundowners Club. Looks like it might be on part of Walton Farm. There's a lot of smoke. If the fire department doesn't get out there fast, the whole place is going to be up in flames."

"Thank you, sir. Can you—?"

The phone went dead on the other end of the line.

5

The fire trucks arrived at 2:54 a.m. Chief Woodrow "Woody" Monroe had been fast asleep when he received the call from dispatch and was still groggy as he walked through the tree-lined dirt path that led to the clearing. Woody had lived in Pulaski all of his life except for the eleven months he had spent in Vietnam in 1967 chasing Charlie. He had seen things during those 337 days in Southeast Asia that still haunted his dreams.

What he saw now as he stepped through the smoke and into the clearing was as bad as anything he'd seen in the Vietnamese jungle. "Oh, Jesus," he whispered, involuntarily retching and dropping his hands to his knees.

"Chief, are you all right?" A young sergeant, Bradley Hill, had put his arm around Woody. "Chief . . . ?"

"I'm OK, Brad. It's just . . ." He pointed, and Brad nodded, his eyes wide with shock and horror.

"I know, sir. What should we do?"

Woody started to respond, but his words were drowned out by the most piercing scream he had ever heard in his life. Woody turned to see a woman in a bathrobe, her hands covering her mouth.

Woody had known Maggie Walton for over fifty years, and he had never seen her outside her home when she wasn't dressed to the nines, her hair always perfectly coiffed. Now here she was, one of the wealthiest women in all of the state of Tennessee, dressed in a green bathrobe, her white tresses tousled all over her head, tears streaking her eyes.

"No!" she screamed, running toward the fire.

"Oh, shit," Woody said, stepping toward her, but she was already past him. "Ms. Maggie, you can't—"

"Andy!" she screamed. "Andy!" She fell to her knees ten feet from the flames.

"Ms. Maggie, you need to back away." Woody dropped to one knee beside her.

"Don't tell me what to do, Woody. This is my land. *Mine*. And that's . . ." She pointed. "That's . . . my . . . my . . . Andy!" She rose and tried to step closer to the fire, but Woody grabbed her around the waist and held tight. He felt the woman's strength as she tried to wiggle free from him. "Ms. Maggie, I'm so sorry."

Eventually, she stopped trying to break away from him and again fell to her knees. "Andy," she whimpered. "No."

"Chief Monroe, we have to—" Brad started, but Woody cut him off with a wave of his hand.

"The fire hasn't spread past that tree," Woody said, squinting harshly at the young sergeant. "We've probably got five minutes before it does. The sheriff will want photographs. Take at least five from every angle you can get. Then start hosing it down. Tell the other men to hold steady until you've taken the pictures. I've got to make some calls."

"Yes, sir."

As Brad began barking instructions to the other men, Woody took out his cell phone and dialed the home number of Sheriff Ennis Petrie.

On the fifth ring Ennis's groggy voice answered. "Hello."

"Ennis, we got a situation out here at Walton Farm."

"What is it?" the sheriff asked, his voice more alert.

Woody started to talk, and then another bloodcurdling scream came from below him, followed by a low, almost-guttural moan. "Ms. Maggie," Woody whispered, squatting and patting her back. Maggie Walton gazed with dead eyes toward the fire.

"What in the hell was that?" Ennis asked, now hyper.

"That was Maggie Walton, Sheriff. She's . . . very upset." He paused, turning away from the woman so she wouldn't hear what he was about to say. Glancing back at the fire, he spoke into the phone, forcing the tremor out of his voice. "Sheriff, Andy Walton's body is hanging from a tree on the northeast corner of his farm with a noose tied around his neck and one half of his face shot off. He's . . ." Woody Monroe paused, closing his eyes, this time unable to keep the whine from his voice as Maggie Walton continued to moan in agony behind him. "He's on fire, Ennis. He's been shot and hanged . . . and his body is on fire."

6

Bocephus Haynes opened his eyes when he heard the sirens.

He was still half-asleep, the dream lingering as it always did. Seeing his father's stretched neck. Flailing at his father's legs as they dangled below the branch of the tree. Hearing the laughter of the white-robed men mixed with his own screams . . .

He gazed upward at the ceiling fan as the sounds from the dream gradually subsided, replaced by the sirens. *Getting closer?*

Bo rolled out of bed, forcing himself to sit up straight, and the sudden movement made him dizzy. His throat felt like sandpaper, and when he tried to swallow he nearly gagged on the half-chewed cigar that still hung out of the corner of his mouth. He spat the remainder of the stogie on the floor and rose to his feet.

The nausea hit him like a freight train.

He stumbled through the law office to the back door, fumbling in the dark for the knob. He took hold and twisted, then stepped outside and vomited over the railing. Blinking his eyes and clutching the railing tightly, he vomited again. And again. Finally, after a last dry heave, he relaxed his frame and sat on the top step, placing his elbows on his knees and taking several deep breaths.

The sirens were now even louder, and the sound of them pounded in Bo's head as he began to look himself over. He was still wearing his clothes from the day before—khaki slacks, oxford button-down, and brown Allen Edmonds loafers. Since he'd moved out of the house and into the office, it wasn't unusual for him to have slept in his clothes, or, for that matter, his shoes. What caught his eye was the dried, caked mud covering the heels and soles of both loafers.

Bo blinked, his mind starting to work despite the horrific hangover. What happened last night?

Everything after he left Kathy's Tavern was a blur . . .

He slipped off his shoes and set them on the top step. Then he shuffled on socked feet back into the office. When he turned on the light in the hallway, he noticed that he had tracked mud the entire length of the hall. Looking through the open door of the library, he saw that the tracks ended at the pullout sofa he now called a bed. An empty pint of Jim Beam lay on its side, top off, on the hard-wood floor below the sofa. He must have dropped it there before he crashed. Again, he asked himself, *What happened last night?*

A collage of images began to play in his mind, and he felt a cold chill on the back of his neck.

"No," he whispered.

The sirens were now deafening, and through the cracked blinds at the end of the hall, Bo saw three sets of blue and white flashers. "No," he whispered again. He swallowed and tasted the bile in his throat. He turned for the back door but stopped in his tracks when he saw them.

Ennis Petrie, the sheriff of Giles County, Tennessee, and Hank Springfield, his chief deputy, stood in the doorway. Behind them, Bo saw two more deputies and four squad cars, all with their flashers on.

Three squads in the front and four in back, Bo thought. *No.*

"Bo," Ennis said, taking a cautious step toward him. "You left the door open."

"Sheriff," Bo said, wiping his mouth and hoping he didn't have vomit on it. "Hank. What can I do for you fellas?"

"You're under arrest, Bo," the sheriff said, removing a pair of handcuffs from his belt buckle.

"For what?" Bo asked, his heart pounding in his chest.

Ennis took another step toward him, eyeing Bo with detached curiosity as he placed the cuffs on the attorney's wrists. "For the murder of Andrew Davis Walton."

7

The holding cell wasn't much bigger than a closet. Three of the walls were yellow cinder block, fading white with age, while the wall to Bo's right was made of glass, presumably so someone could watch the questioning from behind it. The floor was concrete, and the sealed sliding door had a small plexiglass window. Inside the cramped space the cell smelled of disinfectant mingled with traces of sweat and body odor. Bo had visited the Giles County Jail on numerous occasions and remembered that his suits always contained this same stale scent when he took them off at night, sometimes making him gag.

Outside the cell the hallway reverberated with a cacophony of sounds. Bo covered his ears to the noise: officers yelling unintelligible jailspeak to each other, the jingle-jangle of inmates shuffling along the floor in their shackles, the whooshing and slamming of doors opening and closing . . .

Bo sat at a metal desk that filled up most of the cell, gazing at his massive reflection in the window. With his size and strength, he knew he could be an intimidating physical presence. But he felt anything but intimidating now. Dressed in orange prison garb—his clothes had been taken for "testing"—his head throbbed from a hangover, and his stomach felt like acid. Outside of a Styrofoam cup of water they'd given him, he'd had nothing to eat or drink since throwing up at his office, and he knew he wouldn't be hungry for several hours. He placed his forehead on the desk, relishing the cold feel of the metal, and rubbed the back of his head.

Two loud knocks jarred him upright. The door slid open, and Sheriff Ennis Petrie walked inside, taking the seat across from Bo at the metal desk. Ennis wore a tan button-down shirt with his name stenciled over the front pocket. He was about five foot eight with thinning, reddish-blond hair, a mustache that matched his diminished mane, and a potbelly that hung over his belt. Though physically unimpressive, Ennis had a calm, cool manner that had made him an effective lawman.

"Bo, I read your Miranda rights to you at your office immediately after you were arrested. You agree with that, right?" the sheriff asked.

Bo said nothing, gazing back at Ennis with blank eyes. He had seen too many clients burned by their own tongues at this stage of a case. Bo also knew that there was a video camera rolling from just behind the glass, recording every word, every sound, and every movement. Bo had represented enough criminal defendants to know the way this song and dance worked.

"No problem," the sheriff said, pulling out a card from his pocket, prepared for Bo's lack of cooperation. "You have the right to remain silent," Ennis began, speaking in a clear, deliberate voice as he read from the card. When he finished, he put the card back in his pocket and peered at Bo.

"Bo, we've known each other a long time." He paused, narrowing his eyes. "So I'm going to forego any bullshit. The physical evidence that we have found against you in the first eight hours of this investigation is conclusive and overwhelming. If that weren't enough, you're the only person with the necessary motive to commit this kind of atrocity, and it's been simmering for decades. There are four eyewitnesses who heard you threaten to kill Andy Walton at Kathy's Tavern just a few hours before we found him hanging from a tree on his farm. An eye for an eye, right, Bo?"

Bo stared blankly back at Ennis, thinking about the confrontation at Kathy's and the words he had used. *No,* he thought, sitting still, in no way betraying his fear. *Jesus Christ, no.*

Finally, after Bo hadn't said anything for several seconds, Ennis sighed. "Bo, the evidence reflects that earlier this morning, just three hours after you threatened to make Andy Walton pay for his sins eye for eye, tooth for tooth, you shot and killed Andy in cold blood and then hung his body from the same tree limb where you have always claimed your father was lynched by the Ku Klux Klan." Ennis spoke in a measured voice, but his eyes blazed with fury. "Then you set his corpse on fire and almost burned his farm to the ground." He paused. "Do you have anything to say for yourself?"

Bo maintained his blank stare for a couple of seconds. Then, slowly and deliberately, he began to nod his head.

Ennis blinked, caught off guard by the gesture. "OK . . . what?"

Bo took a sip of water from the Styrofoam cup on the table, his eyes never leaving the sheriff's. Finally, he spoke. "I'd like to call my attorney."

The sheriff smirked and gave a quick nod in the direction of the glass wall. Bo knew the cue. The video had been turned off.

"So that's how you're gonna play it?" Ennis asked, a rhetorical question, as he knew Bo was not going to respond. The sheriff started to say more, but his voice was drowned out by the swooshing sound of the metal door opening and sliding shut, and then the clacking of high heels on concrete.

Helen Evangeline Lewis, District Attorney General for the 22nd Judicial District of the State of Tennessee, walked into the cell, a faint smile playing on her lips. At almost sixty years old,

Helen was a striking figure, with her pale skin, black hair, and bright-red lipstick, and these features were only intensified by the black suit and high heels she typically wore. Though her face was a bit tight from Botox, she was not an unattractive woman. Scary looking maybe, but not unattractive. The confidence and self-assurance with which she carried herself made her both intimidating and seductive. And a holy terror to deal with in the courtroom.

The sheriff rose from his seat and gestured for Helen to take his place. As she did, Bo watched her, noticing how her body almost slithered, her movements smooth and calculated. Like a poisonous snake.

"So the great Bocephus Haynes wants a lawyer," she said, her voice reeking with sarcasm. "Don't you find that comical, Bo?" She smiled, but there was no humor in her eyes.

"A lawyer who represents himself has a fool for a client," Bo said. "I'm sure you've heard that one before, General."

She cackled. "I have. But *you*? Bo, you've de-balled almost as many lawyers in this town as I have. I can't imagine you trusting your life to anyone in the defense bar here."

"I didn't say I wanted *a lawyer*," Bo said, glaring at her. "I said I wanted *my lawyer*." He paused. "*My lawyer* ain't from around here."

Helen abruptly stood and looked down at Bo, her green eyes burning with intensity. "Well, he better be good." She started to turn away but then returned her gaze to Bo. "Given the mutilated condition of the body and the multiple felonies involved, we don't have a choice in the punishment we'll seek." She paused, her eyes and voice betraying no emotion. "I'll ask for the death penalty."

Out of the corner of his eye, Bo thought he saw Ennis Petrie flinch, but Bo didn't look at the sheriff. He kept his gaze locked on Helen, forcing himself to remain calm, though he felt goose bumps breaking out on his arms and the back of his neck. "I'd like to call my attorney now."

8

Thomas Jackson McMurtrie winced as the cell phone vibrated in his pocket. He had silenced the phone at the beginning of the mediation but had forgotten that the damn thing would start vibrating if a call came through. His bladder had been scoped yesterday afternoon, and though the news was good—he was clean as a whistle—the procedure was still uncomfortable and made him stiff and sore. Being seventy years old probably didn't help much either, a fact his urologist and longtime friend, Bill Davis, teased him with every time Tom complained. "Cancer-free for a year, old man," Bill had said, slapping Tom on the back at the end of yesterday's appointment. "That peace of mind is worth a little 'torture,' isn't it?" "Torture" was Tom's word for the scope, the chemo washes, and pretty much everything Bill had done to treat the masses that had popped up in Tom's bladder last year. But his friend was right. A clean scope was worth a little pain.

Tom tried to remind himself of this fact as the vibration from the phone caused his stomach and pelvis to tighten, which sent a shot of pain through his groin. His right foot had also fallen asleep, and he wiggled his toes in his loafers to increase the circulation.

Tom was curious about the call—few people had his cell number—but he could not answer it. The mediator was making his final plea.

"Tom, I think everyone agrees that the driver of the rig was negligent when he pulled out in front of Mr. London. Jameson just believes you guys should come off the policy limits to account for your client's"—he paused—"possible contributory negligence in not being able to stop or avoid the collision."

Before responding, Tom glanced to his right. Next to him, his partner, Rick Drake, leaned forward in his seat, elbows on the table, looking ready to pounce. Their eyes met, and Tom nodded at him to take the lead, stifling a smile. *That boy is always itching for a fight,* he thought.

"Jerome London was a sixty-two-year-old grandfather of three who was on his way to pick up his granddaughter from preschool at the time of this accident," Rick said, his voice sharp and edgy. "Mr. London had a perfect driving record—no tickets and only one accident in his whole life—and his pickup truck was in mint condition, having been serviced just one week earlier. The two eyewitnesses at the Waffle House on McFarland, who were sitting in booths with an unobstructed view out their window when the collision occurred, both say that Mr. London hit the brakes immediately once the 18-wheeler pulled onto the road. The only person in the world who says different is Jameson's accident reconstructionist, Eugene Marsh, who has *never* given an opinion that a commercial truck driver was negligent. We took Jameson to verdict last year in the Willistone case in Henshaw County, and the jury came back with a verdict of ninety million dollars. I'm sure Jameson remembers that case very well. Marsh was Jameson's expert in Willistone, and the jury's verdict shows just how impressed they were." Rick paused, licking his lips and placing his hands palms down on the table. "George, Mr. London lost his life in this accident. The policy limits here are one million, and if you ask us the defendant is getting a bargain. Mr. London's son, Maurice, wants this to be over, so he has agreed to accept the limits today at this mediation, but there is no way on God's green earth that we are going to let him take less." Eyes burning with intensity, Rick held up his index finger. "One last thing, and it has to be said. This case is pending here . . . in *Tuscaloosa, Alabama.* You know, George, the home of the Crimson Tide. My partner was a member of Bear Bryant's 1961 national champions, and a video clip of him sacking the quarterback in the Sugar Bowl is shown every fall Saturday on the Jumbotron at Bryant-Denny Stadium as a hundred thousand fans go crazy. He was a law professor for forty years at the University of Alabama, and every judge and lawyer in this state, including you, George, has a copy of his Evidence hornbook in their office."

Rick snorted and stood from his chair. "The bottom line is that we have the facts, and no jury in Tuscaloosa, Alabama is going to find against us. Jameson would have better luck getting a jury of elves to convict Santa Claus at the North Pole."

Rick began to pack up his briefcase, his face red and his hands trembling slightly. Tom also stood, placing his hands in his pockets and eyeing the mediator.

George McDuff Jr. rubbed his neck and smiled. "Rick, I know all about the Willistone case in Henshaw County. I think every lawyer in the state of Alabama has heard about that verdict. And you don't have to tell me about the Professor's accomplishments. I think I was ten when Tom left my dad's practice to be a law professor." He looked at Tom, his eyes turning sad. "I think it was one of Dad's biggest regrets that he couldn't get you to stay."

Tom nodded, looking past George out the window of the conference room. In the distance he could see the lights to Bryant-Denny Stadium. "I believe your father knew that I had to come to

the university," Tom finally said, meeting George's eye. "That I . . .
was made an offer I just couldn't refuse."

"He said Coach Bryant asked you to come."

Tom nodded.

"Well . . ." George clasped his hands together and looked from
Tom to Rick. "I can't say I blame y'all for not backing down from
the policy limits. I'll pass the word on to Jameson. Did you want to
stick around to see—?"

"No," Rick interrupted, shutting the briefcase. "Jameson knows
where to find us."

———

They walked down the stairs in silence. George McDuff's law office
was a two-story stand-alone building on University Drive, eight
blocks from Tom and Rick's own office off of Greensboro. As they
stepped outside into the sunlight, Rick finally spoke. "You think
I came off too strong in there?" His tone was defensive, and Tom
glanced at him, smiling.

"Oh, no, you were very subtle." He paused. "The Santa Claus
thing might have been a bit over the top . . ."

Now it was Rick who smiled. "I guess I got a little carried away."

They reached Rick's car, a thirteen-year-old Saturn the color
of rusted gold, and Rick slipped his briefcase in the back, and they
both took off their jackets.

"You ever gonna trade in this ball and chain?" Tom joked, tapping the top of the Saturn with his palm. "I think you can probably
afford an upgrade." Though Tom and Rick were not able to collect
anywhere close to the full ninety million awarded in the Willistone
case—Jack Willistone was sent to prison, and he and his company
had declared bankruptcy—they had received the three million in
policy limits, resulting in a legal fee of one million dollars. And
in the twelve months since the verdict, the firm of McMurtrie &

Drake had obtained seven-figure settlements in three other cases. They were on a roll, but you sure wouldn't be able to guess it by looking at Rick's car.

"You sound like Dawn," Rick said, climbing in the driver's side of the Saturn and leaning over to manually unlock Tom's door.

"You should listen to her sometimes," Tom said, getting in. "She's probably the smartest member of the firm."

"True enough," Rick said, putting the car in gear and backing out of the parking space. As he straightened the car to exit the lot, a figure was blocking their way, palms out to stop them.

"Should I hit him?" Rick asked, his voice giving away only the slightest hint of humor.

"Nah," Tom said. "I think your little stunt back there may have just paid off."

Rick left the car running, and he and Tom got out of the Saturn. The man blocking their exit walked briskly toward them, a toothy grin playing on his face.

"Gentlemen, aren't we being a little rash? The mediation hasn't even been going an hour."

"Jameson, you knew our position before we ever got here," Rick said. "You knew we wouldn't settle for less than the limits. This was a dog and pony show for your client so a mediator could tell them to pay out. You know what's going to happen at trial. It will be Willistone all over again."

Jameson Tyler, managing partner of Jones & Butler, the largest law firm in the state of Alabama, crossed his arms, his smile fading away. "Big talk for a boy who didn't have much to do with that verdict. As I recollect it, the Professor here saved your ass in Willistone while your case was dying on the vine." Jameson took a step closer. "Must be nice riding Tom's coattails, Rick."

Rick's face flushed red, and he started to step forward, but Tom moved in front of him. "That's enough, Jameson. Rick is right. We told you beforehand that we wouldn't budge from the limits."

Jameson sighed in exasperation. "Tom, practicing law is as much a business as it is a profession. My clients are businesspeople. They deal in dollars and cents."

Tom squinted at Jameson and stepped toward him, invading his space so that the other lawyer had to take a step backward. "You continually disappoint me, Jameson. Exactly when did you sell out, son? When did the billable hour become your moral compass in life?"

Jameson didn't flinch or blink. "You're one to talk, Professor. You're nothing more than an ambulance chaser now, collecting settlement checks like the rest of them. Have you tried a case since Willistone?" He paused, leaning forward. "Willistone was a fluke, Tom, and we both know it. But you and your minion here have used it to scare a few insurance companies into shelling out big money to settle instead of dealing with the circus of trying a case against you in Alabama. Here's a news flash for you, Tom. We're all sellouts, and you're no different than anyone else."

Tom felt his cell phone vibrate again in his pocket, but he didn't move to answer it. He was shaken by Jameson's words. Like his former student, though, he didn't flinch. His expression and demeanor remained exactly the same. "See you in court, Jameson."

Tom turned to go, motioning for Rick to do the same. When his hand touched the door handle, Jameson's voice stopped him.

"No, you won't."

Tom glanced at Rick, who was unable to suppress a smile. Then he peered back at Jameson. "Excuse me?"

"My client doesn't want to go to the circus either. They'll pay the limits."

———

Twenty minutes later the mediation settlement agreement was signed, and Rick and Tom were back in the Saturn, heading toward the office. Rick had just called Maurice London with the good news and, after clicking the "End" button, plopped his cell phone in the drink holder.

"How was he?" Tom asked.

"Ecstatic," Rick said. "He just kept thanking me over and over again."

Rick smiled, but it was obvious to Tom that the boy was still perturbed by Jameson's comments in the parking lot. His young partner seemed to carry a perpetual chip on his shoulder, never appearing to be satisfied with the success the firm achieved. It was like Jameson Tyler's voice was always ringing in the boy's head, telling him that he wasn't good enough.

Rick had been given an offer to work for Jones & Butler when he was in law school, but the offer was withdrawn by Jameson when Rick got into an altercation with Tom after a law school trial competition. Though Tom and Rick had reconciled and had eventually teamed up for the huge verdict in the Willistone case last summer, Rick still carried the scar of his rejection with him like a badge. Tom wondered if that was why Rick clung to the old Saturn, not able to allow himself any enjoyment of their success until . . .

. . . until what?

As Rick pulled to a stop in front of the McMurtrie & Drake, LLC sign, Tom was about to compliment his young partner's handling of the London case but winced as his cell phone vibrated again. He had forgotten to turn the sound back on.

"Goddamnit," Tom said, twisting in the seat to get his phone out of his pocket. He looked at the face, and the caller ID showed a 931 area code.

Tennessee? Tom thought. There were several people in Tennessee that had his cell phone number, including his son, Tommy, who lived in Nashville, but all of those folks had numbers Tom would recognize. This number was unfamiliar.

"Hello."

"Professor, where have you been?"

Tom instantly recognized the voice. "Bo?"

"Yeah, dog. Listen . . ." There was a pause on the other end of the line, and Tom thought he heard someone shouting in the background. Then Bo's voice again, strained, a harsh whisper. *"I need your help."*

PART TWO

PART TWO

9

On Monday morning, three days after the murder of Andy Walton, Tom rose early and decided to walk the half mile into downtown Pulaski. He had stayed the night at Ms. Butler's Bed & Breakfast, a charming white-frame house on Jefferson Street three blocks from the Giles County Courthouse. After a hearty breakfast and two cups of black coffee, Tom grabbed his briefcase and began the trek down Jefferson. By the time he reached the town square, he had to wipe the sweat off his forehead.

Built in 1909 after a fire destroyed the old building, the Giles County Courthouse was an architectural marvel. Eight columns lined the east and west entrances, and a dome and clock surmounted the entire structure. As he climbed the grand staircase to the second floor, Tom couldn't help but gaze up at the top of the rotunda, noticing that the centerpiece of the dome contained the Tennessee state seal, the scales of justice, and a sheathed sword, all on a shield background. Stained-glass windows adorned the north and south walls. To Tom, the building felt more like a cathedral than a courthouse.

At the second-floor landing, Tom turned to his left toward a closed door with a sign above it that said "District Attorney General." Tom was about to knock when a voice rang out from down the hall.

"She's not in there."

Tom turned and saw a plump middle-aged woman wearing horn-rimmed glasses heading his way. "Where . . . ?" he started, but the woman walked past him and pointed toward a set of double doors. Adjacent to the doors was a sign that read "Circuit Court." The woman cracked open the door and peeked inside. Then she waved toward Tom. "She's in the courtroom," the woman said, pointing through the doors. "Do you have business with the General?"

"Yes, ma'am," Tom said, slightly jolted by the woman's use of the military title. He was going to have to get used to hearing the word "General" in reference to the head prosecutor, which was a practice peculiar to the state of Tennessee.

"OK," the woman said, opening the door wider and motioning with her head for Tom to enter. "In the jury," she whispered as Tom stepped through the opening. Before he could say thank you, the door closed behind him.

For a few seconds Tom took in the scene. He had been in a lot of courtrooms in his lifetime, but he had never had his breath taken away until now. The first thing that stood out was the balcony. Eerily reminiscent of the courtroom in the movie version of *To Kill a Mockingbird*, there was a balcony where spectators could sit if the main area was full. Of course, in *To Kill a Mockingbird*, which took place in rural south Alabama, the black spectators sat in the balcony and the whites sat on the main floor. Tom figured that the original intent of this balcony was also segregation. He doubted many cases these days required upstairs seating.

But this one might, he thought. When Bocephus Haynes was tried for the capital murder of Andy Walton, former Imperial

Wizard of the Tennessee Knights of the Ku Klux Klan, Tom figured every seat might indeed be taken.

Tom lowered his gaze to the gallery on the main floor, where he saw four separate seating areas with five or six rows of built-in wooden chairs that folded up like theater seats. The gallery converged on a railing, which separated spectators from the lawyers and the judge. Just beyond this railing were two tables, one of which Tom knew would be the prosecution's table, and the other the defense table. Between the two tables was a built-in box with a high-backed chair inside. *Is that the witness stand?* Tom wondered, squinting at the box and walking toward it. He ran his hand over the wood and then swept his eyes around the courtroom again. *Has to be,* he thought, noticing that this box faced two rows of six built-in high-backed swivel chairs. *The jury,* Tom thought, seeing that just beyond the jury chairs was the judge's bench, which rose twice as high as the witness box.

"Interesting setup, huh?" A sharp female voice cut through the air, and Tom felt his entire body tense. He moved his eyes to the jury chairs and at first didn't see her. Then a hand shot up from the back row.

Tom took a couple more steps and finally saw General Helen Lewis slumped in a jury chair with a file jacket in her lap. She wore a black suit, and her lips were painted bright red with lipstick. Scratching one stockinged calf with the toe of her other foot—her heels were lying in a pile underneath her chair—Helen smiled at him. "Tom McMurtrie."

"Helen," Tom said. "Been a long time."

Over the years Tom had run into Helen Lewis at various seminars put on by the American Bar Association, where they both had been speakers. Though not friends, they had developed a mutual respect for the other's abilities and reputation. He extended his hand, and she stood to shake it, looking him directly in the eye.

Her handshake was firm, and her eyes were the greenish-blue color of the Gulf.

"Are you lost, Tom?" she asked, her bright-red lips curving into a grin. "You are a long way from Tuscaloosa."

Tom chuckled and then turned away from her. "This setup *is* interesting," he said, pointing at the witness box. "I haven't seen anything like it. In every courtroom I've ever been in, the witness stand has been adjacent to the judge's bench. Here, it's—"

"Right in the center of the room," Helen finished his thought, and walked toward the witness chair.

Tom noticed that she made no move to put her heels on. Her comfort level made him a bit uneasy. It was as if she were walking around in her own home. She stopped when she reached the witness box and turned to him.

"Front and center, facing the jury and the judge." She paused, smiling. "I think it's the way a courtroom should be. Everything that's important happens right here," she said, patting the back of the chair. "All testimony. All evidence." She paused. "Everything else is just for show." She stepped toward Tom, the smile gone from her face. "You're here because of Bo Haynes, right?"

Tom nodded.

"You taught him in law school, didn't you? He was on one of your trial teams."

Again, Tom nodded. "You seem to know a lot about me."

"Not really," Helen said. "I just know a lot about Bo Haynes. He's the only black trial lawyer in town, and he's very good. He used to do a lot of criminal defense back in the late '80s and early '90s, and we had dozens of cases against each other." She paused. "I always do a study of my opponents when I face them in court."

"And what did you learn about Bo?" Tom asked, smiling at her. But the gesture wasn't returned. Helen's emerald eyes blazed with intensity.

"Having grown up in Giles County myself, I knew a lot already. I was just starting in the DA's office here when Bo was an all-state football player at Giles County High. I remember when Bear Bryant came to Pulaski to watch him play. You woulda thought the president was in town. Police escort to the stadium with sirens blaring. State troopers everywhere. It was the damnedest thing I'd ever seen."

Tom smiled, thinking of a similar scene from his own past. "The Man knew how to make an entrance."

"*The Man*," Helen mocked. "I think I've heard Bo call him that too. *The Man*. Is that an inside thing?"

Tom shrugged. "I guess. If you played for Coach Bryant or spent any time around him, he was . . . *the Man*. It's a hard thing to describe."

"Whatever," Helen said, waving a hand in the air. She returned to her seat in the back row of the jury and crossed her legs. Again, Tom was taken back by the familiarity with which she treated the courtroom. "Anyway, everyone in Pulaski followed Bo's college career. It was hard not to. The local newspaper always mentioned how many tackles he had made in a game, stuff like that. The articles stopped after he blew his knee out." She paused, squinting up at him. "The rest I learned from doing a little digging. Law School at Alabama, where he was on your national championship trial team. Clerked a summer at Jones & Butler, the law factory in Birmingham. Then back here after law school. Hung a shingle on First Street a block north of First National Bank, and he's been in that same office for the past twenty-five years." She paused, chuckling with what sounded to Tom like admiration. "Starting out as a black lawyer in this town in the mid-'80s was not much different than being a female prosecutor. Not many of us around. In Bo's case, none. He cut his teeth on criminal defense and workers' comp cases and then started attracting the lucrative personal injury plaintiff cases by the mid-'90s."

"I always thought it was strange that he came back here," Tom said, purposely testing Helen's knowledge, as he had learned the answer to that riddle himself last year.

"Not to me," Helen said. "Or to anyone else in Pulaski." She cocked her head at Tom. "And I think you might be playing possum with me, Tom. I think you know the reason too."

Tom kept a poker face, giving away nothing. Helen Lewis was a different animal. Unlike almost every other lawyer he'd been around for the past several decades, male and female alike, Helen paid Tom no deference for being a longtime law professor. She didn't address him as Professor, as so many of his colleagues did, and she didn't seem awed in the least by his association with Coach Bryant.

"Why don't you remind me?" Tom asked.

Keeping her head cocked to the side, Helen glared up at Tom. "Because ever since he was five years old, Bocephus Haynes has claimed that Andy Walton and twenty members of the Ku Klux Klan murdered his father. Bo came back to Pulaski for revenge." She paused, crossing her arms across her chest. "And early last Friday morning he got it."

"Sounds like an opening statement," Tom said, forcing a smile. Tom knew he had just heard the theme of the state's case against Bocephus Haynes.

This time Helen returned the smile. "I thought you were a law professor, Tom."

"I was. For forty years. But now I'm practicing again."

"And you and your partner hit Willistone Trucking Company last year for ninety million dollars in Henshaw County, Alabama."

Tom was impressed. He figured most lawyers in Alabama had heard of the verdict, but Helen was a Tennessee prosecutor. "How did you hear about that?"

"Because it was in the goddamn *USA Today*. Legendary law professor hits big verdict in Alabama. Yada, yada, yada. Aren't they making a movie about it?"

Tom shrugged, his face turning red. "I hadn't heard anything about that."

"Well, they should." She chuckled. "The best part of that verdict is that you beat that arrogant, overrated prick Jameson Tyler."

Now Tom laughed. "You know Jameson?" Tom asked.

"Unfortunately, I've met him at several ABA meetings. You taught him too, right?"

Tom nodded.

"I was also glad to see Jack Willistone put out of business," Helen continued. "Jack had been running trucks up and down Highways 64 and 31 for years, collecting speeding tickets that always seemed to mysteriously disappear before we could prosecute them." She paused, shaking her head in disgust. "One of Jack's biggest customers was Andy Walton. If you hadn't put Jack in jail where he belongs, I bet his sorry ass would be at Andy's funeral tomorrow."

For a moment an awkward silence fell over the courtroom. Then the smile faded from Helen's face.

"What can I do for you, Tom?" she asked.

"Helen, we need to obtain some discovery from you," Tom said. "What do I—?"

"Hold it," she interrupted, raising her hand to stop him. "Tom, are you telling me that you are going to represent Bo in this case?"

Tom nodded, forcing a smile again. "Yes. What did you think I was doing here?"

Helen didn't smile back. "I was hoping you were here as a concerned friend and former teacher." She paused, recrossing her legs. "Bo is charged with capital murder, Tom. He shot Andy Walton in cold blood, hanged him from a tree on Andy's farm, and then set his body on fire. The evidence is overwhelming."

"We'd like to see some of this *evidence*," Tom said.

Helen peered up at him. "Tom, you are barking up the wrong tree coming down here out of state, having been out of the courtroom as long as you have. As an old friend, I would strongly encourage you to not get involved. One big trucking verdict in Alabama doesn't mean you're ready for a capital murder trial in Tennessee."

"We'd like to get some discovery from you," Tom said, keeping his voice calm despite the surge of anger he felt. He was tiring of Helen's act.

Helen sighed and shook her head. "There is no discovery in a criminal case in Tennessee before the grand jury issues an indictment and the defendant is arraigned, Tom. You would know this if you tried criminal cases in Tennessee on a regular basis. I really wish you would reconsider what you're doing." She gazed at him with mock sympathy. "I would hate for your legacy to be tarnished."

Tom managed a grin. "I'm not worried about that, Helen." He held out his hand, and she stood to shake it. "My notice of appearance will be filed first thing tomorrow morning."

Tom started to walk away, and Helen's voice called after him. "You'll need local counsel, Tom. You can't just waltz down here from Tuscaloosa and enter an appearance in a capital murder case. Since the primary thrust of your practice is in Alabama, you'll need local counsel."

When he reached the double doors, Tom turned to face her.

"And don't think I'm going to educate you the whole way," Helen continued. She had sat back down and had begun flipping through her file again. "That's really not my—"

"Raymond Pickalew will be our local counsel, General," Tom interrupted, addressing her for the first time by her formal title. "I believe you know Ray Ray."

Helen looked up from the file, her eyes widening in bewilderment. She opened her mouth to speak, but the words didn't come. He had finally rattled her.

"And if you aren't going to be forthcoming with the state's evidence, we'll be requesting an expedited preliminary hearing."

Tom opened the door.

"The prelim is the defendant's right," Helen said, her voice as hard as iron as she scowled at Tom from across the courtroom.

"I know it is," Tom said, smiling at her and closing the door behind him.

10

The law office of Raymond Pickalew was located on First Street, about a block south of the courthouse square and two doors down from Bo's office. The receptionist, a big-busted redhead named Bonnie who dressed in jeans and a low-cut sweater, said that her boss was working from home today. He lived in a cabin just off the Elk River about twenty minutes south of town. She had no qualms giving Tom the address of the cabin and Ray Ray's cell number but said, "He's bad about not answering it."

On the way to the cabin, Tom called Rick and filled him in on the meeting with Helen.

"I need you to research the requirements for change of venue in a capital murder case in the State of Tennessee." He paused. "If there's any way possible, we need to get this case out of Pulaski."

"It's that bad?" Rick said.

"Pulaski is a small town, kid. Everyone here is probably familiar with Bo's backstory, which is entirely consistent with a revenge killing." He sighed. "We have to try."

"What does Bo say?"

"I haven't seen him yet. Still doing the groundwork. Visiting hours at the jail are this afternoon, and I'll discuss venue with him then."

"Professor, do you think he did—?"

"Doesn't matter what I think right now," Tom interrupted. "It's too early to be making snap judgments. The bottom line is that Bocephus Haynes is my friend, and he saved my ass last year when I was feeling sorry for myself on the farm." Tom paused, feeling heat behind his eyes. "I owe him."

"I do too," Rick said. "He saved Dawn's life during the trial last year. If he hadn't found her when he did, Willistone's henchman might've . . ." He trailed off, and Tom began to slow down as he saw the sign for the Buford Gardner Bridge. Bonnie had said to take a left on Highway 31 just past the bridge. Tom clicked his blinker, knowing it was time to end the call.

"Listen, Rick, that reminds me. Can you talk to Powell?"

"Of course, but why?" Powell Conrad was an assistant district attorney in Tuscaloosa County. He was also Rick's best friend.

"Because Andy Walton was thick as thieves with Jack Willistone."

"Really?" Rick asked, his voice incredulous.

"That's what General Lewis said. Anyway, we need to get an update on Willistone from Powell." He sighed. "And we may have to pay the bastard a visit in prison. We need to know all we can about the victim."

Silence for several seconds on the other end of the line. Then: "OK." The trepidation in Rick's voice was palpable, and Tom felt a little himself. Neither one of them relished the idea of seeing Jack Willistone again.

"One last thing," Tom said, seeing Ray Ray's cabin up ahead. "I need you to research the requirements for out-of-state admission to Tennessee in a criminal case and draft the necessary paperwork."

"We'll need local counsel, right?" Rick asked.

"Right," Tom said, turning into the gravel drive that led up to the small cabin. "And I'm about to speak with Ray Ray now."

"Ray who?"

Tom smiled. "I'll call you later."

———

He found Raymond Pickalew fishing off his pier. His old friend sat in a lawn chair and wore a navy-blue T-shirt, tattered khaki shorts, and a crimson visor with the letter *A* stenciled on the front. Even sitting down, his bare feet propped on a cooler, Ray Ray displayed the long, wiry muscles that had made him an excellent wide receiver.

"What do you say, Ray Ray?" Tom said, smiling at his old teammate.

Raymond Pickalew had been called Ray Ray since he was a baby. His father had suffered from a bad stutter, and when he tried to say "Ray," it always came out "Ray Ray." His mother had wanted him to just go by Ray, but when his two-year-old sister started calling him Ray Ray, she adopted it too, and before long everyone in town did. Ray Ray made all-state at Giles County High in football and went on to play at Alabama, graduating in 1960. Law school followed, and then back to Pulaski, where Ray Ray had been a general practitioner specializing in divorce since the late '60s.

Ray Ray had a grin that seemed to curl up past his cheekbones, which made him always look like he was up to no good. It was his trademark, and though he hadn't seen Tom in years, he gave it now, standing from his lawn chair. "Well, shit fire and save the matches. Tommy goddamn McMurtrie." He set his rod and reel down and gave Tom a bear hug, and the strong scent of Miller High Life enveloped Tom's nostrils. "How in the hell are you?"

"Just fine, Ray Ray."

Ray Ray sat down and pulled two Miller High Life cans from his cooler. He pitched one to Tom and popped the top on the other one. "How about a taste of the champagne of beers?" he asked, smiling and taking a long sip from the can. "Goddamn, it's good to see you, Tom. How long's it been?"

Tom smiled and opened the beer. Though it was a little early in the day for a cold one, Tom figured it was best to be agreeable. After all, he was about to ask the man for a favor. "Oh . . . maybe five years. Didn't we meet up after the spring game in Tuscaloosa a few years back?"

Ray Ray took a sip of beer and gazed down at the pier. "Actually, I saw you after that . . . at Julie's funeral."

Tom winced. He remembered little about his wife's funeral. Everything a blur of handshakes, hugs, and pain. "That's right," he said, feeling a lump in his throat.

"Sure was sorry about that. Goddamn cancer . . ." Ray Ray had lost his sister and mother to breast cancer.

"How . . . is Doris doing?" Tom asked, and Ray Ray took a long swallow of beer, wiping his mouth and looking out at the river.

"Same," Ray Ray said. "Still at the nursing home. The Alzheimer's has completely taken over now. She don't remember me at all. Used to, I'd have one day every two weeks that she'd say, 'Ray Ray, where the hell am I?'" He chuckled bitterly. "Now I don't even get that. I even tried that thing the guy did in the movie. What's it called . . . ?"

"*The Notebook*," Tom offered.

Ray Ray snapped his fingers. "That's right. *The Notebook*. Well, I tried that mess. Wrote the whole story of our courtship out and read it to her every morning. Course it wasn't as pretty a tale as the one in the movie. Anyway . . . she don't remember shit, and I've stopped going out there every day. Now I go every Friday at lunch and then come out here." He stopped and took down the rest of his beer in one swallow. Then he crushed it in his hand and set it beside the cooler next to two similarly crushed cans. He opened another one and set his foot on top of the cooler, still watching the water. "No one ever said life was fair, Tommy old boy. I put Doris through hell for thirty years. Boned pretty much every secretary I ever had, drank like a fish, and chased cases and tail like there was no tomorrow. And then one day I wake up and tell Doris it's all over. I'm quitting the booze. The other women. All of it. She cries and we go on a second honeymoon trip to the Keys." He took a sip of beer. "A week after we get back, the clerk at Davis & Eslick grocery tells me that Doris is down there and can't remember why she came. The rest . . . well, you know the rest, Tom."

"Jesus Christ, listen to me," Ray Ray said after several seconds of silence. He took another long sip of beer and turned to Tom. "So how's Musso doing?"

Again, Tom winced. "Dead. He killed a bobcat on my farm last year. Saved my life actually, because the bobcat was rabid and was going for me. He died from his wounds."

Ray Ray whistled. "Goddamn. Sure sorry to hear that Tom. Damn, I loved that dog too."

"It was hard not to love Musso," Tom said, clearing his throat. "Got me a new dog, though. Bo gave me a white and brown bull-dog last year. I named him Lee Roy."

Ray Ray smiled. "Good name." Then just like that the smile was gone. "You came out here because of Bo."

Tom nodded.

"He's in a world of shit," Ray Ray said. "I mean a fucking F5 shit tornado."

"He is," Tom agreed.

"So are you out here as his friend or his lawyer?" Ray Ray asked, and the wide grin was back. Had his face been painted white and his lips red, he would've looked a little like one of the main villains from the Batman movies. In fact, Coach Bryant had always referred to Ray Ray as Joker.

"Both," Tom said. "I plan to make my notice of appearance tomorrow morning." He paused. "I need local counsel."

"Oh, hell no," Ray Ray said, standing abruptly and walking past Tom up the pier. "Hell . . . fucking . . . no!" he bellowed from halfway down the pier.

Tom watched Ray Ray ascend a rocky hill toward his one-story cabin. Thirty seconds later he was pacing back down the hill, shaking his head the entire way. In his right hand he held a large bottle of brown liquid.

"Tommy, you are dumber than a box of hammers, you know that?" Ray Ray said. The bottle was a handle of Evan Williams whiskey.

"Drinking the good stuff I see," Tom said.

"Fuck you," Ray Ray said, taking a pull off the bottle and handing it to Tom.

"I'll pass," Tom said, holding his hand up. "I'm still working on this beer."

"Whatever," Ray Ray muttered. He started to lift the bottle to his lips but then set it on the pier. He plopped down in the chair again and reached into the cooler and popped the top on another beer.

"What can you tell me about Andy Walton's murder?" Tom asked.

"Nothing really," Ray Ray said, squinting at Tom. "Just what's been in the papers. *General* Lewis is usually pretty good about keeping a closed lid on information in important cases."

This Tom believed, having just been stonewalled by the General herself. "Well, how about Andy Walton? What can you tell me about him and his family?"

Ray Ray belched, picked up the bottle of whiskey on the ground, thought about it, and then put the bottle back down. "Goddamnit." He wiped his mouth and sighed. "The Curtis family was actually settled in Pulaski long before Andy Walton showed up. In fact, the parcel of land now called Walton Farm was where Maggie Curtis and her brother, George, were raised as kids. Andy was from Selmer, Tennessee, over in McNairy County. He made a fortune running bootleg whiskey before Buford Pusser became sheriff. Instead of going to war with Buford like the other State Line Mob folks did, Andy came over this way and started buying up land and businesses. When George and Maggie's daddy was about to lose the farm, Andy bought the old man out and all the surrounding land too." Ray Ray laughed as the sun began to seep behind a few clouds and the sound of thunder echoed from a good distance away. "It'll be on us in a few minutes," he said.

"How did Andy end up with Maggie?"

Again, Ray Ray laughed. "Some say old man Curtis offered her as part of the deal." He shook his head. "I never bought that. I think Ms. Maggie just couldn't bear to part with that land or the status associated with owning it. I think she made the deal with Andy more so than the old man, and Andy took it because a wife like Maggie could help him in a new town. She was big in the church. The DAR. All the little foofoo women's clubs."

"What happened to George?"

"He was in medical school when the old man was losing the farm, so there wasn't anything he could do to help." Ray Ray shrugged. "I'll say this for George, he's a survivor. I'm sure he had to be bitter that the family farm went to Andy, but he moved on and opened his medical practice after the old man's death and has been a local fixture ever since. But . . ."

"But what?' Tom asked.

"I don't know, he's just a strange bird. Never married. Lives in a small house two doors down from his office. Kind of a loner. Outside of going to medical seminars every so often in different places, I've never known him to leave town."

"Can he shoot a twelve-gauge?" Tom asked, smiling.

Ray Ray chuckled. "I 'spect everybody in Giles County can shoot a shotgun."

"We need another suspect," Tom said.

Ray Ray shook his head and again grabbed the bottle of whiskey. He took a long pull off the bottle and wiped his mouth. "No. What you need is to be talking a plea deal with the General, Tommy boy."

It had begun to rain, and Ray Ray fished out an umbrella from behind his chair and opened it. "We probably need to move this party inside."

"Ray Ray, I need you, man. I'm filing the notice of appearance tomorrow morning. Can I put your name on it?"

Thunder clapped hard from the east, and a bolt of lightning lit up the sky. Ray Ray Pickalew gave the umbrella handle to Tom and stepped out from under the cover. "I'm just a washed-up old drunk, Tom. Bo will tell you. I'd be a cancer to his defense. You need a criminal defense guy anyway, not a divorce thug like me. Go with Lou Horn. His office is a block north of mine. Or Dick Selby. Horn and Selby have cases against Helen all the time."

"Which means she has both of their dicks in a jar above her mantle at home," Tom said. "You've beaten her before, Ray Ray. And you know this county like the back of your hand."

"He's guilty, Tom," Ray Ray said, the alcohol slurring his words. "It's a barking dog of a case. Have you read the papers? Helen ain't going to stop until Bo is lethally injected. You understand what I'm saying."

"He's our friend," Tom said.

"Wrong," Ray Ray said. "He's your friend." He took another sip from the bottle, closing his eyes and grimacing as the liquid burned his throat. "If I was lit on fire and Bo had to piss, he might shoot a few drops my way, but that's the extent of our relationship. The last time I tangled with Bo in court, we about ended up in a fistfight on the steps of the courthouse."

"That's because you're a brawler, Ray Ray. And that's what Bo needs now."

Ray Ray laughed and took another belt of whiskey. He was soaking wet. "What Bo needs is a Catholic priest. Now get the hell off my pier, Tommy."

"Ray Ray—"

"Go on," Ray Ray said, gesturing with the bottle and sloshing whiskey out of it before taking another sip. "Get. I've had enough of this mess. I'd rather drink myself to death than fight at the Alamo, and that's what going to war with Helen Lewis in Giles County will be like."

"OK, Ray Ray," Tom said, holding up his hands in surrender. "I'll leave you here with your buddy Evan Williams. But before you get too far gone, I want you to ask yourself a question. What would the Man think about all this?"

"Tom, I'm warning you—"

"What would Coach Bryant say about you just turning your back on life? Sitting out on this pier and drinking yourself to death."

Ray Ray heaved the handle of whiskey at Tom, and Tom ducked down, the bottle whizzing past his ear and falling into the river. "Get the fuck off my property."

Tom turned and began to walk away. "I'll see you tomorrow, Ray Ray. I'll be at Bo's office. Just meet me there around nine thirty."

"I'll meet you in hell, Tommy. That's the next time you'll see me."

———

As Tom pulled his Explorer out of the gravel drive, he could still see Ray Ray sitting on the pier, the rain pelting down on him. It looked like he was talking to himself.

For a split second Tom considered the possibility of associating one of the criminal defense lawyers Ray Ray had mentioned.

Horn or Selby. Then as the rain continued to pound the windshield, Tom shook his head.

Ray Ray Pickalew had a lot of problems. He was a drunk. A womanizer. And he'd been written up a couple of times by the Tennessee Bar for ethical violations. A saint he was not, and he probably couldn't teach a class on criminal law.

But he's not afraid of a fight, and the nastier the better, Tom thought. Once engaged, Ray Ray would be on this case like stink on a pig, and there would be only one acceptable outcome.

Winning.

He'll come around, Tom thought, nodding his head and pulling onto Highway 31. *Just give it some time . . .*

—

On the pier Ray Ray Pickalew lay on his back, gazing up at the cloudy sky. His legs dangled off the dock, and he was humming a song to himself. He had taken his rain-drenched shirt off, and the wooden dock would probably have been uncomfortable if he wasn't piss drunk. He closed his eyes, seeing Doris for a split second. In her bathing suit in the Keys, sitting on the bed, watching him get dressed. Then . . . at the nursing home, the orderly coming in to change her diaper. He squeezed his eyes shut, forcing an image of his secretary Bonnie's tits into his brain. It didn't hold. The images kept coming, a whirlwind of them, mostly of Doris at the nursing home. Slowly and painfully forgetting who she was until there was none of her left. The day he knew her mind was gone for good, he had sat on this same pier all night with a pistol in his hand. Putting the barrel in his mouth a few times but never doing the deed. Never pulling the trigger . . .

Before he passed out, he saw another image. One that came to him in black and white like an old TV reel. Tommy McMurtrie, sweat pouring off his forehead under his helmet as he took his place on the defensive line. Then Trammell under center, looking at Ray Ray down the line of scrimmage just before the ball was snapped and giving him the slightest of nods. Then the ball . . . in the air, a perfect spiral, hitting Ray Ray right in the hands.

Then he was running, the football tucked tight under his arm.

Then a loud sound, like rushing water in his ears, and a crimson 54 rolling over him.

"Bingo!" came a faraway voice. "That a boy, Lee Roy. That's a way we do it. Now let's do it again."

Then he was on the ground, nose pressed to the grass, blinking, managing to roll over, the wind knocked out of him. Then the voice again, louder and coming from high on the tower. "Hey, Pickalew. Get up. Next play, Joker. Get up."

Was it the voice of God or the voice of the Man?

In 1960 Ray Ray Pickalew hadn't been sure if there was a difference. Now, just before he passed out on his pier along the Elk River, he still wasn't so sure.

11

The Giles County Jail had a "consultation room," where defense lawyers could meet with their clients. The room was not much bigger than a closet, decorated with the same yellow cinder-block walls as the holding cell.

When they were alone, seated in aluminum chairs and saddled up to a square-shaped folding table, the two men just looked at each other for several seconds. Tom was stunned by his friend's appearance. Bo wore orange prison clothes, and his eyes burned red from lack of sleep. His shoulders hunched forward as he placed his elbows on the table, and his fatigue was palpable. In addition to shock, Tom felt a wave of guilt wash over him. He had not seen Bo in over a year, not since Bo left Tom's farm in Hazel Green after dropping off Lee Roy in a small crate the previous June.

Finally, Tom broke the silence. "You look like crap."

Despite his predicament, Bo chuckled, and the sound warmed Tom's heart. "Thanks for doing this, Professor. So how did the morning go?"

For the next few minutes Tom took Bo through his conversation with Helen Lewis and his discussion afterward with Rick. The
only detail he omitted was his trek to the Elk River to see Ray Ray.

"Sounds like the General," Bo said, shaking his head. "Our first
peek at her case will be at the prelim. She always builds a stone wall
around the evidence."

"Bo, so far you haven't told me much over the phone. We
can't wait for the prelim to start our investigation. I need some
leads." He paused. "What can you tell me about the night of Andy
Walton's murder?"

Bo sighed and looked down at the table. "I got myself in a real
fix."

"In order to help you, Bo, I have to know the deal. Why are
you in here?"

"The deal, Professor . . . is complicated."

"Tell me."

Bo kept his eyes fixed on the table and smiled. "You remember
what I told you last year in Hazel Green about why I came back to
Pulaski to practice?"

"Unfinished business," Tom said. "Your father was murdered
by the Ku Klux Klan, and you . . . saw it happen." Tom paused. "You
never told me the whole story."

"I will now," Bo said, raising his head and looking at Tom with
bloodshot eyes.

—

"I was only five years old when they hung my daddy. We lived on
Walton Farm. My momma worked at the Big House as a house-
maid for Ms. Maggie, and my daddy worked the fields. Anyway,
on the night of August 18, 1966 there was a big party to celebrate
Ms. Maggie's birthday. Momma was working late at the Big House,
and I was home with Daddy. One second I was listening to the

radio and throwing a baseball up in the air. Next thing I see these men—I've always said there were twenty of them, but it could've been ten or twelve. Things look bigger to a five-year-old. Anyway, you get the drift. They had the robes. The hoods. They burned a cross in the front yard and told my daddy to get out there or they would set the house on fire. Before he walked out the door, Daddy told me not to watch, but I didn't listen. I followed them . . . and I saw it all.

"They drug him about a half mile from the house to this clearing that had a pond that me and some of the other farmhands' kids would swim in during the summer, encased in a large thicket of trees. They tied my daddy's hands behind his back and put him on top of a horse and walked the horse over to one of the trees on the edge of the clearing. I swear, Professor, when I saw my daddy tied up, I wanted to run. I wanted to but . . . my feet wouldn't move. You know that nightmare you have where you can't move? I lived it. I watched those bastards wrap that rope around a tree branch and tie a noose around my daddy's neck, and . . . I couldn't move.

"The leader of the men wore a red hood, and I recognized his voice. I had been around Andy Walton all my life, and I *knew* that the man under the red hood was Andy. Well, Andy says to my daddy—I'll never forget it—he says, 'Roosevelt, the Knights of the Ku Klux Klan understand that you have laid your filthy nigger hands on a white woman.'" Bo mimicked the voice. "My daddy then spits in Andy's face and says, 'That ain't what this is about. You and me both know what this is *really* about,' but Andy punches him in the nose before he can say anything else. Then Andy whispered something in my daddy's ear and kicked the horse.

"I . . . I really can't remember exactly what happened next. My feet started working when I saw Daddy hanging. All I remember is grasping at his legs, crying, and hearing those bastards laugh. Then I saw a boot coming at my face . . ." He paused, shaking his head. "Next thing I know I'm waking up by that clearing, and my daddy is gone. I see his clothes are down by the bank of the pond, so I dive in. I . . ." Bo's voice had started to shake. "I . . . found his body . . . at the bottom of the pond."

Bo sighed, looking at Tom. "I told my momma everything that happened, but she was scared. She didn't want to go to the police. Said they wouldn't do nothing." He paused. "She was right. When she wouldn't go, I got my Uncle Booker, my momma's brother, to drive me down to the sheriff's office. The sheriff back then was a man named Hugh Packard. A friendly sort but bought and paid for by Andy Walton. He said he couldn't prosecute anyone if I couldn't say that I saw who it was. He laughed and said he'd be run out of town on a rail if he prosecuted Andy Walton 'cause a five-year-old boy recognized his voice. And besides, it looked like a clear case of drowning." Bo shook his head. "And that's what they ruled it. Drowning."

"What about your mother?" Tom asked. "Did she ever—?"

"She left," Bo interrupted. "Two weeks later I woke up and she was gone. Not even a note."

"Why?" Tom asked.

"I really don't know. I . . . was never as close to Momma as I was Daddy. Sometimes before Daddy was killed, I'd be playing in the house or outside, and I'd catch Momma staring at me like she was mad or something, even when I hadn't done anything." He shook his head. "But I don't know exactly why she left. I've always thought it was because she was scared. I overheard her talking to my Aunt Mabel a few days after the hanging. Said she knew she was next. Said 'that monster ain't goin' stop till I'm as dead as Roosevelt.'" He sighed again. "She was gone the next morning."

"How—?" Tom started, but Bo raised a hand up to stop him.

"I'm getting there." He crossed his arms and squeezed them tight against his body, staring down at the table again. "Aunt Mabel woke me up that morning, and it was still dark outside. Said I needed to put some clothes on and pack my bags. I was goin' go stay with her and Booker for a while. I asked about Momma, and Mabel said Momma wanted me to stay with her and Booker for a few days. She was trying to sound calm, but her voice seemed off. Like she was out of breath. I knew something was wrong, but I didn't know how bad until I got outside and saw Uncle Booker. He was standing by his truck, holding a shotgun, watching the road that led up to the shack. I had never seen my uncle with a weapon of any sort, not even a knife. He was the pastor at the Bickland Creek Baptist Church, and he always preached against violence. He didn't even go rabbit or squirrel hunting." Bo shook his head. "But he had a gun that day. Aunt Mabel picked me up and carried me out of the house, and Uncle Booker wasn't even watching us. He had his gun on his shoulder, his eyes moving up and down the road. Once I was in the truck, I sat in between them, and they didn't say a word on the way to their house. I must have asked a hundred questions about Momma, but they were stone silent. The only sound I heard was the vibration of the steering wheel that came from Booker's hands, which were shaking like crazy.

"When we got back to their house, which was the parsonage next to Bickland Creek Baptist, Booker took me inside the sanctuary, and we sat in the first pew, looking up at the pulpit. He didn't say anything for a long time." Bo's lip started to quiver. "Then he told me that Sister—that's what he called my momma—had left the previous night, and she had asked Booker and Mabel to take care of me. I asked him where she had gone, and he said he didn't know. I asked him when she would be back, and he said he wasn't sure. Then he told me that I was welcome to stay at the parsonage for as long as I wanted." Bo paused, returning his eyes to Tom. His whole body had tensed at the retelling, and his glare was harsh. Tom had to look away for a second. "That turned out to be thirteen years," Bo finally continued. "I never heard from my momma again."

"I'm sorry, Bo," Tom said, feeling another pang of guilt. Bocephus Haynes was probably his best friend in the world. *How could I not know that his mother had abandoned him?*

"It's not something I share with a lot of people," Bo said, seeming to sense Tom's thoughts.

Watching his friend, Tom had the strange premonition that perhaps Bo's father's death, while unimaginably horrific for a young boy to watch, might in some ways have been easier to deal with than his mother's abandonment. The lynching was black and white. He could explain it because he saw it. But his mother leaving . . . How could a five-year-old boy ever understand that?

"I'm sorry, Bo. I . . . can't imagine." It was all Tom could think to say, and it was the truth.

Bo nodded and wiped his eyes. "They were good to me, Booker and Mabel," he said. "Never pretended they were my parents, and for the most part never told me what to do. They fed me, kept me in decent clothes, and made sure I went to school." Bo smiled. "And their kids, LaShell and especially Booker T., became like siblings. LaShell was older. A beautiful girl. Milk-chocolate skin with these thick lips and big"—Bo made a gesture with both palms over his chest—"breasts. I remember walking in the bathroom one day when she had forgotten to lock the door and catching her coming out of the shower, those boobies just bouncing like basketballs." Bo laughed, and Tom heartily joined in. Both men were relieved to release some of the tension that had enveloped the small room.

"Booker T. now, he was my boy," Bo continued. "Big old baby-faced son of a gun. Grew up to be a refrigerator of a man, just like that defensive lineman for the Bears. Remember ol' William Perry? Anyway, we were inseparable growing up." He shook his head. "A lot of the black folks at the church shied away from me after Daddy died and Momma left. Almost like I had some kind of disease or something they didn't want to catch. But not Booker

T. He didn't treat me no different than he had before. He . . . was my only friend during elementary and middle school. My brother."

"Did things change in high school?" Tom asked.

Bo shrugged. "Not with Booker T. He was still my brother and always will be. But things did change with everyone else. In the ninth grade I grew seven inches. By tenth grade I was six foot four and weighed over two hundred pounds. I went from being a benchwarmer on the junior high football team to starting at linebacker as a sophomore at Giles County High. At the beginning of my senior year, Coach Bryant came to Pulaski and watched me play. The next week Coach Gryska, one of the Man's assistants, called the parsonage and offered me a scholarship to play for Alabama."

Tom gave a knowing smile. Clem Gryska had also recruited him to play at Alabama almost twenty years before Bo.

"You met Jazz toward the end of college, right?" Tom asked.

"Yeah. Jazz grew up in Huntsville and ran track at Alabama. I met her at an athletic banquet a few months after I blew my knee out." Bo smiled at the memory. "Funny, I met you and Jazz in a span of a few weeks during the worst part of my college career."

Tom remembered that Coach Bryant had asked him to talk with Bo about his future after the knee injury. Tom had requested that Bo shadow him during some classes, and Bo had reluctantly agreed, still sullen over the loss of a possible career in the National Football League. Bo's attitude changed when the Tuscaloosa district attorney asked for Tom's help on some evidence issues in a murder trial, and Tom arranged for Bo to be a runner for the prosecutor during the trial.

"I've never seen a student who wanted to be a lawyer more than you," Tom said. "Once you watched that criminal trial—"

"I was hooked," Bo finished the thought. "When I saw that jury hand down a guilty verdict and the sheriff's deputies lead the defendant away in shackles, all I could think about was Andy

Walton being done the same way. I remember I ran back to the campus after that verdict. I didn't have a car back then, so I pretty much walked wherever I went unless I hitched a ride. When I got to Jazz's apartment, I was dripping with sweat and out of breath, and she had to fix me some water before I hyperventilated. Once I had cooled off, I told her I was going to law school. That I didn't care how long it took or what my grades were, I was going to be a lawyer. A lawyer, goddamnit!" Bo slammed his fist down on the table, and for a flickering moment Tom saw the twenty-two-year-old student he'd first met those many moons ago. Bright-eyed with an energy that knew no bounds.

"How did Jazz react?"

"She said I could do whatever I wanted. That *I*, Bocephus Haynes, could do whatever I wanted and she'd be proud of it." He paused, looking past Tom to nowhere in particular. "Then she told me she loved me for the first time." Bo sighed. "Honestly, Professor, I think it was the first time since I was five years old that anyone had said those words to me. I mean . . . I knew that Uncle Booker and Aunt Mabel loved me, but they didn't say it. And Booker T. and LaShell were kids. That's just not something kids say to each other. I thought I must have misheard Jazz, so I leaned close to her and asked her to repeat what she had said. Then she took my face in both her hands and said, 'I love you, Bocephus Haynes. *I love you*.'"

A hush fell over the room as Tom gave the memory its proper respect. Finally, in a voice just above a whisper, Bo said, "I wish I could say that I hugged her and told her that I loved her too, but . . . I didn't. I was scared, and I just stood there, my face blank. Like I'd just gotten off a roller coaster and was going to be sick. But Jazz . . . she didn't act disappointed. She just smiled and whispered in my ear that her roommate was gone for the afternoon. Then she led me by the hand into her bedroom . . .'"

Bo leaned back in his chair, and his eyes met Tom's. "I applied to law school the next week and . . . you pretty much know the rest."

"You were the best student I ever taught," Tom said. Then, knowing it was time to move the conversation from memory lane to present day, Tom leaned his elbows on the table and squinted at his friend. "Bo, what specifically is the business you came back to Pulaski to finish?"

Bo's bloodred eyes blazed with fury. "To put Andy Walton and every one of the bastards that lynched my daddy in a prison cell." He paused. "And to find out the *real* reason my father was killed."

—

For several seconds Tom said nothing, processing everything he'd just been told.

Then, taking a deep breath, he asked the question he'd waited thirty minutes to ask. "What happened the night Andy Walton was killed, Bo?"

"Honestly . . ." Bo began, shaking his head. "I'm not exactly sure. I . . ." He paused and looked at Tom. "It's going to sound bad, Professor."

"I don't care," Tom said. "To be able to defend you, I have to know everything you remember."

Bo sighed and leaned back in his chair. "I went to Kathy's Tavern on First Street, intending to get drunk and then go to the clearing."

"The clearing—"

"Where my father was lynched," Bo interrupted. "I go every year on the anniversary of his death."

"So what happened at Kathy's?"

Bo grimaced. Then he relayed his confrontation with Andy Walton and the conversation with Ms. Maggie afterward.

When he was through, Tom let out a low whistle. "Jesus, why didn't you just handwrite a confession?"

Neither of them laughed.

"You really quoted line and verse the 'eye for an eye' line from the Bible?"

Bo nodded.

"And then he's found hanging from a noose on his farm from the exact tree where your father was lynched."

Again, Bo nodded. "The same limb, according to Ennis. I . . . had pointed it out to him on a number of prior occasions when I tried to get the sheriff's department to reopen the investigation."

Tom pulled at his hair, trying not to despair but hearing the words of Helen Lewis play in his mind. *Bo came back to Pulaski for revenge.*

"Bad, huh?" Bo asked, but Tom ignored him.

"You said the four eyewitnesses to the confrontation were the bartender Cassie . . ."

"Dugan," Bo said, completing the sentence as Tom wrote the name down on a yellow legal pad. "The others were Clete Sartain—who was probably in the Klan with Andy, though I can't confirm that—Andy's wife, Ms. Maggie, and his brother-in-law, George Curtis."

Tom wrote each name on the pad, one under the other. "OK, that gives me a place to start. What happened after Kathy's?"

Bo shrugged. "I got a pint of Jim Beam from my office and took a walk. Ended up at our house on Flower Street that's now for sale. Just feeling sorry for myself . . . and tying one on pretty good." He sighed. "Then I went to the clearing on Walton Farm where my father was lynched. I don't remember much about being there that night, but I know I was there. It had rained a good bit beforehand, and I noticed that my loafers were muddy the next morning." Bo paused and looked down at the table. "That's really all I can recall."

"So you threatened to kill him in front of four eyewitnesses, and you admit to being at the murder scene?"

Bo made no response. He just continued to stare at the table.

"Was anyone with you when you went to the farm or . . . at any time after you left Kathy's?"

Bo shook his head. "No. I was alone."

Damnit, Tom thought. He began to pace back and forth over the concrete floor, working through the problems in his mind. Bo had no alibi, he had motive out the yin-yang, and the physical evidence, which they probably wouldn't see until the preliminary hearing, was described by the sheriff as "conclusive and over-whelming." Tom quickly came to a stark and rather obvious conclusion. *I'm in way over my head.*

He returned to his seat and looked his friend dead in the eye. "Bo, I appreciate your faith in me and Rick, but you really need an experienced criminal defense attorney to take this on, preferably someone with local ties. Have you thought about—?"

"I *am* an experienced criminal defense attorney," Bo interrupted. "What I need is a good trial lawyer who can talk to a Giles County jury. Someone who hasn't been roughed up by the General and . . . someone I trust. I realize that we'll need to retain local counsel, but I don't want a Pulaski lawyer as lead." He paused, looking Tom dead in the eye. "I want you."

When Tom didn't say anything, Bo chuckled, and the bitterness in his laugh was palpable. "I don't blame you for being scared. I'd be scared too if you asked the same of me in the face of the story I just told you." He paused. "I *am* scared."

"Bo—" Tom started, but Bo held up his hand to stop him.

"Professor, I haven't made a lot of friends in the legal community in this town over the years. Some of that is probably because I'm the only black trial lawyer in Pulaski. Even though we're in 2011, I can still feel a subconscious awkwardness around my white brethren of the bar." He shrugged. "And some of it is just me. I practice alone. I've never had a partner, and I typically blow off the social functions the bar puts on. And I am unapologetically aggressive and relentless when it comes to working a case. That approach has made me a successful attorney." He paused. "But it hasn't made me many friends . . . and it's probably cost me my wife and family."

"Are things with Jazz really over?"

Bo sighed. "I don't know. Right now we are separated, and Jazz is living with her parents in Huntsville. She's enrolled T. J. and Lila in the city schools there for the year, so . . . it ain't looking good." Bo chuckled bitterly. "I doubt that being charged with capital murder is going to help my cause."

"When did things start going south?"

Bo shrugged. "They've been strained for a long time. She has always thought my obsession with my father's murder wasn't fair to her, to our family . . . and she's probably right. When the kids really started getting dragged into it, she finally had enough."

Tom felt another pang of guilt as he saw the anguish on his friend's face. *All that time he was looking out for my butt last year, his own life was in shambles.*

Tom tried to shake off his shame and stay on point. "Bo, I'm sure any number of high-profile criminal defense attorneys from across the country would take this case."

Bo creased his eyebrows. "You think a jury in Pulaski, Tennessee is going to believe some Yankee lawyer over their own elected district attorney?"

"But that happens all the time," Tom said. "Remember the OJ case. He had lawyers from all over the place."

Bo smiled and kept his eyes on Tom. "The Juice's jury was mostly black and all from Los Angeles, and the lead attorney was a brother from LA."

"You don't think a high-profile lawyer will be convincing to a jury in Giles County, and you don't believe a local attorney will take the case," Tom said, attempting to sum up Bo's thoughts.

"Not exactly. I'm sure there are a couple criminal defense guys in town that would represent me if the price was right, and we'll probably have to associate one of them as local counsel regardless. But . . ."

"Not as first chair," Tom offered.

"I'd be bringing a knife to a gunfight," Bo said, shaking his head and sighing. "The General has not lost a case since she took office eight years ago." He paused. "What I need is a lead lawyer who hasn't been manhandled by Helen but who still knows the terrain and can talk to the folks on the jury on their level. You're from Hazel Green, Professor. That's less than thirty miles from here as the crow flies, forty-five by car. You may live and work in Tuscaloosa, but your roots are in this neck of the woods."

For several seconds neither of them said anything. Then Bo finally broke the silence. "Professor, I know taking on a capital murder case in another state several hours from Tuscaloosa will be a hardship on your new firm, so I'll agree to pay whatever fee you quote. If it were me, I'd charge a flat fee of two hundred fifty thousand dollars, half now and half when it's over. Win, lose, or draw. I'm certainly prepared to pay that sum or more. You just name the price."

"Bo, you don't have to pay—" Tom started, but Bo slammed his fist down on the table.

"Yes, I do. You get what you pay for in this world, and I don't want my lawyers going hungry."

"Bo, this is *your life*," Tom said, exasperation finally getting the better of him. "I've tried exactly one case in the last forty years. My partner has tried one case in his whole career. Yes, I'm from this neck of the woods, which I guess will help a little, but as your friend, I'd advise you to think this through a little longer and retain counsel with more experience."

Bo brought his hands together and folded them into a tent. "I have done nothing but think about this decision since the minute I was arrested last Friday morning. My decision now is the same one I came to within two seconds after the handcuffs were slipped over my wrists. I want you, Professor."

"*Why?*" Tom asked.

"Because there's no one else I trust with my life," Bo said, his voice cracking with emotion and fatigue. "No one but you."

12

At 5:00 p.m. sharp, Tom parked the Explorer in front of a red-brick house on Jefferson Street about a block east of Ms. Butler's. The sign in the yard was black with gold stenciled letters. "Curtis Family Medicine." Finding Dr. Curtis had been easy—the manager at Ms. Butler's had just pointed out the front door of the bed and breakfast and said, "Two football fields that way on the left. There's a sign out front."

The rain that had poured all afternoon had subsided to a slow drizzle, and the air felt sticky as Tom stepped out of his vehicle and walked up the path to the front porch of the house. He started to knock on the door but then heard a voice to his right.

"Can I help you?"

Tom turned to see a man that looked to be in his sixties sitting in a rocking chair on the porch. Tom was a bit taken back that he hadn't seen the man on his approach.

"Uh . . . yes, my name is Tom McMurtrie. I was looking for Dr. Curtis."

"Well, you found him," the man said, gesturing to himself and standing up. "George Curtis."

As they shook hands, Tom looked the doctor over. He was medium height with thinning salt and pepper hair. A pair of round wire-rimmed glasses adorned his face, and he was dressed casually in a short-sleeve button-down and khaki pants. His hand felt soft and small, his grip weak.

"Please," George said, gesturing toward the wicker couch adjacent to his chair. "Have a seat. I just finished with my last patient and was about to make a batch of lemonade. Would you like some?"

Tom accepted, and a few minutes later he was seated across from George on the porch, sipping from a plastic cup. If anything, the air had gotten stickier, and Tom felt sweat pooling underneath his white dress shirt.

"So what can I do for you, Mr. McMurtrie?"

"Please, call me Tom."

"OK," George said, not offering Tom the same courtesy.

"I've been retained by Bocephus Haynes to represent him on the murder charges brought against him by the state."

George blinked several times, but his face and body remained perfectly still. Tom thought again of how he had approached the office and not even seen the man sitting on the porch. The doctor's calm demeanor was a bit unnerving.

"OK . . . Why is it that you want to talk with me? I'm sure you know that the victim, Andy Walton, was my brother-in-law."

George's voice betrayed no emotion, but Tom now heard the accent. Southern aristocrat. The kind of voice an actor would use to portray a Southern plantation owner.

"You saw my client and the victim just a few hours before the murder."

"That's right," George said. "Your client threatened to kill my brother-in-law. Said he was going to 'make him bleed.'" George held up the index and middle fingers of both hands to make the quotation symbol. "I guess he made good on that promise."

"Were you concerned for Mr. Walton's life at that point, Doctor?"

George shrugged and took a sip of lemonade, his eyes never leaving Tom's. "Not really. Andy's always been able to take care of himself." He paused. "To tell the truth, I'm shocked that Andy would let anyone, much less Bo Haynes, kill him in the way it went down. Andy . . . was a hard man."

"He was also dying, right?"

Again, George blinked. "How did you know that?"

Tom considered his response. So far George Curtis hadn't told him anything he didn't already know. Tom thought Andy's cancer was a bad fact for the defense. He could almost hear Helen Lewis in her opening—*If Bo hadn't taken his revenge when he did, he might never have gotten the chance.* But after several seconds he came clean. "Your sister told Bo at Kathy's. She told him to let Andy die in peace."

George grimaced, his first outward show of emotion. "That's why she blames herself," he said, shaking his head. "I knew it had to be something like that." He paused. "She hasn't said a word since she saw Andy hanging from the tree."

"She saw?" Tom asked. This was new information.

"Yeah. When the fire department arrived on the scene, the chief said that Maggie arrived just a few minutes after he did." He paused and shook his head. "I'm not sure she'll ever be the same."

"I'm very sorry," Tom said, meaning it. "Would it be possible to talk with your sister?" Tom knew he was pushing his luck, but Maggie Walton was an important witness.

"No," George said, his voice hard. "That wouldn't be possible right now. It's just too soon."

The conversation lulled for several seconds, neither of them speaking, and Tom's sense of discomfort grew. George had an intense gaze that made Tom feel like he was being inspected.

"Doctor, can you think of anyone besides Bo who might have a bone to pick with your brother-in-law?"

George shrugged. "Andy was a polarizing figure in this town. I think there was a general *distaste* for him. You have to understand, Andy didn't grow up in Pulaski. He came from over in McNairy County. A lot of folks thought his money was dirty. Then there was his association with the Klan. Not sure many people ever got over that. The people here have always had to deal with the town being the birthplace of the Ku Klux Klan, but it's a past that Pulaski has tried to distance itself from. Andy's involvement as Imperial Wizard of the Tennessee chapter was another black eye for the town. But . . . no one wanted him dead. Andy gave a lot of his *dirty* money to the town. To its businesses and to Martin College and the church." Curtis chuckled. "What is the old saying? 'He's a son of a bitch, but he's our son of a bitch.' I think that's how the town viewed Andy."

Tom watched the doctor tell the story. *He's enjoying this*, Tom thought. It was time to give him a jolt. "Did you resent Andy for buying the family farm and saving your father from bankruptcy while you were in medical school?"

"Who told you that?"

"Raymond Pickalew," Tom said, his lips curving into a smile. "Ray Ray's an old friend of mine."

George returned the smile, but there was no humor behind his eyes. As with Helen, the mention of Ray Ray's name seemed to rattle the doctor. "Professor McMurtrie, it seems as if you are friends with all of the riffraff in town."

Tom's grin widened. "Dr. Curtis, it seems as if you might have a—how did you put it?—*distaste* for Ray Ray."

"Raymond Pickalew is a no-count drunk, and he always has been," George said, the slightest hint of an edge in his voice. Then, relaxing his shoulders, he leaned back in the rocking chair and wrapped his hands behind his back. "But getting back to your question, the truth is that I was relieved that Andy bought the farm. We all were. He saved our ass and allowed my father to die with dignity. We were all indebted to him for that."

Bullshit, Tom thought but didn't say. He decided to switch gears.

"Do you know Clete Sartain?" Tom asked.

"Everyone knows Clete," George said, chuckling. "He sacks groceries at the Johnson's Foodtown and looks just like Santa Claus. He's lived in Pulaski forever."

"Was he with you, Andy, and Mrs. Walton at Kathy's on the night of the murder?"

George scoffed. "He was there, but I wouldn't say he was *with* us. He just happened to be there. Clete is a regular at Kathy's."

"Was Clete in the Klan when Andy was the Imperial Wizard of the Tennessee chapter?"

George shrugged and drank the rest of his lemonade. "He might have been. I wouldn't know."

"Were you?"

The humorless smile returned to the doctor's face. "Well . . ." He abruptly stood up. "I'm sorry to have to run, but I have an engagement at the church later tonight, and I'm going to be late if I don't go now."

He didn't offer his hand to shake.

"Thanks for your time," Tom said, also standing, but George did not acknowledge him. The doctor walked past his visitor through the front door of the office and closed it behind him.

The sound of the sliding dead bolt was unmistakable.

—

It wasn't until Tom had reached the Explorer that he felt the cold chill on the back of his neck. *Professor McMurtrie, it seems as if you are friends with all of the riffraff in town.* The comment by George had struck Tom as defensive at the time, and he had gotten caught up in the back and forth, missing the hidden significance.

Professor McMurtrie . . .

Tom had not told George that he had been a professor in his former life. How could he possibly know that? As far as Tom knew, today was the first time that he had ever met George Curtis. Unless George had seen the same *USA Today* article that Helen had . . .

No, Tom thought. *Helen would have paid attention to that kind of news because she's an attorney and she already knew of me.*

It didn't make sense. Tom had yet to even file an appearance as Bo's lawyer. George shouldn't have known anything about Tom.

Maybe he has a source in the DA's office or the sheriff's department, Tom thought, sliding into the front seat and cranking the ignition. He had met with Helen this morning and told her his intention to file an appearance. Perhaps she had updated the family. He had also visited Bo at the jail this afternoon, and a sheriff's deputy could have called George and given him Tom's name. Either way George could have then googled Tom and learned all about him.

That's got to be it, he thought, easing the car forward and dialing Rick's number on his cell phone. As his partner's voice came over the line, Tom took a last look at the medical office. Behind the open blinds of the front window, he saw the shadow of a man watching him. Ray Ray was right, Tom thought, feeling gooseflesh break out on his arms.

The good doctor was a *"strange bird."*

13

George Curtis watched McMurtrie leave from behind the blinds and followed the Explorer with his eyes until it stopped out in front of Ms. Butler's Bed and Breakfast. *That's convenient,* he thought, remembering something his late brother-in-law had always said.

Keep your friends close and your enemies closer.

George packed up his briefcase and locked the office. Then he walked two doors down to his house and opened the door. His cat, a black-and-white-striped feline named Matilda, came running toward him, but he paid her no mind, lost in thought over his encounter with Bo Haynes's lawyer.

McMurtrie bothered him. When he had learned earlier in the day that McMurtrie would be Bo's lawyer, George had done some digging, and he hadn't liked what he'd found. It had been McMurtrie, a former law professor, who had spearheaded the big trial win in Henshaw, Alabama over Jack Willistone, whose trucks had routinely carried loads for many of Andy's businesses in Giles County. Over the years George had come to know Jack pretty well.

George knew that anyone who got the jump on Jack Willistone had to be pretty tough.

George's encounter a few minutes ago with McMurtrie had done nothing to ease his concerns. The lawyer had already gotten some of the history. Knew Andy was an interloper. A scalawag who had come in and saved the day. And McMurtrie's question to George had contained some challenge.

Did George resent Andy for saving the farm?

George lit a cigar and sat down in the den, turning on the television set. As an old episode of *Friends* came on, he scanned the dark house. He rarely kept lights on inside, as they gave him a headache, but the glow from the tube allowed him to see the familiar surroundings. The painting of Count Pulaski above the mantle of the fireplace to his left. The old rocker to his right that his mother had rocked him and Maggie in as kids. And beyond the television, the short hallway leading to the home's two bedrooms, one of which was his, while the other was the "guest" room.

At the thought of the guest room, George subconsciously smiled. He could count the "guests" that had stayed in that room over the past thirty years on one hand. There had, however, been one frequent guest.

Matilda crawled into his lap, and he stroked her behind the ears, his thoughts returning to McMurtrie. And the history . . .

Of course he had resented Andy. Hated the son of a bitch. But not because of the farm. George had never loved the property like Maggie. Sure, he had enjoyed hunting dove in the fall and had always been a good shot, but the lure of the land held nothing for him. He would rather have moved when their father hit hard times. Had even talked with Maggie about it. *Let's take what we can get for the farm and move the family to Nashville. Or even Atlanta. Anywhere . . .*

George sighed, and hearing the sound, Matilda purred. George had never wanted to save the farm. He had only wanted . . .

His cell phone chirped in his pocket, interrupting his thoughts with the indication that he had a new text message. He pulled the phone out and clicked open the message.

Coming over in a few.

George rose from the couch and slowly walked to his bedroom. He opened the closet door and retrieved his gun case from the shelf below, where his suits hung. He brought the case over to his bed and flipped the latches.

Inside there were only three guns.

A .30-30 deer rifle. A .38-caliber pistol. And, of course, a twelve-gauge shotgun. Dove season was just around the corner, but George wasn't thinking about doves. He removed the twelve-gauge and aimed it at the mirror across the room, seeing Andy in his mind. Handsome, cocksure, luckier-than-smart Andy. He flipped the safety off the gun and squinted, looking down the barrel. He tensed when he saw someone else's reflection in the mirror.

"Never know when one of those is going to come in handy," the familiar voice said.

George smiled at the other face staring back at him in the mirror.

His guest had arrived.

14

As the sun set over the Strip in Tuscaloosa, Rick Drake and Powell Conrad sat in wrought-iron chairs on the outside patio of Buffalo Phil's, devouring a plate of wings and splitting a pitcher of Bud Light. "Jack Willistone is serving a three-year sentence at the state pen in Springville for blackmail and witness tampering," Powell said, dipping a wing into a plastic container of ranch sauce and taking a bite. "Eligible for parole in eighteen months for good behavior."

"What about the bastard that tried to kill Dawn?"

"James Robert Wheeler," Powell said. "Goes by the name of JimBone. He left his El Camino behind after his failed attempt to murder Dawn, and we took some prints off the steering wheel. After a couple of weeks we got a match in the army database."

Rick raised his eyebrows.

"Yes, sir, James Robert Wheeler was in the US Army from 1992 to 2000. His specialty was explosives. In 2000 he quit, and there is really no official record of him since. It's like he dropped off the face of the earth. But remember Mule Morris?"

"How could I forget?" Rick asked, feeling goose bumps break out on his arm. Mule Morris, a key witness in the Willistone case, had died two months prior to trial when he lost control of his truck on Highway 25 in Faunsdale. The official cause of the accident had been brake failure, but Mule's cousin Doolittle had swore up and down that Mule kept his truck in mint condition. "What about him?"

"There wasn't much of Mule's truck left after the accident, but the forensics team in Faunsdale did find a few stray fingerprints on the wreckage."

"No way," Rick said, anticipating where Powell was going. "Wheeler?"

"Bingo," Powell said. "Doo was right all along. Wheeler messed with the brakes on that car. We ran the artist sketch by several folks at Ca-John's, and a waitress remembers seeing a man who meets his description sitting in the restaurant that night. In fact, she remembers that he was sitting alone very close to where Mule was talking to a young man and an attractive young lady."

"Jesus," Rick said. He and Dawn had met with Mule at Ca-John's just a few hours before his wreck. He hadn't remembered seeing any strange people at the tables nearby, but he was so focused on Mule he probably hadn't paid any attention. "So he killed Mule?"

"There's not a doubt in my mind," Powell said. "And we know he tried to kill Dawn."

"You think he's still alive?"

"They never pulled him from the Black Warrior, so we have to assume so. From Bo's investigation in the Willistone case, we knew Wheeler had spent some time at that strip joint outside of Pulaski, so we contacted the sheriff of Giles County, Ennis Petrie, and put out an APB on him. Now every county sheriff's office in Alabama and Tennessee has him on their 'Most Wanted' list." Powell shrugged. "So far nothing has turned up."

"How did you hear he goes by JimBone?"

Powell smiled. "That came from Jack Willistone. After we got the prints back from the army, me and Wade went over to Springville and paid Jack a visit. Jack said Wheeler goes by JimBone and sometimes he shortens it to Bone." Powell shook his head and drained the rest of his beer. "Unfortunately, that's all we got. Jack said JimBone was an acquaintance and nothing further."

"Do you believe him?"

"Hell no!" Powell said, waving his hands up in the air, both of which were stained with wing sauce. In his lifetime Rick had met few people louder or more gregarious than Ambrose Powell Conrad. He had also met few who were smarter or better in a courtroom. "We just can't find a link," Powell continued. He wolfed down another wing and pointed at Rick. "But we will. It is a top priority of the Tuscaloosa County Sheriff's Office and the DA to haul his ass in. We've been monitoring Jack Willistone's visitor's log, but so far we haven't seen anything suspicious."

"Do you know if Andy Walton ever visited him?"

"Not off the top of my head," Powell said. "But I'll check after the verdict comes back in Arrington." Powell had just finished up the two-week murder trial of a middle school teacher named Foster Arrington, who was accused of abducting, raping, and murdering one of his students. The trial had concluded earlier today, and all that was left was the reading of the verdict. The judge had dismissed the jury for the day, so Powell had readily accepted Rick's offer of wings and beer.

"Thanks, man."

"No problem. Even if Walton's not on the visitor's log, it's probably time to make a visit to Springville. With Willistone in jail, JimBone needs someone else to bankroll him."

Powell put a buffalo wing in his mouth, and his sauce-stained lips curved into a shit-eating grin. Rick knew that grin well. "You've got a plan?" he asked, incapable of stopping his own smile.

Powell raised his eyebrows, and his grin widened. "Don't you think Jack Willistone is getting tired of prison food?"

"A deal," Rick said, nodding along with Powell. "You really think Jack Willistone might deal?"

"I don't have a clue," Powell said, wiping wing sauce off his mouth, but the grin remained. "But when I get through with Arrington . . . I think it's worth a road trip to the state pen."

15

When Tom arrived at Bo's office at 7:00 a.m. the next morning, he had a surprise waiting for him. Leaning against the front stoop and dressed in a rumpled coat and tie was none other than Ray Ray Pickalew.

"Figured you'd get an early start," Ray Ray said, curling his lips up into his patented Joker face.

"I take it you're in?" Tom asked, smiling at his old teammate.

"I'm in," Ray Ray said.

"What made you change your mind?"

Ray Ray shrugged. "Oh, I guess I . . . just had to pray on it."

"I didn't realize you were the praying type, Ray Ray."

"Oh, I talk to God all the time," Ray Ray said. "He just don't listen."

Tom laughed and started to unlock the door, but Ray Ray put his hand up to stop him. "So, I've got some information that I think you'll find helpful." He sighed and wiped sweat from his forehead. "But first I need some breakfast."

Now that he was closer to him, Tom smelled the strong odor of whiskey. "Are you hungover?"

"No," Ray Ray said, beginning to walk across the street. "I'm still drunk."

———

A minute later they were sitting at a back table at the Bluebird Café, a favorite local breakfast spoon caddy-corner from Bo's office and just two blocks from the courthouse square. The smells of bacon grease, coffee, and pancakes fueled the air, and Tom breathed them all in as he sipped from a mug of black coffee.

"The body was moved," Ray Ray said after the waitress had taken their orders.

"What?" Tom asked, feeling his pulse quicken.

"From the Sundowners Club, a little strip joint on the edge of town that Andy liked to visit. He was shot in the parking lot at the Sundowners with a twelve-gauge, and then his body was moved a quarter mile down 64 to Walton Farm. There is a dirt road entrance there that goes right past a small clearing." Ray Ray paused and sipped his coffee. "This is the place where Bo's daddy was lynched by the Klan in 1966. The area is surrounded by trees, and the killer hung Andy from the same tree limb where Bo's father was hanged."

"How can someone get in the farm? There's got to be security, right? A gate or something?" Tom fired off the questions, but something else that Ray Ray had said had begun to nag at the back of his mind. The name of the strip club . . .

Ray Ray nodded. "Yeah, there's a gate and also a surveillance camera."

Tom felt his heart beat even harder at the mention of a camera.

"Cops found the camera lens smashed in," Ray Ray continued, shaking his head. "The last thing on the tape is Bo's ugly mug swinging a baseball bat at it."

Tom covered his face with his hands. "Jesus Christ."

"Exactly," Ray Ray said.

Tom turned the information over in his mind, remembering what Bo had said during their meeting at the jail. "Bo said he visited the clearing every year on the anniversary of his father's death."

"That doesn't surprise me," Ray Ray said as the waitress set their food down on the table.

When she was gone, Tom grabbed a piece of bacon and pointed it at Ray Ray. "But how could he get in if there was a gate and camera?"

Ray Ray shrugged. "That I don't know. I suspect he may have had some help from his cousin."

"Who?"

"Bo's cousin, Booker T., leases a lot of farmland in Giles and Lawrence Counties, including the Waltons' property. If Bo wanted to get on Walton Farm without being seen, I bet Booker T. helped him." He leaned back in his seat as the waitress refilled his coffee cup. Once she was gone, Ray Ray grimaced. "And I bet the General has been on him like stink on shit ever since Bo was arrested."

"If the body was moved from the strip club, it had to be taken by car, right?" Tom asked.

"Probably," Ray Ray said, shrugging. "But Bo is a very strong man. It's conceivable he could have carried Andy a quarter of a mile."

"But to hang him and burn him?"

"He could've set the gas and rope down at the clearing and gone back for Andy. The video of him breaking the camera lens was around eleven thirty. My source says Andy didn't even leave the Sundowners until closing time, which is around one in the morning. So Bo was definitely at the clearing before the shooting." Ray Ray put a healthy helping of eggs in his mouth and spoke with his mouth full. "I figure he probably got the code to the gate from

Booker T., and after breaking the camera at eleven thirty drove through a couple hours later with Andy's body in the car."

"You mean you think that is the prosecution's theory?" Tom asked.

"Of course."

"OK . . . so why would he have gone to the clearing earlier?"

"To scout out the area and to break the surveillance camera."

Tom paused to eat some of his pancake, which was delicious, but stopped after several bites. He had lost his appetite. Ray Ray's breakdown of how the prosecution would view the evidence made sense.

And he knew it would also make sense to a jury.

Despite the bad vibes he was feeling, Tom smiled at his friend. "How might I ask did you find out all of this so quickly?"

The Joker grin was back. "The sheriff's department is a volatile place, Tommy boy," Ray Ray said, wolfing down the rest of his plate. "A lot of divorces. I got a pretty good settlement for one of the deputies a few years back, and he owed me one."

Tom shook his head and smiled. This was why he had wanted Ray Ray Pickalew on the team. "Good work, partner."

"There is a lot of work left to do," Ray Ray said, his grin gone. "We obviously need to meet with Booker T. and find out everything he knows."

Tom nodded. "Did your source mention that Bo was at Kathy's Tavern earlier in the night?"

Ray Ray chuckled. "Yep. My guy said Bo told Andy he was going to give him an 'eye for an eye' in front of several eyewitnesses. Do you have the names?"

Tom rattled them off, and Ray Ray said they should split up the interviews. "I've known Clete forever. Let me take him. Why don't you go down to Kathy's and talk with Cassie? Ms. Maggie is probably off-limits for now and—"

"I've already interviewed George Curtis." Tom paused. "By the way, you were right. He is a bit odd."

"He's as queer as a football bat, if you ask me," Ray Ray said. "But he's too goddamn proud to come out of the closet. I think his problem is that he's lived a lie his whole life."

Tom rubbed his chin, pondering that idea. *Could be,* he thought. But it didn't feel right to him.

"We also need to get over to that strip joint and interview any of the employees who came into contact with Andy Walton on the night of the murder," Tom said, and Ray Ray grinned again.

"That sounds like a job for Ray Ray. I'm already acquainted with the talent there."

"Don't enjoy it too much," Tom said, but the thought that had nagged him earlier was back. "What is the name of that place again?"

"The Sundowners Club. It's a dive on the outskirts of Pulaski on Highway 64. It's owned by a sorry son of a bitch named Larry Tucker, who I went to high school with back in the day. Been around since the early '80s or so. I'm pretty sure Andy Walton bankrolled Larry's operation. Andy and some other guy . . ." Ray Ray snapped his fingers. "Oh, who was that asshole? Made a fortune in long-haul trucking. Big SOB from your neck of the woods, Tom. You would know him if I said the name. Jack . . ." He snapped his fingers again. "Oh, shit, what's his last name? Jack . . ."

"Willistone," Tom finished Ray Ray's sentence, his blood going cold. "Jack Willistone."

16

When they were back at Bo's office, Ray Ray said he was going to walk over to the courthouse and poke around the clerk's office. He knew everyone over there, and he might be able to get a feel for who the judge might be for Bo's case. Ray Ray said the judge would make all the difference in deciding whether to challenge venue. "If we get Harold Page, we're fucked and we need to seek a change of venue immediately. Page is an ornery old bastard who seems to hate everyone but Helen Lewis. But if we get Susan Connelly . . . then the choice is not so black and white. Susan is tough on crime, but she's also fair and, most importantly, smart. Run that by Bo, but I think he'll agree."

"Will do," Tom said, still reeling from the information disclosed by Ray Ray at the Bluebird. *The murder scene is the Sundowners Club . . .*

Tom and Rick's star witness in the Willistone case last summer had been a stripper employed by the Sundowners Club named Wilma Newton, whose husband was the driver involved in the accident. She had agreed to testify against the company, saying that her husband was forced to speed by the driving schedule he was put on by Jack Willistone. It had been a great plan—the trucker's widow sticking it to the company. Unfortunately, Jack got to Newton before the trial, and she did a 180 on the stand, testifying that her husband's schedule was fine. Luckily, Bo had investigated the Sundowners in the days prior to trial and had learned that Jack Willistone and another man—his "henchman," Bo had called him—had been meeting with Newton in the weeks leading up to trial. Bo's investigation had given Tom the ammunition he needed to cross-examine Newton on the stand when she had changed her story.

Jack Willistone was now presumably in prison somewhere. But the last time Tom or anyone else had seen his henchman was when he jumped off the Northport Bridge into the Black Warrior River. His body was never found.

"What about the jury pool?" Tom finally asked, trying to stay focused. Venue was a huge consideration going forward. "With everyone knowing Bo's history with Andy Walton in Giles County, shouldn't we move for a change of venue regardless of which judge is appointed?"

Ray Ray was shaking his head before Tom finished. "I think that would be an overreaction. By the time Helen is finished, whichever jury is selected is going to know Bo's backstory, that he was threatening biblical revenge, and on the night of the murder was seen at the very clearing where both his father and Andy Walton were lynched. Revenge, revenge, revenge. The General will saturate the jury with her theme. Plus this case has already received national news coverage. I saw several stories on CNN over the weekend, all of which mentioned that Bo has claimed since he was five years old that the Ku Klux Klan lynched his father." He paused. "The bottom line is that every jury pool in this state, if not the whole southern United States, has already been poisoned by Bo's history."

"But the folks here know Bo. They've heard about his back-story their whole life."

Ray Ray shrugged. "They also know Andy Walton and his Klan history. I think it's a wash. People here may not like Bo, but no one really liked Andy either. Again"—he held up his hands—"a wash."

"So it all comes down to the judge," Tom said.

"Yep. If we get Susan, we stay. If we get Page, we punt." He paused again. "And pray."

———

After Ray Ray had left for the courthouse, Bo's secretary, Ellie Michaels, came into the conference room with several documents under her arm. Ellie was a plump black woman in her late fifties who had served as Bo's secretary, paralegal, and receptionist for the past twenty years. Last night, after his interview of George Curtis, Tom had met Ellie at Bo's office to discuss the case.

Ellie hadn't hesitated when Tom had asked if she would stay on to help him and Rick with the trial. "I've been with Bo Haynes since he was a pup lawyer and had an Afro haircut. In the early days we were lean and times were tight." She had laughed loud and hearty. "But these last ten years—lordy mercy, Professor. Every time Bo has won or settled a big case, he has given me a bonus off the top." Wiping tears from her eyes, she had said, "I've sent all five of my children and two grandbabies to college off the money I've made working for Bo Haynes. I'd walk barefoot through glass for that man."

Unfortunately, Ellie knew nothing of relevance from the day of the murder. Yes, she knew that August 18 was the anniversary of Bo's father's death, and like every year on the anniversary Bo had been in a foul mood. She also knew about Bo's split with Jazz, and that he was living at the office. "Such a shame, Professor. Those two are still so much in love." She had grunted. "They're just both too stubborn to realize it."

The office had been plundered by the sheriff's department all weekend, but Ellie had not let them touch any of Bo's case files without a court order. "I told 'em straight up no one's going to be violating the attorney-client privilege on Ellie's watch, and they shut up quick." Tom had laughed and been genuinely relieved that Ellie was willing to stay on for the trial.

Now she put the papers that would announce their entry into the fray in front of him side by side. All of the documents had the style of the case front and center: *The State of Tennessee v. Bocephus Aurulius Haynes.*

"This is the notice of appearance for you, Mr. Drake and Mr. . . . Pickalew." Ellie said the word "Pickalew" like she had a bad taste in her mouth.

"I get the feeling you don't like Ray Ray, Ellie."

She wrinkled up her nose. "One whiff of the man is enough to give a teetotaler like me a buzz." She snorted. "I bet if you stuck him with a pick, you could fill up a barrel of whiskey."

Single-barrel Ray Ray, Tom thought, stifling a smile. "He's good, though, Ellie."

"I won't disagree with you on that. I just don't like smelling him." She pointed at the other two documents. "This is you and Mr. Drake's motion for admission to the state of Tennessee *pro hac vice.*"

"And this is the motion for an expedited preliminary hearing," Ellie continued. "Mr. Pickalew has already signed everything, so you just need to sign for you and Mr. Drake."

Tom looked over the paperwork, feeling his heart rate quicken. There was no backing out now, he knew. He signed the documents and handed them to Ellie, who put them back under her arm. Then she smiled down at him.

"What?" Tom asked.

"Wide ass open."

Tom creased his eyebrows, not getting it.

"It's what Bo says every time a case is about to start moving." Her voice began to tremble as she spoke. "He . . . always rubs . . . his hands together and says, 'All right now, dog, you know what speed we've got to take it to now.'"

Tom smiled as Ellie wiped her tears. "Wide ass open," he said.

17

On the way to the jail, Tom called Rick.

"The Sundowners Club? You have to be kidding?" Rick's voice was hyper, and Tom could almost feel the kid's energy from across the phone line.

"I'm not," Tom said. "Andy Walton was shot and killed at the Sundowners Club, and his body was moved to Walton Farm, where it was hanged from the same tree where Bo's father was lynched in 1966."

"Then the body was set on fire."

"Yep." Tom pulled into the jail and cut off the ignition. "Listen, Rick, I don't have much time. I need to go over all this with Bo. Have you talked with Powell yet?"

"Yeah, last night. Powell said Jack Willistone is incarcerated at the state penitentiary in Springville, serving out a three-year sentence. He also said that the Tuscaloosa County Sheriff's Office is still investigating Willistone's henchman, whose name is—get this—James Robert 'JimBone' Wheeler. Anyway, Powell said he'd be glad to go with us to interview Jack, but he's finishing up a two-week murder trial himself right now."

"Arrington?" Tom asked.

"Yes, sir."

"Leave him alone then," Tom said, climbing out of the Explorer. "But as soon as it's over—"

"We'll go to Springville."

"Good man," Tom said.

"Professor, do you think it's possible that Jack Willistone or JimBone Wheeler could somehow be involved in Andy Walton's murder?" Rick asked as Tom opened the door to the visitor's entrance to the Giles County Jail.

"I don't know," Tom said. "But I don't believe in coincidences."

18

In the consultation room of the jail, Bo was anxious and on edge, pacing as Tom summarized everything Ray Ray had told him. He seemed to be having a difficult time coming to grips with the fact that Raymond Pickalew was going to be part of his defense team.

"Professor, I know we need local counsel, but I hate that motherfucker," Bo said, scowling, his hands balled into fists after Tom had finished the recap. "The last case I had with Ray Ray, I just about took his head off."

"The reasons you hate him are exactly why we need him," Tom insisted. "He's a brawler, and he's gone toe to toe with Helen before and whipped her ass."

Bo raised his eyebrows. "You talking about her divorce."

Tom nodded. "She may be the meanest prosecutor in the state of Tennessee, but her ex-husband took her to the cleaners in their divorce. And you know who his attorney was?"

Now Bo smiled. "Ray Ray."

"When I mentioned that we would be associating Ray Ray as local counsel, I thought the General was going to faint."

Bo sighed, the smile fading from his face. "OK, Professor, I trust you. But dealing with Helen Lewis as a party in a divorce proceeding is a little different than going to battle with her in a capital murder trial."

"Can you think of anybody in Giles County who would be a more effective local counsel than Ray Ray?"

When Bo didn't answer, Tom held out his palms.

"OK, you got me," Bo finally said, plopping down in the aluminum chair across from Tom.

"Bo, did you go to the Sundowners Club the night of Andy Walton's murder?"

Bo shook his head. "Absolutely not. I haven't been to that place since I investigated it during the Willistone trial last summer."

"You're sure?"

"Positive."

"OK," Tom said, satisfied. "Ray Ray is going to go out there today and start interviewing employees. Any thoughts?"

Bo nodded. "The owner of the Sundowners is Larry Tucker. Tucker is still a card-carrying member of the Tennessee Knights of the Ku Klux Klan. Outside of Andy Walton, who I know was there, the only other person that I am almost positive participated in my daddy's lynching is Larry Tucker. I seriously doubt that Tucker will want to be helpful or cooperative to our defense, but Ray Ray's a good person to send out there. I'm sure he's dropped a lot of dollar bills in the Sundowners." Bo sighed, then snapped his fingers. "The bartender, Peter Burns, should be helpful if he can. Burns is who gave me the information you used to cross the trucker's widow in the Willistone trial. He owes me, because I represented him a few years back on a DUI and he was acquitted. If he's still around, you need to talk with Burns. From what I recall, if anything happens in that joint he knows about it."

"Anything else?"

"Talk with the dancers. I bet Andy had a favorite."

Tom jotted some notes down on his pad and then looked Bo in the eye. It was time to change direction. "Why did you break the surveillance camera at the gate to Walton Farm?" Tom asked.

Bo sighed. "Honestly, Professor, I don't remember doing that. I was . . . very drunk."

"You told me yesterday that you went to the clearing every year on the anniversary of your father's death. How could you do that if the farm had a gate and video surveillance."

"In years past I would park along Highway 64 and hop a low part of the fence a good distance away from the cameras. This year Andy put a new barrier around the place. I mean, it's like the Great Wall of China now."

"So how did you get to the clearing on the night of the murder?"

Bo stared down at the table. "My cousin, Booker T., he farms the land out there . . . He gave me the code."

It was the answer that Tom expected, but it was no less damaging or significant. "I need to speak with him as soon as possible," Tom said. "Can you give me his number?"

Bo did, shaking his head as he called out the digits. "You think Helen will charge him with something?"

"You tell me," Tom said. "Sounds like it's a decent possibility. Accessory to trespass or even—"

"Accessory to murder," Bo finished the thought, closing his eyes.

19

George Curtis stood in the kitchen, watching his sister through the open slit in the blinds. Even at sixty-nine years old, her once-golden hair now solid white, Maggie Curtis Walton was still a beautiful woman. When they were younger, George had always thought of Linda Evans from her *Big Valley* days when he would watch his sister, six years his senior, ride horses on the farm. These days, with her white hair cut shorter, she often reminded George of Ellie Ewing from the nighttime soap *Dallas*.

Now, four days removed from her husband's brutal murder and just an hour after his graveside funeral service, Maggie sat in a rocking chair on the porch, holding a leather-bound copy of the Holy Bible tight to her chest. Her exhaustion was palpable.

George knew that getting through the funeral had been torture for his sister.

Due to the mutilated condition of Andy's body and Maggie's shock at the gruesome nature of her husband's murder, George had decided against a visitation, and a viewing had been out of the question. Instead, he had organized a private graveside service at

Maplewood Cemetery. So, with temperatures hovering just under one hundred degrees, approximately fifty people, most of them friends of Maggie's from church and the Junior League, sweated and fanned their way through the ceremony, which was officiated by the Reverend Walter Griffith of First Presbyterian. General Helen Lewis, Sheriff Ennis Petrie, and several deputies were on hand as well, but they were mostly there to keep curiosity seekers out. Andy's longtime attorney, Charles Dutton, as well as the mayor of Pulaski, Dan Kilgore, were also present. Mayor Kilgore seemed especially sad, though George suspected that the politician's demeanor had more to do with the bad publicity the town was receiving in the aftermath of the murder than any grief he felt over Andy's death.

All of the guests, at George's request, stayed clear of Maggie, who spent the service sitting on the front row of chairs, her hands clutching the same Bible she clung to now. Even after Reverend Griffith had finished his eulogy and people began approaching the coffin to pay their respects and leave flowers, Maggie remained glued to her seat, her posture perfectly erect as she stared blankly at her husband's coffin.

Maggie's eyes carried the same listless look now as she gazed over the railing at the night sky. Below her and in all directions the hills flattened into fifteen hundred acres of the best farmland in all of Giles County—property that had been in the Curtis family since before the turn of the century. Above her a ceiling fan whirled full blast, cooling the porch slightly, but the unrelenting heat still made the setting a bit uncomfortable. Sweat rolled down Maggie's cheeks and neck, but she made no effort to wipe it off.

Feeling a pang in his heart, George forced himself to turn from the window and look at the three men who had gathered in the kitchen parlor. Counting George, they were the last remnants of the lynch mob that hanged Franklin Roosevelt Haynes on the northeast corner of this farm in 1966.

Originally, there had been ten, but in the years since the lynching, their number had gradually dwindled as accidents, bad health, and age began to catch up with them. With Andy's murder, there were now just the four of them left. George made eye contact with each of the other men in the kitchen. Then, taking off his glasses, he spoke. "She hasn't said a word since seeing the body."

The other men remained silent, their eyes focused intently on George.

"I've given her several Valium, and I'm sure I'll have to give her an Ambien to sleep." He sighed. "I've never seen her like this. Not even after Drew . . ."

Drew Walton had been the only son born of the marriage between Andy and Maggie Walton. Drew had been a straight-A student at Giles County High and then went on to David Lipscomb in Nashville to study music. At nineteen years old he'd been found lying in a bathroom in a bar on Music Row, a heroin needle stuck in his arm. Dead of an apparent overdose. Though Maggie never let anyone utter the word "suicide" around her, George had always thought the boy had killed himself.

"Drew wasn't lynched like a field nigger, Doc." Larry Tucker, owner of the Sundowners Club, spoke in a whiskey-soaked Southern drawl and rubbed his scruffy beard, a toothpick stuck in the corner of his mouth. "Andy was." Larry paused and stepped into the middle of the parlor, moving his eyes around the room. "On *her* land." He looked George dead in the eye. "Your family's land, Doc."

"He was killed at your club, Larry," George said.

"That's right," Larry said, his bloodshot eyes again moving wildly around the room. "He was. The question, gentlemen, is what are we going to do about it?"

"Nothing." The voice came from behind Larry, and he turned around to face it. "Nothing?" Larry asked, squinting at the man.

"Nothing," Sheriff Ennis Petrie repeated. "If he's guilty, then Helen Lewis will make sure that he is put to death. The General is undefeated as a prosecutor, and the preliminary investigation indicates that Bo is guilty as sin."

"I don't think we should trust a cunt to do a man's job," Larry said, stepping closer to the sheriff, spittle flying from his mouth as he spoke.

"Helen Lewis has bigger balls than you do, Larry," Ennis said. "There is *nothing* for us to do."

"Spoken like a yellow-bellied, chicken-shit politician if there ever was one," Larry said, placing his hands on his hips and continuing to gnaw on the toothpick.

"That's enough, Larry," George said. "Ennis has a point."

"Ennis can suck my dick," Larry said, pausing with his mouth open, toothpick dangling.

"No, thanks," Ennis said. He was still wearing his badge and uniform and lowered his thumb to his gun holster. "Don't fuck with me, Larry."

Larry smiled at the sheriff, but there was no humor in his eyes. "Your backbone has gotten almost as soft as your belly, Ennis." Then he turned his head and looked around the room. "Goddamnit, fellas, come on! Andy Walton would roll over in his grave if he thought his family and friends were just gonna lie down and let a damn lady prosecutor avenge his death. Tape up those vaginas and remember who you are and where you came from. Tennessee chapter for life, remember?"

Ennis stared back at him, making no attempt to hide his disgust. "The rest of us got out of the Klan a long time ago, Larry. Andy got out too, remember? You're the only one still carrying the banner."

"Oh, come off it, Ennis. Everyone in here knows the only thing you care about is that precious badge on your chest. What? Don't you think we can take the nigger out without you being implicated?" His mouth curved into a wide grin. "I know a guy, Ennis. A guy used to come in my club last year. A *fixer* of things, you might say. He actually approached me earlier tonight. Called me from a pay phone and offered to take Haynes out. Said he had a score to settle with the nigger." Larry paused and licked his lips, his eyes dancing around the room before they returned to Ennis. "My guy could take Bo out, and everyone in here would be as clean as the brass on that badge of yours. Come on, man. Don't you see Ms. Maggie out there? How can you stand there and tell us to back off?"

Ennis took a step forward and stuck his index finger into Larry's chest. "The fact of the matter, you ignorant redneck piece of shit, is that some of us here have more at stake than others." The sheriff nodded at the other remaining guest in the room, and they both stepped toward the door. When Ennis grabbed the knob, he turned and looked only at their host. "Doc, I'm sorry about Andy, and I'm damn sure sorry that Ms. Maggie saw him hanging from that tree. But my advice is to stay the hell out of Helen's way and let her do her job. Pride and family honor don't change the situation. Bo is guilty and is going to be put to death for it. There is *nothing* for us or anyone else to do."

When they were gone, George looked out the window again and watched the sheriff's cruiser move steadily down the long and winding gravel driveway to Highway 64 below.

"Well . . ." Larry said. "What's it gonna be, Doc? Are we gonna hold our dicks and do nothing? Or are we gonna do something?"

When George didn't answer, Larry continued. "George, if we're gonna leave things to Helen, we at least need to address McMurtrie. He's the reason Jack Willistone is sitting in a prison cell instead of filling my club up with truckers wanting lap dances. If we can take McMurtrie out, we'll make Helen's job a lot easier."

Still looking out the window, George lowered his eyes to his sister, who continued to rock slowly back and forth in the chair. Finally, he turned back to Larry. "You said you knew a guy."

20

On the outskirts of Lawrence County, Tennessee, about thirty miles north of Pulaski, is a small village called Ethridge. Within this village is the largest per capita Amish settlement in the southern United States. Everyone in Ethridge wore the community's traditional gear. Black pants, black jackets, and black hats on bearded men. Long black and white dresses with white bonnets for the women. Transportation was limited to horse-drawn buggies, and the only food eaten was grown in the fields nearby.

If a person was aiming to disappear from society, it was a pretty good place to be. It was also a good place to stow away valuables taken from another life, as the police were unlikely to stop a man pulling a horse-drawn carriage.

Inside the dark log cabin, JimBone Wheeler, a.k.a. the Bone, lit a lantern with a match and smiled, enjoying the genius of his setup. People left the Amish alone, and for the most part the Amish left their own alone. When he had come to visit Martha Booher, his "aunt," back in June, Martha told the village folks who had asked that he was her nephew from the Franklin village whose wife and unborn infant had died in childbirth in the spring. He would be helping her with the chores around her house from time to time on weekends when he could spare a trip.

No one had asked a single further question. Everyone was too busy tending to their fields and tackling the daily grind of living.

As the police had never been able to snap a photograph of him and all the descriptions from Tuscaloosa and Henshaw had been vague, the drawing the police had put out among the neighboring counties, including Lawrence County, looked nothing like Bone. The picture showed a large man with a strand of stubble on his face and short dirty-blond hair, wearing a golf shirt and khaki pants. Now Bone had a full beard dyed a dark brown, with long brown hair and, of course, the black hat, pants, and jacket of an Amish man. He suspected he could probably walk into the sheriff's office and ask for directions and no one would pay him a second's mind.

"How long are you staying?" Martha asked as Bone took the lantern and walked to the back of the cabin. They had barely spoken on the buggy ride from Lawrenceburg to Ethridge. Martha, having been raised Amish, was not a big talker anyway, which to Bone's way of thinking made her the perfect companion.

"Couple hours," he said, feeling for the cell phone in his pocket. He'd left his number when he'd reached out to Tucker this afternoon, and he knew the phone would ring soon. *They won't be able to resist . . .*

Bone stepped out the door of the cabin and walked toward the barn in back. It was over ninety degrees outside, but Bone barely noticed. Weather had never bothered him much. Cold, cool, warm, or hot, it made no difference. There was only the job at hand. That's probably why the military had suited him so well. But the army hadn't paid for shit, and being a fixer for people like Jack Willistone did. For Bone it all came back to the moolah. Spend a few years of your childhood hungry, and a person gains an appreciation for the almighty dollar and its importance in life. Let the hypocrites worship Jesus, Muhammad, or whoever. The Bone sat at the altar of Benjamin Franklin.

That's why the end of his partnership with Jack bothered him so much. Haynes and old man McMurtrie had cost him over one hundred thousand dollars cash and put Jack in jail. Bone had promised himself when he crawled to shore after jumping off the Northport Bridge that he would get even with both of them, and now the pieces were finally in place. Of course, as sweet as the revenge would be, it would come with a price.

JimBone Wheeler never worked for free.

Once inside the barn, Bone shut the door, leaving him in darkness except for the glow from his lantern. He walked past the two horse stables to the rear and knelt on the saw grass floor, feeling around for the loose plank. When he found it, he set the lantern down and pulled. Underneath, Bone saw his goodies.

Putting his gloves on, Bone quickly made sure everything was there. Two rifles, three twelve-gauge shotguns, a six-pack of revolvers, a toolbox full of knives of all sizes, and, finally, several work tools that could double as weapons. Satisfied that he had everything he needed, he put the plank back in place and stepped on it, making sure it was secure.

Then, retrieving the lantern, he started to walk away. He was halfway to the barn door when he felt his cell phone vibrate in his pocket.

He answered on the second ring, listened for several seconds, and then said, "I'll take care of it."

Smiling, he slid the phone back in his pocket and walked the rest of the way to the house. He had been right. *They couldn't resist.*

When he reached the bedroom, Martha was nude from the waist down, sitting on the edge of the bed with her legs crossed. Her blouse and bonnet remained.

"Are you ready to pay rent?" she asked, the slightest hint of a smile playing on her lips.

Looking her over, Bone was relieved to see that Martha continued to violate the Amish rule prohibiting the shaving of body hair.

"I probably need to go soon," Bone said, but he was already taking off his suspenders. His business wouldn't start for several hours and . . . he needed to keep his "aunt" happy.

At forty-six years old, Martha Booher was just a few years older than Bone, but the plain-Jane wardrobe of the Amish, combined with the age difference, made it easy for her to pass him off as her nephew.

"You can spare an hour for a lonely Amish woman, no?" She ratcheted up the Pennsylvania Dutch accent and began to unbutton her blouse, revealing two of the largest and fullest breasts Bone had ever had the pleasure of fondling. For some reason they made him think of whole milk and Nebraska.

"Leave the bonnet," Bone said, placing the lantern on the bedside table and climbing onto the bed. Bone loved the bonnet . . .

21

Booker Taliaferro Washington Rowe Jr. had been called Booker
T. since the time he was born to distinguish him from his father,
whom everyone just called Booker. Booker T. had played left tackle
for Giles County High School on the same team with Bocephus
Haynes and even now, as he approached middle age, maintained
the massive build of an offensive lineman. "You won't be able to
miss Booker T.," Bo had said. He was right. A few minutes after
arriving at the Legends Steakhouse—Booker T.'s only condition for
the meeting was that Tom buy him dinner—Tom saw a mountain
of a man enter the restaurant. Arms like pythons, a barrel chest,
and a neck that rose to his chin like a tree trunk. Tom held his
hand up, and the massive man nodded and headed his way.

"Booker T. Rowe," he said, extending a heavily calloused
right hand that felt like sandpaper when Tom shook it. Dressed
in a sweat-stained, gray button-down with "Rowe Farm Systems"
on the front pocket and dusty jeans, Booker T. plopped down in
the chair across from Tom and let out a long breath, his face the

picture of exhaustion. He held his hand up for the waitress, and a plump redhead bustled over with a smile on her face.

"You want a single or a pitcher?" she asked, and it was evident that Booker T. came here often.

"Beer?" Booker T. asked, giving Tom a tired smile.

"Sounds good," Tom said.

"Let's make it a pitcher, Louise," he said.

———

Thirty minutes later, with one pitcher down and another well on its way, Booker T. took the last bite of his steak and shook his head. "So, Trammell was really the toughest player you ever played with?" Though Tom had drunk a couple of beers, Booker T. was drinking two to every one of his. The huge man wasn't drunk, but he was getting loose and, having been a lifelong college football fan, was enjoying Tom's war stories of playing for Coach Bryant in the early '60s. Tom had hoped to direct the conversation toward Bo's case, but something held him back. He sensed that Booker T. needed to relax, to blow off some steam, and Tom didn't want to press it.

"It's not even close," Tom said. "Billy Neighbors used to say if he saw Trammell coming down the street, he'd change paths so he wouldn't have to face him. It was a joke—Billy loved Pat—but there was a hint of truth in it. We were all a bit scared of Pat. He was the bell cow of that team."

"He died before he was thirty, didn't he?"

Tom felt his throat constrict a little. Even over forty years after his friend's death, it was still hard to talk about. He nodded. "Only time I ever saw Coach Bryant cry."

Booker T. shook his head. "The by God 1961 National Champions." He poured the last remnants of the pitcher into his mug and leaned back in his chair. "Well . . . as much I'm enjoying your stories, Professor, that's not why you wanted this meeting, is it?" Tom just waited, knowing the question didn't really need an answer. After Booker T. took another swallow of beer, he placed his elbows on the table and leaned toward him. "The General owns my ass."

"How so?" Tom asked, his spirits beginning to sink.

"Because I gave Bo the code to that gate." He shook his head. "Stupidest thing I've ever done. But how could I have known that Bo . . . ?" He trailed off and drained the rest of his glass. "General Lewis says she's going to wait until after Bo's trial to decide whether to charge me with accessory to murder or aiding and abetting a trespass."

"What have you told her?" Tom asked, dreading the answer.

"Just the God's honest truth. That Bo asked me for the code to the gate early last week. Said he always pays his respects to his father at the clearing, and what with the big wall that Ms. Maggie had me construct this year, he couldn't just sneak in like he'd done in the past." He paused. "I just couldn't say no. Me and Bo are cousins, but we're more like brothers. Besides, Mr. Andy knew that Bo visited that clearing from time to time, and he never said nothing."

"What?" Tom asked. This was interesting.

"Sure enough. I been leasing that land to farm for ten years, and seem like every year on the anniversary of his daddy's death and sometimes on Christmas or Bo's momma's birthday, Bo would end up out there. A few times on those nights I'd come back in the morning and he'd still be there, curled up and sleeping on the banks of the pond. One of those times Mr. Andy was with me."

"Really?" Tom asked.

Booker T. nodded. "And he didn't say nothing neither. Just looked at Bo, sighed, and drove away."

"So I guess it doesn't surprise you that Bo would want to come to the clearing on the anniversary of his father's death?" Tom asked.

"Not at all. Like I said, he came every year on the anniversary, and I knew he was coming this year because he asked me for the code."

"Do you think Andy Walton would have known that?"

Booker T. shrugged. "I don't know. But I'm sure it wouldn't have surprised him.

"Were you on the farm last Thursday night?" Tom asked.

"No."

"So you didn't see anything."

"No, I did not."

"Is there anything else you can tell me?" There was a hint of desperation in Tom's voice.

"Nothing you want to hear," Booker T. said, draining the rest of his mug and standing from the table. "Want to know something else that doesn't surprise me?"

"What?"

Booker T. threw a few dollar bills on the table for a tip. "It doesn't surprise me a bit that Bo finally snapped and killed Mr. Andy. He's been thinking about it his whole life. I probably heard him say a hundred times that he was going to kill Andy Walton one day. And with Jazz gone . . ."

Tom's thoughts leapfrogged a few weeks to trial. Booker T. on the stand and General Lewis finishing her examination with this doozy: "Did the defendant ever tell you that he was going to kill Andy Walton?"

Only about a hundred times.

"Mr. Rowe, what did Bo think about you working for the man that murdered his father?" It was a question that Tom had intended to ask Bo, but he thought he'd try it out on Booker T. When he saw the big man's reaction, he immediately knew he had made a mistake.

Booker T. stood there, stunned for a second or two, just staring. Then he slowly leaned over the table and brought his face to within an inch of Tom's. "Now you listen here, Professor. I work for *myself*. I farm that land the way *I* want to farm that land. All I do is cut the Waltons a rental check. I don't work for them at all. I use their ass and their land to make a buck." He scowled, and Tom thought the temperature in the room had dropped ten degrees in a few seconds. "Bo didn't have no problem with that at all." He started to walk away, then stopped. "You tell my cousin that I'm pulling for him but that I'm not gonna lie. I'm not going to go to jail for his ass."

As Booker T. stormed out of the restaurant, Tom flagged the waitress down for the check. After paying the tab, he was heading for the door when he heard his cell phone chirp. He read the text from Ray Ray, which was short and sweet.

Bad news from the Sundowners. We need to talk. Bo's office at nine?

Tom replied, *Better make it 9:30. I still need to hit Kathy's.* Then he sighed as he walked out into the muggy night.

22

Kathy's Tavern was beginning to fill up when Tom walked in the door ten minutes after leaving Legends. As he made his way to the bar, he noticed that most of the patrons were starting to filter to the back room, where a band appeared to be tuning instruments. According to the flyer in the window, the music would start at nine.

Tom took a seat at the bar and ordered a beer, taking in the place. It was 8:45 p.m. He had forty-five minutes to hopefully find and interview Cassie Dugan before his meeting with Ray Ray.

Kathy's was a block north of the courthouse on First Street. According to Bo, Kathy's had the best cheeseburger in town and usually attracted an up-and-coming country singer or band on the weekend. The layout was basically two areas—a front room with four tall tables to the right and a long bar to the left, and a back room with a stage in front of several tables. As he looked around, Tom was struck by the diversity of the crowd. To his left at the bar were two college boys who had probably both just turned twenty-one. They wore jeans and collar shirts with the shirttail out, and they were splitting a pitcher of beer. Martin Methodist

College was just a stone's throw away, and Tom figured these boys were aiming to catch a buzz before the party on campus. To his right was a bearded man who appeared to be middle-aged wearing a gray T-shirt, a dusty camouflage cap, and khaki work pants and boots. He was drinking Natural Light from a can and staring straight ahead, lost in thought or something else. Across at one of the tables was a fiftysomething couple, the man's face covered with a white Kenny Rogers–style beard and both wearing cowboy hats. Next to them was a much younger couple, probably in their thirties.

As a steel guitar cranked up in the back, the waitress brought Tom his beer. She wore a white Kathy's T-shirt with blue jean cutoffs, an outfit which showed off her large breasts and long, tan legs, and Tom could almost feel the eyes of the two college boys on her.

Brushing her brown hair out of her eyes, she smiled. "Just drinking, or would you like to order some food?"

"Just drinking," Tom said, returning the smile. As she started to go, Tom held up his hand and leaned across the bar. "Can I ask you a question?"

She nodded, her eyes curious.

"Do you know Bocephus Haynes?"

The smile disappeared. "Who wants to know?"

"Tom McMurtrie," Tom said, extending his hand across the bar. "I'm Bo's attorney."

"Cassie Dugan." She shook his hand, eyeing him like he might be a dangerous animal. *Bingo*, Tom thought, cautioning himself to ease into the questioning. *Don't scare her off.*

"I'm told he was in here last Thursday night. Is that true?" Tom asked.

"He was here a lot of nights," she said, leaning in close so that only Tom could hear.

"But Thursday?" Tom pressed.

She nodded. "Look, mister, we're starting to get crowded—"

"Did you wait on him?"

Another nod. "Bo always sat at the bar when he came in, and that's normally my station."

The familiar "Bo" as opposed to "Mr. Haynes," Tom thought. *Interesting . . .*

"Cassie, do you know Bo pretty well?"

She blinked, hesitating only slightly. "Just from his time in here. Like I said, he came a lot the last couple of months."

Right after the separation, Tom thought, feeling a twinge of anxiety. "Was he with anyone on Thursday night?"

She shook her head. "No. He was alone." She paused. "He was usually alone."

"Did he speak to anyone?"

"Look, mister, I gave the police a statement with everything I saw and heard. I don't have time—"

"One last question," Tom said. "Did he say anything to you while you waited on him? Anything at all that you thought was strange or unusual?"

She shrugged. "Bo liked to talk to me, OK? I think he was lonely. He and his wife were separated and"—she paused—"I don't think he had anyone else to talk to."

Another twinge of anxiety. "Did he say anything that—?"

"All I remember about last Thursday night was that Bo seemed very tense and angry. He normally flirted with me and asked me questions about my day. Small talk mainly, but he barely said a word last Thursday. Just smoked a couple of cigars and had several bourbon and waters. Then he scared Clete to death, and that's when Mr. and Mrs. Walton and Dr. Curtis came up." She shuddered. "I thought I was going to have to call the police."

"Why didn't you?" Tom asked.

"Because it was just talk. Nobody hit anyone. Just talk." She glared at Tom. "In hindsight I guess I should've called the police."

Tom asked her about the confrontation, and Cassie reiterated what everyone else had said. Bo had threatened to make Andy "bleed" and quoted the "eye for an eye" verse from the Bible.

"Is there anything else you can tell me?" Tom asked.

"Not really," Cassie said, pouring a pitcher full of beer. "Clete Sartain hasn't been back since last Thursday. I'm sure he's staying away so he doesn't get pestered with questions from people like you."

She turned to walk away, and Tom couldn't think of anything else to ask her. The day wasn't getting any better.

It was about to get a lot worse.

———

"Another Natty Light?" Cassie asked the man with the camouflage hat and gray T-shirt.

Bone nodded, watching McMurtrie from the corner of his eye. He could tell the old man was disappointed by whatever Cassie had told him. Bone knew it was risky being out in the open like this, but it was a calculated risk. The police sketch only vaguely resembled his current appearance, and the long hair, cap, and work clothes were almost as perfect a disguise as his Amish getup.

After an hour of "paying rent" at the cabin, Bone had asked Martha to drop him off at an Amish trading post just outside of Lawrenceburg. He had then walked from the trading post to the hotel where his truck was parked and arrived back in Pulaski around 8:00 p.m., just in time to get to Kathy's a few minutes before McMurtrie.

As Cassie set the beer can in front of him, Bone stole a glance at the old professor, who had now stood up and was digging in his wallet for some cash. *He's leaving,* Bone thought, fighting the urge to smile.

As the band in back started its first set with a cover of an old Eddy Raven number—"I Got Mexico"—Bone took a long sip of beer and followed McMurtrie out the door.

This was going to be so much fun.

———

Out on the sidewalk, McMurtrie was heading back up First Street toward the courthouse.

This should be easy as pie, Bone thought, reaching inside his work pants for the hammer as McMurtrie crossed Jefferson Street. Bone gripped the hammer tightly and held it by the head so that only the handle was visible. Then he reached under his left pant leg, where the revolver was strapped to the back of his calf. He put the gun in his left pocket. Just in case . . .

As McMurtrie passed Reeves Drug Store, Bone noticed that the sidewalk had darkened. All the businesses along this stretch were closed. *Perfect,* Bone thought, sliding his hand up the hammer to the handle and taking a deep breath. Then he began to count. A thousand one, a thousand two . . .

. . . *now.*

———

As he approached the intersection of First Street and Madison, Tom fiddled in his pocket for the keys to the office, dropping them on the sidewalk. He chuckled and bent down to pick them up. When he did, he saw movement out of the corner of his eye. He whirled around, and the head of the hammer was coming right at him.

His arms instinctively went up to block the blow, but it was too dark and he wasn't fast enough. He felt a sharp pain on his forehead and then the sensation of falling.

Then everything went black . . .

—

The job took all of thirty seconds. Bone had parked his truck two blocks west of the square and he walked briskly toward it. A minute later he was leaving Pulaski on Highway 64 toward Lawrenceburg. On the way there he rolled the windows down and let the hot, humid air engulf him. He remembered the feel of his testicles being squeezed a year earlier in Tuscaloosa by Haynes, and though the old man hadn't been the one who had done it, Bone held him partly responsible. *Now we're close to even,* he thought.

But not entirely. Haynes and McMurtrie had cost Bone a lot of money. And his El Camino . . .

Tonight's job was just the beginning.

It was nice being paid to get revenge, Bone thought, taking out his phone. He dialed the number, and it was answered on the first ring.

"Done," Bone said.

PART THREE

PART THREE

23

"ALL RISE!" the bailiff bellowed. "The Circuit Court of Giles County, Tennessee is now in session."

Rick and Ray Ray stood from their chairs at the defense table and watched as General Helen Lewis and Sheriff Ennis Petrie did the same from across the courtroom. Behind them, spectators lined both sides of the galley. The judge had not barred the press from the preliminary hearing, and they had come out in droves. She had, however, barred television and news cameras, though Rick wondered whether she would do that for the trial. Surely, Rick thought. Then he heard Powell's voice in his mind telling him "Don't call me Shirley," the familiar refrain from the movie *Airplane!* Rick probably would have smiled if he wasn't about to soil himself. His heart was beating so fast and hard that he could feel it.

"You OK?" Ray Ray asked to his right. Rick thought he smelled the slight undercurrent of whiskey on his local counsel's breath, disguised by mouthwash and a hefty chunk of aftershave. There had been a basketball coach at Henshaw High that gave off that same smell. It didn't bring back good memories.

"Yeah," Rick said, glancing around the packed courthouse. After several seconds Judge Susan Connelly strode into the courtroom. Her Honor was an attractive, petite woman in her early forties with short brown hair. Ray Ray had told Rick that drawing Connelly as judge was the first break the defense had received in the case, and Rick had no basis to disagree.

"Henry, please have the defendant brought in," the judge directed once she was seated behind the bench.

The bailiff turned and walked past Rick out the doors to the courtroom. A few moments later two armed police officers escorted Bo to the defense table and unlocked his handcuffs.

"Rick," Bo said, patting Rick's shoulder. Then for the first time in the case, Bo came eye to eye with Raymond Pickalew.

"What, no hug?" Ray Ray asked, but Bo just gawked back at him. Then, sweeping his eyes over and around the defense table, Bo realized what was wrong, "Wh-where's the Professor?" he stammered, his eyes cutting wildly to Rick.

"It's a long story," Rick said. "I'll fill you in after the hearing."

"He's OK," Ray Ray added, extending his hand and leaning over to whisper in Bo's ear. "Just shake my hand and act like everything is fine."

Bo paused. Then his face cleared in an instant and he shook Ray Ray's hand, feigning a smile. "God help me," he said under his breath.

"When Gabriel is busy, God sometimes sends Ray Ray," Ray Ray whispered back.

"General, are you ready to present the evidence?" the judge asked, turning to the prosecution table.

Helen Lewis stood and spoke in a clear voice. "Yes, Your Honor."

"Very well then, please proceed."

—

As Sheriff Ennis Petrie had warned on the day of his arrest, the evidence presented by the State of Tennessee at the preliminary hearing for Bocephus Haynes was "conclusive and overwhelming." First and as expected, the state proved motive through the testimony of Cassie Dugan, Dr. George Curtis, and Clete Sartain, who all recounted the confrontation between Bo and Andy Walton at Kathy's Tavern a few hours before the murder. Sheriff Petrie then testified to Bo's numerous attempts over the past two decades to reopen the investigation of his father's murder.

The next piece of evidence introduced by the prosecution was the testimony of the county coroner, Melvin Ragland. After a few questions to establish his credentials, Ragland opined that, on the morning of August 19, 2011 Andy Walton was shot to death from close range with a twelve-gauge shotgun. The time of death was approximately 1:15 a.m.

Last came the surprises, and none of them were pleasant. Larry Tucker, owner of the Sundowners Club, was called to play the surveillance tape from the club the night of the murder. When he saw his own Lexus SUV on the screen with the personalized University of Alabama license plate "BO-1982" leaving the scene of the crime at 1:20 a.m., Bo had to squelch a groan. Then there was the DNA evidence. Blood and hair samples matching those of Andy Walton were found in the cargo area of Bo's Lexus. And though it was impossible to conduct a ballistics check of a shotgun, the medical examiner was able to determine that the twelve-gauge seized from the backseat of Bo's vehicle was the exact type of weapon used to kill Andy Walton. Finally, a shell casing found underneath Andy's truck in the parking lot of the Sundowners was an exact match to the shells seized from the glove compartment of Bo's car.

—

When Rick informed Her Honor that the defendant would be calling no witnesses, Judge Connelly recessed for a short break. When court resumed fifteen minutes later, her ruling was short and to the point. "Based on the evidence presented by the State of Tennessee in this preliminary hearing, it is the ruling of this court that there is probable cause to believe that, on August 19, 2011 the defendant, Bocephus Aurulius Haynes, committed the crime of first-degree murder in wrongfully causing the death of Andrew Davis Walton. This case will now be bound over to the grand jury." Connelly paused and leaned back in her chair. "Court adjourned."

24

After Judge Connelly left the bench, Helen Lewis made a beeline for the defense table. She held her hand up to stop the two sheriff's deputies who had entered the courtroom to take Bo back to the jail.

"Gentlemen, you heard the evidence," she said, looking at each of them for a second before setting her gaze on Bo. "And unlike most cases, I didn't hold anything back. I have never seen a more open-and-shut, black-and-white case." She smiled, her eyes tight. Mean. "I'll offer life in prison, but only if the defendant accepts before the arraignment. Mrs. Walton is acceptable to this plea, though I frankly believe that it is very generous, given the heinous nature of this crime." She paused, still looking at Bo.

Bo held her gaze. "No," he said. His voice was low and did not waver. "No deals."

Helen glanced at Rick, then back at Bo. "I'm going to forget I heard that, Bo, and give you time to discuss this deal with your counsel."

"We'll get back to you," Rick broke in, stepping in front of Bo so that he didn't have to look at Helen anymore.

"Let me hear from you no later than the day of the arraignment," Helen said. "Knowing Susan, she will have this case in front of the grand jury within a week. There's not a doubt in my mind that the grand jury will issue an indictment, and the arraignment will be scheduled a few days later. You have some time, Counselor, but not much. If Bo pleads not guilty at the arraignment, there won't be any more deals coming from my office."

"You thinking trial in late September?" Ray Ray asked.

Helen smiled again, turning toward him. "Why, Ray Ray, I almost forgot you were over here. You were so quiet during the hearing."

Ray Ray smiled his Joker grin. "I'm a sneaky bastard, Helen. Plus I think all you've got here is a first-rate frame-up. Ain't no way a jury in this county is going to believe that Bocephus Haynes would convict himself with that crock you introduced today."

"A *frame-up*?" Helen asked, her voice high and filled with glee. "How much are you drinking these days, Ray Ray?"

"Not as much as your ex," Ray Ray said, his grin widening. "Butchie boy likes the good stuff." He paused, lowering his voice. "He sure appreciates you maintaining his lifestyle for him."

Helen's pale face turned crimson red, and her hands balled into fists. "You son of a—"

"Easy, General," Ray Ray cut her off, nodding at the press corps assembled in the gallery. "You wouldn't want to make a scene."

Helen gave a quick jerk of her head and turned back to Rick. "Let me hear from you by the arraignment."

25

Though the Giles County Jail was air conditioned, the cramped space of the consultation room felt combustible as Bo paced in front of them, alternately glaring at Rick, then Ray Ray. Finally, placing his hands on his hips, he fixed his eyes on Rick. "What in the hell is going on?"

"The Professor was attacked last Tuesday night on the courthouse square," Rick said, keeping his voice steady. When Bo's eyes widened, Rick held out his palms. "He's OK, but he's hurt bad. He suffered a couple broken ribs and a severe concussion. He also tore some ligaments in his right knee and can barely walk." Rick paused. "He was in the hospital for five days, but he's out now."

"Why didn't you tell me—?"

"That was the Professor's call," Rick interrupted. "He saw no point in upsetting you before the prelim."

Bo gazed down at the concrete floor. "Where is he?"

"The farm in Hazel Green. The doctor said he needs to be off his feet at least a month."

"Jesus," Bo said, scratching the back of his head and closing his eyes. "He could miss the trial." As they all processed that possibility, Bo opened his eyes. "How did it happen?"

"He was jumped from behind after interviewing the waitress at Kathy's Tavern who served you the night of the murder." Rick kept his voice calm and remained in his seat.

"Cassie?" Bo said, scratching his chin.

"You keep good company, Bocephus," Ray Ray chimed in, and Bo pointed a finger at him.

"When I want to hear from you, I'll ask," Bo said, his eyes on fire.

"Fuck you if you can't take a joke," Ray Ray shot back.

"I can't believe you are in this room," Bo said, keeping his finger pointed in Ray Ray's direction while he turned his glare to Rick.

"The Professor said he had already cleared Ray Ray as local counsel with you," Rick said, not backing down. "He said this case was like a knife fight in a ditch and—"

"That's just my game," Ray Ray finished Rick's sentence, the wide grin back on his face.

Bo turned to Ray Ray, looking at him for a long time. "I should've kicked your ass on the courthouse steps last year," he finally said.

"Why didn't you?" Ray Ray asked.

Bo shook his head and whispered an obscenity underneath his breath. Then he resumed his pacing. After a full minute he turned to Ray Ray. "You saw how bad it looks," Bo said.

"It looks like warmed-over dog shit," Ray Ray said. "But I don't care. I never liked the son of a bitch."

"You think I killed him?"

Ray Ray shrugged. "If you did, nothing would make me happier than seeing you walk."

"I didn't," Bo said.

"Well . . . good," Ray Ray said. "I'd hate to have that eating at my conscience."

After a two-second pause, Bo managed a weak smile and sat down at the table. "All right then," he said. "Where are we?" He looked at Rick, who in turn nodded at Ray Ray to begin.

"The night Tommy was attacked, I went out to the Sundowners Club to interview anybody that had any contact with Andy on the night of the murder." He squinted at Bo. "What you told Tommy was right, Bo. Andy did have a favorite."

"And?" Bo asked, placing his elbows on the table.

"She's gone."

26

Larry Tucker was worried. It had been two weeks since Andy Walton's murder, and Darla Ford had not reported back to work. Darla had always been one of his most reliable dancers, so this wasn't like her. Plus it was beginning to hurt the bottom line. Not only was Darla reliable, Nikita—Darla's stage name—was probably his most popular dancer. Several regulars had stopped coming in after Darla's third day gone, and more would probably follow.

"Any ideas?" Larry asked, gazing bleary-eyed across the bar at Peter Burns. It was 10:45 p.m. on Thursday night—prime time for business—but the club was almost empty.

"Nope," Peter said, drying off a beer mug with a towel. "Ain't like Darla to do this. She's pretty conscious about money, and I just don't see her walking away from this job. She did well here."

"Damn straight," Larry said. "And so did we. It's killing the bottom line to have her gone." Larry drank the rest of his bottle of Bud. "She have any family in the area?"

"Not that I'm aware of," Peter said, cracking the top on another Bud and putting it in front of Larry.

"Shit," Larry said, shaking his head and then taking a long swig of beer.

"You think Mr. Walton may have left her a chunk of change when he died?" Peter asked.

Larry shrugged. "Andy wasn't thinking all that clearly in his last few months, so nothing would surprise me."

"Well, that's all I can think of," Peter said.

"Me too," Larry said. Then under his breath, "*Shit*."

———

Almost three hours later, at just past 1:30 a.m. on what was now Friday morning, Peter Burns sat in the driver's side of his 1997 Ford Ranger truck and sipped on a cold Miller High Life. The other five beers that comprised the six-pack lay in the passenger-side seat, and the radio blared a favorite from Kenny Chesney. "No Shoes, No Shirt, No Problems."

Peter was still dressed in his work clothes, which consisted of a pair of khaki shorts, an untucked navy-blue golf shirt, and flip-flops. A faded Atlanta Braves hat was perched on his head, which covered his long but thinning dirty-blond hair. He had two days of stubble on his face, and he scratched it before taking another sip of beer.

Then he peered up at the second-floor apartment. No lights on inside, though that wasn't unusual. Darla was religiously frugal and wouldn't allow a light on in her place unless it was being used to read. So she could be in there, but Peter doubted it. He had tried to call her several times in the last two weeks with no answer, and like Larry he was worried. But—and he would never tell Larry this—he was also excited.

Peter finished the rest of the beer and grabbed the carton from the passenger seat. Then he opened the door to the truck and trudged his way to Darla's apartment, his heart racing.

His relationship with Darla was not something he had pub-
licized. He didn't want Larry to know, because he knew Larry
wouldn't like it. Larry could have all the girls at the Sundowners
he wanted, but he didn't want any of the other male help touching them. The bouncer, big Steve, was gay, so it didn't make much
difference to him. But Saint Peter, as the dancers called him,
liked the opposite sex, and it was a little much to ask him not to
be interested in the women whom he watched dance naked all
day long.

So he had gotten with a few over the years, including Darla
Ford, a.k.a. Nikita. But Peter quickly figured out that Darla was
different than the other girls. Darla was smart. Not book smart,
mind you. She didn't quote Shakespeare or read the classics every
night. But she was smart in the ways of the street. She knew how
to make money and she knew how to save it. And Peter had always
felt that she wasn't long for the Sundowners.

It seemed like every dancer that became employed by the
Sundowners had a story of some kind. Studying up to be a doctor, a nurse, a hairdresser, an actress, screenwriter, and on and
on. You name it, Peter had heard it. And though the stories all
sounded good, Peter had never seen any of these girls ever follow through with their dream. To Peter's mind, dancing nude for
money had a way of killing the soul. A girl might start working
toward her goal—sign up for school, start taking classes during
the day or take a job in that field—but the nightly grind of dancing the pole would wear them down. As would the cocaine, the
meth, the liquor, or whatever else a girl put in her system to allow
her to take her clothes off and rub her tits into the faces of men
twice her age who reeked of body odor and whose breath smelled
like castor oil.

Darla Ford was different. She did no drugs and limited her
alcohol intake to one Seven and Seven, which she'd sip on all night
and which Peter would refill with just 7 Up. Every night Darla's goal

was always the same. To take home as much money as humanly possible. To do that she had to give the best show, and no one at the club had ever danced like Nikita. She was the most requested dancer for lap dances, and, outside of Tammie Gentry, a.k.a. Sweet & Nasty, and Wilma Newton, a.k.a. Smokey, the only other dancer asked to go up to the VIP room and make the big bucks.

In the VIP room Peter knew that Darla had sex for money. She had so much as told him. "But only a small minority get to sample the merchandise," she had said. "Only the really deep pockets who I think might come back for more."

Andy Walton had fit the bill to a tee. A lonely seventysome-thing-year-old billionaire looking for a good time because his wife had gone cold between the sheets.

Peter wasn't sure how much money Darla had stored away, but one night, after a romp on the mattress in her apartment, she'd volunteered that she was just about ten grand short of being able to place a down payment on her dream.

"I'm going to have the best oyster bar on the Gulf Coast, you just wait," she had said.

By the time Peter reached the door to Darla's apartment, he had already popped the top on beer number two. He knocked, because it was the polite thing to do, but he knew there would be no answer. Then, taking out the key that Darla had given him two years ago, he opened the door.

No lights, no sounds . . . no Darla.

She's gone, Peter knew, involuntarily smiling. He remembered that scene at the end of the movie *Good Will Hunting* when Ben Affleck goes to Matt Damon's house and doesn't find him there. Affleck smiles, knowing that his friend has finally moved on.

Walking back into the kitchen, Peter noticed the note on the table. It was handwritten on a three-and-a-half by five-inch index card. The message was short and to the point.

"Saint Peter, I'm out of here. You know where to find me. I hope you will come. If not, you are welcome to whatever's left in the apartment."

Peter Burns closed his eyes, the smile still playing on his lips. Her ship had come in.

The *arrangement* with Andy Walton had finally paid off.

———

Peter decided to spend one last night in Darla's apartment. He drank the rest of the six-pack and watched old *Seinfeld* episodes on one of the three channels Darla had on her TV. Then, not quite drunk, he lay on the mattress in her bedroom and thought through his options.

He had lived in Giles County all his life. He hadn't gone to college, and, outside of the occasional trip to Nashville, he had barely left town. He had only been to the beach once in his life. A spring break trip to Gulf Shores, Alabama in high school.

I can pour whiskey anywhere, he knew, imagining the emerald-green waters of the Gulf.

By the time he closed his eyes, he could almost smell the salt water . . .

———

He woke up hungover but motivated. Though not as frugal as Darla, he had saved a few bucks here and there. Enough to make the trek to the coast and put a down payment on a new apartment. *And that's all I'll need,* he thought, smiling with excitement. *I'm really going to do it,* he told himself. *I'm going to get the hell out of here.*

He pulled into his apartment and literally jumped out of the seat. *No looking back now,* he thought. He didn't want to lose his gumption. He'd call his landlord, pack a bag, and stop at the Sundowners on the way out of town.

I can be eating oysters on the coast by sundown.

As he began fiddling for the key to his apartment, which was a ground-level unit in a complex popular with the Martin College kids, he was startled by a voice from behind him.

"Mr. Burns?"

Peter turned and saw a young man wearing a shirt and tie walking his way. The top button on the man's shirt was unbuttoned, and his tie was loose and wrinkled. *College kid?* Peter initially thought, but then he changed his mind when the man got closer and Peter saw his bloodshot eyes and the yellow pad he was holding.

"Who wants to know?" Peter asked, crossing his arms, annoyed that his momentum had been interrupted.

"Rick Drake," the man said. "I'm a lawyer for Bo Haynes. Do you have a minute to talk?"

"I'm busy right now, kid," Peter said. "I'm actually about to leave town for a while."

"I've been waiting in the parking lot all night," Rick said. "I tried to reach you at the Sundowners, but each time I called they said you were 'busy.'"

"I couldn't talk there anyway," Peter said. "Too loud." He smiled. "And too many distractions."

Rick smiled back. "I'm sorry to just show up here. My client had apparently met you here before, so he gave me the address."

"So you just been waiting this whole time?" Peter asked.

"Since midnight," Rick said. "I figured you'd get off work around then and come home."

"I usually do," Peter said. "But I got lucky last night." He smiled, knowing that it wasn't entirely a lie. He *had* gotten lucky. Just not the kind of lucky he was implying.

Rick chuckled. "I figured as much, but I was afraid to leave for fear of missing you. And if you're about to go out of town—"

"Well, I don't know how I can be of help," Peter started, putting the key into the lock. "But I can at least fix you a cup of coffee for your trouble."

"Thank you," Rick said, sighing with relief. "That would be great."

27

"I knew Andy a long time," Peter said, handing Rick a cup of scalding black coffee. Rick took it and blinked his eyes to get his bearings. After seven hours cooped up in the Saturn, his mind drifting in and out of consciousness, Rick was glad to be anywhere but the front seat of his car. He felt sluggish and tired, but he knew he had to snap out of it. Burns was an important witness. "And I've known Bo my whole life," Peter continued.

"Bo said he represented you a few years ago."

Peter chuckled. "Yeah. Possession of marijuana and a DUI. Since it was my second DUI charge, I could have gone to jail. But Bo tried the case and won."

"I thought Helen Lewis hadn't lost a case as DA," Rick said, feeling a pang of hope in his heart.

"Wasn't Helen," Peter said. "It was one of her assistants. Though I was stoned out of my mind that night, I had only blown a .09, which is just barely drunk. I did the field sobriety tests better than the officer, which really wasn't fair because I work all day about half-cocked. I walk straighter after a few joints and a couple beers than I do stone sober." He laughed and sipped from his coffee. Rick did the same, beginning to feel the caffeine kicking in. "Bo said we had a chance, and sure enough he won it." Peter shook his head. "Bo's a good lawyer now, I'm goin' tell you."

"Bo said in lieu of payment for his work, you agreed to give him information."

Peter nodded. "And I have. I gave him some information on a stripper last year that was involved in one of his cases in Alabama."

"Wilma Newton," Rick said.

"That's right."

"That was actually my case," Rick said. "Bo was lending a hand because Wilma was a key witness and she lived and worked here in Pulaski." He paused. "Whatever happened to Wilma?" Rick asked. "I haven't seen her since—"

"Wilma's . . . not with us anymore," Peter said. "Look, I'd rather not talk about that. Everyone at the club liked Wilma. It . . . was a sad situation."

Jesus, Rick thought. He wanted to press Peter for more information, but he stopped himself. *Stay focused. That's not why we're here.*

"Did you see Andy Walton on the night he died?"

Peter nodded. "I did. Andy was a regular at the club, so I saw him a good bit."

"And he also saw a dancer named Darla Ford the night of the murder. Is that correct?"

"Yeah, Darla. Her stage name was Nikita."

"*Was?*" Rick asked. "What . . . ?"

"Shit," Peter said, standing up and refilling his cup. "Is, I mean. Her stage name *is* Nikita."

"Is she not there anymore?" Rick asked, and Peter closed his eyes.

"Ask me something else, OK, kid?" Peter said, his agitation evident.

"How long had Andy been seeing Darla?"

Peter sat back down and sighed, shrugging his shoulders. "A year maybe. Ten months?" He shrugged. "A while I guess."

"What happened the night of the murder?"

"Just what I said in my statement to the police. Andy came to the club around eleven that night. Had a beer with me and then went upstairs with Darla to the VIP room."

"How long did Mr. Walton stay in the VIP room with Ms. Ford?"

"Hour or so," Peter said. "Give or take fifteen either way."

Rick sipped his coffee. Despite his fatigue, he was alert now, hanging on every word. "What would . . . go on up in that room? Would . . . ?"

"You want to know if he was fucking her?" Peter said, his lips curving into a grin. Rick noticed a small gap in the man's teeth.

Rick also smiled, playing along. "Well . . . was he?"

"The on-the-record answer to that is, of course, no."

"And off the record?"

"Her brains out. Every time he came in." He fiddled with the handle of his coffee cup. "You have to understand. Andy Walton was a self-confessed 'man of the flesh.' He wasn't getting any at home, so . . ."

"How often did he come in?"

"Two . . . maybe three times a week."

"Always the same pattern?"

"Pretty much. He'd shoot the bull with me for a beer or two, and then head up the stairs with Darla."

"Did he ever say anything to you about his health?"

"No," Peter said, gazing down at the floor. "But Darla . . ."

"What?" Rick pressed, sensing he was getting somewhere.

"A couple weeks before Andy was killed, Darla was crying as she left the club. I asked her what was wrong, and she said something was about to happen. Something big. She couldn't tell me what it was, but she said Mr. Walton was going to take care of her."

"Did Andy ever tell you he thought someone might want to kill him?"

Peter shook his head. "No. He never said nothing to me. We mostly just shot the bull. He liked to come to the club and blow off steam. He spent the majority of his time with Darla."

"Mr. Burns, where is Darla? We've tried to meet with her, and no one at the club seems to know where she is."

Peter stood and emptied the remains of his coffee in the sink. "She's gone."

"What do you mean?" Rick asked.

"Just what I said. She's gone." Peter sighed. "Look, what was your name again?"

"Rick Drake."

"OK, Rick, you got a business card?"

Rick fiddled in his wallet and then handed Peter a card.

Peter examined it. "Look, I got no dog in this hunt. I'd like to help Bo because he saved my ass from jail. But I was awful fond of Andy Walton. He was a friend and a great customer. If Bo killed him, then Bo deserves what's coming to him."

"Mr. Burns, with all due respect, Andy Walton was the Imperial Wizard of the Tennessee Knights of the Ku Klux Klan," Rick said, his exasperation and fatigue palpable. "He and his brethren in the Klan murdered Bo's father forty-five years ago."

Peter shrugged, unmoved by Rick's show of emotion. "He was never charged, was he?"

"That doesn't mean it didn't happen," Rick said. "I don't understand the people in this town. Bo *helped* you. If it wasn't for Bocephus Haynes, you'd be rotting away in a jail cell. Bo helped a lot of people in this town. Why is everyone so quick to throw him under the bus? What about Andy Walton's sins, for God's sake?"

"Are you finished?" Peter said, yawning.

"You just don't care, do you?" Rick asked, putting his hands on his hips and glaring at the bartender. "Nobody . . . seems to care."

"Nobody's got time for it, boy. People in Pulaski trying to make a buck just like any other place. Stuff like this just makes it harder. You know how many businesses will close down over the next year because of Bo's trial? Ask me how much in tips I've made in the last week since Andy's murder." When Rick didn't say anything, Peter stuck a finger in his chest. "I haven't made shit. And you know what? I'm sure I ain't the only one. I bet sales are down across the board. Here's what you need to know. Win, lose, or draw. Guilty or innocent. It don't make a damn. People just want it to go away. Now if you'll excuse me—"

"Mr. Burns, it is imperative that I speak with Darla Ford. Can you tell me how—?"

"I'll call you, OK?"

Rick started to protest, but Peter held a hand up. "That's the best I can do," Peter said. 'Now I'd like you to leave."

He walked to the door and opened it, gesturing with a hand for Rick to go.

At the door Rick again wanted to protest, but there was nothing else he could think to say. "Best number is the mobile," he managed.

28

Fifteen minutes later Rick and Ray Ray were sitting at a back table at the Bluebird Café.

"I bet he calls," Ray Ray said, crossing his legs and taking a sip from his own mug. "I don't know Burns like Bo does, but based on him letting you in the apartment, I bet he will call."

Rick shook his head. "I doubt it. Not after I got on my soapbox about Andy being in the Klan and lynching Bo's father. I . . . think that pissed him off pretty good."

"Fuck him," Ray Ray said, taking a bite of bacon. "You're too sensitive, kid. Peter Burns isn't. He just told you like it is."

"You think he's right about the town just wanting it to go away?"

"I think he told you the God's honest truth. Pulaski, Tennessee has a history that the town can't seem to escape. It's like the damn town hall has a big scarlet *R* on it for 'racist,' because of the Klan being born here." Ray Ray scoffed. "When Bo's trial is discussed by the national media, what you'll hear over and over again until you're sick to death of it is 'Pulaski, Tennessee, birthplace of the

Ku Klux Klan.' The broadcaster will be hyping the trial, and they'll be showing images on the screen of houses in Giles County that sport the Confederate flag on the front porch and dozens of other pictures of Klansmen marching on the square. It won't matter whether Bo is acquitted or found guilty. Whether he walks free or is lethally injected, Pulaski will take another hit. The shine on that scarlet *R* will be back. We can turn plaques around and shut the town down for a day, but we can't change the national spin." He paused and took a sip of coffee. "Burns shot you straight." Then Ray Ray smiled his Joker grin. "I still think he calls you back."

"I hope so," Rick said, not feeling as confident. "He's our only way to get to Darla Ford."

"Maybe not. She might have been close to some of the other girls out there. I'll head out to the Sundowners tonight and take another look."

"Ray Ray . . ." Rick eyed his new partner suspiciously across the table.

"Business only, I promise. We have to find her, right?"

Rick nodded. "We have to find her."

"Then I'm going."

"I'll go too," Rick said.

"No, God, hell no. I've known Larry Tucker for years, and it's not like I've been a stranger to the Sundowners. I'll blend in better. Like I was telling Helen at the prelim"—he gave his Joker grin and sipped from the mug—"I'm a sneaky bastard."

"All right then," Rick said, leaning back as a waitress placed a steaming plate of blueberry pancakes, bacon, and scrambled eggs in front of him. "But be careful. With what happened to the Professor . . ." He trailed off.

Ray Ray patted the front pocket of his pants. "Ray Ray always packs a nine-millimeter friend with him." Then, pausing to put a huge bite of pancake in his mouth, he asked, "Have you heard from Tommy?"

Rick shook his head and swallowed a mouthful of eggs. "I tried to call him after the prelim yesterday but got no answer."

"He took a hell of a beating," Ray Ray said.

"He's also just coming off some cancer treatments," Rick added, and Ray Ray wrinkled up his face. "Yeah," Rick continued. "Bladder cancer. The treatments have worked. He's been cancer-free for a year, but he had just been scoped a couple days before he got down here."

"Jesus," Ray Ray said. "So—"

"He may be out of commission for a while," Rick completed the thought, feeling a sense of dread and anxiety come over him.

Ray Ray looked down at his food. Then he chuckled, and the grin was back. "He'll be back sooner than you think."

"You played for Coach Bryant with the Professor, didn't you?" Rick asked.

Ray Ray nodded. "Graduated in 1960, the year before the first national champion," he said, his eyes narrowing. "You know, us boys on that team—Tommy, Lee Roy, Billy, Benny, Darwin, Pat . . ." He shook his head. "Hell, all of us. We're different. We've had our struggles in life like everyone does, but we don't quit." He paused, shaking his head again. "You go through what we went through, you . . . *can't*. It's just not possible. Those boys that went with the Man to Junction when he was at A&M get all the publicity. And they was tough as nails, don't get me wrong. Beebs was one of our assistants. I know. But . . . us boys in Tuscaloosa in '58, '59, '60, and '61 . . . we didn't have no choice but to win. Coach demanded it. He willed it to happen. You'd look in that man's eyes and hear his voice coming at you from up on that tower, and by God you had to whip the man in front of you. I was a receiver, and I didn't just catch the ball when it came my way, I swallowed the damn thing. I was so focused I could see the laces on the ball." He dug his fork into the plate of eggs and pointed it at Rick. "I can't tell you how many times I've wanted to quit in my life, and before I could do it, before I could walk away or stop what I was trying to do or . . ." He paused, blinking his eyes, and the hand holding the fork began to shake. "Or *pull the trigger*, I'd always hear that goddamn gravelly voice in my head. 'Get up, Pickalew. Get up, goddamnit.'" Ray Ray wiped his eyes and slammed his right hand down on the table, causing the ice in the water glasses to rattle and Rick to jump back from the table. "Sorry," Ray Ray said.

Rick didn't know what to say. He was taken back by the intensity resonating from across the table. And for the first time he was glad that Ray Ray Pickalew was on the team.

"Anyway," Ray Ray continued, scraping his teeth on his fork as he wolfed down a bite of eggs. "Tommy may be down right now, but he'll be back. Us boys . . ." He gave a quick jerk of his head. "We just don't know any different."

29

Hazel Green, Alabama is a small town just a few miles south of the Alabama-Tennessee border. In 1967, led by a rugged all-state center named Rickey Clark and a skinny sophomore shooting guard named Stanley Stafford, the Hazel Green Trojans won the 2A Alabama state basketball championship. Most folks in Hazel Green of a certain age will tell you they remember two things about high school sports during the '50s and '60s. They remember Stanley Stafford hitting a jump shot at the buzzer to win the state championship in '67.

And they remember when Coach Paul "Bear" Bryant came to Trojan Field in 1959 to see Tom McMurtrie play football.

It had been homecoming in late October. The Trojans were playing Sparkman in an important game in the race for the county championship. The air was crisp and cool, and many of the crowd had paper cups filled with hot chocolate. There had been rumors all week that Coach Bryant might come to the game, so the stands were packed an hour before kickoff, everyone turning their heads this way and that to see if the great man would actually visit.

He arrived midway through the first quarter. The referees literally stopped play as they got word that the Bear was on the premises. Coach Bryant rode in a black Cadillac marked by two state trooper sedans in front and one behind. The motorcade pulled to the front of the stadium, and according to Principal Ebb Hanson, the Bear was out of the back seat before the wheels had stopped rolling. Principal Hanson shook Coach Bryant's hand and escorted him into the stadium as fans from both sides of the field rose and clapped. The Hazel Green band even broke into a rendition of "Yeah, Alabama." The black-and-white pictures taken of the event show Coach Bryant in a dark suit, white shirt, and tie, with a black overcoat to keep off the cold. His head was covered with his trademark houndstooth fedora.

Principal Hanson led Coach Bryant into the stadium, flanked on the sides and in the back by four uniformed state troopers. Eventually, the Bear and his entourage were seated in the home stands on the fifty-yard line.

Coach Bryant, pursuant to his request, sat right between Sut and Rene McMurtrie, the parents of the boy he had come to see. Tom, watching from the field, heard one referee whisper to the other, "Sweet Jesus, look how big the son of a bitch is," as the Bear shook Tom's father's hand and kissed his momma on the cheek.

The Trojans actually lost the game 17–14, but no one ever talks about that. They only talk about Coach Bryant's entrance to the stadium, and the eight minutes of the first half that he watched.

Eight minutes in which Tom McMurtrie sacked the quarterback three times, had two tackles behind the line of scrimmage, caused a fumble, intercepted a pass, and blocked a field goal. Though his daddy couldn't understand much of what Coach Bryant had said, given the noise in the stadium and the Bear's gravel-like voice, Sut had told Tom later that he did hear the word "stud" several times. "Besides," Sut had said, rolling his eyes, "he spent most of his time listening to your momma."

Sure enough, a *Huntsville Times* cub reporter had gotten a great snapshot of the three together and put it on the front page of the sports section, which Sut said summed up the experience better than words could ever do. In the picture Sut is sitting bolt upright, arms folded, eyes focused intently on the game. Coach Bryant, smiling pleasantly, is leaning toward Tom's mother, Rene, who is pointing at the field and telling the Bear something.

The next afternoon, seated at the kitchen table of the McMurtrie home, Coach Bryant offered Tom a scholarship to play football for the University of Alabama.

———

Sitting now in the same chair that his father had sat in those many years ago, Tom leaned his elbows on the table and held the framed newspaper photograph in his hand. Tracing his finger over the three faces—his daddy, Coach Bryant, and his momma—he knew that these three people had probably had the most influence on who and what he had become in life. Sometimes, like last year in the courtroom in Henshaw, he could still hear their voices. Encouraging him. Still teaching him lessons long past the grave.

And as he rubbed the wounds on his face, still raw from the beating outside of Kathy's Tavern, and felt the bandages on his ribs, he thought he could hear one of their voices now. Crystal clear and spoken firm and direct. *"Don't ever tolerate a bully . . ."*

Tom had been in the fifth grade and had come home from school with a black eye. A seventh-grader had been picking on him, taking his lunch, and when Tom attempted to fight back, the boy had punched Tom in the face. Tom had tried to defend himself, but it was no use. The boy was bigger and stronger, and Tom got his ass whipped. He had hung his head in shame when he got home, not wanting to face his daddy. His momma had found him crying in his bedroom. She had hugged him and kissed his eye. Then she had made an egg custard pie, Tom's favorite.

After they had eaten their pie and washed it down with some sweet tea, his momma had taken him by the shoulders and looked him directly in the eye. She did not mince her words. "Tom, if that boy *ever* picks on you again, I want you get a stick and beat the tar out of him, you hear me?"

"Yes, ma'am," Tom had said, too scared of the look in her eye to question her.

"And you don't stop beating him until they pull you off."

Tom had swallowed hard, but he had nodded. The next day at school he had hit Justin Ledbetter in the face with a fallen tree branch, sending him to Huntsville Hospital with a broken jaw and nose. The boy had tried to take his lunch again so Tom *"did exactly what his momma told him to do,"* Rene McMurtrie told Principal Hanson when she and Sut had come up to the school that afternoon.

When Hanson said he had no choice but to suspend Tom, Tom's momma had placed her hands on her hips and said, "Oh no you're not. *You will do no such thing.*"

Flustered, Hanson had looked to Sut for help. "Sut, I'm the principal. She can't tell me what to do."

But Tom's father just crossed his arms and smirked. "Ebb, I fought for George Patton in the Third Army. I'd rather disobey a direct order from him than have to deal with the war you are about to start. If I were you, I'd fix the bullying problem you've got at this school. I would not pick a fight with my wife."

Tom had been sent home for a two-day cooling-off period, but he was never officially suspended. And Tom noticed that Ebb Hanson always walked in the other direction when he saw Tom's momma headed his way.

After the Justin Ledbetter incident, no one at Hazel Green High School ever messed with Tom again. In fact, no one had picked a fight with him in over fifty years. Tom had grown to be six foot three and well over two hundred pounds. He had played football at Alabama for the toughest coach that ever lived on a defense that believed it was a sin to give up a point.

But someone was messing with him now.

Tom had no doubt that whoever was responsible for the attack on him had framed Bocephus Haynes for the murder of Andy Walton. It was the only explanation for what had happened. Downtown Pulaski was not known for violence.

But his theory had fallen on deaf ears. Helen Lewis had visited him in the hospital, but she had scoffed at the idea that anyone could possibly have killed Andy Walton but Bo Haynes. "You're not thinking clearly, Tom. Give it some time."

Tom had given it some—a whole week at the farm—and his gut feeling had only intensified. Bocephus Haynes was framed for murder, and the person or people responsible would stop at nothing to keep the truth buried. If it meant nearly killing Tom, then so be it. These people didn't give a damn about playing fair. They were bullies, no different than Justin Ledbetter.

And it was high time they were taught a lesson.

Tom limped into the living room and carefully placed the framed newspaper photograph back on the mantle. Then he edged his way to the rear of the house, using a cane for balance.

The gun case hung on the wall in his bedroom. He opened the latch and pulled out a Remington deer rifle and a .38-caliber pistol, complete with a holster, and placed them side by side on the bed. Tom grabbed the rifle and pointed it at the mirror in the corner, looking through the scope and thinking about his momma again.

During the first day of his cooling-off period, he had asked his momma why she had told him to get a stick. He had never forgotten her response: "Don't ever tolerate a bully, son. Bullies are people whose goal in life is to keep you or other folks down. They're so stupid and insecure in who they are, their whole identity comes from the suppression of others." She had paused then, creasing her eyebrows and looking over Tom's shoulder with an expression that reeked of disgust. *"And there's only one way to deal with them."*

"You fight them," Tom had volunteered, trying to be helpful, but his mother's eyebrows had creased even further, and she brought both fists down on the table.

"No. You fought the other day when you came home with a shiner."

"So . . . the stick."

She nodded. "Bullies always slant the field in their direction. They don't play by the rules, so the rules of fairness don't apply. It doesn't matter how big and strong a bully is if you bring a stick to the fight." Then she'd said something he'd never forgotten. *"Bullies are only scared of two things. People who aren't scared of them . . . and people who won't tolerate them."*

Tom attached the holster to his hip and put the .38 inside. Then he threw the rifle's strap over his shoulder and slowly limped to the front of the house.

When he finally returned to the kitchen, he saw the two men through the bay window. They were standing outside, leaning against a black Dodge Charger and drinking coffee from Styrofoam cups.

Tom set the guns on the kitchen table and, using the cane again, walked outside into the humidity. The hot sun felt good as it warmed his face and arms, but it was so bright he had to squint at his visitors.

"Professor," Powell Conrad said, extending his hand. Powell wore a blue button-down, jeans, and Ray-Ban sunglasses. "You growing a beard?"

Tom nodded, shaking Powell's hand. "Doctor's orders. He doesn't want me to irritate the skin."

"Well, it looks like shit," the other man said, and Tom smiled, grabbing the man in as much of a bear hug as he could muster.

"Wade, how the hell are you?"

"I'm bored, Tom," he said, running his hand through his thick salt and pepper hair—mostly salt these days. He wore black jeans, a black T-shirt, and a bushy mustache that matched the color of his hair. Tom had always thought Wade favored the Sam Elliott character in *Roadhouse*.

"You coming out of retirement for this?" Tom asked.

"You might say that." Wade Richey had been a detective in the Tuscaloosa County Sheriff's Office for thirty years, retiring last summer. Over the years he and Tom had become friends, with Tom assisting the sheriff's office in several key investigations where there was a critical evidentiary question. Tom knew that Wade had always been considered the best homicide detective on the force. "The sheriff's office is pretty serious about catching this JimBone fella. And they've always had a lot of respect for your ideas."

"It may be a bust," Tom said.

Wade shrugged. "Maybe . . . but that would be a first."

Tom nodded and turned to Powell. "You get what I asked for?"

"Yeah." Powell reached into his pocket and pulled out several sheets of paper.

"And?"

Powell smiled. "And it's interesting."

"All right then," Tom said. "Time to go to work."

30

Rick woke to the sound of his cell phone ringing. Stumbling off the bed, he grabbed the phone from the nightstand. The time in the upper right hand corner said 2:30 p.m. Jesus . . . he had slept for five hours. After breakfast at the Bluebird, he had only intended to take a catnap at Ms. Butler's and then head back into town. He sighed. The caller ID was a number he didn't recognize.

"Yeah," Rick said, his voice a low croak.

"Drake, this is Peter Burns, the bartender at the Sundowners—not the author of *Sliding Down a Pole*."

Rick's grogginess was gone in an instant, and he looked wildly around the room for pen and paper. "Yes. How are you?"

"Jesus, you sound terrible."

"Thanks," Rick said. "Been taking a nap."

"Well, I hope you got a few winks, because if you want to talk to me or Darla Ford, you need to come over to my apartment. I'm leaving in fifteen minutes."

"Leaving? Where . . . ?"

"Just get over here," Peter said, and the phone clicked dead.

—

Fifteen minutes later Rick pulled into Burns's apartment complex. *Déjà vu all over again*, he thought, parking in the same place he'd spent eight hours last night. He had managed a quick shower and grabbed a Coke on the way out of Ms. Butler's. On the drive over he'd tried the Professor again on his cell phone, but there was still no answer. *Where the hell is he?* Rick wondered, stepping out of the Saturn and seeing Burns heading toward him, carrying a duffel bag under one arm.

"I hope you've got a full tank of gas," Peter said, throwing his bag in the back of Rick's car and climbing in the passenger seat.

"What are you doing?" Rick asked, tensing as the man, basically a complete stranger, started fiddling around with the radio.

"Jesus Christ, man. When did you get this car? When Clinton was president? I thought lawyers were supposed to all drive Mercedes. Where's the USB port for an iPod?"

"Don't have one," Rick said, still stunned by Burns's presence in the car.

"Well, you got any CDs?"

"Uhhh . . . there's some in the glove compartment. Mr. Burns—"

"Just drive, all right. I'll tell you on the way."

"On the way . . . where?" Rick asked, hesitating a second before backing out of the space.

"Destin," Peter said, rolling down the window and howling.

"Destin?" Rick asked. "Destin . . . Florida?"

Peter howled again. "The Redneck Riviera, baby. If you put this dinosaur in gear, we'll be eating oysters on a half shell and drinking Coronas with limes in just under"—he turned his wrist and made like he was looking at his watch, but he wasn't wearing one—"nine hours!"

Rick stopped the car. "Are you telling me that you want me to drive you all the way to the panhandle of Florida?"

"My piece of junk won't make it to Birmingham, and I got no other options that ain't gonna cost me at least two or three hundred dollars. But you can take me for free."

"What's in it for me?" Rick asked.

"Do you want to talk with Darla Ford?"

"Yes, but—"

"Good," Peter said, pointing his finger out the window. "Then take my ass to Destin."

Rick hesitated with his hand on the gear shift. *This is crazy,* he thought.

"Yes!" Peter screamed, pulling the worn George Strait CD out of the glove compartment and sliding the disc into the player.

As George started singing about "oceanfront property in Arizona," Rick finally put the car in drive. *This is crazy,* he thought again, pulling onto Highway 64.

Headed due south . . .

31

Bone hated surprises.

And this definitely qualified, he thought, watching Drake's Saturn pull out of the apartment complex with Peter Burns, the bartender from the Sundowners Club, in the passenger seat. Parked in the back corner of the complex, Bone eased the truck forward, wondering what this was all about.

Bone had laid low since the attack on McMurtrie, which according to his benefactor had achieved the desired effect—the old professor had left town to recover from his injuries, and it was doubtful he'd be able to try the case. Even if he did, he wouldn't be 100 percent, and the kid would have to do the heavy lifting.

Bone knew the police would give up on finding the assailant after a few days, so he'd stayed clear of Pulaski, playing his role as Martha Booher's "nephew" at the Amish settlement in Etheridge, doing his chores during the day and paying "rent" to "Aunt" Martha every night. It had been good, but he was restless. Ready to be back in the game.

He'd resurfaced in Pulaski this morning, picking up Drake's scent at the Bluebird Café. He'd been a bit surprised when Drake drove to the bed and breakfast instead of the office. After all, it was Friday, a workday for those fools who made an honest living in this world. Maybe the boy was going to work from the house today. Or maybe he was about to head back to Tuscaloosa. Bone's new employer had indicated that the case was now in limbo until the grand jury issued its indictment. Bone thought there might not be anything for him to do for a while.

I thought wrong, he knew as he watched the Saturn take the I-65 South ramp. *Where in the hell are they going?*

From a safe distance of about four hundred yards behind, Bone followed them onto the interstate. Then, taking out his cell phone, he dialed the number of his employer.

32

The warden of the St. Clair Correctional Facility in Springville was gracious enough to let them use his administrative conference room for the meeting. Fearing that he wouldn't be strong enough for the walking required at the jail, Tom had reluctantly agreed to let Powell push him in a wheelchair. After they had gone through security, a corrections officer took them down a long hallway and opened the door to the conference room. Before going inside, Tom looked up at Powell. "Any word from Wade?"

The three had split up at the farm, with Wade taking the Dodge Charger to Pulaski while Tom and Powell took Tom's Explorer to Springville.

"Nothing yet, but you know Wade. He's not one to call or text unless he has some information."

Tom nodded and let out a deep breath. "All right," he said. "Let's do this."

The prisoner was waiting for them when Powell pushed Tom's wheelchair inside the room.

Jack Daniel Willistone was thinner than Tom remembered, and his formerly clean-shaven face was now bristled with salt and pepper whiskers. But even wearing the dark-green jumpsuit of a state prisoner, he still gave off an air of strength and power, sitting straight in the chair, his head up, eyes moving slowly back and forth between Tom and Powell. Finally, he focused on Tom and crossed his arms.

"Well, Jesus Christ Superstar," Jack said. "McMurtrie, right?"

Tom nodded. "Mr. Willistone, you look . . . pretty good. Have you lost weight?"

"As a matter of fact I have. When all there is to eat is turd sandwiches and turd stew, you tend to drop a few." Jack paused, squinting at Tom. "What happened to you, McMurtrie? Did you get run over by a bus?"

"A hammer," Tom said. "I got hit in the head and ribs with a hammer. Tore ligaments in my knee trying to block the blows."

Jack continued to squint at Tom. "Well . . . that's unfortunate." Then he shifted his eyes to Powell.

"Conrad," Jack said. "Always such a pleasure to see you."

Sitting next to Jack was an unnaturally tan man with dark, oily hair who had introduced himself as Gregory Zorn outside the conference room. Zorn had been one of several lawyers who represented Jack in the criminal case and had granted the visitors permission to speak to his client. Of course, as the conversation would center around a possible deal for less jail time, granting permission was a no-brainer.

"Gentlemen, Mr. Willistone has agreed to listen to your questions," Zorn said, his voice loud and official sounding. "That is all he has agreed to, and if I feel that the questioning is inappropriate, then I'm going to cut it off and send you on your way. Understand?" According to Powell, Zorn was a greaseball who got his reputation defending DUI cases. A lot of bluster and a limited supply of brains. On the bigger cases he tended to plea, which is what he'd done in Jack's blackmail and witness-tampering cases, though no one could have faulted him for that. The evidence against Jack had been overwhelming.

"Thanks, Greg," Powell said, but his eyes were on Jack, ignoring Zorn. "But we don't look at this meeting as an opportunity for Mr. Willistone to do us a favor. We look at it as a chance for us to consider doing him one if he provides us with helpful information." Powell paused, still only looking at Jack. "Understand?" Powell repeated Zorn's line, the intensity in his voice and behind his eyes palpable.

Jack smiled. "Could one of you boys spare a cigarette? I think a little better after a shot of nicotine."

"Mr. Willistone, I don't think smoking's allowed . . ." Zorn started to say but stopped when Powell pulled out a pack of Marlboros from his front pocket and slid them across the table. Then he pitched a lighter toward Zorn—a little too hard, Tom thought—and Zorn dropped it on the table. "Light it for him, would you, Greg?" Then without missing a beat, Powell turned to Tom. "83 woulda caught that."

Tom couldn't help but smile. "83" was Kevin Norwood, a young wide receiver on Alabama's football team. Powell had asked the warden before going in the room if it was OK if he gave Willistone cigarettes to get him talking, and the warden had simply said, "Whatever works, potnah."

"Norwood, right?" Jack said, taking a draw on the now-lit cigarette, and Powell nodded. Next to Jack, Gregory Zorn's face had turned crimson red. He was being ignored by his client and the prosecutor.

As smoke fumes filled the room and Tom leaned away to breathe, Powell put both elbows on the table. "Here's the deal, Mr. Willistone. We have reason to believe that your old buddy JimBone Wheeler has surfaced in Giles County, Tennessee. We think he may have involvement in multiple crimes in that area, including the attack on Prof. McMurtrie. As we have linked Wheeler to a murder in Faunsdale, Alabama *and* an attempted murder in Tuscaloosa, catching him has become a top priority." Powell paused. "We think you may have information that could lead us to him."

"What makes you think that?" Jack asked, tapping an ash out in Zorn's coffee cup.

"Based on the civil trial in Henshaw last year, we know that JimBone Wheeler was seen inside the Henshaw County Courthouse sitting by your side. We also know that he was spotted at the Sundowners Club outside of Pulaski on multiple occasions with you."

Jack took another drag on the cigarette and blew smoke across the table in Powell's direction. His face gave away nothing. "So what are your questions?"

"Tell us what you know about Andy Walton," Powell said.

Jack shrugged, tapping another ash in Zorn's cup. "When Andy made all his money in the '70s, he started a lumber and logging business over in Lawrenceburg. Walton Lumber. He needed someone to haul freight to various parts of Tennessee and Kentucky, so . . ." He shrugged again. "That was one of our biggest contracts at the time. We had been around for twenty years but were mostly limited to Alabama and the eastern tip of Mississippi. Walton Lumber doubled our coverage and probably led to a half-dozen other contracts." He stuck the cigarette in his mouth but didn't puff on it. "Landing that deal really put us on our way." Jack lowered his eyes to the table, the Marlboro hanging out of his mouth like a toothpick.

"Why you?" Powell asked. "Of all the trucking companies out there, why you?"

Jack raised his eyes from the table, glaring at Powell. "Because we were the best. The fastest, the most dependable, and the best bang for your buck."

"Did you have a prior relationship with Andy?"

"Not really. I knew of him, I guess, when he was running with the State Line Mob over in McNairy County. But our paths really didn't cross until he started looking for a freight hauler."

"How did you find out he was looking?" Powell asked, and Tom was struck by Powell's skillful interrogation techniques. The questions were so natural that Willistone barely blinked at them. *But we are getting close to the heart of it,* Tom knew. *Just a few more questions . . .*

"We had a mutual friend. Larry Tucker. I had just helped Larry with the down payment on his club and—"

"The Sundowners?" Powell interjected, and Jack nodded.

"Yeah. Anyway, Larry owed me, and Andy and he were friends from way back to Andy's Klan days."

"Did you keep up with Andy over the years?"

"Oh, yeah," Jack said, taking a drag on the cigarette. "He was a big client, so of course. I'd go dove hunting every fall on his farm, and he normally threw a big party in Knoxville every other year for the Alabama-Tennessee game. We'd return the favor when the game was in Birmingham or Tuscaloosa."

"How about JimBone Wheeler?" Powell asked. "When did you meet him?" Again, Tom was impressed with the change of direction.

Jack smiled and tapped the cigarette several times on Zorn's cup, though there were no ashes about to fall off. Stalling . . . "Oh, I don't know. A few years ago."

"How did you meet him?"

"I can't remember."

Powell glared at Jack. "Greg, perhaps your client needs a reminder of why we're here."

"If he doesn't remember, he doesn't remember," Zorn fired back.

Jack dropped his cigarette in the coffee cup and pulled another Marlboro from the pack that still lay on the table. Zorn lighted it, and Jack blew a smoke cloud in the air. "Next question," he said.

"Describe your relationship with JimBone Wheeler."

"Casual acquaintance."

"Why was he at the trial in Henshaw last year?"

"I can't remember."

"Did you ever pay him to do . . . jobs for you?"

"Not that I recall," Jack said.

Powell crossed his arms and sighed in frustration. "Sticking to the same old script, huh, Jack? You must really like prison."

"Fuck you," Jack said.

"Ditto," Powell said, starting to stand. "Come on, Professor. I told you this guy would be no help."

But Tom didn't move. He was glaring at Jack Willistone, who was giving it right back to him. Finally, Jack laughed. "McMurtrie, why don't you cut the bullshit and tell me what you want?"

Tom nodded at Powell, who slid several sheets of paper across the table.

"What the hell is this?" Jack asked, beginning to leaf through the papers.

"It's a list of visitors to the jail," Powell said. "Each sheet has the date, the name of the visitor, and the name of the inmate the visitor has come to see. It also has the check-in time of the visitor and the checkout time. The highlighted names are the people who came to see you."

"OK . . ." Jack said. "So what do you want to know?"

"Why did Larry Tucker come to see you on July 20, 2011?" Tom asked. "It's on the third sheet of paper."

"Money," Jack said without turning to the sheet.

"Be more specific," Tom said, feeling a twinge of excitement. Money was a powerful motive.

"He said the club's income was down almost half from the year before. A lot of the reason why was that my trucks weren't rolling."

"What do you mean?" Tom asked.

"I mean you boys shut me down last year. We had over a hundred drivers, and on any given week anywhere from twenty-five to fifty of them would be hauling ass down Highway 64 to one of Andy Walton's businesses in Pulaski, Columbia or Lawrenceburg. We wore that stretch of road out, and the Sundowners was a regular stopover. The Tennessean Truck Stop in Cornersville is just thirty minutes away, so the boys could go off duty at the Sundowners, have a few beers, and look at some skin, and be asleep in their berths less than an hour later, ready for the next haul in the morning. Those that got too drunk would just stay parked in the lot until they were sober. Larry didn't mind." Jack took a quick drag on the cigarette. "But that all changed last June. When I was arrested, the Feds launched a full-scale investigation of my company, and all operations came to a halt for ninety days." He shrugged. "That's a long time, gentlemen. When my drivers stopped getting paid . . ." Jack paused and took a last drag on the cigarette before tapping it out in Zorn's coffee cup. "I can't blame them for leaving. A man's got to eat."

"So . . . are you saying that the federal investigation put Willistone Trucking Company out of business?" Powell asked.

"Actually, no. McMurtrie over there is who put me out of business." He paused, chuckling bitterly. "We had to bankrupt after that jury in Henshaw came back with its ninety-million-dollar verdict."

"If it makes you feel any better, all we ended up receiving was the policy limits," Tom said.

"It doesn't. I'd have rather paid the ninety million and stayed in business. But we were mortgaged to the hilt, and my arrest, followed by the Feds' investigation . . . we just couldn't withstand all of that going on at once." He took another cigarette out of the pack and placed it in his mouth. "Sad thing is that my logs were clean as a whistle, and they got nothing from any of the boys. Not one damn thing. But for that ridiculous verdict, we'd still be rolling." Jack squinted at Tom from across the table. "You shut me down, you son of a bitch. You, showing up at the trial when you did."

"What did Tucker want?" Tom asked, trying to redirect the conversation back on point.

"A loan," Jack said. "Anything I could spare." Jack leaned toward Zorn, and his attorney lit the new cigarette. "He also wanted to know why the drivers had stopped coming in. He knew about the verdict and my arrest, but he hadn't heard about the bankruptcy." Jack puffed on the cigarette. "So I filled him in on the bad news."

"And he went away empty-handed?" Tom asked.

"Like everyone coming in here wanting handouts."

"Why didn't Tucker ask Andy Walton for money?"

"You'd have to ask Larry about that," Jack said.

"During Tucker's visit, did he mention any other problems he was having?" Tom asked.

"No, just the money."

"Did JimBone Wheeler's name ever come up?" Powell asked.

Jack shook his head. "No."

"Mr. Willistone, I've done the math and it appears that outside of your wife and son, the person who came to see you the most was Andy Walton. Does that sound correct?" Tom asked.

He shrugged. "I don't know."

"It looks like he came four times, starting on March 1, 2011. His last visit was August 11, just a week before his murder."

"If you say so," Jack said.

"Look at the last page of the stack."

Jack put the cigarette in the cup and flipped through the documents to the last page. He held the sheet out from him and then brought it closer, like someone who needed bifocals might do. Then he smiled.

"Something funny?"

"Just you boys," Jack said. "All right, I see it."

"You see the name Andy Walton and the date August 11, 2011?"

"Yes."

"Why did he come to see you on August 11?"

"I really don't remember much about that day. The first time Andy came, he had a bunch of questions about other freight haulers. Who was good? Who would I recommend? Anyone I'd stay away from? That kind of stuff. When we'd gone under, every Tom, Dick, and Harry had come to Andy, wanting his business. The last couple times . . ." Jack paused, smiling again.

What is he smiling about? Tom wondered.

"The last couple times all he wanted to talk about was prison life. How were they treating me? The food? Was I able to sleep? That kind of stuff. I got the feeling . . ." Jack paused.

"What?" Tom pressed.

"I got the feeling he was worried he might end up here. In prison I mean."

Tom glanced at Powell. Now they were getting somewhere. Based on the documents, "the last couple times" would be August 1 and August 11, 2011, less than a month from Andy's murder. Powell nodded for Tom to continue the questioning.

"Did he ever say why or what he had done that might make him so curious about prison life?"

"Nope. He never said anything at all about that. It was just . . . *weird* that Andy would take so much interest in my predicament." Jack laughed and took a quick drag on the cigarette. "I mean, I'd known Andy for thirty years. He was a hard-ass like me. Cared first and foremost about his business. About making money. When we were together, we talked business, and that's the way we both liked it. After the first visit about freight hauler recommendations, there was no reason for him to come see me. It wasn't in his interests to visit me and ask a bunch of questions about prison life unless . . ."

"Unless he was worried about ending up in the same place," Tom offered.

Jack nodded. "Nothing else makes sense."

"Did he ever say anything to you about his days as the Imperial Wizard of the Tennessee Knights of the KKK?"

Jack shook his head. "Never. I think that was a part of Andy's life that he'd just as soon forget. But I knew about it."

"Did he mention anything to you about the killing of a black man named Franklin Roosevelt Haynes in 1966?"

Jack looked down at the table. "Nothing specific." Then, looking up, he squinted at Tom. "I do remember him saying on one of his visits that 'your bad decisions in life have a way of catching up to you.'" Jack laughed. "Course I knew all about that, and I agreed with him."

"To your knowledge, did Andy know JimBone Wheeler?" Tom asked.

Jack smiled, his eyes mean. "Andy knew everyone."

Tom glared back at him once more, fed up with Jack's song and dance. "We are *really* not in the mood to play, Mr. Willistone."

"I don't give a shit about your mood, McMurtrie. And let me tell you something, you sumbitch. When I get out of this hellhole, I am going to make it *all* back. Every last cent. You didn't break Jack Willistone. You just slowed me down a little."

"And when you get out of here, *you sumbitch*, don't you think JimBone is going to come looking for his payday?" Tom asked, his voice low. "How much did he charge you to trip Mule Morris's brakes? How about trying to kill Dawn Murphy? Did he do that for free, or did he charge you a fee?" Tom pulled himself up from the wheelchair and leaned his hands on the table, bringing his face to within an inch of Willistone's. He could smell the inmate's stale scent. "I'm betting he charged you, and I'm also betting that your financial difficulties have kept you from paying." Tom lowered his voice to a whisper. "I'm betting that the first person you see when you get out of this 'hellhole'"—Tom made the quotation symbol with his fingers—"is going to be JimBone, and I bet you're going to look a hell of a lot worse than me when he's through with you."

"Now that's enough," Greg Zorn said, placing a hand on Jack's shoulder and pointing at Tom. "Prof. McMurtrie, please sit down and stop harassing my client."

"Don't get your panties in a wad, Greg," Powell said, his eyes on Jack. "Mr. Willistone, we think it is in your best interests to cooperate," Powell said, still sitting in his chair, his voice matter-of-fact.

Jack Willistone slowly rose from his seat. He smiled, then chuckled. "You boys think you're so goddamned smart." He paused, turning to Tom, the smile gone. "You aren't paying attention, old man. The answers you want are right under your nose. You're just not looking." He sighed. "I have to say I'm disappointed in you, McMurtrie. Fucking Yoda, letting a storm trooper like Bone get the best of you."

"Mr. Willistone—" Powell started.

"Get me out of here, Zorn," Jack interrupted. "These turds have upset my stomach."

As Zorn stood to usher Jack from the conference room, Tom held up his hand. "Not yet, Jack. Just a couple more questions. We need to finish going through that list." Tom pointed at the visitor log on the table.

"My client is done here, Mr.—"

"We'll be quick, Greg," Tom interrupted. "Now, the visitor log lists a grand total of five people who have come to see you since you were incarcerated."

"What can I say?" Jack said, grunting. "I'm a popular guy."

"Your wife, Barbara, son, Barton, Larry Tucker, Andy Walton, and . . . one name we didn't recognize."

Jack shrugged. "Just spit it out, McMurtrie."

Tom reached across the table and flipped the log to the page he was looking for. Holding his finger on the name, Tom eyed Jack

Willistone. "On June 10, 2011 a lady came to see you around 10:30 in the morning. Check-in time is 10:32. Checkout time is 10:45." Tom tapped the times with his finger. "See that?"

"I do."

"It's right under your nose, isn't it?" Tom said, smiling at Jack.

"Strong in the Force, are you," Jack said.

"Who is she?" Powell asked. Then, stealing a glance at Tom, who nodded, Powell leaned across the table and put his finger on the highlighted name: "Who is Martha Booher?"

33

The Boathouse is an oyster bar that sits on Destin Harbor. As he and Burns waited for a table on the wooden deck outside the establishment, Rick gazed across the water to Holiday Isle, which was the last stretch of beach before the bridge to Okaloosa Island. *Beautiful,* he thought, watching a yacht slowly make its way through the harbor to the gap that led to the Gulf of Mexico.

Feeling a tap on his shoulder, he turned to see Burns holding two longneck Coronas. "Ask and ye shall receive," he said, passing the cold beer to Rick and looking out at the harbor.

The trip hadn't been too bad, Rick had to admit. The Saturn stayed in one piece, and they had only made two pit stops, one just outside of Birmingham and another in Andalusia. In Andalusia, at Burns's urging, Rick bought a six-pack, and Burns took down five of them before they hit the Mid-Bay Bridge, which took them into Destin. Rick had only had one and didn't finish it. He knew he needed to keep his wits about him.

They had parked a few doors down from The Boathouse at a place called The Fisherman's Wharf. After a beer at the outside bar there, they'd left the car in the parking lot and walked the hundred yards down Highway 98 to The Boathouse.

"Where's Darla?" Rick asked Burns. They were both leaning their elbows on the wooden railing, eyes fixed on the dark water in front of them. In the daylight Rick knew the water would be emerald green. But at 10:30 p.m. it was dark and foreboding.

"Coming," Peter said. "Just be patient." He took a sip of his beer. "Beautiful, isn't it?"

Rick nodded. Last fall he had taken Dawn on a weekend getaway to Destin. They had stayed at a place on Holiday Isle and had eaten dinner at The Fisherman's Wharf. Their waitress at the Wharf had recommended they have a beer and listen to the band at The Boathouse and told them they'd be better off leaving their car at the Wharf and walking. So they had, just as Rick and Burns had done tonight. Rick and Dawn had actually stood right where Rick now stood with Burns, holding hands and talking about nothing in particular.

"Hey, man. You OK?" Peter asked.

Rick blinked and turned to his unexpected traveling companion, seeming to see him for the first time. Burns had a three-day growth of brown stubble, with messy dirty-blond hair thinning at the temples and in the back. He wore a Hawaiian shirt and tattered khaki shorts with flip-flops. Rick, who had not had time to change or even pack a suitcase, was wearing gray slacks and a white button-down, no tie, with his sleeves rolled up.

"Yeah, fine. Just thinking about my girlfriend."

"Gotcha," Peter said, nodding his head as if he understood. "Well, listen, dude. I really appreciate the ride. That was a lifesaver."

"When is Darla going to be here?" Rick asked, growing impatient.

Burns started to say something, but his words were drowned out by loud screams inside and outside the restaurant as the band struck the opening riff of "Sweet Home Alabama."

"Yeah!" Peter said, whooping and slapping Rick on the back, forcing him to turn around and look inside the restaurant. Rick saw several nice-looking college-age women swaying back and forth in front of the stage. As if on cue a waitress came up to the two men holding a tray with two shot glasses, a salt shaker, and two limes.

With no hesitation Burns shook some salt on his wrist, sucked it, and then turned the shot glass up. He took it down in one swig, then shook his head and put the lime in his mouth. "Ah, tequila!" he yelled, putting the other shot glass in Rick's hand and shaking salt on Rick's wrist. "Come on, dude, you're paying for all this. At least do a shot with me."

Thinking what the hell, Rick licked his wrist, turned up the shot glass, and then sucked the lime.

"That a boy," Peter said. Then, leaning into him, "Now, let's forget about that girlfriend of yours, and let's find us a wife for the night. What do you say?"

"Darla," Rick managed, coughing the words out, his throat burning with the taste of the tequila.

"She'll be here," Peter said, his words a bit slurred. "But until she arrives . . ." He gestured toward a group of girls wearing bikini tops and blue jean cutoffs. If they were twenty-one years old, they had just turned it. "Let's be social. What do you say?"

———

Thirty minutes later the men were seated inside the restaurant at the table closest to the band. Burns had ordered two dozen oysters, but he wasn't eating them, having moved his chair to the neighboring table, where the group of bikini-clad college girls—four sorority sisters from Jacksonville State on a last trip to the beach before classes started—reveled in Peter's stories from the Sundowners Club. Either that or they were just putting up with him because he kept buying them beers and shots and charging them to Rick's credit card.

I'm going to have a three-hundred-dollar bill, Rick thought, putting an oyster drenched with cocktail sauce on a cracker and popping it in his mouth. He washed the concoction down with the remains of another Corona, his second, and leaned back in his seat. Taking out his phone, he went to check his e-mail and see if he'd missed any calls, but his phone was now dead.

Damnit. In his haste to leave Pulaski, he'd forgotten to juice up his phone and had left the charger on the dresser at the bed and breakfast. Stealing a glance at Burns, he made his way to the restroom, wondering if Darla Ford was really going to show, or if this was just one big hoax. A con played by a strip club bartender who had spent his whole life playing folks like Rick. *Maybe,* he thought, *but what are my other options?*

When he returned to his seat, the band was playing John Anderson's "Straight Tequila Night," but Rick wasn't hearing anything. He looked at the barely touched plate of oysters, and he wasn't hungry.

"Another beer?" the waitress yelled from behind him, and Rick gave her the thumbs-up sign. Blinking his eyes, he realized that the table of bikini-clad girls was gone, and there was no sign of Burns.

Rick turned all the way around in his chair, his eyes frantically scanning the crowd. Where the hell was Burns?

He stood and did a sweep of the bar with his eyes, still not seeing him, and then began to walk around the place, which was packed, his eyes darting to every corner, nook, and cranny. Nothing.

Rick lumbered back to his seat in a daze. "Have you seen the guy that came in with me? Hawaiian shirt, shorts, stubble?" he asked the waitress, who was setting a Corona down at his place at the table.

"The guy talking with the table of girls?" she asked, pointing to the now-empty table.

"Yes," Rick said, nodding. "Did you see—?"

"I'm pretty sure he left."

Rick just stood there, unbelieving, as the waitress walked away from him. He slunk down in his seat. Burns was gone. He'd driven the bastard to Destin, Florida, and now he was gone. And Rick had no idea where. Had he left with one of the girls at the adjacent table? Or had he just split the minute he saw Rick head to the bathroom?

Damnit. Rick held the cold longneck to his forehead and closed his eyes. The band started in on "Whiskey River," by Willie Nelson, and Rick couldn't think of a more appropriate song. He drained half the beer in one gulp and slammed the drink on the table.

All for nothing, he thought. The whole trip. He'd been played a fool. He should've known Burns would split the minute Rick let him out of his sight.

Rick drained the beer with two more sips and gave the signal to the waitress as she passed by to bring him another. For an instant he thought of Bocephus Haynes, alone in his cold jail cell, and guilt washed over him. Bo had put so much faith in the Professor and Rick. And the Professor had been beaten up and . . .

. . . *I'm getting drunk in an oyster bar on the Gulf Coast.*

Rick took the beer out of the waitress's hand before she could set it down and took a quick sip. Too quick, in fact, as most of the drink went straight up his nose. He set the bottle down and it bubbled over, making a mess.

"That won't do you any good," a voice said from behind him, and Rick spun around to see a smiling woman. She was short, maybe five foot two, if that, and was wearing a black tank top and khaki low-cut shorts. Her skin was tanned golden brown, and her eyes, also brown, gave him a curious glance. "The lawyer, right?" she asked, and Rick nodded as she took the seat across from him.

"Are you—?"

"Darla Ford," she interrupted, extending her small hand.

Rick blinked at her in disbelief. Then as relief flooded his veins, he wiped his right hand on his pants and reached across the table.

"Rick Drake." When his hand clasped Darla's, she held on to it for a second.

"Well, Mr. Drake, if you don't mind me saying so . . . you look like you could use a friend."

34

Three hundred miles away, in his cell on the A Block of the St. Clair Correctional Facility, Jack Willistone lay on his cot, staring at the concrete ceiling above him. It had been lights-out for at least three hours, but Jack couldn't sleep.

He'd answered the questions about Martha Booher as well as he could. "An old friend. Met her in Nashville many years ago. She had been a barmaid at Tootsies, the famous bar in Nashville on Broadway Street." They'd "spent some time together" on Jack's trips to the Music City, but he hadn't seen her in years. She'd heard the news and just wanted to say hello and that she was pulling for him. It was . . . "sweet," Jack had said.

And all of it was true. He'd just left out one minor detail.

Our mutual friend sends his regards. He says he's looking forward to seeing you when you get out of jail.

It had been the last thing Martha said. Completely innocent, in case their conversation was being recorded. But the meaning came in loud and clear, and it was just as McMurtrie had predicted.

Bone will come for me, Jack knew. *He'll come for me, and if I can't pay . . .*

Jack closed his eyes, unwilling to allow himself to panic. A lot had happened since Martha's visit. He had gotten a break.

Someone *had* come to see him, and he *had* referred that person to Bone. Bone wasn't stupid. He would know the source of his newfound income. The question, though, was would it be enough?

Jack propped himself on his elbow on the cot and gazed through the steel bars. McMurtrie had put him here. In his whole life, a journey spent hustling some of the smartest and shrewdest businessmen in the country, McMurtrie was the only son of a bitch that ever got the best of him.

He'll figure it out, Jack knew, chuckling to himself. *And when he does, Bone will either be dead or in prison for life.* Either way he couldn't get at Jack.

Jack knew he could answer the riddle for them. But if he did that, he was committed. If they failed, Bone would most certainly come for him. And the referral wouldn't make a damn. Not paying was one thing. Outright betrayal was another. *I'd be a dead man walking,* Jack knew.

So he'd stay on the fence and hope that McMurtrie would figure it out. Martha Booher was certainly part of it. Booher might lead them right to Bone . . .

. . . if they ever find her.

But she wasn't the only clue. There was something else.

Something else . . . right under their nose.

35

Bocephus Haynes lowered his chest to the concrete floor. "Forty-five," he said out loud as if anyone in the cell could hear him. He did five more push-ups and then switched to planks. Five minutes later, when he had reached the point of physical exhaustion, he crumpled to the concrete and rolled over on his back.

Because of the press the case had garnered, Ennis had decided to keep Bo in the holding cell as opposed to moving him to general population. The decision suited Bo just fine, as he had no wish to rub elbows with any of the other patrons of the Giles County Jail. But he'd now been incarcerated for over two weeks, and the boredom and monotony had become almost unbearable.

The cell was pitch dark, but Bo was used to the shortage of light. It was also deathly quiet in the small space, the constant noise of the day ceasing after the warden called for lights out. Bo gazed at the ceiling, trying not to think about the Professor licking his wounds in Hazel Green. *My fault,* he knew. *I shouldn't have dragged him into this mess.* Bo sighed and closed his eyes. Images of Jazz, T. J., and Lila floated through his brain, causing his heart to ache. They had not come to see him, and in all truth he was relieved. He didn't want his son and daughter to see him here. And Jazz . . . he couldn't bear to see her look of disappointment and shame. *I've let them all down . . .*

Bo rolled over into push-up position and started another set, trying to will the negative thoughts out of his brain. He had reached ten when he heard the sliding door swoosh open. Figuring it was a corrections officer doing some type of nightly sweep of the jail, Bo continued his push-ups. He stopped when he saw the loafers come into view. That wasn't the footwear of a corrections officer.

"Got a minute, Bo?" a weary but familiar voice asked.

Bo shot to his feet and wiped the sweat from his eyes. Blinking inside the dark room, he recognized the round face of Mayor Dan Kilgore. The mayor was a bullnecked man with thinning silver hair who usually had a broad grin plastered on his face.

But he wasn't grinning now.

"What—?"

"Relax," the mayor said, taking a seat in one of the metal chairs at the desk. "I've been meaning to visit you, but I didn't want to come during normal hours when the press leeches are out."

"Well . . . thanks. I guess," Bo said, taking the seat across the small desk from the mayor.

Dan Kilgore had been the mayor of Pulaski for twelve years. Back when he was a city councilman, Kilgore had been a big part of the Klan rally boycott in 1989, and since becoming mayor was constantly pushing progressive programs and measures.

"Bo, nothing we say in here can be used against you. I've already covered that with the General, and she understands."

Bo smiled. "Sure."

"Believe what you want to believe, but you can talk freely."

Bo shrugged. "Why are you here, Mayor?"

"To ask you to plead guilty."

For a moment Bo didn't think he'd heard him correctly. *"What?"*

"There's still time. Take the deal the General has proposed. It's . . . better than the alternative."

"I didn't do it," Bo said. "I'm not pleading to nothing."

"Bo, the evidence—"

"I was framed, Mayor."

Kilgore smiled sadly. "If you say so. Bo, Pulaski . . . has changed so much over the past two decades. So many good things are happening here, and you've been a big part of that. Do you really want all of our progress to go out the window?"

"I didn't kill Andy Walton. I'm not going to rot away in a prison cell to save this town. My daddy was lynched when I was five years old, and I saw the man that did it. And no one here has done one damn thing about that. Not even you, Mayor."

"Bo—"

"Let me finish. No one lifted a finger for me, and you want to know why? Because they were scared. Just like you, Mayor. Scared that if Andy Walton was charged with the murder of my father, then Pulaski would be dragged into another story about the Ku Klux Klan."

"Bo, you know that's not true."

"It is true!" Bo screamed, bringing his fist down on the table. "Now you just want me to take one for the team. Plead guilty to a crime I didn't commit? Why should I do that, Mayor? When has this town ever had my back?"

Kilgore sighed and stood from his chair. He began to pace back and forth in the small space. "You know they'll come, don't you?"

"The Klan?" Bo asked.

Kilgore nodded. "My office has been inundated with calls all day long from different factions. Permits have been requested by the Klan for every single day from mid-September until the end of October."

Bo said nothing as Kilgore continued to pace and rant.

"It'll be the Heritage Festival on steroids," the mayor said, referring to the annual rally organized by various Klan sympathizers that was held on the Giles County Square every fall in Pulaski. He sighed again and stuffed his hands in pockets. "Won't just be them either. The NAACP's been calling too. And the press . . . it's going to be the circus of all circuses."

"What's the pulse of the town?" Bo asked.

Kilgore let his hands fall to his side. "Nobody knows what to do, Bo. I mean . . . no offense, but you look guilty as hell. And with Jasmine leaving town and resigning from the college . . . I don't know, I think everyone just feels paralyzed."

For almost a minute neither man said anything. Finally, Bo spoke. "I'm sorry, Mayor, but I'm not going to plead guilty to something I didn't do."

Dan Kilgore nodded solemnly and walked away. When he reached the sliding door, he said, "I'm sorry too, Bo."

—

Out in the hallway the mayor's face told the story.

"No dice?" Helen asked.

Kilgore shook his head. "He says he didn't do it."

"Just like every person who's ever been charged with a crime."

"Bo Haynes is not a common criminal, General."

Helen nodded in agreement. "No, Mayor, he's not. But on August 19, 2011 he killed Andy Walton in cold blood, moved his body to Walton Farm, and then hung him from the same tree where the Ku Klux Klan lynched his father."

Kilgore smirked. "That's going to sound good on TV, General. What are you going to do after the trial? Run for governor?"

Helen started to say something but then stopped herself. She'd let the mayor have that one.

Trudging down the hall, the mayor sighed. "You're gonna be the only winner in this deal, General. The town will lose. Bo will lose. Even if he were to somehow win the case, he'll still lose. The college will lose. Every damn body will lose except General Helen by God Lewis." He paused and turned to face her. "You'll win. You'll win even if you lose, and the damnable part of it is *you already know.* This case is going to make you a national celebrity."

"You may not believe this, Mayor," Helen said, speaking in a calm tone, "but I get no joy in prosecuting Bo, and I certainly don't relish the idea of putting him to death. Bocephus Haynes is one of the finest lawyers in this state. I have a great deal of respect for him."

"He says he didn't do it," Kilgore said.

"But he did," Helen replied, her voice devoid of any doubt. "The evidence is overwhelming. If I had any question about Bo's guilt, I would not be charging him, but . . . he did it." She paused, crossing her arms against her chest. "I'm sorry, but I have to do my job."

Kilgore nodded. *Déjà vu all over again,* he thought. Then: "I'm sorry too."

36

They left The Boathouse five minutes after Darla arrived. They were sitting too close to the band to be able to talk, and there weren't any other empty seats. Rick closed his tab, and then Darla led him by the hand through the crowd of people to the exit.

A few minutes later they were walking along the dock of boats that lined the harbor, the music from The Boathouse band still playing faintly in the background. Darla had yet to let go of Rick's hand, and Rick wasn't exactly sure how to take that. He felt woozy, his head spinning from the alcohol, the panic over having lost Burns, and fatigue and stress from the last few days. He breathed in the salt air, feeling his arms involuntarily shake.

"Thanks for coming," Rick said, trying to direct his jumbled thoughts back to his purpose for being here.

"You're welcome," she said, taking a seat on a white bench that looked out over the harbor. Rick glanced to his left and right, and they appeared to be alone. There were still a few stragglers drinking beers at the outside bar of The Boathouse, but they were well out of earshot. Still holding his hand, Darla patted the place next to her. "Pop a squat," she said, and Rick smiled. His mother used to say that when she wanted him to sit.

Rick sat on the bench, self-conscious of his right hand, which Darla was still holding, now with both of hers.

"You don't like holding my hand?" Darla asked, puckering her lips, feigning that her feelings were hurt.

"Uh . . . I . . ."

Darla punched his shoulder and laughed. "Relax, Counselor. I'm just joshing you." She turned to face him, propping her left knee on the bench so that it touched his side and wrapping his right hand again with both of her own. "I'm sorry, it's just a habit."

"What is?" Rick asked, looking at her. The breeze coming off the water flittered her hair, but she made no move to fix it.

"Being touchy-feely. I was a dancer for eight years and"—she paused, smiling at him—"you learn things about men."

"What things?" Rick asked.

"Most men want to be touched."

When Rick raised his eyebrows, Darla giggled. "No, silly. Not a sexual touch. *All men like that.*" She lowered her voice and narrowed her eyes, and Rick felt a warmth come over him that he tried to fight off.

"I'm just talking about physical touch," she said. "Like this." She held up their interlocked hands. Then she let her left hand slide up his arm, resting it on his shoulder. "And this."

Rick felt his cheeks reddening and was glad for the dark.

"Most men are starved to be touched like this," she continued, running her hand up his neck. "At least . . . the men that came into the club seemed to be."

"Was Andy Walton?"

The smile faded from Darla's face. "Very much so," she said. "Mr. Walton . . . was a very sad man."

"Sad about what?" Rick asked.

Darla shrugged and leaned into him, wrapping her arms through Rick's. "Everything. He was dying, did you know that?"

"Pancreatic cancer, right?" Rick asked.

Darla nodded. "He didn't tell me right off. The first few times he came in, we just sat in the back of the bar, talking. He really liked talking to me. And . . . I could tell he liked the way I touched him."

"How would you . . . ?" Rick's voice faltered. Questioning a stripper about how she touched a patron was not something you learned in law school.

"Just like this," she said, turning to face him. "I'd brush his hair, hold his hand, or wrap my arms through his." She leaned into Rick, and he blinked his eyes, trying to focus.

"Did you eventually, you know . . . ?" Again Rick faltered.

"Dance naked for him?"

"Yeah," Rick said, looking away from her.

"Of course," she said. "Eventually . . ." She shrugged. "My approach to dancing was different than most of the girls. Most of them would prance around in their G-string and throw their boobs in the men's faces. Every few seconds they'd ask if they could give them a lap dance." She paused. "Larry always said he needed a few foot soldiers like that. Tall, horsey-looking girls with big breasts who could work the pole and get the small bills from the day laborers and the truck drivers who would stop by. That was important for the success of the club. It set the tone and allowed me to work my magic." She stopped and eyed him curiously. When he didn't say anything, she asked, "Don't you want to know what my magic is?"

"I . . ." Rick gazed into her brown eyes and then looked away, focusing on a boat floating slowly along in the water. "I didn't want to insult you by asking. I'm pretty sure I know what it is."

"Then tell me," Darla said, leaning into him and elbowing him under the rib cage. "Don't be shy, Counselor."

"It's . . . this," Rick said, shrugging. "What you're doing right now. The touching. The way you talk. The way you smell . . ."

"Do you like me?" Darla asked.

"Very much," Rick said.

She smiled. "That's the magic. Stripping at the highest level is no different than any other business. It's all about building relationships . . . and I'm good at that." Darla placed her elbow on the bench and let her hand drop onto Rick's shoulder.

Beginning to feel warm again, Rick tried to stand. One leg had gone completely asleep, and he stumbled, almost falling into the harbor. *Jesus Christ . . .*

Behind him, Darla was laughing.

Rick gazed down at her and wiped sweat off his forehead. He needed to regroup. "You said Andy told you about the cancer."

"You're a cutie, you know that?" She was smiling at him. "I bet you have a girlfriend."

"Ms. Ford, please . . . I . . ."

"*Ms. Ford*? Oooooo . . ." She narrowed her gaze and wrapped her arms around her left knee, her smile widening. You're starting to turn me on, Counselor."

Before Rick could protest again, Darla yawned and stretched her arms above her head. "There is a VIP room at the club," she finally said. "After Mr. Walton requested that I dance for him, I began to take him up there. The VIP dances cost a hundred dollars for thirty minutes, but Mr. Walton didn't care about the money. He'd let me dance with him for two or three hours. There were some weeks where he would be the only customer I'd have at night and I'd take home six grand, while some of the foot soldiers had done the pole all night along with ten lap dances and only had two hundred dollars to show for it." She paused, shaking her head and crossing her arms. "Anyway, after about a month he told me about the cancer."

"Do you remember when that was?"

Darla shrugged. "Wasn't that long ago. Maybe the beginning of summer. May, I think."

"Did he say how bad it was?"

"Just that it was terminal. I think at some point he said he wasn't sure how long he had left. Could be a year. Could be a few months."

Rick nodded. *Keep her going . . .*

"You said he was a very sad man," Rick began. "How so? Was it just the cancer?"

"No. That was a big part of it, but there was something else. Mr. Walton . . . had something weighing on him. A secret, you might say."

Rick felt his stomach catch and took a step closer to her. "A secret?"

Darla nodded and leaned forward on the bench, resting her elbows on her knees. When she didn't say anything, Rick prompted her. "Did he tell you this secret?"

"Not in so many words," she finally said.

"What does that mean?" Rick pressed, sitting down again on the bench.

She shifted her gaze to the water. "Mr. Walton said he had done a lot of bad things in his life and he was scared."

"Scared of what?"

"Of dying." She looked back at him. "He was scared of dying. He said the truth would die with him."

"The truth?"

"About what he had done."

They were going in a circle. "What had he done? Did he tell you about the bad things?"

This time Darla did shiver. "He said he done them when he was in the Klan, and a man got killed." She stopped and squeezed her knees together with her arms. "He said it was his fault. He was responsible."

"Did he say who he was talking about?"

Darla shook her head. "No, he didn't. But I've lived in Pulaski a long time. You hear things, and I knew the rumors about Bocephus Haynes's father being lynched on Mr. Walton's farm. So I asked him about it."

"How . . . did you ask him?" Rick asked, involuntarily scooting closer to her on the bench.

"I just blurted it out—not subtle at all. I said, 'Mr. Walton, is Bo Haynes's father the man that was killed while you were leading the Klan'?"

"What did he say?"

"He didn't say nothing at first," Darla said. "He just got the saddest look on his face I'd ever seen. Then he just started nodding." Darla paused, shaking her head. "It was weird, like I wasn't even in the room. Then . . ." She trailed off and stood from the bench.

"Then what?" Rick asked.

She wiped her eyes, and Rick realized that she had begun to cry. "Then he said he was going to confess."

Rick felt the blood almost go out of his body. "*What?*"

Darla turned to him, fresh tears running down her cheeks. "He told me that he was going to confess. That he wasn't going to let the truth die with him. Then"—she choked the words out—"he told me that he'd done something for me. Something special that would help me move down to the coast." She paused. "I had told him many times about my dream to move down here and open up an oyster bar. Anyway, sure enough the Monday after he died I got a call from his lawyer. Said I needed to come down to his law office and pick something up. When I got there, the lawyer gave me a manila envelope. He said, 'Mr. Walton asked that I personally deliver this to you.' When I got back to my car, I opened it, and there were ten smaller envelopes inside of it. I opened them one by one when I was back in my apartment, and they all had ten thousand dollars in them." She paused. "A hundred thousand dollars." She stopped and looked at Rick. "I left for Destin the next morning."

For a moment Rick didn't say anything. Andy Walton had bequeathed a stripper one hundred thousand dollars. Probably just pocket change for a guy like that, but still . . . It was a noble act, Rick thought. Inconsistent with the view he held in his mind of the man. "Going back to the night he said he was going to confess," Rick began. "When did this conversation take place?"

Darla shrugged. "A couple weeks before he died."

"Did he say anything else to you?"

She nodded, and fresh tears formed in her eyes. "He gave me the same warning the last few times I saw him."

"Which was?"

"To not . . . tell . . . anyone." Her lip quivered with emotion, and Rick felt gooseflesh break out on his arm.

"Did you?" Rick asked.

Darla Ford crossed her arms tight around her chest and bit her lip, looking down at the ground.

"Ms. Ford, did you tell anyone that Andy Walton was going to confess to killing Roosevelt Haynes?"

Slowly, she nodded.

"*Who?*" Rick asked.

"Larry," Darla said, sniffling and leaning her head on his shoulder. "I told my boss. Larry Tucker."

37

Bone watched them from the deck of The Boathouse. He held a Bud Light bottle that he had barely touched and was dressed in a "Fisherman's Wharf" T-shirt he'd bought while Rick and Burns were having a drink at the place next door, a tattered red cap with the cursive *A* of Alabama's Crimson Tide on the front, khaki shorts he kept in a duffel bag in the back of the truck, and a pair of old flip-flops. With his scraggly beard and his hat pulled down low over his eyes, he blended into the crowd perfectly.

This can't be good, he thought. Drake had talked with the stripper for at least forty-five minutes now, and the conversation had turned heated. For a while Drake had paced in front of the bench, asking her questions.

He's getting something out of this, Bone knew. He had placed calls and sent texts to his benefactor on a regular basis, and so far the instructions had been to follow and report what he saw. He took the cell phone out of his left pocket and texted, *They've talked for forty-five minutes, and the kid seems to be excited.* Bone returned the phone to his pocket and waited.

When Burns had snuck out of the restaurant alone while Drake was in the bathroom, Bone had thought for a moment that the kid had been taken for a ride. Burns had scampered off down the dock a ways, so Bone wasn't sure where he had gone. His orders were to stay with Drake.

He figured the night was probably over—a wasted trip no different than Drake's—until he saw Nikita emerge from the shadows of the front parking lot a few minutes after Burns had left.

Bone recognized her right off from his nights at The Sundowners Club. Nikita—Bone did not know her real name—had always dressed relatively conservatively as far as strippers went, and this contrast made her stand out at the club. It also made her easy to recognize now.

The phone in his left pocket vibrated, and Bone grabbed it, never taking his eyes off Nikita and Drake. He looked down at the message on the screen and felt his body temperature drop a couple degrees.

Kill the girl. And the lawyer if necessary.

Bone felt his heart pick up a beat as he read and reread the message. Not exactly what he was expecting, but . . .

A second message came in on top of the first.

And make it look good.

Bone smiled. He always did.

He glanced at his watch, then looked around. It was already past 1:00 a.m., and outside of the few stragglers in The Boathouse, Bone saw no one around. The dock below was completely deserted except for Drake and the dancer, and there was very little light.

Perfect, he thought, taking a small sip of beer and placing it on the railing. Bone felt for the gun inside the front of his shorts. His pockets were too tight for the .38, so he'd stuffed it down the front of his shorts and let his loose-fitting T-shirt hang over it.

Slowly and softly, Bone began to walk down the wooden steps to the dock. Both the stripper and Drake had come to The

Boathouse from the parking lot. When he got to the bottom of the steps, he saw them.

Drake's life is over, Bone knew, stepping behind the stairs and into the shadows. Killing the lawyer, he'd already determined, was going to be necessary. The boy, along with McMurtrie, had cost Bone a lot of money last year. And the El Camino . . .

He took the gun out of his shorts and waited. They would have to come back to these steps to get to the parking lot. When they did . . .

He flipped the gun so that he was holding the weapon by its barrel. He'd hit them both with the butt end and toss their limp bodies in the harbor. Bone could almost see the headline in the paper. "Accidental Drowning Claims Lives of Young Man and Woman."

Bone smiled, waiting . . .

38

"Hey, I'm talking to you," Darla said, squeezing her hands into fists and lightly tapping Rick on the stomach. "Do you think Larry could be involved in Mr. Walton's murder?"

Rick hadn't even heard the question the first time she'd asked it. He was still looking at the water, thinking it through in his mind. Assuming that Larry Tucker was one of the ten men who participated in the lynching of Roosevelt Haynes in 1966, then he would have every reason to want to stop Andy Walton's confession.

Motive, Rick thought. Larry Tucker had motive. He was also the owner of the Sundowners Club, the scene of the crime. Opportunity. Rick felt his heart pounding in his chest. *We might have an alternative theory . . .*

"When did you tell Mr. Tucker about Mr. Walton's plan to confess?"

"The same night Mr. Walton told me about it."

"So two weeks before the murder?"

Darla nodded, and her eyes were wide with fear. "Do you think Larry—?"

"I don't know," Rick interrupted. "I think it's possible that Mr. Tucker was involved. We represent Bocephus Haynes, who has been charged with the murder, but he has pled not guilty. If Bo is innocent of the charges, then—"

"Someone else did it," Darla completed the thought. "And you think it might be Larry."

"Was Larry in the Klan with Andy?"

Darla crossed her arms and shrugged. "I don't know. I just know they had been friends for . . ." She stopped and placed her hand over her mouth. "There were others. Of course . . . Mr. Haynes was killed by the Ku Klux Klan, and Mr. Walton was just one of the men." She paused, her eyes wide. "You think Larry was one of them." It wasn't a question.

"I do," Rick said. "But I can't prove it right now. Assuming he was and he found out that Andy was going to confess . . ."

"Oh, Jesus, it's my fault then," Darla said. "I'm the one who told him." Her voice cracked, and she sat down on the bench. She crossed her arms and began to rock back and forth. "After all Mr. Walton did for me . . ."

"You didn't know," Rick said, sitting beside her. "Besides . . ." He sighed. "It's just a theory."

For several minutes they both just sat there. Arms crossed, gazing out at the water. The only sounds were Darla's sniffles. Finally, she wiped her eyes. "I would have made it here without him," she said, her voice determined. "I was two years away from saving enough. I didn't need a sugar daddy." She sighed. "But he helped me. I . . . no one ever did anything for me before. If I'm somehow responsible for his death . . ."

"He was dying," Rick said. "It wouldn't have been much longer."

She nodded. "Still . . . it's not right."

"I agree, but you can't blame yourself. You did what you thought was right. That's all anyone can do." Then a thought struck him like a thunderbolt. "Did you tell the sheriff's department or

DA's office about any of this? Andy saying he was going to confess, and you telling Larry Tucker about it?"

"They didn't ask. All they wanted to know was what I saw the last night Mr. Walton was with me, and they told me to write a statement. They said they would schedule another interview with me, but I guess I left town before they could talk to me again."

Rick turned and gazed into the depths of the dark water. *Larry Tucker is our killer,* he thought. *Has to be . . .*

"It's late," Darla said, snapping Rick back into the present.

"Ms. Ford, I really appreciate your time tonight. You've been very helpful."

She looked at him and smiled. "You got a place to stay tonight, sailor?"

Rick creased his eyebrows. "Ms. Ford, I really can't—"

"Relax, I'm not going to seduce you. Though if you keep calling me Ms. Ford, I may have to." She laughed. "Come on," Darla said, taking him by the hand.

Walking on worn-out legs, Rick followed her.

—

Where are they going? Bone thought. The stripper and Drake were not walking toward him. They were moving in the opposite direction.

Bone started to move, but then just as quickly he stopped and became calm, realizing what was happening. They were walking down a series of docks that would all wind back to these stairs. After they strolled around, looking at the boats, they'd have to come right back here.

Bone took a deep breath and wiped his hands on his shorts. *Patience,* he thought. *Patience.*

—

"Where are we going?" Rick asked, curious as to why they were walking farther down the dock as opposed to going up the stairs and back out to the highway.

"My place," Darla said.

Rick started to ask another question when Darla abruptly stopped and gestured with her right arm. "Ta-da," she said.

It was a pontoon boat. One of the fog lights was on, and Rick could make out that the boat was a tan color with green trim. The word "Sweetness" was etched on the side.

"What do you think?" Darla asked, her voice expectant.

"This is your place?" Rick asked, noticing that Peter Burns was sprawled out on two of the seats, either asleep or passed out. Darla stepped down into the boat and held out her hand.

"No, silly," Darla said. "This is my boat. My place is over there." She pointed to Holiday Isle, and Rick couldn't help but smile. The day just kept getting crazier and crazier.

———

Son of a . . .

Bone started walking when he saw them step onto the boat. Then he broke into a run, knowing he would be too late.

A boat. The stripper had a boat. How could that be? He'd seen her enter the restaurant from the parking lot. How could he possibly have known she'd have a boat?

He ran down the dock, holding the gun at his side, his eyes darting in every direction. The other boats appeared to be empty. As the boat with Drake and the stripper left the dock and began to merge into the harbor, Bone pointed his weapon at them. With the silencer he might still be able to . . .

"Mr. Wheeler!"

The killer spun around at the sound of his name and saw a man with a salt and pepper beard wearing a black cowboy hat who was pointing a pistol at his chest.

"JimBone Wheeler, I presume?" The man was walking toward him. "Put the gun down and get on your knees."

Bone cut his eyes wildly to his left and right.

"Nowhere to go, JimBone," the man said. "Or do you prefer Bone for short?"

How could anyone possibly have found him? Bone wondered, forcing his mind to remain calm. "Who are you?"

"Wade Richey, Tuscaloosa County Sheriff's Office," the man said, holding up a badge. "And you're under arrest."

As the man stepped into the light, Bone saw that Richey resembled the actor Sam Elliott from his *Tombstone* and *Roadhouse* days.

"Not today, friend," Bone said.

And then he jumped into Destin Harbor.

39

"I think I may have hit him," Wade said, talking rapidly into the phone. "I got two shots off, and I think I may have nicked him on the leg."

"Are you sure it was Wheeler?" Tom asked, his voice barely registering under the hum of police sirens. Twenty-five minutes had passed since JimBone Wheeler took a dive into the harbor, and the place was now crawling with officers from the Destin Police Department and deputies from the Okaloosa County Sheriff's Office.

"Positive," Wade said. "I called him by his name, and he spun around immediately. He looked the part too. Same height. Had a beard. I didn't get a good view of his eyes because he had his hat pulled down low, but it was definitely him."

Out on the water, three police boats were moving slowly up and down the harbor. Officers on board were shining lights in every direction, and one man spoke into a bullhorn. "Mr. Wheeler, get out of the water. Mr. Wheeler, you are surrounded. Get out of the water now."

"All right, keep me posted, Wade," Tom said. "Wheeler survived a jump off the Northport Bridge last summer and was able to make it out of the Black Warrior River alive. He's a survivor."

Wade watched as police lights continued to flood the harbor in every direction. "I don't see how he makes it out of this harbor, Tom. It's covered with cops on both sides. Unless the son of a bitch is half fish, I just don't see it. We'll either apprehend him, or his body is drifting along the floor of the Gulf."

There was a pause on the other end of the line as Tom took in the information. "What about Rick?" he finally asked.

"He left the harbor by boat with the stripper. They were out a ways when I shot at Wheeler, so I doubt they heard it."

"He left with her by boat?"

"Yeah," Wade said.

"Find him, Wade. If Wheeler somehow did survive . . ."

"Ten-four," Wade broke in. "I'll have him before the sun rises."

40

As the sun began to peek its head above the eastern horizon, Rick Drake's eyes shot open, and both hands grabbed for his left calf muscle. *Cramp, cramp, cramp,* he thought, holding in a scream of pain as he twisted and rolled off the cushioned seats of the boat and onto the floor. He tried to straighten his leg, but the muscle had completely seized up on him, and he writhed on the floor of the boat in pain.

"Kid, are you all right?" a voice came from behind him in the dark, and Rick turned, eyes wide, as adrenaline poured through his body. What . . . ? Who . . . ? He squinted, seeing a dark shape on the dock above, crouching to look at him as he lay on his back, holding his calf. He rubbed the muscle hard, but it was still seized, and Rick bit his lip.

"Cramp?" the voice asked.

"Yeah," Rick managed, continuing to rub furiously on the calf as his leg slowly began to relax, the cramp gradually easing. Rick sucked in a quick breath. "Who are you?"

"Wade Richey," the man said, flashing his badge. "Detective, Tuscaloosa County Sheriff's Office."

Rick creased his eyebrows. "Tuscaloosa?"

Wade nodded. "Our office has escalated its investigation into the whereabouts of JimBone Wheeler." He paused. "Your partner suggested that he thought JimBone was following him and you, so I trailed you last night to Destin and"—he sighed—"I think we got him."

"My partner?" Rick scratched his head and tried to stand, putting both hands on one of the seats and pulling himself up. He stumbled when he tried to put any weight on his left leg. "The Professor asked you to trail me?" Rick blinked his eyes, adjusting to the dark, which was becoming lighter by the second as the sun slowly rose behind them. Peter Burns was still passed out on the seat across from him, snoring loudly and oblivious to anything that was going on.

"Yeah, it was Tom's idea. And it worked. Wheeler was here, and I . . . think we got him."

Rick felt his body go cold. "He was here. You mean . . . ?"

"He was watching you and the girl. When y'all stepped into the boat, he ran down the dock and was about to shoot at you, but I got there first."

"Jesus," Rick said. "I didn't have a clue. I . . ." He felt his calf begin to seize again, so he plopped down on the seat below him, rubbing the muscle with both hands. "JimBone Wheeler was here," Rick said, still not believing it.

"He was."

"How do you know it was him?"

"Because I called his name on the dock and he turned around. I spoke to him using his name, and he didn't try to correct me."

"What happened? Where is—?"

"He jumped in the harbor," Wade interrupted. "The city and county police have been patrolling the area all night, looking for him." Wade pointed, and squinting out over the water, Rick could see several police boats moving back and forth.

"Any word?"

Wade shook his head. "None. I think I may have shot him, so—"

"He might be dead," Rick offered, involuntarily shivering.

"Maybe," Wade said. Then, correcting himself, "Probably. I just don't see how he could not have turned up by now, and I never saw his head come up out of the water."

"I can't believe we didn't hear the shot," Rick said, scratching the back of his neck.

"With the breeze coming off the Gulf, it's hard to hear anything. I wouldn't sweat that. Listen, where is the girl? Before we go, I need to warn her about Wheeler."

Rick pointed toward a small duplex that fronted the dock and stood on wobbly legs. "In there."

41

Rick watched as Detective Wade Richey briefed Darla on JimBone Wheeler and the attempt on their lives the night before.

"We will arrange for a security detail to watch you for a few weeks, Ms. Ford, just as a precaution," Wade concluded. "Like I said, we think Wheeler is probably dead, but just to be safe we'll have someone with you until we know something for sure."

"Thank you," Darla said, her voice distant.

"You're going to be OK," Rick said, but he heard the unease in his own voice.

Wade set his coffee cup on the steps and stood. "Give you a ride back to your car, kid?" he asked, his voice containing a sense of urgency that made Rick also stand.

"Yeah."

Darla Ford remained seated on the steps and placed her chin in her hands. Rick squatted so that he could look her in the eye.

"We're gonna have to call you as a witness at trial," he said. "About the confession and who you told."

Darla nodded. "So be it," she said, her voice cold. "If I'm called to testify, I'll tell the truth." She gave her head a quick shake and stood. "I have to go to work now," she said, brushing past Rick without saying good-bye.

He watched her go and then felt a hand squeezing his arm. "Time to go, kid," Wade said, releasing his grip and heading away from the dock.

Rick sighed and closed his eyes, wishing for a breeze off the harbor that wouldn't come. Instead, the air was hot and sticky, and he sucked in a humid breath.

I'm lucky to be alive, he thought.

But all things told, the trip had been a success. Darla Ford could be a key witness for the defense, provided they could obtain more evidence linking Larry Tucker to the murder of Andy Walton. So the nine hours in the car, the three-hundred-dollar bar bill at The Boathouse, the exhaustion at having barely slept for forty-eight hours, and the cramping in his left calf that was making it difficult to walk had all been worth it.

The defense of Bocephus Haynes for capital murder had improved. An alternative theory was beginning to take shape.

He knew he should feel grateful for his good fortune.

But as he began to limp away from the dock, Rick Drake felt neither grateful nor fortunate. Truth be known, the events of the last forty-eight hours had left him numb. His instincts had proved to be both successful and almost fatal. His persistence had been rewarded, but it had almost resulted in him and an innocent bystander being shot and killed.

He felt like he was walking a tightrope with no net beneath him.

And he was scared. For the first time since Wilma Newton changed her testimony during the trial in Henshaw the year before, Rick Drake was scared.

42

"You look different with a beard," Helen said, her eyes flashing with amusement. "More rugged."

"It's not by choice," Tom said, managing a smile as he rubbed the purplish bruise on the side of his face.

"I'm sorry, Tom," she said. "A mugging is extremely rare for Pulaski." She lowered her voice. "I told you not to get involved."

"So you admit that the attack on me is related to our defense of Bo?" Tom crossed his arms, his eyes fixed on hers.

Sheriff Ennis Petrie sat next to Helen, but he had yet to utter a word, and outside of shaking his hand, Tom had not looked at him. Tom had called the sheriff's office that morning, saying he had news with respect to JimBone Wheeler. Two hours later he was here, meeting with Helen and the sheriff. In the center of the conference room table was Tom's cell phone, which he had turned to speaker so that Wade Richey could also attend.

"No," Helen said. "I admit nothing. Your wallet was stolen, so a mugging is the correct call. But"—she tapped her fingernail on the table—"I don't believe in coincidences. You show up in town to represent Bo, and you become the first victim of a mugging in downtown Pulaski since I've been DA . . ." She stopped, shaking her head. "I will admit that it is very strange."

"Big of you," Tom said, his voice hard.

"You said you had new information," Helen said, placing her elbows on the table.

Tom nodded. "I do. My partner, Rick Drake, went to Destin, Florida on Friday to meet with Darla Ford, the dancer at the Sundowners Club who Andy Walton saw the night of the murder."

Helen gave a slight twist of her head, and for a split second her eyes darted at the sheriff's. Tom could tell she was unaware that Ford had left the county. "OK . . ."

"He was followed," Tom said. "JimBone Wheeler, a suspect in several felonies in the state of Alabama, followed Rick to Destin and tried to kill him and Ford."

Helen raised her eyebrows. "Tell me."

On the speakerphone Wade's voice came in loud and clear. Introductions had already been made, so Wade got right to it, explaining in detail his tailing of Rick to Destin, concluding with Wheeler's leap into the harbor.

"Has he been found?" Sheriff Petrie asked, his first words since introductions were made.

"No," Wade answered. "The Okaloosa County Sheriff's Office and the Destin PD have been patrolling the harbor for the past fifty-six hours, and they have found nothing. They have also scoured the Holiday Isle section of Destin, which is located on the other side of the harbor and where Ford lives in a duplex, but so far nothing has turned up. The preliminary conclusion is that Wheeler drowned."

Helen slapped her hands. "So that's that. He drowned. Good work, Officer Richey. You have taken care of a significant problem. We appreciate you all letting us know."

"It's not that simple, Helen," Tom broke in. "First of all, Wheeler managed to survive a fall off the Northport Bridge in Tuscaloosa last year, and he did not drown in the Black Warrior River, which was the preliminary conclusion in Tuscaloosa. We think it is a bit presumptive to think he is gone at this point."

Helen shrugged. "OK. So if he's alive, he's in Destin, and the authorities there are looking for him. What do you want us to do?"

"We have two requests," Tom said, knowing they had finally reached the point of this meeting. As per their strategy session beforehand, Wade explained the first.

"General Lewis," Wade began, "though we were unable to apprehend Wheeler, Tom's idea worked. Tracking Drake led us to Wheeler. We would request that the Giles County Sheriff's Office assign a security detail to Rick and Tom."

Helen laughed. "Let me get this straight," she started, looking at Tom and crossing her arms. "You are asking us to assign officers to follow you around as you conduct your mission-impossible task of trying to defend Bocephus Haynes on a charge of which he is one hundred percent guilty."

Tom smiled. "Actually . . . yes. We obviously disagree with your conclusions, but . . . yes. That's what we're asking. If JimBone Wheeler is still alive, then we have no doubt that he will come back to Pulaski. If so, the best way to catch him would be to have someone close to me and Rick." Tom paused. "If you catch Wheeler, you will likely be able to apprehend whoever it is paying Wheeler to try to hurt or kill me and Rick. Find that person, and you will find the true killer of Andy Walton."

Again, Helen laughed. "You've been a law professor too long, Tom. This whole thing sounds like an incredibly complicated law school fact pattern, but I'm not buying any of it. If JimBone Wheeler is following you and Drake around, it's because you two almost caused his death last year in Tuscaloosa. We see no connection between Wheeler and the murder of Andy Walton. On the contrary, all of the evidence points toward your client as the killer." She paused, shaking her head and sighing. "As much as I would love to assign an officer—heck, a whole team of officers—to follow you and your partner around, we simply don't have the manpower here for that kind of goose chase. Do we, Ennis?"

Petrie was looking down at the table. "No, ma'am."

"What is your other request?" Helen asked.

"OK," Tom began, undaunted by Helen's rejection. "We know that Wheeler was seen with Jack Willistone, a trucking magnate from Tuscaloosa, at the Sundowners Club last summer. Willistone is now serving a prison sentence at a correctional facility in Springville, Alabama. Though Willistone denies that Wheeler ever worked for him or his company, it is our contention that Willistone likely owes Wheeler money in light of his arrest and his company's subsequent bankruptcy. In looking at the visitor's log at the Springville prison, a name came up that we didn't recognize." Tom paused. "Martha Booher."

Helen shrugged. "So what?"

"So, Willistone says that Booher is just an old friend. He said he met her in Nashville years ago." Tom paused, licking his lips. "We think it's possible that Booher may be a friend of Wheeler's. Perhaps she was sent to the jail to deliver a message to Willistone."

"You're reaching, Tom," Helen said, scratching her chin. "You're back in law school fantasy conspiracy land."

"Maybe," Tom admitted, smiling. "But it is a rock we haven't turned over yet."

"Sheriff Petrie," Wade said, breaking in on the speakerphone, "we'd like the Giles County Sheriff's Office's cooperation in trying to locate Martha Booher. Our preliminary investigation has turned up an address in Nashville, but the phone number is disconnected, and we have no other leads. Willistone says he met Booher at Tootsie's bar, so we plan to talk to the people there, but we haven't gotten that far yet."

"Our office cannot—" Helen started, but the sheriff cut her off.

"We'll assist in any way we can, Officer Richey," Petrie said, his voice firm.

Helen shot him a look, but Petrie gave it right back to her. Tom watched, knowing that while the sheriff would obviously listen to the district attorney general, it was the sheriff's decision whether to cooperate with Tom's requests. Tom was glad to see Petrie take a stand on Booher.

"Is there anything else, Tom?" Helen asked, making no effort to hide her exasperation.

"Yes," he said, smiling again. "Could I buy you a cup of coffee?"

43

They sat at a table at Reeves Drug Store, two full mugs of steaming black coffee in front of them.

"You really do look different with a beard," Helen said, smiling at him.

Tom shrugged, involuntarily scratching the white whiskers that now grew on the sides of his face. "You have a nice smile," he told her. "You should use it more."

"He needs to plea, Tom," Helen said. Smile gone. Back on subject. "Life in prison. It's better than the alternative, and it would save the town a lot of bad publicity."

Tom shook his head. "Never." Glancing around the store, Tom saw several kids enjoying ice-cream cones and an elderly lady working on a Coke float with a spoon. "I like this place," he said.

"Pulaski or Reeves?" Helen asked.

Tom shrugged. "Both. Reminds me of home."

"Tuscaloosa?" Helen asked, her voice incredulous.

Tom chuckled, shaking his head. "No. Tuscaloosa is my home now, but I was thinking more of home when I was a kid. I grew up in Hazel Green. Right on the border. When I was young, my parents would take drives on the weekend to pass the time, and I would tag along. On a Saturday or Sunday afternoon, we'd just get in the car and drive somewhere. A lot of times we went up to Fayetteville and would have lunch or dinner at Rachel's."

Helen smiled. "Great place."

Tom nodded his agreement. "And sometimes we'd come here. Get some ice cream and a nickel fountain drink, just like those kids over there," Tom said, pointing. "My daddy fought in the war, and my momma was a math and history teacher. They'd get to talking. Dad telling stories about the war, and momma pestering him with questions . . ." He trailed off.

"Are you married, Tom?"

He looked at her, surprised by the question. "I was," he said. "She died four years ago."

"I'm sorry," she said. "How long—?"

"Forty-two years," Tom interrupted, now holding his mug with both hands.

For a minute neither of them spoke. This happened to Tom a lot when he told people he was a widower. A moment of silence, so to speak, for the dead.

"How about you, Helen? Did you remarry after . . . ?"

She snorted, and Tom stopped his question, smiling at her. "I was never cut out for marriage, Tom. Butch always said I was married to the job, and he was probably right." She sighed. "It irks me, though. Marriage is the only thing I've ever failed at."

"Never too late," Tom said, but Helen crossed her arms and narrowed her gaze. Small talk was over.

"What do you want, Tom?"

"I want you to know that this case is going to go all the way to verdict. Ain't no two ways about it."

"I already know that," she said. "Are you sure you're physically up to a trial?"

Tom gritted his teeth. "I'll manage. I also want you to know that Darla Ford told my partner that Andy Walton confided to her that he was going to confess to the murder of Bo's father."

"Double hearsay," Helen said. "Good luck getting that in."

Tom stared at her. "Is that all you care about, Helen? Christ, woman, Bo Haynes's life is on the line here."

"Bo Haynes took Andy Walton's life in cold blood. It is Andy's life that I am concerned with. The *victim*."

"Darla also said that despite Andy's admonition to remain quiet about his intentions, she told Larry Tucker about Andy's plans to confess."

Helen blinked and pursed her lips. "When?"

"Two weeks before Andy was murdered."

"Doesn't change anything. You're still grasping at straws."

She stood from her chair, and Tom followed suit, pulling a folded piece of paper out of his pocket. He handed it to Helen.

"What's this?" she asked.

"It's a page from the St. Clair Correctional Facility visitor's log. I gave you the full log back at the office."

She raised her eyebrows. "OK . . ."

"The log shows all the visitors who have come to see Jack Willistone in jail. Helen . . . Larry Tucker is on the list. He came to see Jack on July 20, 2011, less than a month before the murder."

Helen looked at the document. "Why do you want me to know this?"

"Because there are folks in this town who do not want Bocephus Haynes to get a fair trial. I was nearly killed, and my partner escaped death by a nose hair."

"What do you want me to do, Tom?" Helen asked.

"I've already asked for it, and you said no."

"The security detail?" She snorted again. "You can't be serious. This is Giles County, Tennessee. We don't have enough manpower for that."

"Then perhaps you should call in the National Guard."

Helen raised her eyebrows in mock amusement. "You must be joking."

"The Ku Klux Klan has already requested a permit to be here during the trial. I read that in the paper today. They'll be out in full force. Things are only going to get crazier . . . and more dangerous."

"They're clowns, Tom."

"Maybe so, but why do they want to be here? Have you asked yourself that?"

"They want to be here because a long-lost former leader of theirs has been murdered by a black man seeking revenge. It's a straight-up racial revenge hate crime, and the Klan lives for that kind of mess. Don't be so obtuse, Tom. If this same thing happened in Tuscaloosa or Birmingham, the Klan would be there too."

"Maybe so. But would lawyers be getting attacked?"

"I thought you were implying that Larry Tucker was responsible for your attack." She waved the page from the visitor's log in front of his face. "Is it the Klan now?"

"Larry Tucker *is* the Klan," Tom said. "He was in it in 1966, the same as Andy."

"You can't prove that."

"Maybe not, but we both know it's true."

"Andy Walton got out of the Klan in the '70s," Helen said, keeping her voice steady. "The Klan's only relevance to this case is in regard to your client's motive. Bocephus Haynes believed that Andy Walton and a group of other Klansmen killed his father in 1966, and forty-five years later, on August 19, 2011, he murdered Andy Walton out of revenge."

"That's a great impact statement for your opening, Helen, but this case goes deeper than that. That's why I wanted to talk with you. Andy Walton had pancreatic cancer. He was about to die, and before he did he was going to put a bow on a forty-five-year-old murder. He was going to bring a bunch of people to justice, some of whom, like Larry Tucker, still live in this town."

Tom held his palms out and smiled. "We think it is highly probable that one of these people, most likely Larry Tucker, hired JimBone Wheeler to kill Andy to keep the truth buried."

Helen chuckled, shaking her head. "Well, that is quite a story. One that I'm sure a jury might enjoy. But here's the problem. You don't have any physical evidence linking JimBone Wheeler, Larry Tucker, or anyone else to Walton's murder. All the physical evidence points to Bo."

"He was framed," Tom said, exasperation leaking into his voice. "Can't you see that?"

When she didn't answer, Tom crossed his arms, his smile gone. "Andy Walton had cancer, Helen. Don't you think it's possible that he wanted to make things right before he died? That he didn't want blood on his hands when he passed through the Pearly Gates?"

Helen shook her hand. "Tom, you are the world's last noble man. Andy Walton wasn't like that. Not the Andy I knew."

"You might be surprised," Tom said, standing up and tossing a five-dollar bill on the table. "Things aren't always as black and white as they seem, Helen."

44

At exactly 1:30 a.m. the lights in the storage closet for Unit 203 flicked on—just as they had the three previous mornings. As there was no way to see inside the closet from the outside, no one passing by could tell that the lights had been turned on.

No one was up that hour of night anyway. The grounds crew for the condominium left at 5:00 p.m. sharp, and though some of the units were occupied by guests, there wasn't a huge crowd. Each of the owners in the complex had their very own one-car garage as well as a private storage unit. Though there were several signs on the wall urging the tenants to make sure to close their garage doors each night, sometimes people forgot.

Sometimes teenage girls might go out for a swim through the garage door and forget to close it when they scampered back in. Or perhaps a tired father had gone across the highway for groceries and in the process of trying to load up everything and take it upstairs to his condo, forgot to hit the button for the door.

JimBone Wheeler enjoyed thinking over these scenarios as he recounted his good fortune. He had always been a good swimmer, and the distance from the dock at The Boathouse to the other side of the harbor was about a thousand yards. Ten football fields. Bone had made it across, spending most of his time under the water, in about twenty-five minutes. Literally just seconds before the place was covered with cop cars.

He'd come ashore at a restaurant called Louisiana Lagniappe and had immediately begun walking down the sidewalk of Gulf Shore Drive. He knew he didn't have much time, so he began to jog. He had managed to keep his cap, so he twisted it on backwards, hoping that a man out for a run at just past midnight wouldn't cause any alarm. Luckily, he saw no one on the sidewalk.

At first Bone thought he'd steal a car and try to get out of town, but the sounds of the sirens backed him off that plan. He'd have to squat somewhere for a time, so he started looking for a quiet place to do just that. About midway down he saw a white building with tennis courts and a pool out front and, like all the complexes along Holiday Isle, the Gulf of Mexico in the back.

Of greater significance, Bone saw an open garage door.

As nonchalantly as he could manage, he walked through the entrance. Seeing what appeared to be a series of one-car garages side by side, Bone scoured the place, looking for a place to hide. He noticed numbers on a series of doors, and he started trying to open each one of them, hitting pay dirt when he came to Unit 203. Quickly, he stepped inside and locked the door, hiding behind a large orange inflatable boat that covered almost half of the space.

For over twenty-four hours Bone stayed in the storage closet, barely moving, knowing that the owners of the unit could open the door at any moment. However, after a while his body demanded that he move, so he explored the closet, striking pay dirt again. Next to the light switch there were two hooks, each with a set of keys. One set had a keyless entry device attached, so Bone knew it had to open a car. The device had the word "Porsche" etched on the side.

What kind of place was this? Bone wondered, eventually coming to the conclusion that it was a private condominium where only owners were allowed on the premises. Perhaps one of the wealthy owners kept his Porsche down here full-time to ride around town during his trips to the Gulf.

The other set contained three keys that were color coded. Knowing he couldn't stay in the closet forever, Bone had opened the door on Sunday morning at 1:30 a.m. The garage area was deserted, so Bone turned to the closet and began seeing if any of the color-coded keys fit in the lock. The orange one did.

Heart rate picking up, Bone looked at the door to the closet. It had the number 203 written on it. Then he inspected the other two keys. If one of the keys opened the closet, then one should open the door to the unit. And if no one had opened the storage closet with all the beach toys in over twenty-four hours . . .

. . . *they aren't here,* Bone knew, smiling.

He took the stairs up to the second floor and tried the other two keys in the lock to Unit 203. The purple one wouldn't fit, but the door swung open when Bone inserted the green one.

Bingo, Bone thought as he quickly scanned the empty unit. Two bedrooms, two baths, a fridge with some food and beer in it, and a bathroom with a toothbrush, razor, and other essentials. Whoever owned this condo obviously came on a regular basis.

In the master he'd found a drawer full of summer clothes and, in the master bath, a rack of beach caps.

Bone knew that the owner could show up at any moment, but he doubted he or she would come at two in the morning. Turning as few lights on as possible, Bone began to go about his work.

First he took scissors and began to cut his hair. When he had all of the chunky parts off, he took the razor and shampoo and shaved his head. The entire process took an hour. Then after a quick shower, he applied the scissors to his beard. Then the razor. When he was done, he looked like Mr. Clean. He put on a pair of loose-fitting athletic shorts he'd found in the clothes drawer and an extralarge T-shirt that read "The Back Porch." Then, heading into the kitchen, Bone made himself two peanut butter sandwiches and wolfed them down in less than three minutes. He cleaned up his mess and then went into the bedroom and allowed himself to sleep for two hours on the bed. Before the sun started to rise, he locked the unit back up and returned to the storage closet.

For two days he followed this same routine, going up to the unit at 1:30 a.m., eating, bathing, shaving, and sleeping for two hours. The hardest part of staying in the closet all day was using the bathroom, but luckily there were plenty of sand buckets around. He'd fill a bucket of piss daily and then take it up to the condo and dump it out in the toilet.

If he was anything, JimBone Wheeler was a survivor.

On this, the third night of his stay, he knew he'd pressed his luck long enough. Given how nice and fresh everything in the unit was, the owner was a frequent visitor, and Bone couldn't chance another night. After following his routine, Bone cleaned up his mess and trudged back down the stairs, dressed in a faded khaki hat that said "Destin" in blue letters, black athletic shorts, and another T-shirt. Since the owner didn't wear the same size shoe, Bone was barefoot. But Bone figured no one would raise an eyebrow at that. After all, this was the Gulf Coast. People walked around barefoot all day.

Opening the storage closet at just past 2:00 a.m., Bone took the other set of keys off the hook and shut the door. There was only one possibility. A crimson Porsche 911 in a space about three rows down from the closet. Carefully and confidently, Bone hit the garage door button and climbed into the sports car.

Straight shift heaven, he thought, backing the Porsche out of the garage. Not one to leave anything to chance, Bone stepped back into the garage and hit the button again. Then he ducked his head under the door as it began to close behind him.

Three minutes later a crimson Porsche 911 pulled onto Highway 98, driven by a clean-shaven man with a cap who looked like a hundred other doctors on vacation. If anyone paid him any attention at all, they'd figure he was making a late-night Krispy Kreme run or . . . maybe going down to AJ's bar to see if any of the cougars were still on the prowl. Either way he'd fit right in.

Bone rolled the windows down and flipped the radio on, beginning to relax. A news report came on that interested him, so he turned it up.

"Today, in Pulaski, Tennessee a grand jury indicted Bocephus Aurulius Haynes for the murder of prominent businessman and entrepreneur Andrew Davis Walton. Walton, the onetime Imperial Wizard of the Tennessee Knights of the Ku Klux Klan, rose to prominence in the '80s and '90s by making a number of investments that landed him on the cover of *Newsweek* magazine, which proclaimed he was the 'Warren Buffett of the South.' Haynes, a noted African American trial attorney, is believed to have murdered Walton out of revenge for the suspected 1966 Klan killing of Haynes's father. Judge Susan Connelly, a Giles County Circuit Court judge, has been assigned the case and will likely set a trial date at the arraignment Friday. To be sure, when this case goes to trial the eyes of the world will be on Pulaski . . ."

There was more, but Bone turned the knob to a station that played old country. He'd heard all he needed to hear.

Things were about to get good, he knew. Everyone there, including his employer, probably thought he was dead. They wouldn't be expecting him, and that, Bone knew, was a huge advantage.

He would still collect his paycheck, but as he went over the events of the last year in his mind, he realized that moolah or no, he had grown weary of McMurtrie and Drake. He also owed Bocephus Haynes one from his encounter with the black lawyer last year in Tuscaloosa. Involuntarily, Bone felt a pain in his testicles, which Haynes had squeezed until Bone thought one of them would fall off. "You're as far from Jesus as you're ever goin' be," Haynes had said when he'd pointed a pistol in Bone's face and shamed him for bringing "a knife to a gunfight."

Bone adjusted his balls with his right hand. Then he flipped a switch above him, and the top to the Porsche came down. Feeling the salt air off the Choctawhatchee Bay hit his nostrils as the car ambled across the Mid-Bay Bridge, Bone took a deep breath.

They didn't get me last year. They literally had me by the balls . . . and they didn't get me. And they missed this time too. He knew that in some way Destin had been a trap. Someone else had followed Drake, hoping to catch JimBone.

And they almost had. Almost . . .

JimBone Wheeler chuckled, shaking his head. He would take his time. He would pick his spots. But in the end he would take them all.

McMurtrie . . . Drake . . . Haynes.

Bone almost laughed at the irony. In a month, maybe less, there would be a trial in Pulaski meant to determine whether Bocephus Haynes lived or died. A trial that would hinge on a jury's verdict.

But Bone knew the verdict was already in. Win, lose, or draw at trial, McMurtrie, Drake, and Haynes had been sentenced to death. And not by lethal injection, the gas chamber, or the electric chair.

But by any means necessary . . .

Courtesy of the Bone.

PART FOUR

PART FOUR

45

Dr. George Curtis rarely took on new patients. He had been in practice for thirty years and had all the work he could handle. But there were times he made exceptions. And this was one of those times.

The woman had come without an appointment, and George's longtime receptionist, Dabsey, had told her that Dr. Curtis almost never took on new patients and that she would have to wait for an opening. The woman said she had been referred by an old friend of Dr. Curtis, and that she would wait.

She waited until noon, and after Dabsey had left for her one-hour lunch break, Dr. Curtis ushered her to a patient room. Had the woman not been attractive, George probably would have had Dabsey tell her to leave. But she was attractive in sort of a Midwestern farm girl kind of way. She had long brown hair with brown eyes and was dressed conservatively in an ankle-length navy dress. George figured he could spare five minutes for a pretty woman to tell her story. Besides, there was something familiar about her . . .

Once in the patient room the woman didn't mince words, and George immediately knew why she looked familiar.

"You . . . should . . . not be here," he said, pacing the floor in front of her, agitated almost beyond words. "Our mutual friend should know better than to pull a stunt like this. The cops have been passing your picture around town. They are *onto* you. He should have called."

"Our mutual friend said that no one here would have any idea who I was. He said that wasn't possible, and besides, even if someone here did know me, there was no other way to get his message to you. He lost his phone."

Dr. Curtis stopped pacing and placed his hands on his hips. "Well, they are onto you, sweetheart. I don't know how, but they are." He sighed. "What's the message?"

"That he is alive and ready to finish the game."

"That's it?" Curtis said.

"Yes. He said you would be pleased."

Curtis brushed a lock of silver hair out of his eyes and began to pace again. "I am . . . I guess." He stopped abruptly and closed his eyes. Thinking of something, George quickly walked to the front of the office. When he saw the visitor list, he put his face in his hands. "You gave her your name!" George screamed, finally coming undone. "How stupid are you? You gave her your goddamn name!"

"Like I said"—the woman did not raise her voice—"our friend told me that no one here would have any idea who I was."

George surveyed the visitor's list. "Martha Booher" was written in Dabsey's hand about midway down. Dabsey always insisted on writing the guest names herself so that she'd be able to read them when she called visitors back to see George.

Damnit, George thought. Dabsey wasn't the sharpest tack in the box, so maybe she wouldn't pick up on it. Or maybe she already had . . .

"How did you get here?" George asked.

"The bus. I took a bus from Ethridge at eight this morning."

George looked at his watch. It was twelve thirty. Dabsey would be back in a half hour.

"I was planning to take the bus back to Ethridge at five," Martha offered.

"That's too risky," George said, pulling his keys out of his pocket. "If no one recognized you walking from the bus station to here, they might when you walk back."

He led her by the arm to the front of the office and looked through the blinds, seeing no one coming and no cars on the road-way. There were also no cars in any of the nearby driveways, except the dentist office that was caddy-corner, and he doubted any of the patients there would take notice. Quickly, he thrust the keys into Martha's hand. "Listen, my house is two doors down from the office on the same side of the road. 1404 is the house number. As casual as you can, I want you to walk to my house and use this key"—he pointed to a large gold one—"to open my front door. Got it?"

She nodded.

"Lock the door behind you and don't turn on any lights. Feel free to eat whatever you like from the fridge. Just don't do anything that would draw attention to the house. OK?"

Again, Martha nodded.

"I should be over there a little after six, and we can come up with a plan for getting you home then. Got it?"

"Yes, I—"

"Go," George said, pushing her toward the front door.

George watched Martha walk down the sidewalk and up the front walk to his home, his heart racing the entire time. Once she was inside, he slowly exhaled. Then he grabbed the phone and dialed the number.

Before the person on the other end of the line could even say hello, George was talking into the receiver, making no effort to hide the panic in his voice.

"*We have a problem.*"

46

Michael Capshaw was a patent lawyer in Birmingham at one of the largest firms in the state. Five years ago, after the kids had both graduated from college, Michael finally bought his wife and himself something he'd wanted his whole life.

A two-bedroom condo on the Gulf.

He had long been fond of Holiday Isle in Destin, having had several colleagues buy in the area, and the private-only complex on Gulf Shore Drive was exactly what he'd always wanted. Since in addition to a spacious parking lot the condominium provided a one-car garage for each owner, Michael had decided he wanted to leave wheels at the condo at all times. That way he and Lisa could fly down on a whim if they so desired and would have a car to drive when they arrived.

He'd bought the crimson Porsche a year after closing on the condo.

Michael also had his own plane, a twin-engine Cessna, and he and Lisa boarded it on Friday afternoon at 3:00 p.m. They landed at the Fort Walton airport by 4:30, and a cab dropped them off in front of the condo at five.

Knowing a trip to the grocery store was in order—it had been over a month since they'd been to the condo—and secretly wanting any excuse to take the Porsche for a spin, Michael walked down the aisle of cars with Lisa until they reached the parking spot. Frowning, he looked to his left and right, making sure he was in the right place.

"Honey, where's the car?" Lisa asked.

When Michael opened the storage unit and noticed that the key chain on the side hook was gone, he knew he had an answer to his wife's question.

"It's gone," he said, already pushing the buttons for 911 on his phone.

47

The Sleepy Head Inn was not Lawrenceburg's finest hotel. Not by any stretch. But Bone had done the owner a favor a few years back and in return been granted a free room for the rest of his life. As there were no security cameras in the place, it made for a good arrangement.

Rarely did Bone trade his services for anything but money, but a place to stay when he ran into a snag was a valuable commodity. And like several times in the past, it was paying dividends tonight.

There were twelve rooms at The Sleepy Head, and all were decorated with the same decor. Queen-size bed, an archaic desk with a wobbly chair, and a bathroom. All units were saturated with the smell of lemon disinfectant.

Bone sat in the chair, watching Dr. George Curtis, who stood by the door. He was a thin man with pale skin and soft and pasty features. He wore glasses, and his hair was balding on top with a thin layer of silver on the sides. Dressed casually in jeans and a golf shirt, the doctor looked awkward and nervous. Adding to this impression was the fact that George's hands were shaking so bad that he had to grab his left with his right every few seconds.

"Doctor, it is nice to finally meet you. Larry speaks highly of you."

"L-L-Larry shouldn't have spoken of me at all," George said.

Bone shrugged. "Well, maybe he didn't. I can't remember what I hear and don't hear anymore." He paused. "Tell me what happened."

George pointed toward the bathroom, where the door was closed and the sound of running water could be heard. "Sssh . . . she showed up this morning, asking to see me. She talked to my receptionist, and Dabsey wrote her name down on the guest list." George paused, wiping his mouth with a shaky hand. "The police have been going by stores and offices, showing her picture and telling us all to be on the lookout for a lady named Martha Booher. If my receptionist wasn't overworked and ditzy as hell, I'm sure she would've caught it. She didn't mention anything today, but I won't be surprised if it eventually hits her." George rubbed his eyes, which Bone noticed were bloodshot from either stress or sleep deprivation. Probably both, he surmised, stifling a smile. George Curtis was clearly not someone who had spent a lot of time talking to people like the Bone.

"Anyway," George continued, "Martha hid at my house the rest of the day, which luckily is just a couple doors down from the office. Once it was dark and most of the lights were out on the street, we headed this way."

"Do you know how Martha got on the police radar?" Bone asked, thinking he knew the answer but wanting confirmation.

George shook his head. "No. But they've been passing her name and picture around for a few weeks." He swallowed. "They've also been passing around your name and picture."

Bone smiled. "Does mine look like this?" he asked, gesturing at himself with two thumbs.

George shook his head. "No. You have hair in the photograph. And you look younger in the picture." When his right hand began to shake again, Curtis clasped it with his left and took a deep breath. "Mr. Wheeler, I think it's time to call everything off. Things have gotten . . ." He swallowed again, staring down at the green vinyl carpet. Bone again stifled a smile. "Out of control. The police are so close now, I think it may be time to abort the mission."

Bone slowly shook his head. "I'm not going to abort. I've come too far and expended too much energy."

George shook his head violently, stepping closer to Bone. He almost sat on the bed, then hesitated and remained standing. "Bo is going down anyway, Mr. Wheeler. Helen Lewis is going to convict him of capital murder, and he'll eventually be lethally injected in a few years. You were just an insurance policy, and I think it's time we abort."

"No can do, Doc," Bone said, standing from the chair. "Bocephus Haynes has cost me a lot of money over the last fourteen months, and he's going down. And with any luck I'm going to kill his lawyers. Drake and McMurtrie. I owe them one too."

"Mr. Wheeler, you are a contract killer. We hired you. *You work for us*, and I'm telling you to abort."

"Wrong, Doc. The Bone works for himself, and you agreed to pay me for something I was planning to do anyway. I am not going to walk away." He paused and pulled his .38 out of his waist and pointed it at George Curtis. "Now . . . you can help me finish the game we started, or"—he cocked the pistol—"you can see what's at the other end of this barrel."

The bathroom door squeaked open, and Martha Booher stepped out. George's eyes, wild with fear, glanced at her and held as she walked past Bone and lay on the bed. She was naked. "Doctor," she said, "I believe I would like that physical now."

"I'd like to go," George said, turning back to Bone.

"Not before we come up with a plan," Bone said. "I can't take Haynes while he's sitting in a jail cell, and it's too risky to follow him, because he'll likely have a police escort to the courthouse and anywhere else he's taken over the weekend or during trial. I can't risk being seen downtown either, as while that photo isn't great, it's good enough that someone might make the connection. Plus Pulaski is a small town, and I'm a stranger." Bone paused. "Any ideas, Doc?"

"Abort," George said, the words coming out just above a whisper. Martha Booher scooted to the edge of the bed and put her hands on George's belt buckle. Slowly, she undid the loop. "What are you . . . ?" he started to protest, but he felt the cold steel of Bone's pistol on his forehead.

"Just leave Martha be and answer the question, Doc," Bone said as Martha Booher undid George's belt and the button on his pants.

"I . . . I . . ." George fumbled for the words as his pants and underwear dropped to the floor.

Martha grabbed hold of George's stiffening penis, and Curtis closed his eyes, now dizzy.

"Thank you so much for working me in at lunch today, Dr. Curtis. I'm sorry I couldn't pay, but I hope this will in some way make up for it."

As the feel of Martha's fingers was replaced by her mouth, moist and wet as it moved back and forth, George's knees became weak, and Martha had him sit on the bed as she continued her work.

"Dr. Curtis, is this how you treat all your patients who don't have insurance?" she asked.

George's eyes shot open at the sound of the word "insurance," and the sight in front of him almost made him puke. Bone continued to hold the gun, but in his other hand was a small phone with the camera lens pointed right at the doctor.

"No!" George shot up off the bed, but Bone stepped forward and pressed the gun again into the doctor's forehead. Bone smiled and began talking in a television news anchor voice.

"Dr. George Curtis, longtime family physician in Pulaski, Tennessee was arrested today on charges of assault and battery and third-degree rape as a tape surfaced of him trading medical services for sexual favors. Dr. Curtis is under investigation by the Tennessee Board of Medical Examiners, and it is believed that he may lose his medical license. His reputation, once pristine, is now beyond repair."

"You *son of a bitch*," George said as Martha walked back into the bathroom and closed the door.

"And then some," Bone said. "Now, I want you to tell me how I can get close enough to Bocephus Haynes to put a bullet in his brain."

"It's impossible," George managed, fumbling for his underwear and his pants. "You said it yourself."

"Think, Doc. Come on. How can I get close to Haynes and not be seen?"

George blinked when it hit him, and Bone smiled. "You already know," George said.

"That I do, Doc. It came to me when I was listening to the news about the trial on the way here. But I wanted you to come to it on your own."

"You can get close, and you'll never be seen. It's—"

"Perfect," Bone said, completing the thought. "However, I will need one thing from you to make it work."

"I'll get it," George said. "I'll give it to you in return for the video you just recorded."

"Deal," Bone said, extending his hand.

George Curtis's body trembled with a mixture of fear and relief, but he managed to shake Bone's hand. "Deal."

48

By the time the Giles County Courthouse opened for business at 8:00 a.m. Monday morning, the square was covered in white. At least three hundred members of the Ku Klux Klan surrounded the courthouse, all wearing white robes and hoods. Many held signs saying "Justice for Andy Walton," or the shortened "Justice."

Inside Reeves Drug Store, Emma Jean Waites could hardly believe her eyes. She had lived in Pulaski all her life, long enough to have seen Klan rallies that were organized and well attended. Most of those rallies had centered around some kind of Confederate or Klan tradition. For a few years there was one on General Nathan Bedford Forrest's birthday in July. Forrest had been the first Grand Wizard of the Klan. In other years the Klan had marched on General Robert E. Lee's birthday in January. Emma Jean couldn't remember a time the Klan had rallied in front of the courthouse during a trial. If they had, it was nothing like this.

"Kinda reminds me of that Grisham book *A Time to Kill*," she said out loud.

"Me too," a voice came from beside her. "At least they're not chanting 'Fry Bo.'"

Emma Jean turned to the voice. "Why hi there, Dabsey. Where's Dr. Curtis today?"

"He's not seeing patients this week, so he sent me to drop off the prescriptions. I think he wanted to avoid this circus too."

Emma Jean nodded and turned back to the window. "Don't blame him. It's got to be hard. Is he going to watch the trial?"

Dabsey shook her head. "Can't. He's been subpoenaed as a witness. Witnesses are excluded from the courtroom."

"Really?" Emma Jean asked, again turning to look at Dabsey. For the first time Emma Jean noticed that Dabsey appeared distressed about something. Her brow was furrowed, and she seemed lost in thought.

"Yep," Dabsey said, still watching the Klansmen through the window.

"Hey, you OK, girl?" Emma Jean asked. "You look pale."

"Fine," Dabsey said. "Just a little spooked by this. Normally, when the Klan does their marches I try to stay out of downtown."

"We all do," Emma Jean agreed. "But those rallies are usually one-day ordeals. This thing may last a week. We can't just shut the town down for a week."

"You're right," Dabsey agreed, still watching through the window. She was holding a Styrofoam cup of coffee, but she had yet to take a sip.

"You sure you're OK?" Emma Jean asked.

"I'm fine, Emma Jean," Dabsey said, drinking from the cup. She took too big a sip and almost cried out as the scalding coffee hit the back of her throat. Coughing, she began to walk toward the door. "I have to get back to the office now."

Before Emma Jean could say anything more, Dabsey was out the door and on the sidewalk. Dr. Curtis's practice was on East

Jefferson, just a block away, so Emma Jean expected to see the receptionist take off in that direction.

But Dabsey didn't walk toward Curtis Family Medicine. Instead, she turned down First Street.

Where is she going? Emma Jean wondered. Then, feeling an intuitive nudge, Emma Jean whispered the words she was thinking out loud. "Something *is* wrong."

———

Dabsey Johnson felt her heart beating hard in her chest. Something had been bothering her all weekend, but she hadn't known what it was until thirty minutes ago. At fifty-eight years old, Dabsey was having more and more senior moments, where she forgot what she was about to say or couldn't remember what she'd done the day before. Something about last Friday had bothered her, but she hadn't figured it out until she arrived at work that morning.

When she looked at the sign-in sheets, she noticed that Friday's page was gone. In fact, it appeared that Dr. Curtis had replaced the entire sign-in booklet with a clean one. Which made no sense. The sign-in booklets contained forty pages and were typically thrown out monthly or when they ran out of pages. There had still been a number of pages left to work with for September, but Dr. Curtis had thrown the whole thing out.

Then it came to her. *The walk-in*, she thought, remembering the woman who had come to the office Friday morning. Dabsey had written the name down, and something about it had seemed familiar. Martha . . . Martha something. She had forgotten about it then, because the morning had been so busy. It was cold season, which meant Dr. Curtis's office was crawling with patients, most of them young mothers whose kids were in kindergarten or pre-school. Dr. Curtis had said he would work the woman in at lunch, but by the time Dabsey had come back after a sandwich at Reeves

Drug Store, she was gone. When she had asked Dr. Curtis about the woman, he had just shrugged and said he didn't have room for another patient.

So why hadn't he told her that when she had first walked in the door? Dabsey had figured it was because the woman was attractive. Though Dr. Curtis was a lifelong bachelor, there was never any doubt, at least not for Dabsey, that he was heterosexual. She saw the way he admired women's backsides when they left the office, or the way he would glance down their cleavage when he was doing an examination. The woman from Friday had been attractive. She could see Dr. Curtis at least wanting to talk to her before he showed her the door. So why had it bothered her all weekend?

Martha . . . Dabsey had thought to herself. Then she had said it out loud. "Martha . . ."

She had tried to forget about it by calling her husband, Steve, about dinner. But when she had reached for the telephone, she had seen the flyer. It was hidden under a bunch of magazines on her desk. Something Officer Springfield had dropped off three weeks earlier. Dabsey had snatched the flyer and looked at the photograph. An old driver's license picture that had been blown up. The name below the photo had caused her heart to skip a beat. Martha Booher.

"If you see this woman, please call the sheriff's office immediately," the flyer had said at the bottom of the page.

Walking down First Street, Dabsey removed the flyer from her purse and looked at the photograph again. Then the name below it. Martha Booher.

That's her, she knew. *That was the woman on Friday.* Dabsey knew that she was not a smart woman. But she had been gritty enough to obtain her GED after having to quit high school when she got pregnant. And determined enough to scratch out an LPN degree at Martin Methodist, which allowed her to not just sign patients into Dr. Curtis's office but also to administer medications, take blood, and obtain histories. She wasn't smart, but she wasn't stupid either. Maybe a little slow, but not stupid.

It was her, she knew. The walk-in on Friday had been Martha Booher.

Dabsey took out her cell phone. She felt guilty for not talking with Dr. Curtis first, but he wouldn't be at the office all week, and she didn't want to bother him. She knew he didn't pay attention to those kinds of things anyway. She doubted that he'd ever even seen the flyer.

I'll tell him when he calls in today, she resolved. Then she dialed the number on the flyer.

49

At 8:45 a.m. the courtroom was quiet as a mouse. There were no cameras. No reporters. And outside of Maggie Walton, who sat in the front row nearest the prosecution table, there were no spectators.

Tom scratched at his beard, still not quite comfortable with facial hair, having been clean shaven most of his career. His bruises had basically healed, but there remained a reddish hue that the beard helped to conceal. Below the counsel table he'd conspicuously placed his cane, which he continued to need for walking, though he was now strong enough to eschew the wheelchair. The knee was not going to get better until he could have it surgically repaired, but he had delayed any procedures until after the trial. For now the cane and a boatload of Advil would have to do.

Tom looked across the nearly empty courtroom, allowing his eyes to settle on Mrs. Walton, or "Ms. Maggie" as he'd heard Bo refer to her. She was an attractive, striking woman with her thick white hair and ankle-length black dress, perfectly suited for a woman in mourning. She sat with her shoulders back and held what looked like a Bible in her lap. *She is certainly playing the role of the grieving widow,* Tom thought, wondering if Ms. Maggie's manner of dress and Bible toting were her own idea or something encouraged by the General to play to the jury.

Rick had tried on several occasions in the lead-up to trial to meet with Ms. Maggie, but she didn't return any of his calls. Finally, Dr. George Curtis had left a message that if Rick called his sister again, he was going to notify the police.

Seeming to sense that she was being watched, Ms. Maggie turned her head and looked at him. Caught redhanded, Tom forced a smile, but she didn't return the gesture. Instead, she turned away from him and seemed to whisper something to herself, which Tom would've guessed were words like "Of all the nerve."

"She's a cold glass of water, huh?" Bo said, placing his hand on Tom's shoulder.

"Arctic," Tom said, smiling at his friend. Bo wore a navy-blue suit, white shirt, and light-blue tie. It was nice to see him in something other than jail clothes. "How you holding up?" Tom asked.

Bo shrugged. "Nervous as a long-tailed cat in a room full of rocking chairs," he said. "But I'm glad to be out of that cell." He paused. "I can't believe you're here, Professor. After the beating you took . . ."

"They'd have to kill me to keep me out of this courtroom," Tom said.

Bo's eyes started to water and he looked away.

"I know we've gone over this, Bo, but Rick is going to do most of the legwork in the trial. Opening statements, the examinations, and closing argument. I'm flying copilot this week. My health—"

"I'm just glad you're here, Professor," Bo interrupted. "That's enough for me."

"Awful quiet in here," Rick said, joining them at the defense table. Dressed in a charcoal-gray suit, blue shirt, and red tie, he appeared sleek and ready for battle.

"That'll change very soon," Tom said. "Once the jury is in the box, it's going to be like Bryant-Denny Stadium on a fall Saturday."

Media coverage of jury selection was prohibited by Tennessee law. "But once the jury is selected," Judge Connelly had informed them earlier that morning, "I'm going to allow the case to be televised."

Tom was a little surprised that Helen Lewis hadn't objected. His research regarding cameras in the courtroom revealed that when jurors realized that the case was being seen all over the world, they were more likely to make sure they were being very cautious. The biggest example of this was probably the O. J. trial, where a jury acquitted Simpson of the murder of his wife. But Tom knew that Helen Lewis loved the fact that this case was going to be national news.

"Where is Ray Ray?" Tom asked, turning around in a circle and seeing no sign of their local counsel. "This is his part, for God's sake." The case would begin with jury selection, and the defense team would be leaning heavily on the thoughts and advice of Ray Ray Pickalew. Tom also wanted the jury pool to see Ray Ray sitting at the table with them. Tom and Rick were strangers to the area, but Ray Ray was part of the community.

"I don't know," Rick said.

Tom glanced at his watch. 8:52 a.m. Eight minutes till go time. He looked down at his legal pad but didn't read his notes. His mind was lost in thought. He felt a hand tug on his arm, and he looked up into the eyes of General Helen Lewis.

"Last chance. Life sentence. Eligible for parole after thirty years for good behavior. This will be our last offer." Helen fired off the plea deal like it was coming out of a machine gun.

Tom leaned over the table and whispered the deal into Bo's ear. Without hesitation, Bo shook his head, never looking Helen's way.

"No," Tom said, turning back to her.

"Suit yourself," Helen said, but her voice sounded as if she was not displeased in the least that Bo had refused. In fact, Tom thought he heard a giddiness in her tone, which made him cringe. Again, he couldn't help but think of the O. J. case. Win, lose, or draw, Helen Lewis was going to come out of this trial as one of the most famous lawyers in the country.

"Professor, Bo, look!" Rick whispered loudly, pointing to the entrance to the courtroom. Tom and Bo both turned to see Ray Ray Pickalew standing in the front door. On his right, clutching his arm, was Jasmine Haynes. Behind them was a tall, gangly teenage boy.

"Oh my God," Bo said under his breath as he blinked his eyes to make sure he wasn't dreaming. Feeling a hand on his shoulder, he looked at Tom, who was nudging him toward the door. "Go," Tom mouthed, and Bo forced his wobbly legs to move.

The former Jasmine Henderson, whom Bo had called Jazz since the first time they met, had milk chocolate skin, her hair brown and wavy and cut to just below her neck. She wore an elegant navy dress with an orange corsage above the heart. "You're . . . beautiful," Bo managed.

Jazz smiled, though her eyes had filled with tears. "You're gonna win," she said.

Then, unable to control himself any longer, Bo pulled her to him, and she wrapped her arms around his waist. "*Thank you*," he said. "Thank you for being here."

"Lila is with Momma in Huntsville," she whispered into his ear. "She's just too young . . . but I brought T. J. with me."

Bo looked past his estranged wife to his teenage son. He held out his hand for T. J. to shake, but the boy grabbed him in a bear hug. "I love you, Dad. I'm here for you, dog."

"I didn't do it," Bo said, looking at T. J. first, then Jazz. "I didn't kill him."

Jazz nodded, wiping her eyes. "We know. Ray Ray said you were framed. He said you've been the victim of a rush to judgment."

Bo glanced at Ray Ray Pickalew, who was going over the jury list with Tom and Rick. He started to call his name when the bailiff's voice cut through the air like a knife. "ALL RISE!"

As the attorneys rose to their feet, Jazz kissed Bo on the cheek. "I love you," she said.

"I love you too," Bo said. He gave her one last squeeze, and Rick escorted her and T. J. to a spot on the front row.

"Please be seated," Judge Connelly said. When everyone had followed her instruction, the judge cleared her throat and spoke into a microphone that had been placed on the bench. "The court hereby calls for trial the case of *The State of Tennessee v. Bocephus Aurulius Haynes*. Is the state ready?"

"Yes, Your Honor," Helen Lewis said.

"Is the defense ready?"

"Yes, Your Honor," Tom said.

"All right then," the judge said, turning to her bailiff. "Let's bring in the jury pool."

———

"How in the hell did you get her here?" Tom whispered under his breath to Ray Ray as the jury venire filtered in.

"Who do you think her divorce lawyer is?" Ray Ray said, flashing his Joker grin.

"Ray Ray, no."

"Relax, Tommy. They're just separated. She still loves the son of a bitch. But"—he winked—"even if they did end up breaking the knot, it would be in Mrs. Haynes's best interests if her ex-husband weren't facing lethal injection. Take it from me, it ain't easy collecting alimony from men on death row."

Tom shook his head and smiled despite himself. "Somehow you take a heartwarming moment and shit and piss all over it."

"It's a gift," Ray Ray said. "Now let's find Bocephus a jury of his peers."

50

By 4:00 p.m. they had selected a jury. Eight men and four women. Eleven whites and only one black. The lone African American juror was Delray Bender, who had been on the "maybe" list for the defense team due to his presumed resentment of Bo using a different auto mechanic service.

"This is the jury of my peers," Bo whispered, gazing out at them as they took their seats in the twelve chairs that would face the witness stand. "I should start picking out my coffin."

"It's not the dream team," Ray Ray whispered back, "but Woody Brooks ain't all bad. He's white and a retiree, but he's also fairly liberal. He lives in my neighborhood, and his house was the only one I can remember with an Obama sign in it." Bo watched Mr. Brooks take his seat. When the white-haired man was in his chair, he looked over at Bo with cold eyes.

"If you say so," Bo said.

"Millie Sanderson is also OK," Ray Ray continued, and Bo nodded. He knew Millie as well. She was a civics teacher at Giles County High. Had T. J. not transferred to the Huntsville City School system in the fall, he would have had Millie for civics. Midforties, red hair, and green eyes, Millie was an attractive woman with a nice smile. "I bet Millie was on Helen's strike list and they ran out of strikes before they could get rid of her," Ray Ray continued.

Five minutes later Judge Connelly recessed the trial for the day, saying they'd start with opening statements in the morning.

"If we could buy a little more time, then maybe JimBone would surface," Tom said after the jury had adjourned. "I still think he did the deed at Larry Tucker's beckoning. If we can catch JimBone, he might want to deal."

"Susan would deny any motion to continue at this point," Ray Ray said, heading for the door and looking at Rick. "I'd start working on my opening."

"Where are you going?" Tom asked him.

"My work here is done, fellas. The jury is in the box and my brain is fried. I'm going to get drunk. Maybe try to get laid too. It's been a while. I'll see y'all in the morning."

"Ray Ray . . ." But the shutting of the door cut Tom's voice off.

"Just let him go, Professor," Bo said. "He's right. He finished his role."

But Tom wasn't listening. He left the courtroom and caught up with Ray Ray out in the lobby, grabbing his friend by the arm before he could walk down the stairs. "What the hell, Ray Ray? We need you tonight to prepare for tomorrow."

"No, Tommy. What we need is to prove that Larry Tucker was part of the lynch mob that killed Bo's father. That'll pack Darla Ford's testimony with some bite and provide a clear motive for Larry to do the deed." He paused. "Larry's our best shot, and we both know it. The murder happened at his club. If we can show motive too, we might be able to spread some reasonable doubt on the case against Bo." He slapped Tom on the shoulder. "I'm on it, Tommy, but I won't do any good hanging around Bo's office." He paused. "I'm going to have to go dog-and-bone it."

The two men nodded at each other, and Ray Ray began to descend the stairs.

"Hey, Ray Ray," Tom called after him.

"Yeah."

"Be careful."

51

George Curtis jumped to his feet when he heard the knocking. He had been asleep on the couch with Matilda in his lap, and the cat screeched as she tumbled off of George and onto the floor. The doctor paid her no mind.

He looked at his watch. It was 9:30 p.m. *Who the hell would be knocking on my door at this time of night?* George walked to the front door and peeked through the blinds. Sheriff Ennis Petrie was standing on the stoop, dressed in full uniform. He held what appeared to be a folder in his hand. *This can't be good,* George knew, but there was no use in delay. He undid the dead bolt and opened the door.

"Evenin', Ennis," he said, eyeing the sheriff. "What can I do for you?"

"George, we need to talk."

—

Two minutes later they were holding mugs of instant Folgers. Ennis sipped his with both hands. "Thank you. This hits the spot."

"Long day?" George asked, still unsure of why Ennis wanted to talk to him.

"Yeah. In court all day with the General on Bo's case. Listen, George . . . who is Martha Booher?"

"Who?" George asked, feeling a cold tickle on the back of his neck. *Jesus Christ, Dabsey . . .*

"Martha Booher," the sheriff repeated. "She signed in for an appointment with you last Friday. According to Dabsey, she was a new patient, and you don't normally take on new patients." He paused. "But you saw Ms. Booher."

Behind his glasses, George's mind was a jumbled mess of emotions. He knew he needed to handle this carefully. "Ennis, I vaguely remember talking to a lady that wanted to be my patient during my lunch break last Friday, but I told her I didn't have any additional space."

"Dabsey said she normally tells patients you're full up, but you instructed her that you wanted to see Booher."

George shrugged. "So what if I did? Look, Ennis, all I remember about last Friday is that I had a full slate of patients. I'm almost seventy, and I can barely remember what happened yesterday. I keep patient charts so I can remember their diagnoses, and since I didn't treat this woman you're talking about, I don't have any recollection of her other than telling her I didn't have room. Why is this lady so important to you?"

Ennis pulled a blown-up photograph out of the folder he had with him. "Because Martha Booher is believed to be an important witness in a three-state manhunt for a man named James Robert Wheeler, a.k.a. JimBoneWheeler. Wheeler is the prime suspect in a murder case in Alabama, an attempted murder charge in Florida, and he was seen at the Sundowners Club as early as fourteen months ago. My office has been passing this photograph of

Martha Booher around town for the past month, and I gave one to Dabsey in your office. Dabsey recognized the woman's name from the sign-in sheet at your office, and she said the woman looked very similar to the photograph in the picture."

George inspected the photograph. "I'm sorry, Ennis. I had no idea. I'm in my own little world treating patients, and Dabsey screens a lot of this kind of stuff from me."

"So you had no idea we were looking for her when you spoke with her at lunch last Friday?"

George shook his head. "But I remember her now," he said, smiling. "She's . . . a pretty girl. That's why I told Dabsey to let me talk to her."

"Because she was pretty?"

George held out his palms. "Guilty as charged. I handled it myself, because I wanted to talk to a pretty lady."

Ennis nodded, giving no indication whether he believed George's response or not. "How long did you talk with her?"

George shrugged. "Maybe five minutes. I remember I gave her a few recommendations of other doctors in the area."

"Did she say she was from Pulaski?"

Damnit, George thought. He was laying it on too thick. "Uh . . . no," he said. "I guess I just assumed that she was." He stopped, satisfied with his answer. Who wouldn't assume that?

"Did she drive a car to the appointment?"

"I really don't know."

"Dabsey said she didn't remember seeing a car. Her desk is situated so she can see when cars pull in the driveway to park in the back of your office, and she knows the make and model of most of your patients. She said she would've remembered seeing a strange car, and there wasn't one. She also said she saw no cars parked out in front of your office when she walked to lunch."

"So she didn't drive," George offered, holding out his palms again. "A lot of my in-town patients like to walk to the office if it's a pretty day."

"George, we've checked, and Martha Booher does not live at any house within a three-mile radius of your office, nor was she staying as a guest at any of those homes."

George shrugged. "Then maybe she had a friend drop her off. Or maybe she took a cab."

"Not many cabs in the area that would be running that early in the morning," Ennis said.

George knew that Martha Booher had ridden the bus into Pulaski, so he didn't want to offer that as a suggestion. He held out his palms. "I don't know how I can help you, Ennis. I don't remember anything about my encounter with Ms. Booher other than she was an attractive woman."

"We think she took the bus," Ennis said, his eyes boring into George's.

"This all sounds very interesting, Ennis," George began, feigning boredom and faking a yawn, "but I don't see how any of it concerns me."

Slowly, Ennis stood and brushed past George to the front door. After he grabbed the knob, he snapped his fingers and looked over his shoulder at George. "Oh, yeah, I almost forgot. George, why did you destroy your sign-in book with Booher's name on it? Dabsey said she always kept the sign-in book until the end of the month, but this one was gone when she arrived for work on Monday."

"I spilled coffee on it," George said.

"Convenient," Ennis said, nodding. Then, opening the door, he spoke without looking at George. "George, I'm only going to ask this once. Is JimBone Wheeler the fixer Larry was talking about at the farm the night of Andy's funeral?"

George paused for two seconds while Ennis waited in the opening. Summoning all the strength he had in his voice, George said, "No. Ennis, I swear to God."

Sheriff Ennis Petrie turned his head and glared at George.

"*I swear to God,*" George repeated.

———

Ennis sat in his patrol car for several minutes after the confrontation, watching George Curtis's house. *That prick had better not be lying to me . . .*

George was dirty. Ennis knew it. But the bastard was also slippery as a minnow's dick. Like with the coffee spill on the sign-in book, George always had an answer for everything. *Which is a good thing,* Ennis tried to tell himself. *If George is lying and he and Larry did hire JimBone, he'll have himself covered.*

Which should cover me too.

Sighing, Ennis eased the squad car forward. One thing that made no sense was how any of this related to the murder of Andy Walton. As General Lewis said every time Bo's defense team mentioned the possibility that JimBone Wheeler might be involved, every ounce of physical evidence at the crime scene pointed to Bo Haynes as Andy's killer.

Ennis's cell phone buzzed. He grabbed the phone off the passenger-side seat. "Yeah?"

"Sheriff, this is Lonnie Dupree down at the bus station. I was calling about the video your office requested."

"What?" Ennis asked.

"The video. Deputy Springfield asked me to pull last Friday's surveillance tape of riders getting off and on the buses."

"OK, Lonnie. Thanks for getting back to us. What do you have?"

"We've got her," Lonnie said, his voice rising with excitement and pride.

"What?"

"The girl in the flyer," Lonnie said. "She's on the tape."

52

When Tom entered the courtroom on Tuesday morning, he immediately noticed the cameras in back, already in place to film every
second of the trial. Sweeping his eyes around the courtroom, he
saw that there was not a single open space on either the ground
floor or the balcony. *Sold out,* he thought, limping toward the
defense table, where Rick Drake was flipping through his outline
for the opening statement while Bo sat stoically in his chair.

"Ready to be famous?" Tom asked, and Rick gave a nervous
laugh. He had practiced his opening deep into the night and knew
it by heart.

"Remember the mantra from trial team?" Tom asked.

"Calm, slow, Andy," Rick said, taking a deep breath.

"Glad you were paying attention," Tom said, slapping him
on the back. Before big trial team competitions, Tom had always
advised his students to repeat the line "Calm, slow, Andy" to them-
selves. It was a visual intended to help them relax. If they spoke
to the jury in the same calm and slow manner that Andy Griffith

used in talking to Barney or Opie, they would have a relaxed and confident effect.

"Any word from Ray Ray?" Rick asked, and Tom shook his head.

"No, but he'll be here," Tom said.

"Speak of the devil," Rick said, pointing behind Tom to the doors of the courtroom. Tom turned to see Ray Ray Pickalew walking toward them, his head down and his hands in his pockets.

"Glad you could make it, sunshine," Tom said.

Ray Ray grunted. "Not in the mood, Tommy."

He passed by them and plopped down in the chair next to Bo. Like before, Rick smelled the powerful odors of mouthwash and aftershave, which were still not able to completely mask the scent of alcohol beneath the surface.

"Any luck last night?" Tom asked.

Ray Ray turned and looked at him with bloodshot eyes. "Not yet. But I'm close."

53

By the time the jury was in the box on Tuesday morning, the Giles County Courthouse Square was covered in a sea of white robes and hoods. The Klansmen were split up into what their leader referred to as "brigades."

All of the men in the Lawrenceburg brigade had assembled that morning at the First Church of God. They had been dropped off by the church bus two hours ago on the south side of the Giles County Courthouse square directly in front of the Sam Davis statue. Some of the men had not worn their hoods on the bus ride over, but most had. It seemed that the majority did not want their faces to be shown on television, and they all knew that cameras would be everywhere.

One of the men who left his hood on was Cappy Limbaugh, the owner of the Sleepy Head Inn in Lawrenceburg. Cappy had gotten his girlfriend to watch the front desk for him so he could participate in the rally. Cappy was almost sixty years old and had been a member of the Klan back in the '70s. Eventually, though, he'd grown tired of the Klan and its changing leaders and directions.

He'd gotten out in 1982 and had never looked back. Cappy had decided that there was no point or percentage in being associated with a group that hated black people. Hell, black people needed a motel room too. At the Sleepy Head, if you had the money, Cappy had the room. He didn't give a damn about your color, race, creed, or sexual orientation. If there was one thing he'd learned in his fifty-nine years, it was that money talked and everything else was pure grain bullshit.

And it was money that had put him on the bus that morning. One of his regular patrons wanted to march with the crazies and had paid Cappy a handsome sum to go along so that no one would ask questions.

Rubbing sweat from behind the back of his neck, Cappy turned to his customer, who had sat next to him on the bus ride over and had marched beside him throughout the morning. "Hotter than hell out here, huh?"

Underneath the hood given him by Dr. George Curtis, JimBone Wheeler nodded. "It's only going to get hotter."

54

Helen Lewis gave a thirty-minute opening statement that was both powerful and effective. She methodically laid out the state's case step-by-step, focusing first on Bo's motive to commit the crime and then using a flow chart to list all of the physical evidence against Bo. She finished with the theme of her case.

"Ladies and gentlemen of the jury, this case is about revenge. The defendant, Bocephus Aurulius Haynes, carried around a burning hate for Andy Walton for forty-five years. You will hear his own cousin tell you that the defendant promised on many occasions that he would one day kill Andy Walton. That day turned out to be August 19, 2011. After a heated confrontation with the victim earlier in the night at Kathy's Tavern, the defendant could no longer keep his hate under control. He decided to take the law into his own hands and finally exact revenge on Andrew Davis Walton." Helen paused and took a moment to glare at the defense table and in particular Bo. "I am confident that when you hear and see the mountain of evidence against the defendant, you will find him guilty of murder. Thank you."

Helen strode confidently back to the prosecution table and took her seat.

"Thank you, General Lewis," Judge Connelly said. Then she nodded toward the defense table. "The defendant will now give his opening statement."

As Rick stood, he felt a hand grab hold of his own. He looked and saw Bo's intense eyes, which were so black they reminded him of the water at midnight in Destin Harbor. "Pure, dog. Be pure. Be *you*."

Rick nodded and blinked his eyes. He felt emotion welling in his chest and fought it off. *Be me,* he told himself. *Be me . . .*

"May it please the court," Rick began, talking from behind his chair at the defense table and then moving in front of the table. "Your Honor." He looked at Judge Connelly. "General." He moved his eyes to Helen Lewis, who stared back as if she were looking right though him. "Members of the jury." Slowly, he directed his eyes to the twelve men and women who would decide the case, holding his gaze on the schoolteacher, Millie Sanderson. "There are two victims in this case. The first is obviously Andrew Davis Walton. The second is . . . Bocephus Haynes. Mr. Haynes, would you please stand."

Bo stood to his full height of six feet four inches, and Rick walked to the side of the table and put his arm around him. During trial competitions, the Professor had always instructed them to make sure they put their hands on the defendant in a criminal case. It was important for the jury to see the defense lawyer touch the accused. For the jury to know that, regardless of whatever monstrous crime the defendant had been charged with, he was still a person. A human being. "This is Bocephus Haynes. In August 1966, a mob of the Tennessee Knights of the Ku Klux Klan burned a cross in Bo's family's yard. Then, threatening to torch the house if Bo's father didn't come outside, these men dragged Bo's father, Franklin Roosevelt Haynes, to a tree in a clearing just a half mile away." Rick paused. "There they kicked him and beat him and . . . *hanged him*. Bo Haynes was five years old at the time. Five . . . years . . . old. Much too young to have seen such a gruesome tragedy." Rick paused, and as they had rehearsed the night before, Bo sat down. "But old enough to recognize a familiar voice. The men who lynched Bo's father wore the robe and hood of the Ku Klux Klan. They could not be recognized by appearance, but Bo knew the voice of the one who did the talking. Bo grew up on Walton Farm. His father worked the fields, while his mother worked in the house with Mrs. Walton. Five-year-old Bo Haynes had heard Andy Walton's voice every day of his short life. He knew it, but the sheriff of this county at that time would not prosecute Mr. Walton based on the word of a five-year-old boy."

Rick paused, moving out from the table and standing in the well of the courtroom, that place right in front of the jury. "General Lewis is right. Bocephus Haynes has lived with the tragedy of his father's murder for forty-five years. Can you even *imagine* what this man has gone through in his life?" Rick glanced at Bo, then back to the twelve jurors, again meeting Millie Sanderson's eye. "So let's examine that life more closely. Bocephus Haynes attended elementary school and high school here in Pulaski, graduating from Giles County High. He obtained a scholarship to play football at Alabama, where he played for Coach Paul 'Bear' Bryant." Rick noticed that Woody Brooks, the retired juror who Ray Ray had said voted for Obama, had his arms folded across his chest but was nodding. "Law school followed at Alabama, where Bo graduated in the top ten percent of his class. Bo had offers from all the big Birmingham firms and several firms in Nashville, but he turned them all down. From the day he set foot in a law school class, Bocephus Haynes knew he would always return here. To Pulaski. His home." Rick moved a couple of steps to his right for effect, maintaining eye contact with Woody. "For twenty-five years Bo has practiced law in Giles County, raising a family with his wife,

Jasmine, right here in Pulaski." Rick gestured to the front row of the gallery, just a few feet from the defense table, where Jasmine Haynes sat with T. J. Unprompted, Jazz stood from her seat and leaned over the railing, placing her hand on Bo's shoulder. Rick noticed that she wore the same orange corsage over her heart as she'd worn the day before, though today her dress was hunter green. Bo squeezed his wife's hand and then she returned to her seat.

Surprised but grateful for the gesture, Rick paused so that the jury could take in the moment. All twelve sets of eyes were now trained on the defendant's wife, and Millie Sanderson appeared to smile without opening her mouth. *All it takes is one*, Rick thought, knowing that for Bo to be found guilty the jury's verdict had to be unanimous. If just one juror held to a belief that Bo was innocent, the court would declare the case a mistrial and Bo would win. Rick sensed, as Ray Ray had suggested, that Millie was the soft spot in the jury pool.

After several seconds Rick cleared his throat and returned his eyes to the jury. "For the past ten years Bo Haynes has made every single edition of *Super Lawyers* magazine as one of the top fifty attorneys in the state of Tennessee." Rick walked to the defense table, and Tom handed him the magazine. "In fact, in 2006 he made the cover of *Super Lawyers.*" Rick held the magazine up for the jurors to see. It was a picture of Bo in a charcoal-gray pinstripe suit, standing in the exact spot where Rick now stood. In the well of the jury. "The cover reads 'Pulaski's Bocephus Haynes: Bulldog for Justice.'" Rick paused, hoping the words sunk in. "In addition to summarizing Bo's heroics in the courtroom, this article goes into great length about why Bo came back to Pulaski. Bo is quoted as saying 'I came back to Pulaski because I wanted to make sure the men who murdered my father were brought to justice. I won't rest until every single one of them is in jail.'"

Rick set the magazine back on the table and again faced the jury. "Bo Haynes has never hidden why he came home. But General Lewis has the terminology wrong. Bo didn't come back for revenge. He came back for justice. Bo is a lawyer. One of the very best in this state. He, more than anyone else, knows that justice is done in a courtroom. Justice . . . is delivered by you." Rick held out his palms to the jury. "Bo's mission has always been for the men who lynched his father to be brought to answer before you. And while making a living and raising a family in Pulaski these past twenty-five years, Bo has tirelessly investigated the circumstances of his father's death, trying to do just that."

Rick paused and walked closer to the defense table. "Bocephus Haynes is innocent. As he sits in this courtroom and throughout this trial, Bocephus Haynes is innocent. He is innocent and will remain innocent until the prosecution"—Rick pointed at Helen Lewis for emphasis—"proves to each and every one of you beyond a reasonable doubt that he murdered Andy Walton in cold blood on the morning of August 19, 2011. I am confident that the state will not be able to meet its burden."

Rick approached the jury. "What General Lewis spent the majority of her time talking about was motive. The prosecution asks you to believe that Bo Haynes, a man who has spent a lifetime practicing law in this very courtroom, took the law into his own hands." Rick paused, glaring at the prosecution table while he continued. "What the prosecution chooses to ignore is that there were other men with motive to kill Andy Walton." Rick let that teaser hang in the air for a second before turning to face the jury. "One of the last people to see Andy Walton alive was Darla Ford, a dancer at the Sundowners Club. Darla will take the witness stand and tell you that just two weeks prior to Andy Walton's murder, Mr. Walton told her that he intended to confess to the 1966 lynching of Haynes's father. That left fourteen days for any one of the other Klansmen who helped Andy Walton murder Roosevelt Haynes in

1966 to take the law into his own hands again. To silence Andy Walton and frame Bo Haynes for the crime."

Rick took a couple of steps back, letting the information sink in. "I ask you to hear all of the evidence before you make up your mind. There are two sides to this story. Two very different sides." He paused. "And two victims. Andy Walton . . . and Bocephus Haynes. Thank you."

Rick gave a slight bow and walked back to the defense table. Under the table he felt Bo nudge him with his knee.

"Great job," Bo whispered.

Rick turned to his left, but Ray Ray was staring straight ahead into space. Over Ray Ray's shoulder, Rick caught the Professor's eye, who nodded his approval, and Rick nodded back. He had planted every seed they had. Now it was up to the witnesses to bring in the crop.

"General Lewis," Judge Connelly said, interrupting Rick's thoughts, "please call your first witness."

55

Emanual's Stop is the local Greyhound bus station in Ethridge, Tennessee. It sits on Highway 43—right in the heart of Amish country.

Deputy Hank Springfield leaned against his squad car out in front of the station and spoke in clipped tones to Detective Wade Richey and Powell Conrad. Hank was wired, having barely slept the night before. The tape that Lonnie Dupree had retained at the bus stop in Pulaski showed Martha Booher arriving there at 8:45 a.m. the previous Friday. By looking at the bus schedule, Hank, with Lonnie's help, had determined that the bus Booher had taken would have embarked from Ethridge that morning at 8:00 a.m., with stops in Pulaski, Franklin, and Nashville.

"So you're thinking that if she caught a bus here"—Powell paused to gesture at the farms located on both sides of the highway, some of which were currently being tilled by Amish men— "she has to be here. Why would she come here to catch a bus? I can see why she might want to stop here, especially if she was a tourist.

But why would she start her journey here at eight in the morning unless . . . ?" He held out his palms.

"Great work, Deputy," Wade said, nodding his head.

"It's not great unless we find her," Hank said.

"All right then," Powell said, slapping his hands together. "You got copies of her photograph for me and Wade?"

Hank nodded and pulled a folder out of the front passenger seat of the squad. "Photographs of Booher and Wheeler. My hunch is that JimBone's been hiding out here with her." He paused. "I mean, think about it. What better disguise for Wheeler than to blend in with the Amish? Given how adept he's been at changing his appearance and that he was seen at Kathy's Tavern with a beard, I think that's got to be it."

They all looked at each other, the intensity palpable. If what Hank said was true, they were very close to finding the most wanted man in three states. "Everybody packing?" Powell asked, slapping the holster on his side. It was unusual for Powell to carry a gun, but this was a bizarre situation. Hank was double holstered, and Wade opened up his jacket to reveal a Glock 41 pistol tucked into his pants.

Powell nodded. "Let's roll then."

56

Similar to the preliminary hearing, Helen Lewis began the trial by establishing motive. In order, she called all four eyewitnesses to the confrontation at Kathy's Tavern—Cassie Dugan, Clete Sartain, Dr. George Curtis, and even Maggie Walton. Mrs. Walton had been particularly effective, Tom thought, describing to the jury her private interaction with Bo after the other three had left the bar. "I was just trying to get him to leave my husband alone," Maggie said. "But I fear that finding out Andy was dying sent Bo over the edge." Tom objected to the characterization, and Connelly sustained, but the damage was done.

By day's end Tom knew that there wasn't a shadow of doubt in any of the minds of the jurors that Bocephus Haynes had the necessary motive to kill Andy Walton.

"The first day of trial is always bad for the defense," Tom had whispered to a downtrodden Bo after Judge Connelly had adjourned the jury. "You know that."

"I know. I just hope to hell it gets better," Bo said as the sheriff's deputies led him away.

Me too, Tom thought, closing his eyes and putting his head in his hands. *But not tomorrow,* he knew. Tomorrow the General would put on the physical evidence—the real strength of her case.

It's gonna get worse before it gets better, he knew, opening his eyes and packing up his briefcase.

57

By 6:00 p.m. Hank, Wade, and Powell had covered almost every square inch of the Amish settlement in Ethridge. The good news was that numerous people had recognized Martha Booher's picture, and they were even able to locate her cabin. The bad news was that no one had seen Booher on the settlement in over a week, and a search of her cabin revealed absolutely nothing. It was essentially bare.

Several people remembered that Booher's nephew, whom they all described as a "large man," had come to stay with her for a while a few months back, but none had gotten a great look at him. None were able to identify the man as JimBone Wheeler from the photographs.

Their last interview turned out to be the most productive. Booher's next-door neighbor, Linda Whitaker, said that Martha had been going to Lawrenceburg a lot in the last month. She would take her nephew there in the wagon, and she'd come back without him.

As the sun began to set, they gathered around Hank Springfield's squad car, each drinking black coffee from a Styrofoam cup. Finally, Powell said what they were all thinking. "We've got to cast a net around Lawrenceburg. If JimBone Wheeler is still operating in this area, that's where he is."

"Got to be," Wade agreed.

Nodding along, Hank called the number for the Lawrence County Sheriff's Office.

58

In Room 107 of the Sleepy Head Inn, JimBone Wheeler took off his Klan garb and sat down on the bed. Martha Booher lay on her side next to him.

"Well . . . ?" she said.

Bone shrugged and took a Busch Light Draft can out of the six-pack that Cappy had bought at a convenience store on the way back. He took a long swig from the can and offered one to Martha, but she refused.

"Going to be hard . . . but not impossible. They came out the doors to the east side today, which I suspect is the side they'll always come out. They also entered from the east, and Haynes's office is on the east." He paused, taking another swig from the can. "There are a lot of factors. I need the crowd to be fairly large around them, but not so big I can't get close. With Haynes being brought in and out of the courthouse by the deputies . . ." He shrugged. "I don't know. The trial is probably going to last a couple more days, so I'll have at least four to six more chances."

"What if you can't get close enough?"

Bone shook his head and drained the rest of the beer. "I will."

59

Melvin Ragland had been the Giles County Coroner since 1981. Melvin was a tall, thin man whose typical manner of dress was a pair of khaki pants and a short-sleeve, white button-down with two pens in the pocket. On Wednesday morning Melvin was the first witness called by the prosecution. He had added a blue blazer and red tie to his daily ensemble and took the stand in the calm and easy manner that you would expect from someone who had testified hundreds of times over the past three decades.

Methodically, like a tested surgeon, Helen took Melvin through his experience as a coroner, going over his expertise in determining the cause and time of death in thousands of cases. After establishing his acumen in forensics, Helen got right to the heart of it.

"Dr. Ragland, did you have an opportunity to examine the body of Andy Walton?"

"Yes, ma'am, I did. On the morning of August 19, 2011, Mr. Walton's body was taken to our crime lab, where I performed an autopsy."

"And can you tell the jury your opinion as to the cause of Andy Walton's death?"

Melvin adjusted his eyes toward the twelve juror seats and leaned forward in his chair. "Andy Walton died as a result of one gunshot wound to the head."

"And were you able to determine the type of gun that killed Mr. Walton?"

Ragland nodded, still looking at the jury. "Twelve-gauge shotgun. A shell casing found under Mr. Walton's vehicle was twelve-gauge buckshot. I compared the entry and exit points of the shot to those of a twelve-gauge buckshot shell, and they were identical."

"Were you able to reach a conclusion as to the time of death?"

"Yes. Based on the statements of the witnesses at the Sundowners Club, who saw Mr. Walton alive at just after 1:00 a.m., and the surveillance tape of Mr. Haynes's vehicle leaving the club at 1:20 a.m., it was my determination that Mr. Walton died at approximately 1:15 a.m."

Helen nodded at Dr. Ragland. "Thank you, Doctor. I have no further questions."

"Cross-examination?" Judge Connelly turned to the defense table.

Tom and Rick had long decided not to cross-examine Dr. Ragland, because there were no points to be gained. "We have no questions at this time," Tom said. "However, we reserve the right to recall Dr. Ragland during our case-in-chief."

"Very well," Connelly said. "The witness is excused for now, but Dr. Ragland"—Connelly glanced his way—"don't leave town."

"I haven't in twelve years, Judge," Ragland said, which elicited some laughs from the jurors.

Smiling to herself a little, Connelly turned her attention to the prosecution table. "Call your next witness, General."

—

The next witness called by the prosecution was Dr. Malacuy Ward from the State Forensics Lab in Nashville. Dr. Ward was a scientist who specialized in ballistics. After establishing his credentials as an expert, Helen had Dr. Ward take the jury through the difficulties in tracing whether a particular shotgun was used in the commission of a crime. Dr. Ward testified that there was no way to trace whether a "projectile," as he called it, came from a particular weapon, because a shotgun leaves no barrel markings on the lead projectiles in a shell as it's fired. However, if an empty shell casing was retrieved, it was possible to determine if that shell casing was fired from a particular shotgun by extractor marks on the brass base. Helen concluded in grand style, taking a plastic baggie from the evidence table and handing it to Dr. Ward.

"Dr. Ward, did we ask you to compare an empty shell casing found at the scene of Andy Walton's murder to a particular shotgun seized in the investigation?"

"Yes, you did. I compared the shell you provided with a shotgun registered to Bocephus Aurulius Haynes."

"And you are aware that Mr. Haynes is the defendant in this case?" Helen pointed at Bo.

"Yes."

"And please tell the jury what your testing revealed."

Ward leaned forward and looked at the jury. "After testing the empty shell casing with the shotgun registered to Mr. Haynes, we found an exact match. The extractor marks on the casing from the empty shell matched Mr. Haynes's shotgun."

Almost in unison all of the jurors turned their eyes to Bo. Of all of the physical evidence, Tom knew that this, with the possible exception of the surveillance video from the Sundowners, was the most damning. An empty shotgun shell fired from Bo's gun was found within a few feet of where Andy Walton was killed.

"Thank you, Dr. Ward. I have no further questions."

—

Tom kept his cross-examination short and to the point. "Dr. Ward, you are aware that the lead projectile, or in layman terms, the buckshot that killed Andy Walton, was discovered, correct?"

"Yes, that is my understanding."

"But you performed no testing on the actual buckshot, did you?"

Ward shook his head. "No. As I indicated earlier, you cannot trace the ballistics on the projectile. That would have been a futile exercise. The shotgun does not leave any barrel markings on the projectile."

"And there is no way to test for sure whether the shot that killed Andy Walton came out of the empty shell casing that you examined."

"Correct."

"So, isn't it true then, Doctor, that there is no way to determine whether the empty shell casing traced to Bo Haynes's shotgun actually came from the shell that killed Andy Walton?"

Ward shrugged. "Yes. That is true."

"Thank you, Dr. Ward. No further questions."

60

At 3:30 p.m. Booker T. Rowe was called to the stand, with Helen promising the court that he would be a short witness. As Bo's massive cousin trudged toward the witness chair, Tom let his eyes drift to the gallery, which was again filled to capacity. He noticed that for the third straight day, Jasmine Haynes had attached an orange corsage to her dress just above her heart. Curious, Tom had asked Jazz about the garnish this morning. "When the Klan marched in 1989 with the Aryan Nation, the people here protested by putting orange wreaths and ribbons on all the business doors," she had explained. "Orange is the international color of brotherhood. Bo and I were part of that protest, and I guess I'm . . . trying to send a message."

Tom thought the idea was both subtle and brilliant. And as his eyes moved across the courtroom to the balcony above, he noticed a number of other people wearing shades of orange, and some of the women, white and black alike, had mimicked Jazz's corsage. The message was getting across . . .

Tom eventually lowered his eyes to the front row behind the prosecution table, where Maggie Walton again wore the garb of a widow in mourning—black dress, black gloves, and the Holy Bible in her lap. He couldn't help but be struck by the contrast between the spouses of the victim and the defendant. Maggie, sitting like a statue in her black garments and white hair, and Jazz with the orange flower over her heart, arms locked with her teenage son's. He tried to imagine what the scene looked like on television, and he figured Jazz and T. J. had to appear more sympathetic than Maggie. It wasn't much, but given how bad the first two and a half days of trial had gone for the defense, Tom would take points wherever he could get them.

———

Helen was as good as her word, and Booker T. was in the witness chair less than an hour. First, the General covered Booker T.'s providing Bo Haynes with the code to the gate leading into Walton Farm. "So the defendant would easily have had access to Walton Farm on the night Andy Walton was murdered?"

In a defeated voice, Booker T. had agreed.

Then Helen took Booker T. through his relationship with Bo. That he and Bo were cousins and they had grown up in the same house after Bo's daddy had died and his mother left town. Helen ended with Booker T. testifying that he had heard Bo say on "numerous occasions" that he would one day kill Andy Walton. He could not remember the last time he'd heard Bo say those words, but it was within the last year. Then, unprompted, Booker T. shrugged and volunteered, "He said that all the time."

There was a stirring in the gallery, and Tom saw Jazz take hold of T. J.'s hand in the row behind the defense table. Moving his eyes to the other side of the courtroom, Tom noticed that Maggie

Walton had crossed her arms and was staring at Bo with smug satisfaction.

"No further questions," Helen said, knowing that she couldn't have asked for a better ending to her examination.

At first the flippant manner in which Booker T. had volunteered the statement angered Tom, and out of the corner of his eye he could see Bo gripping his fists underneath the table. Then he saw the opening Booker T.'s demeanor provided. Tom led with it on cross, beginning the first question before he was even out of his chair.

"Mr. Rowe, you never reported Mr. Haynes to the police on any of these occasions when Mr. Haynes said he was going to kill Andy Walton, did you?"

Booker T. shook his head. "No, sir. I didn't." His voice was both annoyed and angry.

"Why?"

"Objection, Your Honor." Helen Lewis was out of her chair, and her own annoyed look made Tom know he had just hit the sweet spot if he could get it in front of the jury. "The reasoning behind why Mr. Rowe didn't report Mr. Haynes on these prior occasions is completely irrelevant."

"Overruled," Judge Connelly said, waving her hand at Helen like she might be a fly. "You opened the door to this, General. I'm going to allow it."

"Thank you, Your Honor. Mr. Rowe, do you remember the question?"

"Very well," he said, his deep voice carrying out over the entire courtroom. Tom imagined that he sounded like a preacher to those watching on television. "I never reported Bo's statements saying he was going to kill Mr. Walton to the police, because I *never* thought Bo would do such a thing."

Having scored the only points he could, the rest of Tom's examination focused on Bo's affinity for visiting the clearing where his father was murdered. Just as he had told Tom during their encounter at the Legend's Steakhouse, Booker T. told the jury that the clearing was "exactly where he would expect Bo to go" on the anniversary of his father's murder.

Finally, Tom walked over to the evidence table and picked up the twelve-gauge, holding it with his palms out, first for the jury to see and then showing it to Booker T. "Mr. Rowe, do you recognize this gun?" Tom placed his thumb on the initials on the handle.

"Sure do," Booker T. said, smiling. "That is Bo's shotgun."

"And how do you recognize it as Bo's gun?"

Booker T. pointed at the handle. "It's got his initials on there. 'BAH.'" Booker T. paused. "I gave Bo that gun, and I stenciled the initials on there. Gave it to him when he came back here to practice law."

Keeping his eyes on the jury, Tom asked his next question. "Mr. Rowe, on the occasions where you saw Bo at the clearing on Walton Farm, did you ever know him to bring this shotgun with him?"

Booker T. smiled and looked directly at the jury. "Every single time."

"And did he ever tell you why he always brought the gun?"

"Didn't have to. I know why. There's wild animals on that farm. Bobcats, deer, snakes."

"Do you carry a gun when you walk the farm during your work?"

Again, Booker T. looked at the jury. "Every single time."

Tom nodded, watching the jurors. "Thank you, Mr. Rowe. I have no further questions."

61

The net thrown over Lawrenceburg had turned up nothing. Hank, Wade, and Powell, along with all available deputies in the Lawrence County Sheriff's Office, had searched every square inch of Lawrence County, and there was no sign of JimBone Wheeler.

On Wednesday evening at 6:00 p.m. they ended the search where it had begun the day before. The Sleepy Head Inn.

The Sleepy Head had seemed like an ideal place for JimBone, because customers typically paid in cash and didn't have to show ID. Every room was searched both days, and there were no clues leading to JimBone.

"I bet he's gone," Hank said, kicking gravel across the parking lot. "On to bigger and better things."

Wade nodded, but Powell gave a quick jerk of his head and grunted.

"We should have gotten him by now," Wade offered, but Powell just grunted again and walked a few paces away, his hands stuck deep in his pockets.

"What now?" Hank asked, the defeat evident in his voice. "I should probably get back to Pulaski."

Wade nodded and extended his hand. "We appreciate your cooperation, Deputy."

"What are y'all going to do?" Hank asked, taking out his keys.

Wade turned to Powell, who had kneeled down and was skipping a few stray stones across the lot as he gazed at the setting sun. "I think we're gonna stick around for a little while longer."

Hank nodded, then leaned in close to Wade. "Is he OK? He hasn't so much as said a word in the last few hours."

Wade smiled. "He's fine. That's just his way."

As Hank pulled out of the gravel lot, Wade squatted next to Powell. "Well, brother, what's our play?"

Powell skipped a few more stones and finally stood, wiping his hands on his jeans. "You're the investigator, Wade. What do you think?"

"I think my partner is onto something, and I'm out of suggestions. Come on, brother. I see it in your eye. Let's hear our play."

Powell slowly nodded. "See that Huddle House across the street?"

Wade stood and turned his head, seeing the red and blue neon lights of the Huddle House. "Yep."

"I want you to go over there and get some eggs and coffee. Get you a booth where you can keep both eyes on this parking lot. If you see anyone leaving the lot or walking around, anything suspicious, call me."

"And what are you going to do?"

Powell grunted and turned back to the Sleepy Head. "I'm going to get a room."

62

Cappy Limbaugh rented a room to the sandy-haired prosecutor, never letting the smile leave his face. "Sure am honored that you'd choose my place to stay the night," Cappy offered. "Where did your friends go?"

"They left," Powell said, throwing three twenty-dollar bills on the counter.

Cappy took the money and put it in his cash register. Then he slid the key to the room across the counter. Instead of a card, like most hotels provided these days, this was actually a rusted silver key. "Room 110. It's on the back side of the property." He paused. "Have a nice night."

Powell took the key and examined it, rolling it over in his hand before looking up at Cappy. "Mr. Limbaugh, you be sure and buzz my room if you see anything suspicious."

"Gladly, Mr. Prosecutor. Like I said, I'm proud to have a *law dog* stay at my establishment."

Powell smiled at him. "I bet."

———

Once the prosecutor had left the lobby building, Cappy strolled behind the counter to the garage in back. The prosecutor and the detective from Tuscaloosa had searched the garage high and low for almost an hour before the detective had left and the sandy-haired bastard had decided to get a room. Cappy wasn't stupid. He knew the detective was close by. He'd seen him turn into the Huddle House. And he knew the prosecutor didn't take a room because he was wowed by the accommodations.

The garage was littered with lawn equipment, including a five-year-old John Deere riding lawn mower that Cappy used to cut the grass on the grounds of the hotel. There was also a weed eater, assorted cans of paint, and an electric- and gas-powered leaf blower. Against the right-hand wall next to the lawn mower was a crowbar, and Cappy quickly grabbed it. He knew he couldn't be away from the front desk more than a couple minutes. Especially not with that goddamn prosecutor snooping around.

In the center of the garage Cappy had parked his 1969 orange Dodge Charger, which he'd bought a few years after *The Dukes of Hazzard* had first come out. Involuntarily, Cappy smiled at the car, his pride and joy, and then opened the driver's-side door and climbed in. The prosecutor and the detective had both made over the car during their inspection, but neither had come close to figuring anything out. Cappy felt with his fingers along the floorboard next to the accelerator and pulled up the carpet. Underneath, he could see the concrete garage floor. As the floor was littered with cracks from years of settlement, the jagged crevice underneath where the Charger sat wasn't noticeable in any way. Just another crack in a garage full of them. Cappy took the crowbar and placed it in the fissure and pulled. Putting his face in the opening, Cappy pulled back the concrete block and looked underneath.

When Cappy Limbaugh had first opened the Sleepy Head thirty years ago, he had gotten in a scrape with the Feds over unpaid taxes. Knowing he needed a good place to hide, he'd built the room underneath the garage so he would have a place to camp out when federal agents came by to interview him or, worse, if they wanted to arrest him. And considering his membership in the Klan, Cappy figured it couldn't hurt to have a "safe room," as he'd heard such places called.

The room was five feet by eight and fit two people rather snugly. As he peered inside, the light from a flashlight caught him directly in the eyes and he looked away, blinking to get his bearings.

"What's up?" Bone asked from below.

When Cappy turned back around, he saw the muzzle of a .38-caliber revolver pointed at him. Bone held the gun steady, but his eyes, typically calm and cold, were bloodshot red and wild, having not seen the outside in almost twenty-four hours.

"That prosecutor from Tuscaloosa took a room. He's staying the night, and his detective friend is camped across the street at the Huddle House."

"Shit," Bone said.

"Shit is right. You've got to get out of here. If I'm caught harboring a fugitive—"

"Shut up. Just get back in there and act cool. Is my Klan outfit in the trunk?"

"Yes."

Bone nodded to himself. "Good. All right. Look, tomorrow morning, before we leave for the bus, I want you to put on your Klan garb and walk outside the hotel. Stretch, fart, walk around. Let them see you. Then come back inside to the garage. I'll be ready."

"How the—?" Cappy stammered, but Bone waved his hand to cut him off.

"Don't worry about it. I've got it all figured out. Just leave your car keys with me and get the hell out of here."

"Leave my keys? What—?"

"Just do it, goddamnit."

Cappy dropped the keys into the hole and peered into Bone's wild eyes. He started to say something else, but Bone's look stopped him.

"See you in the morning," Bone said, shutting off the flashlight.

For a moment Cappy thought about the girl. She was in there somewhere, but it was so dark Cappy couldn't see her. *Is she asleep?* he wondered. Then a cold chill came over him. *Is she dead?*

"Cappy, don't make me shoot you," Bone said, his voice cold as ice.

Cappy Limbaugh moved the concrete block back into place, silently praying that tomorrow would be the last time he'd ever see JimBone Wheeler. Thirty seconds later he was back behind the counter in the lobby. His heartbeat had not stopped racing as his eyes bounced around the small room, making sure that everything was the same as he'd left it. As there were no customers and he saw no cars pulling in the parking lot, he reached into his pocket for a pack of Marlboros and headed for the door to the outside. Some fresh air and a hit of nicotine sounded good.

It was going to be a long night.

———

Powell checked into Room 110 and first did a clean sweep of everything. The bed, the shower, even the walls. He saw nothing that worried him about the room, other than the fact that it adjoined Room 109. He made sure the adjoining door was locked and then called Wade.

"Where are you?"

"Back booth at the Huddle House. Drinking a cup of coffee and eating some raisin toast. How's your room? Free Wi-Fi, I'm hoping."

Powell laughed. "Free cable's about it. Look, Wade, that Limbaugh cat is as dirty as a French whore. I'm going to explore the grounds a little. It's probably nothing, but . . . it's been a while since my antennas were up like this. Something's wrong. I can feel it."

"Ten-four. I'll be here until I get further word from you."

Powell clicked the "End" button and then called Rick.

"Whatcha got?" Rick asked.

"Jack shit," Powell said, looking through the room blinds. The back side of the hotel looked out upon a field of weeds and brush. The room didn't have much of a view and, worse, it was the farthest unit from the hotel lobby. "There's no sign of him, and we've searched every square inch of Lawrence County." Powell paused and stepped out of the room into the cool night air.

"What are you going to do?" Rick asked. "Go back to Tuscaloosa?"

Powell walked down the sidewalk and turned the corner so the lobby was now back in view. Beyond the lobby and across the street, he saw the red and blue lights of the Huddle House and a figure sitting in the back booth. Powell nodded, though he figured Wade was too far away to recognize the gesture. "Nah, it's not quitting time yet. I'm going to hang out in Lawrenceburg tonight. There's something here . . ." Powell moved his eyes to the lobby building and saw Cappy Limbaugh step outside. The hotel owner turned his head left and right and then lit up a smoke as Powell slunk back a few steps into the darkness. "That's just not right. How about y'all?" he asked, knowing that the trial would crank back up in the morning. "How are things going there?"

There was a long pause. Then, his voice solemn and detached, Rick said, "Not good."

63

Larry Tucker had an alibi.

"He was with Tammie Gentry all night," Ray Ray said, waving his arms and sloshing bourbon on the polished mahogany of Bo's conference room table as Tom and Rick watched him with wide eyes. "All goddamn night."

"How did you—?" Rick started, but Ray Ray held up his palm.

"Doesn't matter," Ray Ray said, slurring his words. "If you cross Tucker on him knowing Andy was going to confess, it ain't gonna make a hill of beans, because the General is just going to stuff his alibi right up our ass."

"Ray Ray, calm down," Tom said. He'd never seen his friend this agitated. He wondered if he'd slept the last two nights.

"Calm nothing," Ray Ray said, turning up the bottle. "We're fucked, Tom. We're fucked six ways from Sunday."

64

At 7:30 a.m. on Thursday morning Cappy Limbaugh stepped outside and lit a cigarette. He wore his Ku Klux Klan robe and gripped the hood in the crook of his armpit. Luckily, outside of the Tuscaloosa prosecutor, there was only one other patron who'd stayed at the Sleepy Head last night—a trucker on his way to Memphis—and he'd already checked out. Walking around in KKK regalia wasn't the best way to attract or keep business, but Cappy figured for what Wheeler was paying him it was worth the risk. He took a long drag on the Camel and glanced around his hotel, knowing that at least two sets of eyes were watching him now. The detective's unmarked car was still parked outside the Huddle House across the street, and the prosecutor was no doubt watching from some corner of the property. *Get a good look, boys,* Cappy thought, smiling and stretching his arms above his head.

After waiting a full minute, Cappy flicked the cigarette to the ground and crushed it out. Then, making a show of it, he looked at the hood and placed it on his head. Then he went back inside and walked through the lobby to the garage in back.

—

"See him," Powell croaked into the phone. He hadn't slept at all during the night and desperately needed a cup of coffee.

"Got him," Wade said. "I don't remember him telling us he was going to a Klan rally this morning."

"I don't remember us asking," Powell muttered.

"Garage door is opening," Wade said. "He must be on the move."

"If he's moving, we need to move," Powell said, and despite his fatigue he felt the adrenaline pulse through his veins. *Pulaski,* he thought. *He's going to Pulaski.*

"On my way," Wade said.

Less than a minute later Cappy Limbaugh's orange Dodge Charger pulled onto the highway.

Wade eased his car to a stop in front of the motel, and Powell climbed inside, accepting the cup of coffee that Wade offered with a sigh of relief. "Thanks, brother."

Wade and Powell turned onto the highway and picked up Limbaugh a quarter of mile later. "Hang back a little," Powell said, taking a scalding sip of coffee and feeling the caffeine mixing with the adrenaline. Up ahead he could see the back of Limbaugh's white hood from the front seat of the Charger. Without provocation Powell started to chuckle. Then he broke into a belly laugh.

"Mind telling me what's so funny?" Wade asked, sipping from his own cup.

"Oh, nothing," he said, his face still contorted in laughter. "It's just . . . you realize that we are in hot pursuit of the General Lee?"

Wade glanced at Powell, then moved his eyes back to the road. Finally, he shook his head and also began to laugh. "Well . . . I guess you know what that makes us?"

Powell nodded, barely able to get the words out he was laughing so hard. "Rosco and Enos."

For a full minute they laughed as they kept a respectable distance behind the Charger.

The laughter stopped when the Charger's turn light came on and the bus came into view. It was parked in the front parking lot of a church, and the words "Lawrenceburg First Church of God" were painted down the side of it. Thirty or forty white-robed and hooded Klansmen were milling about the parking lot beside the bus, some beginning to embark the steps and climb inside.

"You don't think . . . ?" Wade began as the Charger turned into the entrance to the church.

"Yep," Powell nodded, feeling another wave of adrenaline. "They're going to Pulaski."

65

Ray Ray Pickalew didn't show for court on Thursday morning. Given the man's condition the night before, Tom couldn't say he was all that surprised. Still, it was disappointing.

Damnit, Ray Ray, Tom thought, feeling the first pangs of regret at having associated his old teammate as local counsel. *He's come up lame at the finish line.*

"Any word from Ray Ray?" Rick asked as the jury began to filter into the courtroom.

Tom turned to him, and his young partner had the bloodshot eyes of a trial lawyer entering the latter stages of a courtroom battle.

"Nothing," Tom said. As he eased himself into his seat, using the cane for balance, Tom could feel his own fatigue setting in. His knee was also throbbing, and the Advil had stopped providing any relief. *We'll probably finish today,* he told himself. *Tomorrow at the latest. Suck it up, old man.*

As he started to ask Rick a question, his cell phone vibrated in his pocket. As nonchalant as he could be—he didn't want the jury to see him checking his phone—he took it out and set it on the

table between him and Rick. He tapped the screen so that the text
message would be visible. Glancing down at the screen, he felt his
breath catch in his throat.

The sender was Ray Ray Pickalew, and the message was short
and sweet: *I think I've found a witness who puts George Curtis AND
Larry Tucker at the scene of Roosevelt Haynes's lynching. Will bring
him this afternoon.*

Tom nudged Rick with his elbow and tapped the screen again,
which had gone black after a few seconds. Tom watched as his
young partner's eyes grew wide. "So that's what he's been doing,"
Rick whispered.

Tom nodded and turned his eyes back to the witness stand. He
stifled the urge to smile. *How could I have ever doubted Ray Ray?*

For the first time since being retained as Bo's lawyer, Tom
allowed himself to think of victory.

If Ray Ray Pickalew had indeed found a witness who could
place Dr. George Curtis and Larry Tucker at the scene of Roosevelt
Haynes's lynching in 1966, then Andy Walton's intention to confess would be a powerful motive for murder. And with motive . . .

Again, Tom fought the urge to smile as his heart raced in his
chest.

. . . we might just win this thing.

66

By the time the Lawrenceburg First Church of God bus arrived on the Giles County Courthouse square, the time was 9:15 a.m. Bocephus Haynes and his legal team would have long since arrived and gone inside the courthouse.

JimBone Wheeler followed the brigade of Klansmen off the bus, knowing that he would likely only have one shot to complete his mission. But that was OK. One shot was better than no shot—especially after spending all of yesterday in the safe room at the Sleepy Head—and he was pleased with the plan he had developed in just a matter of seconds last night.

He knew the prosecutor who'd stayed the night at the Sleepy Head and the detective who'd camped out at the Huddle House had followed the bus into Pulaski. From his seat in the back row, he'd caught sight of an unmarked black police car tailing the bus about a mile outside of Lawrenceburg.

Bone knew that had to be them, and the knowledge had made him smile under his white hood. *Gotcha*, he had thought.

Now, standing on the square surrounded by hundreds of other white-hooded and white-robed men, Bone waited for part two of his plan to unfold.

———

In the trunk of the orange Dodge Charger, Cappy Limbaugh knew they'd waited long enough. He turned the lever in the back of the trunk down and leaned into the carpeted wall, and the wall folded down into the backseat of the car. Moving as quickly as his stiff limbs would carry him, he crawled through the opening, with Martha Booher right behind him. He shut the opening and then slowly raised his head to look around. The parking lot of the church was full of cars, but he saw no people and no sets of eyes. "Let's go," he whispered. Grabbing the keys that Bone had left on the floorboard of the passenger-side backseat, Cappy cracked open the door just a hair and stepped outside, motioning for Booher to do the same. Then he shut the door, clicked the keyless entry lock button—he had modernized the car just a bit—and tried to walk as nonchalantly as possible across the parking lot full of cars to the Chevy Silverado parked near the rear of the church, where Pastor Leo Jacobs's house was located.

As he climbed in the front seat of the unlocked truck and grabbed the keys from under the mat on the floorboard, Cappy saw Pastor Leo staring at him through the blinds of the large picture window at the front of the house. The reverend nodded, and Cappy returned the gesture, turning the key as Martha Booher climbed into the passenger side of the truck.

Pastor Leopold Jacobs, minister of the First Church of God, was for all intents and purposes as fine a man as Cappy had ever known. A great preacher in the pulpit and unafraid to handle a rattlesnake if it meant the collection plate would rise. Church attendance had doubled since Pastor Leo had taken over as minister in 2002.

But Pastor Leo was a bachelor—his wife lost her battle with breast cancer in 2006—and he had certain primal needs that his occupation hamstrung him from fulfilling.

So every Thursday night for the past three years, Pastor Leo had met Ann Reynolds, whose husband was a trucker and was rarely at home, in Room 106 of the Sleepy Head Inn. Cappy understood and embraced the hypocrisy of it all. To Cappy Limbaugh, it made perfect sense that a minister who preached the gospel on Sunday would commit adultery with one of his married parishioners every Thursday. To Cappy's mind, the sooner a person embraced the hypocrisy of life, the sooner he might find real happiness.

Regardless, Pastor Leo was indebted to Cappy, a situation that had paid great dividends when Bone said he needed a place to hide his truck. Raising his right hand in salute, Cappy put the Chevy Silverado in gear and pulled out of the driveway.

Behind him Pastor Leo closed the blinds in the picture window.

———

"What do you make of this?" Wade asked.

They had followed the bus all the way to Pulaski and were now parked in front of Reeves Drug Store on the east side of the square.

Powell grunted and continued to stare out the windshield. Finally, he sighed. "I'm sorry, partner. I guess I've led us on a wild-goose chase. I . . ." He stopped, shaking his head. He grabbed the door handle and then took his hand off of it. "I swear, though. Something about all this has my antennas up. It stinks. Why the hell is Cappy Limbaugh marching in this damn parade of clowns?" He surveyed the square, where there were now hundreds of Klansmen marching.

Wade pointed at the door to Reeves. "Come on, partner, let's grab some more coffee. A shot of caffeine may open our eyes."

Powell followed Wade out on to the sidewalk and then did a sweep of the entire square with his eyes. "Wade, just for shits and giggles, could you call one of those Lawrenceburg deputies and see if that orange General Lee look-alike is still parked out in front of that church?"

"Sure thing. Whatcha thinking?"

Powell grunted. Then: "I was just thinking that if I wanted to kill someone on this square, I'd be dressed in a white hood and robe. Unless you had a bird's-eye view, how could you tell who was doing the shooting?"

"Brother, I think you really need that cup of coffee. We saw Cappy Limbaugh in his car. We saw him drive to that bus and get on it. There was no one else with him."

"He was wearing a costume the whole time. We never saw his face."

For a long moment Wade just looked at Powell. Then, sighing, he nodded his head. "True." He walked to the Charger and reached inside the open window, grabbing the microphone. "Yeah, give me the Lawrenceburg Sheriff's Office," he blared.

"Wade," Powell said, his voice scratchy from lack of sleep, "have them search the car."

"There's no probable cause for a search, partner. What crime do we suspect him of?"

"Harboring a fugitive," Powell scratched back. "Abandoning his car on private property. Anything. Just see if someone can get in that car."

"What will they be looking for?" Wade asked.

"The trunk," Powell scratched. "See if there's anything in the trunk or backseat showing that another person could've been in the car. And have someone drive by the Sleepy Head. If Limbaugh is sitting in there right now running the front desk, then someone else drove to that church. *Someone else* could be out here." Powell pointed to the Klansmen, most of whom were now gathered on the south side of the square, milling in front of Rost Jewelers and the Sam Davis statue.

"Powell, that's crazy talk."

"Just do it, brother," Powell said, walking over to the wrought-iron bench in front of Reeves and sitting down. He was exhausted, but he couldn't remember the last time he'd had such a bad premonition. As a prosecutor and a trial lawyer, you learned to trust your instincts and hunches, and Powell knew something was terribly wrong.

67

As expected, the first witness for the prosecution on Thursday morning was Larry Tucker. After the surveillance video was introduced showing Bo's Lexus pulling out of the exit at 1:20 a.m., Helen asked Larry where he was on the night of the murder.

"I was at the home of Tammie Gentry, one of the dancers at the club." Then he added, "I've been seeing Tammie for almost a year."

Short, sweet, and devastating, Tom thought.

At 11:30 a.m., after concluding her case with testimony from a DNA specialist showing that the blood and hair follicles found in the cargo area of Bo's Lexus matched that of Andy Walton, General Helen Lewis addressed the court. "Your Honor, the state rests."

68

Judge Connelly recessed for lunch, but Tom didn't want to leave the courthouse, not when Ray Ray could show up any minute with the most important witness in the case. He sent Rick out for sandwiches and waited at the counsel table. When his knee began to ache so bad he couldn't stand it any longer, he got up to move around, walking with his cane through the second-floor lobby and finally stopping to look out a window.

The number of Klansmen on the square was enough to take his breath away. He had heard of Klan rallies and gatherings that rivaled this, but he had never seen one. Tom also noticed a few orange ribbons attached to the front doors and windows of some of the businesses. In fact, as he surveyed the square more closely, it appeared that the majority of people who weren't wearing the white robe and hood of the Klan were dressed in orange. Tom smiled, thinking again of the subtle brilliance of Jazz's corsage.

"It's a circus, isn't it?"

Tom turned toward the harsh voice, and Maggie Walton was standing behind him. As on the three prior days of trial, she wore a conservative black dress, and black gloves covered her hands. Her face carried little makeup, and the lines of age were visible on her forehead. But standing right next to her, Tom had to admit that she had a natural beauty about her.

Without waiting for Tom to answer, Maggie added, "Andy would have hated this." She crossed her arms and stood next to him. "He spent the last three decades of his life trying to distance himself from the Klan." She sighed. "And now here they are. Using his murder as a pretext to try and rally support for their cause."

"It's pretty sad," Tom said, not really knowing what to say. "What do you make of the orange ribbons everywhere?"

She scoffed. "Just as ridiculous. Like holding an umbrella up during a hurricane. I wish everybody here would just ignore the Klan. What? Do they think dressing up in orange and supporting a murderer makes the town look any better?" She paused. "Idiots. Just like Bo's wife with her stupid corsage."

Tom raised his eyebrows and turned to face her.

"Oh, I've noticed that. She must think she is so smart." Maggie smirked and then let out another sigh. "This whole thing is an outrage and an embarrassment." Her voice was clipped and hard. "Bo could end this circus if he would just plead guilty."

"He won't do that, Mrs. Walton. Bo didn't kill your husband."

She scoffed and shook her head. "He's going to end up getting the gas chamber."

"Lethal injection," Tom corrected. "Tennessee uses lethal injection to put prisoners to death."

"Whatever."

Tom felt stung by the coldness of her tone. "Aren't you the least bit concerned that someone else might have done this?" Tom asked.

"No, I'm not," Maggie said, her voice devoid of any doubt. "Bo did this. I've never been more sure of anything in my life."

"Really?" Tom said. "Were you aware that Andy was going to confess to murdering Roosevelt Haynes?"

Maggie creased her eyebrow and placed her hands on her hips. "That's the most ridiculous thing I've ever heard. Why would Andy confess to something he didn't do?"

She's either in total denial or she's a pretty good actress, Tom thought, deciding to press the issue. "Mrs. Walton, Darla Ford is going to testify that a few nights before his murder, Andy told her that he intended to confess to killing Roosevelt Haynes. Interesting, isn't it? Seems like a lot of folks would have motive to kill Andy if he was about to confess." He paused. "Your brother, for instance . . ." He left it hanging out there and started to walk away.

As he entered the courtroom, he saw Maggie Walton's reflection through the glass in the doors. Her hands remained on her hips and her mouth was open in shock.

Tom hoped he would see the same reaction when Ray Ray's witness testified that her brother participated in Roosevelt Haynes's lynching.

69

Darla Ford did not look like a stripper when she took the stand as the first witness for the defense on Thursday afternoon. On the contrary, in her navy suit and medium-length brown hair, she gave the appearance of an affluent businesswoman. Over the course of an hour, Darla took the jury through a quick summary of her life story. From high school in Pulaski to not having enough money for college, to taking a job first as a waitress and then a dancer at the Sundowners. Rick covered it all. The money she made and saved up as a stripper, her relationship with Andy Walton, and Andy's bequeathment to her of a hundred thousand dollars upon his death. He ended this line of questioning with Darla's current quest to be a restaurant entrepreneur in Destin.

While Darla testified, Tom couldn't help but glance at Maggie Walton, sitting as stoic as ever in the row behind the prosecution table. If Darla's testimony bothered her, it didn't show. She held her Bible and stared straight ahead, not even looking at the witness stand. He wondered if Maggie knew about Andy and Darla, and he guessed that she probably did. Tom took Maggie for the kind of woman who would look the other way if her man decided to stray, just as long as he continued to provide her with the kind of life to which she was accustomed.

Through the entire direct examination, Darla came across calm, confident, and likeable. Best of all, Rick thought, she was believable. It was Darla who had called what she did at the Sundowners "stripping," making no bones about her role. "My job was to take my clothes off for money, and I was very good at it. I had a regular client list of at least fifteen men . . . and two women."

Rick concluded his direct examination by covering Darla's interactions with Andy Walton during the last two weeks of his life.

"Ms. Ford, did Andy Walton ever tell you that he killed Roosevelt Haynes?" Rick asked.

"Objection, Your Honor," Helen said. "Hearsay."

Connelly moved her eyes to Rick, and he did not hesitate with his response. "Your Honor, a witness's statements against interest are an exception to hearsay."

"Overruled," Connelly said. "The witness may answer the question."

"Yes," Darla said, speaking to the jury and not Rick. "He said he was responsible for the killing, and he was worried that the truth wasn't ever going to come out."

"Did he tell you why he was worried about that?"

Helen was on her feet. "Again, Your Honor, the question calls for rank hearsay."

This time Rick responded before Connelly could even call for a response. "Your Honor, this entire line of questioning will ask Ms. Ford to recall statements made by Mr. Walton against his own interest. Also, we are not offering Mr. Walton's statements for the truth of the matter asserted, but rather for the state of mind of Ms. Ford."

Connelly pondered for a few seconds and then nodded at Rick. "I'm going to allow it."

"Ms. Ford?" Rick prompted.

Again, Darla turned her eyes to the jury. "He had pancreatic cancer. It was terminal. He wasn't sure how long he had left, and he was afraid the truth was going to die with him. He said he wanted to make things right."

"And did he ever say what he meant by 'making things right'?" Darla nodded. "He was going to confess."

"When did this conversation with Mr. Walton take place?"

"In early August, about two weeks before he died."

"Ms. Ford, did you tell anyone about Mr. Walton's intention to confess to the murder of Roosevelt Haynes?"

"Yes," Darla said.

"Who?" Rick asked.

"My boss," Darla said, sweeping her eyes over the jury. "Larry Tucker."

"And when did you tell Mr. Tucker about it?"

"The same night that Mr. Walton told me."

"Which was two weeks before Andy Walton's murder?"

Darla nodded. "Correct."

"Ms. Ford," Rick began, moving his own eyes over the jury. "Was Larry Tucker in the Ku Klux Klan with Andy Walton?"

"I don't know," Darla said.

"No further questions, Your Honor," Rick said.

Given the circumstances, Rick knew it was the best he could do. He turned to his partner for approval, but the Professor was not looking at Rick. Instead, he was focused on the double doors to the courtroom, which had just opened behind the defense table. Rick followed the Professor's gaze and felt a wave of relief at what he saw.

Ray Ray Pickalew, sporting a charcoal-gray suit, white shirt, and crimson tie, was standing in the opening.

Helen's cross-examination focused on the things that Darla Ford did not know. Though she was with Andy Walton an hour before he died, she did not witness his murder. She did not see who killed him. At the time she left the Sundowners that night, Larry Tucker had long since gone for the evening.

The last thing she remembered was Andy Walton walking slowly to his pickup truck in the parking lot of the Sundowners Club.

Darla actually teared up during this part of the questioning, clearly upset at the image of Mr. Walton alone in the moments before he was killed.

When Helen finished, Rick said he had no further questions for Ms. Ford.

As she descended the witness chair, Darla gave Rick a quick wink and walked out of the courtroom.

"The defense may call its next witness."

—

Tom turned to Ray Ray. "Is your witness out in the lobby?" he asked, his voice a scratchy whisper. Other than nodding when Tom had asked if the witness was at the courthouse and ready to testify, Ray Ray had yet to utter a word. Of course, there was no way they could really talk during Helen's cross-examination of Ford.

Ray Ray shook his head. "No, Tommy boy."

"What?" Tom felt his stomach turn. "You said he was here."

"Mr. McMurtrie," Judge Connelly said, her voice rising, the annoyance in it clear, "call your next witness. We have a jury waiting."

"Ray Ray, go get the witness," Tom said, grabbing him hard by the shoulder. "Rick just set it up with Ford on the stand. If you have someone that puts Tucker and Curtis at that clearing when Roosevelt Haynes was lynched, we need to call him now."

"He's here," Ray Ray said.

"Then go get him, for God's sake." Tom's voice rose well above a whisper. He was breaking one of his long-standing rules for behavior in a courtroom. He was losing his cool.

"I can't," Ray Ray said, standing from the table.

Tom also stood, forgetting the pain in his knee and putting both hands on Ray Ray's arms, shaking his old friend. Had he lost his mind? *"What do you mean you can't? What are you talking about? Why?"*

Connelly banged her gavel on the table. "Mr. McMurtrie, what is going on . . . ?" Connelly said more, but Tom didn't hear it.

"Because *I'm the witness,*" Ray Ray said. "Me. Raymond . . . James . . . Pickalew."

Tom staggered back away from him. He tried to speak, but the words wouldn't come.

Connelly banged her gavel again, and then Tom heard his partner speak from just to the side of him.

"Your Honor, the defendant calls Raymond James Pickalew."

———

Helen Lewis literally jumped to her feet as she saw Ray Ray swagger toward the witness stand. "Objection, Your Honor. May we approach?"

Her words were barely heard as the courtroom stirred to life.

Connelly banged her gavel and glared at Rick. "I want all counsel in my chambers this instant. You too, Mr. Pickalew." She turned to the jury. "Members of the jury, we are going to take a fifteen-minute break."

Connelly strode off the bench toward the door that would take her to her chambers, her black robe flowing behind her.

Tom felt a rough hand on his shoulder and heard a ragged voice. "What's going on?" Bo asked.

Tom turned to his client, his mind and body still in shock.

"Professor, what's happening here?" Bo asked again.

"I don't know," Tom said, forcing his lips to move. Then his feet. "Come on, let's go."

"She only said counsel," Bo said.

"You should be in on this, Bo," Tom said, having fully gained his composure. "Whatever this is"—he looked to the witness stand, but Ray Ray was gone, having followed Connelly to her chambers—"you need to hear it."

70

Once they were all in the judge's chambers, Helen did not waste any time.

"Your Honor, Raymond Pickalew is of record as counsel for Mr. Haynes. A lawyer cannot testify in a case he is trying."

Tom cleared his throat, shooting a glance at Ray Ray. The Joker grin covered Ray Ray's broad face.

"All I did was help pick the jury, Your Honor," Ray Ray said. "I haven't examined a single witness, and I haven't even sat at the table for all of it. Me testifying will be no different to that jury than when Ennis testified, and Ennis has sat at the prosecution table the entire case."

"Your Honor, Mr. Pickalew was not included on the defendant's witness list. This is an outrage. An ambush." Helen's fists were clinched at her sides. "And it should not be allowed. I move for sanctions against Mr. McMurtrie, Mr. Drake, and Mr. Pickalew for this outrage on our court."

"Your Honor, we had no idea that Mr. Pickalew would be a witness for the defense," Tom said, thinking as fast as he could as he went through what Ray Ray had indicated "his witness" would say. "Based on what this witness will reveal, it is our position that justice demands that Mr. Pickalew be heard."

"And just what is this witness going to reveal?" Connelly asked, her voice awash with frustration and annoyance. "Really, Mr. McMurtrie, I agree with the General. I cannot imagine how Mr. Pickalew can testify in this case."

"This witness"—Ray Ray began, and everyone else in the room stopped talking. Ray Ray, who had been standing near the back of the office, took a step forward. He did not look at Judge Connelly. Instead, he focused his eyes on Bo—"is going to reveal the names of the men who were present at the clearing at Walton Farm when Roosevelt Haynes was murdered."

The room remained utterly silent as Ray Ray took another step into the room. He was now standing right in front of Bo, his side to the judge.

Bocephus Haynes rose to his full height of six feet four inches tall.

"And just how in the hell are you going to do that, Pickalew?" Helen asked, her voice a high-pitched whine. "Good grief, how much have you had to drink today?"

But no one else in the room moved or spoke. All eyes were on Ray Ray and Bo.

"I'm stone sober," Ray Ray said.

"How?" Bo asked, his voice an anguished crackle. "How can you name those men?"

Tom rose and stepped between his two friends.

"How?" Bo repeated, looking over Tom's shoulder and into the eyes of Ray Ray Pickalew. "*How?*"

"Because I was one of them," Ray Ray said.

71

Seconds after Ray Ray's pronouncement, Sheriff Ennis Petrie and two deputies burst into the judge's chambers. When Ray Ray had begun talking only to Bo, Judge Connelly had pressed the security button. Everyone in the room turned to Ennis, who was looking at Connelly.

"Sheriff, please take Mr. Pickalew into custody and hold him in my clerk's office across the hall."

The sheriff did as he was told, taking Ray Ray by the arm.

"I'm sorry, Bo," Ray Ray said. "I'm so sorry."

As Ray Ray was led out of Connelly's chambers, Bo slowly sank to his seat, his legs wobbly.

"Judge, it would be highly prejudicial and improper to allow Mr. Pickalew to testify in this case," Helen began. "This case is about Andy Walton's murder. Not Roosevelt Haynes. Besides, Mr. Pickalew has rights. He will be confessing to murder."

Connelly leaned back in her chair and rubbed her eyes with her hands. "Son of a . . . *bitch*," she said, shaking her head as if to rid it of the memory of what she had just seen. Her eyes shifted to Tom for a response.

Tom glanced down at Bo, who was clearly in shock. "It is very *ironic*," Tom began, "for General Lewis to be concerned about Mr. Pickalew's *rights*. Based on what Mr. Pickalew has already admitted to all of us here, I do not think he will have any hesitation to testifying on the stand to what he saw . . . and what he did. It is our expectation that such testimony will place Larry Tucker and Dr. George Curtis as participants in the lynching of Roosevelt Haynes. We have already heard testimony from Darla Ford that she informed Larry Tucker that Andy Walton intended to confess to this murder in the two weeks or so before Andy was killed. Mr. Tucker's phone records from the Sundowners show multiple calls to Dr. Curtis in the fourteen days prior to Mr. Walton's murder. Combined with Darla Ford's testimony, Mr. Pickalew's expected testimony will provide a strong motive for either Curtis or Tucker to have committed the murder of Andy Walton."

"Judge, there is not a shred of physical evidence linking Dr. Curtis or Mr. Tucker to this crime. No evidence was found at the scene of the crime implicating either man."

"Your Honor, Larry Tucker's strip club *is the scene of the crime*. How big of a physical link does General Lewis need? Mr. Haynes is on trial for his life. He should be allowed to show an alternative theory for this crime."

Judge Connelly slammed both hands on her desk and abruptly rose to her feet. "I'm going to allow it. The defense is entitled to show evidence of other suspects' motive."

"Your Honor, this witness wasn't disclosed. You should not allow this ambush."

"Mr. McMurtrie, when did you know that Mr. Pickalew would be a witness for the defense?" Connelly asked, turning to Tom.

"A few seconds before my partner called his name. Ray Ray hadn't told us anything."

"Ray Ray is one of Mr. Haynes's lawyers," Helen said, clearly exasperated by this turn of events. "A lawyer should not be allowed to testify in a case where he is also appearing as counsel."

Connelly waved her hand at Helen as if to swat the argument down. "I'm going to allow it. It's relevant to motive, and"—she paused, gazing down at Bo, who still sat shell-shocked in the chair before her—"it's the right thing to do."

72

Helen Lewis walked back into the courtroom in a daze. What in God's name was going on? She could feel the case slipping away. In truth, she had felt it slipping since last night. Since the moment she noticed the portion of the St. Clair Correctional Facility visitor's log she had missed during her first read.

Now, as she swept her eyes over the packed courtroom until they reached the cameras in back, she couldn't escape an inevitable feeling of dread. While Ray Ray Pickalew was sworn in as a witness, the thought that Helen had suppressed since last night came over her like an arctic chill.

I might lose this case.

—

"Would you please state your name for the record?" Rick asked. There had been no discussion about Ray Ray's direct examination when Tom, Bo, and Rick returned to the counsel table. Rick had just plunged in.

Tom was having a hard time keeping his emotions in check—he could literally hear the thudding of his own heartbeat—and he was grateful for his partner's calm. Next to Tom at the defense table, Bo sat in a trancelike state, gazing at Ray Ray as if he were a ghost. *Forty-five years he's waited for this moment,* Tom thought.

"Raymond James Pickalew."

"Mr. Pickalew, were you living in Pulaski, Tennessee in 1966?"

"Yes."

There was a pause, and Tom could tell that Rick was wondering where to go next. He obviously hadn't had time to prepare for this examination.

"Mr. Pickalew, are you aware that the testimony you are about to give may implicate you in a crime?"

"Yes, I am," Ray Ray said.

"Mr. Pickalew . . . were you on Walton Farm in 1966 when Roosevelt Haynes was killed?"

"Objection, Your Honor. Lack of foundation."

"Sustained," Connelly said.

Rick shot a glance at Tom, who mouthed the words he'd taught three generations of trial team students: *"Calm, slow, Andy."*

Rick nodded. "Mr. Pickalew, did you know Roosevelt Haynes?"

Ray Ray nodded. "Not well, but I knew who he was."

"Did you know Andy Walton?"

"Yes."

"How did you know Andy Walton?"

"I first met Andy in 1965. Right after I joined the Tennessee Knights of the Ku Klux Klan."

"How long were you in the Klan?"

"Just over a year. I quit in August 1966."

Rick felt his stomach leap. "Why did you quit?" Out of the corner of his eye, Rick saw Helen Lewis begin to stand, but she only made it halfway to her feet before returning to her seat.

Ray Ray turned his eyes directly to the jury. "I quit after me and nine of my Klan brethren hung Roosevelt Haynes from a tree on Walton Farm."

Rick had thought the courtroom might explode, but it had become dead silent. It was so quiet that Rick could hear the faint hum of the air-conditioning unit kick in from somewhere in the building. He looked to the defense table and watched as his client, Bocephus Aurulius Haynes, slowly rose from his chair, his legs shaking and his arms trembling. Reacting without thinking, Rick walked over to Bo and stood by his side.

"You were there?" Rick asked, returning his attention to the witness stand.

"I was," Ray Ray said. "And I've regretted it every day of my life."

"Mr. Pickalew, how many men were present when Roosevelt Haynes was killed?"

"Ten."

Rick sucked in a breath and glanced down at Tom, who nodded. It was time for the big finish.

"Mr. Pickalew, could you tell the jury who those ten men were?"

Ray Ray nodded, but he did not look at the jury. Instead, he kept his eyes focused on Bo, who remained standing. "Andy Walton was the Imperial Wizard of the Tennessee Chapter. He was our leader, and it was he who organized the mob that night." Ray Ray paused. "Roosevelt's hands were tied behind his back and he was placed on top of a horse. Dr. George Curtis and Larry Tucker held the horse, while Andy wrapped the noose around Roosevelt's neck."

From the jury box Rick heard sniffles. Millie Sanderson was now crying.

"I remember Andy said something right before . . . something about Roosevelt laying hands on Ms. Maggie. Then Roosevelt said something back. Then"—Ray Ray paused and hung his head in shame—"Andy slapped the back end of the horse, and George and Larry let go."

The courtroom had now become a chorus of dismay. From her perch on the front row of the courtroom behind the defense table, Jasmine Haynes unabashedly cried, holding a handkerchief to dab her eyes. Rick felt dampness on his own cheeks as the gravity of the moment sunk in. Forty-five years . . .

"The other seven were Ferriday Montaigne, Samuel Baeder, Bull Campbell, Alvin Jennings, Rudy Snow, myself and"—Ray Ray paused, gazing with blank eyes at the prosecution table—"Ennis Petrie."

There was a collective gasp from the gallery, and Rick turned to look at the prosecution table, where Sheriff Ennis Petrie held his head in his hands. *Unbelievable,* he thought. He turned to Bo, who was likewise gazing at the sheriff in disbelief.

"Your Honor, I have no further que— "

"*Wait.*" Ray Ray's voice shook with emotion as he kept his eyes fixed on Bo. "There's one more thing I need to say."

Bo straightened his back and sucked in his chest as if to steel himself to whatever bombshell Ray Ray was about to hurl now.

Rick knew a speech by the witness was improper, and he expected an objection from the prosecution table. But Helen Lewis remained glued to her chair. "OK, Ray Ray, what do you need to say?"

"On the night of Andy Walton's murder, George Curtis asked me to watch Bo's office. My office is two doors down from Bo's, so I have an unobstructed view. At just before midnight on August 18, 2011, I saw Bo Haynes park his Lexus on the curb on First Street and stumble into his office." Ray Ray paused, looking straight at the jury. "Ten minutes later, while Bo Haynes was still inside his office, I saw another man drive off in Bo's Lexus."

"Who?" Rick asked.

"Dr. George Curtis," Ray Ray said.

73

"Cross-examination, General?" Judge Connelly's voice was somber, as she, like everyone else in the courtroom, was still in shock over Ray Ray Pickalew's testimony.

"No, Your Honor," Helen said, managing to sound calm and collected. "If it pleases the court, the prosecution would ask for a short recess."

Connelly nodded and shot a glance at the witness stand, where Ray Ray Pickalew remained in the chair. "I think that is a good idea, General. I think . . . we could all use a break right now."

As the jury filed out of the courtroom, five sheriff's deputies entered and surrounded the prosecution table.

Judge Connelly addressed one of them. "Deputy Springfield, please take Sheriff Petrie and Mr. Pickalew into custody. And I suspect you will want to dispatch a couple officers to pick up Mr. Tucker and Dr. Curtis."

After two of the deputies led Ennis Petrie out of the courtroom, the deputy strode toward the witness stand. Ray Ray stood and held his hands out as Hank applied the handcuffs.

"Raymond Pickalew," Hank began, looking over at Bo as he continued to talk, "you are under arrest for the murder of Franklin Roosevelt Haynes. You have the right to remain silent . . ."

74

At 4:30 p.m. Judge Connelly called the courtroom back to order. After the jury was seated in their twelve chairs, she cleared her throat and motioned toward the prosecution table. "General Lewis, you said during the break that you would like to file a motion."

Helen Lewis rose to her feet and stood like a statue. "Your Honor, based on new evidence that has just surfaced today, the State of Tennessee hereby moves to dismiss all charges against the defendant, Bocephus Aurulius Haynes."

For a moment a stunned silence enveloped the courtroom. Then several shrieks and one "Hallelujah" came from the gallery. Several members of the print media were already moving toward the double doors. Once they were outside, their laptops and iPads would be out, tweets and blog updates being sent to their hordes of followers. In the front row Maggie Walton sat motionless, gazing into space.

Judge Connelly banged several times on the bench with her gavel. "I'll have order! Order in the court!" After the courtroom had quieted down, Connelly peered down at Helen and nodded.

Then she turned to the defense table. "Will the defendant please rise?"

Tom, Rick, and Bo all stood in unison.

"It is the court's decision to grant the prosecution's motion to dismiss. All charges brought by the State of Tennessee against the defendant, Bocephus Aurulius Haynes, are hereby dismissed with prejudice." Smiling, Judge Connelly looked at Bo. "Mr. Haynes, you are free to go."

75

Bocephus Haynes closed his eyes and let the tears come. He felt hands on his back and looked up into the smiling face of Rick Drake.

"Congratulations, Bo," the boy said, his bloodshot eyes rimmed with tears. "We did it!"

Bo picked his young lawyer off his feet and pounded the lawyer's back until Rick started to cough and both of them began to laugh. "You're all right, Drake. You're my believer."

"Never a doubt," Rick said, wiping his eyes.

Bo turned, searching for Jazz, but the entire courtroom was drowned out by the sight of Booker T. Rowe picking Bo off the ground and hugging him tight.

"So happy for you, cuz," Booker T. said.

Then there was Jazz, smiling through her tears and falling into Bo, letting him hug her and kiss her cheek.

"I'm so sorry, Jazz. I'm so damn sorry. For everything."

"Just shut up and hold me," Jazz said, and Bo did, holding her tight and then embracing T. J. in a three-way hug.

Finally, Bo pulled back from her, and she said the words that Bo was thinking himself. "Where's the Professor?"

Bo turned his head 180 degrees, looking for Tom and initially not seeing him. Then, lowering his eyes to the defense table, he saw his friend.

———

Thomas Jackson McMurtrie sat unmoving in his chair. After Judge Connelly had dismissed the case and told Bo he was free to leave, Tom's legs had given way, and he had almost fallen down into his seat. Now he watched the scene unfolding in front of him like it was a movie. His eyes were moist with tears, but he made no move to wipe them.

"Professor," Bo said, standing above him and gently placing his hand on Tom's shoulder. "Are you OK?"

Tom found he didn't have the words. He gazed up at his friend . . . his best friend . . . but still couldn't say anything. He moved his mouth but no words came.

"We did it," Bo said. "You did it. You saved my life."

Finally, as if he were beginning to come out of a trance, Tom nodded and held his hand out.

Bo took it and leaned over him, grabbing his shoulder and kissing his cheek. "Thank you, Professor."

From behind Bo came Jasmine Haynes, who planted her own kiss on Tom's forehead. "Thank you, Professor. Thank you so much."

Then there was Rick, extending his hand. "We did it, Professor," Rick said.

Coming out of his funk, Tom shook his partner's hand and motioned both him and Bo to come closer. "We need to talk with Ray Ray," he said. Then, holding his eyes on Bo's, "It's not finished yet." He paused and exhaled a ragged breath. "Not all of it."

76

Deputy Hank Springfield led Ray Ray Pickalew down the winding staircase to the lobby floor of the courthouse. Ray Ray's hands were cuffed behind him. On most days the courtroom was empty at 4:45 p.m. Today it was a madhouse, and both the second floor and lobby floor were humming with reporters, spectators, and friends of either Bo or the Waltons. Most of them had either watched Ray Ray's confession live or seen it on television. Questions poured in from every direction. "Why did you wait so long to come forward, Mr. Pickalew?" "Did the state offer you a deal for your testimony?" "Are you still in the Ku Klux Klan?"

Ray Ray ignored all the questions, keeping his head down. He hadn't said a word since Hank had entered Judge Connelly's clerk's office to lead him away.

At the foot of the stairs Hank heard a familiar voice yelling behind him.

"Hank, wait!" Bocephus Haynes shuffled down the stairs, with Rick Drake following behind. The reporters and spectators had crowded around them to the point where movement was becoming difficult.

More questions poured in. "Mr. Haynes, is there anything you'd like to say now that the trial is over?" "Mr. Haynes, do you feel vindicated?" "Mr. Haynes, do you believe Mr. Pickalew's confession to your father's murder?"

At the mention of Ray Ray's name, Bo looked past Hank to Ray Ray, whose hands were cuffed behind his back. Bo stepped forward, his gaze burning into Ray Ray, who lowered his eyes to the ground.

"Why'd you do it, Ray Ray?" Bo asked, leaning toward him so that none of the spectators and reporters could hear him. "Why now?"

"Bo, there is a time and place for those questions," Hank said, beginning to move forward with Ray Ray and motioning for the deputies in front and back to do the same. They walked in what almost looked like a conga line toward the double doors leading out to the west side of the square. "This isn't it."

"Wait," Bo said. "One question, Ray Ray. Right now I have to know."

The deputy in front pushed the doubled doors open, and sunlight poured through the opening. Bo was momentarily blinded and held his arm up to block the sun. He felt a hand on his shoulder.

"Bo, let's go back inside," Rick said. "We can ask him later. It's too crazy out there."

But Bo wasn't listening. He needed to talk with Ray Ray, and he didn't want to wait. He had waited forty-five years, and he would not wait any longer.

He continued to follow Hank, Ray Ray, and the other deputies out the doors of the courthouse.

———

Rick trailed Bo through the doors to the outside, feeling his cell phone rattle in his pocket. He grabbed for it and saw that he had missed eleven text messages. Ten were from Powell. In all the excitement over Ray Ray's testimony, Rick had turned his phone on silent and forgotten to check it.

As he descended the steps, Rick scrolled through them all. The first one read: *Do not exit the courthouse without police protection. Probably nothing, but I think JimBone may be on the square.* All of the others were shortened to: *Don't leave the courthouse without calling me first.*

Damnit, Rick thought, looking up into the bright light and seeing a wave of white-hooded and white-robed Klansmen lining the west side of the square. "Bo, wait!" Rick yelled, but his voice was drowned out by the questions of the reporters closing in around them. The Klansmen, who were being kept at bay by four or five deputies who had cleared a path from the courthouse steps to Hank's squad car, had also begun to hurl expletives and chants of "Murderer" when they recognized Bo.

Pressing forward, Rick tried to catch up.

There were still several reporters in front of him when he heard the first gunshot.

77

A courtroom is an eerie place when a trial is over. In a matter of seconds a room that was filled with energy and people, where life and death hung in the balance, becomes as empty as a vacant lot and as silent as a morgue. In some ways it reminded Tom of the feeling of being on a football field after a game. He had always enjoyed walking the field postgame, looking up at the empty stands and remembering places where key plays had been made. There was a sense of satisfaction, especially after a win, to walk the ground that had just been plowed with competition. Though Tom had never served in the military, he figured it was the same way a general felt when he walked an empty battlefield after the fight was over. *Sacred ground,* Tom thought.

"Professor McMurtrie, OK if I turn off the lights?" The court's bailiff was standing in the doorway to the judge's chambers.

Tom blinked and nodded his head. "Sure, that's fine."

"How about you, General?"

Startled, Tom looked to the prosecution table, but Helen wasn't there.

"Fine, Jerry. Have a nice night."

Tom moved his eyes around the courtroom but still didn't see her.

"In the jury," Helen said, and Tom looked to his right. Focusing his eyes, Tom finally saw his former nemesis. She was sitting in the same chair she'd been in during their first conversation over a month before. She held a white Styrofoam cup in her hand.

Forcing his legs to move, Tom rose from his chair and walked toward her. When he got closer, he saw a pint of Jack Daniel's Black on the floor at Helen's feet and figured it wasn't coffee in the cup.

Helen smacked her lips after taking a sip and smiled at him with tired eyes. "Can I buy you a drink?"

Tom smiled back. "Sounds great."

With some effort Tom walked along the back row and slumped in the chair next to Helen. When he did, she passed over the pint of Jack Daniel's.

"Sorry, no more cups." She shrugged, and Tom twisted off the bottle and took a sip, wrinkling up his face as the hot liquid burned the back of his throat. He gave the bottle to Helen, and she did the same, closing her own eyes as the taste and feel of the sour mash whiskey enveloped her.

"You tried a good case," Tom said.

Helen laughed bitterly. "I lost. That's all that matters."

"We all do," Tom said. "Losing is part of it the same as winning."

"Not for me, Tom. I always win." She gritted her teeth and took another sip from the bottle. *"Always."*

"There's no way you could've known that Dr. Curtis was going to frame Bo for the crime. If Ray Ray would've come forward sooner, you would've charged Curtis and—"

"I'm not sure Curtis did it," Helen said.

Tom took the bottle from her and raised his eyebrows. "How could it not be him?"

"Oh, he's part of it."

"You're saying he had help," Tom offered, nodding his head. "And I would agree with that. At least two people involved . . . maybe three. You thinking Curtis and JimBone Wheeler? Or maybe Curtis, JimBone Wheeler, and Larry Tucker?" Tom paused and took another hit off the bottle. "That might be the most likely."

Helen sighed and slumped even farther in her chair. "Could be, but . . . that's not what I'm thinking." She took the bottle from him and started to take another sip, but then stopped, shaking her head.

"What then?"

"I'd rather not say, Tom. I'm not really sure of it myself, and it could be nothing. But—"

"Come on, spit it out," Tom said. "Now that the charges against Bo have been dropped, I'd like to catch the real killer as much as you would. And I'm sure Bo wants to know who framed him."

Helen finally lifted the bottle to her lips and took a small sip. Then, screwing the top back on, she stood from her chair. "Remember the St. Clair Correctional Facility visitor's log you gave me?"

"Of course," Tom said, also standing.

"Did you read every word of it?" Helen asked, looking down at him.

Tom creased his eyebrows. "Yes. What?"

"Come on," Helen said, waving him toward the prosecution table. "There's something I want to show you."

Tom followed her, thinking again how serene it felt to be in the empty courtroom, sharing a drink with his opponent.

They had not quite made it to the table when they heard the gunshots.

78

Bo caught up to Hank and Ray Ray right before they reached the squad car. The chants coming from the Klansmen on all sides were drowned out by the flashes of photography and the questions from reporters. It was one big hodgepodge of sound, and Bo heard none of it.

"Ray Ray, one question!" Bo screamed, and Hank wheeled on him.

"Bo, so help me God, I'm going to arrest you again if you don't let me do my job."

"Why, Ray Ray?" Bo asked, ignoring the deputy and pushing closer to Ray Ray. "Why did Andy Walton order the hit on my father? You said he laid hands on Ms. Maggie? How?" Bo hurled the questions at Ray Ray one by one, talking loud and fast.

Ray Ray, who up to that point had kept his eyes fixed on the ground, finally raised them to look at Bo.

"*Why?*" Bo pressed. "*Why did the Klan kill my father?*"

Ray Ray pursed his lips as if to speak, and Bo moved even closer to hear. Then Ray Ray's eyes seemed to flicker and move past

Bo. Ray Ray's lips formed the word "no," but Bo heard no sound. Bo started to say something but then felt the air go out of his stomach as Ray Ray lowered his shoulder and plowed into him.

Bo lost his footing and began to fall. He could now hear Ray Ray screaming the word "no" above him.

And before he hit the ground, he heard the deafening sound of gunfire.

79

JimBone Wheeler had changed positions when he saw the squad car pull up to the west side of the square and stop abruptly on the curb. His instincts told him that someone would be coming out of the doors to the west side quickly, and odds were it would be Haynes getting a police escort. He had heard rumblings that the trial had been halted by new evidence. If so, it was possible that the state had finally figured out what happened, and Haynes was going to walk.

Bone gripped the handle of the .38 as he walked at a normal pace around the side of the courthouse. As there were Klansmen in every direction, he knew his movement would be undetected, though it troubled him that he had lost sight of the sandy-haired prosecutor. *Probably went back to Lawrenceburg*, Bone thought, not fretting it too much. He knew their bases were covered tight. Cappy was here on the square, just as would be expected. The Sleepy Head was being covered by Cappy's girlfriend, who had been instructed to say that Cappy was in Pulaski marching with the Klan. And Cappy's Orange Dodge Charger was still parked at the First Church of God and should be empty of any obvious traces of Bone. Even if the prosecutor had an inkling that something wasn't right, there was no trail for him to follow. Finally, and most importantly, Martha was parked a block north of the square in the truck. Once Bone shot Haynes, he'd drop the gun and make a beeline for the truck as pandemonium ensued after the shooting. As everyone should be running to get away from the sound of the shots, he'd blend in with the hundreds of other Klansmen dressed just like him.

When Bone had made it to the west side of the square, he noticed that at least four sheriff's deputies had cleared a path from the top of the stairs to the squad car. Seeming to sense that something was about to happen, numerous television and newspaper reporters had crowded around the steps and just inside the courthouse.

Something is *about to happen,* Bone knew. He had always known when the kill was near. It was a gift. Something he'd had since he first went deer hunting with his father, when he was ten years old. A sixth sense. As if he could smell the blood of his prey.

The doors to the west side of the courthouse flew open. Bone tensed, then immediately began to relax as the movements of the people around him started to slow down. Bone had always figured he would have been a great race car driver, because when everything became very fast for most people, the world slowed down for him, and he was able to see things that most people missed.

Two deputies burst through the doors, first followed by a white man in handcuffs that looked familiar. One of Haynes's lawyers maybe. *What the . . . ?*

Then another sheriff's deputy, whose hand was on the handcuffed lawyer's shoulder and was pushing the prisoner forward toward the squad car.

What the hell is going on? Bone thought. *Where is . . . ?*

There. There he is.

Bone took the pistol out of his pocket as Bocephus Haynes came through the doors right on the heels of the deputy pushing the prisoner.

Bone inched forward to within just a few feet of where the other deputies had blocked the sidewalk. There wasn't much room, but Bone saw an opening. He would have a clear shot if no one got between him and Haynes.

Bone cocked the .38 and sucked in a quick breath, thinking about the moment a year and a half earlier when Bocephus Haynes had cost him a six-figure payday. What had the nigger lawyer said? *Hasn't anyone ever told you not to bring a knife to a gunfight?*

Underneath his hood, Bone smiled as Haynes actually stopped directly in the opening created by the deputies guarding the sidewalk. Haynes was talking to the handcuffed man, and his back was to Bone. His entire back was exposed in the opening.

Now . . .

Bone shuffled forward, moving the gun out from under the robe. The sheriff's deputies also had their backs to him at this moment, looking toward the north side of the square.

Bone brought the gun up and stepped into the opening. He was now just a few feet away from Haynes, with a clear shot.

Though his fellow Klansmen were chanting and reporters were yelling questions, Bone heard nothing. He saw nothing either. Nothing but the back of his target.

Gotcha, Bone thought as he pulled the trigger on the .38.

80

Bone had fired two shots before he realized that the handcuffed lawyer had pushed Haynes out of the way and absorbed both bullets. As the prisoner began to collapse in front of him, Bone pointed the gun at the ground where Haynes had sprawled after being pushed out of the way. The killer started to press the trigger again but felt the wind go out of him as someone's shoulder dug into his lower back. "You son of a bitch!" he heard a voice scream in his ear, but Bone was rolling now. Rolling and coming up to his feet in one motion. Immediately, Bone saw his attacker and instinctively brought his right hand up to fire the .38.

But his hand was empty. The gun was gone. Bone's eyes shot wildly to the ground. *Where is it?*

"I've got your gun, asshole," the sandy-haired prosecutor said. "I picked it up when I went DeMeco Ryans on your ass."

"*You,*" Bone said in disbelief.

"*Me,*" the man said, his voice so loud it rose over the screams of the people, who had fled the moment the gunfire started. "Ambrose

Powell Conrad, assistant district attorney for Tuscaloosa County, *by God*, Alabama."

The prosecutor stepped forward and cocked the pistol at Bone's head.

Bone shuffled backward a few steps, intending to run. He didn't think the prosecutor would shoot him. But when he turned, he looked right into the barrel of another gun.

"Move and I turn your head into a canoe," the man said, and Bone raised his hands, as he saw right off that this man would shoot him.

In his peripheral vision Bone now saw that all of the Giles County sheriff's deputies were kneeling on one knee and pointing their guns at him. If he did anything at this point, it would be an execution.

He felt rough hands grab his own and then the cold steel of handcuffs rolling over his wrists and locking. Bone turned, expecting to see the prosecutor, but instead looking into the crystal-blue eyes of the Sam Elliott look-alike from Destin Harbor.

"Remember me?" the man said, tightening the cuffs and then jerking the hood off of Bone's head.

As he blinked his eyes to adjust to the light, Bone heard an ominous chuckling coming from the ground below him. Then the chuckling rose to loud, wild laughter. Bone looked down, and the handcuffed lawyer was gazing up at him with a crazy grin. If the man's face had been whiter and his lips redder, the grin would give a mind to the Joker from *Batman*. Bone saw blood oozing from the man's midsection from where he had been shot, but the maniac didn't seem to notice. Instead, he gazed up at Bone, laughing hysterically. *"Just like . . ."* More laughter. Then coughing. Then more laughing. *"Scooby Doo."*

81

Bo crawled toward the body of Ray Ray Pickalew, hearing the laughs. The smell of gunpowder was thick in the air, and he coughed as he sucked the scent in. Two sheriff's deputies were leaning over Ray Ray's body, and one of them was screaming into his walkie-talkie for an ambulance.

"Scooby fucking Doo," Ray Ray wailed, grabbing his bleeding midsection. "Only . . . *goddamn* thing Doris watches anymore."

Bo gazed upward from Ray Ray and saw that Powell Conrad and Wade Richey had taken a Klansman into custody. The Klansman's hood had been taken off, and when Bo saw the man's face, a memory came rushing back to him. The man who jumped off the bridge last summer . . .

"Bo . . ."

Bo's eyes immediately shot to Ray Ray as he heard the whimper of a voice. *"Bo, I'm sorry. I . . ."*

Bo looked at the two bullet holes in Ray Ray's stomach and knew his time was short. "Ray Ray," he said. "Please tell me why—"

"I should have spoken sooner. I—"

"Don't worry about that now. I forgive you." Bo was surprised to feel tears welling in his eyes. "*I forgive you, but please . . .*" He leaned as close to Ray Ray as he could and spoke the words directly into the man's ear. "*I have to know why.*"

Ray Ray blinked, and his eyes shot upward, as if he were trying to look at the sky.

"*Stay with me, dog.*" Bo shook Ray Ray by the shoulders. Then he felt his own shoulders being grabbed, and he was being pulled up off his feet. He turned and saw Deputy Hank Springfield.

"The paramedics are here, Bo. Let them do their job."

"He's gonna die!" Bo yelled. "And I've got to know."

"We have to get him to the hospital."

Bo turned and saw Ray Ray being placed on a gurney. He stepped between the EMTs and grabbed Ray Ray by the shirt. "*Ray Ray, tell me.*"

As the EMTs propelled the stretcher forward, Ray Ray Pickalew reached toward Bo and grabbed his hand, pulling him close with an astounding show of strength. "Your daddy's . . . hanging . . . was a present," Ray Ray stuttered.

Bo wrinkled his face in confusion. "What . . . ?"

Ray Ray spat blood out of his mouth and took in a huge breath. Then, turning Bo's head so that he could look him directly in the eye, Raymond "Ray Ray" Pickalew spoke his last words. "*A birthday present.*"

82

George Curtis sat alone in the dark den of his home. His right hand and arm were bleeding from where Matilda had bitten and scratched him. He had euthanized the cat fifteen minutes ago, but in one last show of spirit, Matilda had managed to slice flesh before he could inject the needle.

No matter, George thought, chuckling at the idea of poor old Matilda, who'd never shown a bit of spirit in her life, rearing up to fight just before death swept her away.

Ironic, he knew. But irony was one of his favorite things about life.

George lifted the note he'd written just a few minutes before, reading the words carefully and making sure everything was clear. He knew this was the only way, and, truthfully, he was relieved. He could not have what he wanted in this world. Only glimpses and tastes of it, but never . . . all of it.

He had gotten one last taste today, and the thrill of it had already worn off. Just like it always did. He figured his obsession was probably the way a drug addict felt about crack. In fact, he figured the crack addict had it easy compared to his day-in, day-out torture.

George waited until he heard the sirens outside his house, followed by loud footsteps coming up the front walk and the rustling of more movement around the side of the house. When he heard three swift knocks on the door, he grabbed his Remington shotgun, which he'd had propped beside him on the couch, and clicked the safety off.

Then he paused for two seconds to admire the gun, thinking again of the irony of it all. He was holding the same gun used to kill Andy.

As the front and back doors of George Curtis's home on East Jefferson Street were kicked in, George put the barrel of the shotgun in his mouth. *Sorry to disappoint you, boys,* he thought.

Then he pulled the trigger.

83

Raymond James Pickalew was pronounced dead upon arrival at Hillside Hospital at 5:05 p.m. Tom watched the nurse place the white sheet over Ray Ray's head, thinking how ironic it all was. Ray Ray, who had worn the sheet and hood of the Klan, had revealed the truth behind a four-decade-old murder today. He had figuratively pulled down their sheets and hoods to show everyone the awful, naked truth.

Now, as if to make the circle complete, he was having the sheet pulled back over him.

"God bless, old friend," Tom said, touching the dead man's arm.

Tom walked out of the trauma room in a daze and then down the narrow corridor of the emergency room hallway. He took a seat next to Rick, who was gazing forward with a blank look on his face.

"He's gone," Tom said, his voice low.

Rick gave a quick nod. Then he turned his head to look at Tom. The boy's face was almost ashen. "My ears," he began, his voice shaking, "they're still ringing."

"That's just temporary," Tom said. "It'll go away. Listen . . . why don't you let them check you out here?"

Rick shook his head. "I'll be fine. I just . . ." He sighed, and Tom saw tears forming in the corners of the boy's eyes. "I saw the whole thing. Ray Ray . . . saved Bo's life. He stepped right in front of him."

Tom sighed and put his arm around his partner. "I know, son." Tom started to say more but stopped when he saw two uniformed officers burst through the entrance to the ER. Tom rose to his feet when he recognized Officer Springfield. Before Tom could even say hello, Hank was talking, his voice clipped and edgy.

"Is Bo here?"

Tom shook his head. "No, I—"

"Jazz says that she hasn't seen him since just after the shooting. He walked her and T. J. to his office and then said he was coming over here to check on Ray Ray."

"He was here for a few minutes but left after the doctor said there was no chance to save Ray Ray."

"So Ray Ray's . . ."

"Dead," Tom said. "Pronounced five minutes ago."

Hank rubbed his neck and exhaled. "Professor, did Bo say where he was going?"

"No. I assumed back to the office. Deputy, what's—?"

"We found George Curtis dead on his couch ten minutes ago. Self-inflicted gunshot wound. He left a note confessing to Andy's murder."

"Jesus," Tom said, feeling his legs begin to wobble again.

"Yeah, I know. It's . . . a mess," Hank said, looking down at the floor and shaking his head. "Listen, we haven't been able to locate Larry Tucker yet, and I just want to make sure Bo's in a safe place.

JimBone Wheeler has already taken a shot at him, and if Tucker or someone else is involved they might try to finish it."

Tom took out his cell phone and clicked on Bo's number. Without even ringing, Tom heard Bo's message come across the line: "You've reached Bocephus Haynes. I'm sorry I missed your call. Please leave your name and number, and I will call you back." Tom spoke into the speaker. "Bo, this is Tom. Please call me as soon as you get this message. Thanks, bye." Tom ended the call and looked at Hank.

"Deputy, I know you've probably already thought of this—" Tom started, but Hank's voice cut him off.

"He's not at the clearing. At least not yet. I checked there myself on the way here. He's driving Jazz's Sequoia, and it isn't parked anywhere along 64 near the dirt road turn-in."

"OK, I'll keep trying him on his phone," Tom said, feeling his heart rate quicken. "How about Wheeler? Is he talking?"

"Nothing so far. He's yet to utter a word."

Tom rubbed his chin. "Did Curtis implicate anyone else in his note?"

"No one. In fact, he said the whole thing was a 'solo operation.' That he planned Andy's murder and he pulled the trigger."

"Bullshit," Tom said. "He's covering for someone."

"Agreed," Hank said. "I've known George Curtis all my life, and he was an old-school Southerner. Definitely not a rat." Hank paused and then sucked in a quick breath. "He knew he was about to spend the rest of his life in prison, so he took one for the team."

Tom was nodding along with him. "Makes sense. Helen would have seen to it that he fried for both crimes." At his mention of her name, Tom thought back to his conversation with the prosecutor at the courthouse right before the gunfire erupted on the square. "Is General Lewis down at the station, Deputy?"

Hank let out a low whistling sound. "She was. But when I gave her the news about Curtis . . ." He shook his head.

Tom could only imagine. If Helen could have quickly charged George Curtis for the murders of Roosevelt Haynes and Andy Walton, she might have been able to spin her loss of Bo's murder trial into a long-term victory. Staying the course and brushing herself off from defeat, General Lewis had brought the lynch mob who killed Roosevelt Haynes to justice and solved the Andy Walton murder to boot. Now . . .

"I'm sure she's pretty upset," Tom said, knowing his words were a vast understatement.

"She blew a gasket, Professor. I've never seen the General so angry." Hank started to say more, but the walkie-talkie clipped to his belt sounded off and he grabbed it. "Yeah," he blared into the handheld device. He listened for a few minutes before saying "Ten-four" into the speaker. Then he turned back to the Professor. "We need y'all to come down to the station to fill out statements about the shooting." Hank paused and looked over Tom's shoulder to Rick, who had remained seated in the plastic lobby chair. "He up for it?"

Tom walked over to Rick and kneeled down. "Deputy Springfield needs you to write a statement about what you saw on the square. Can you do that?"

Rick blinked and then he nodded. "Yeah, I think so."

Tom turned back to Hank and gave the thumbs-up sign. "We're right behind you."

"Ten-four," Hank said, walking toward the exit with the other deputy that came in with him right on his heels. At the doors he turned around and looked back at Tom, making the phone symbol with the thumb and pinky finger of his right hand. "Keep trying Bo."

84

As the sun began to set over Walton Farm, Bo pulled into the gravel driveway leading up to the main entrance of the Big House. He pushed the buzzer out in front of the gate and waited.

Bo had spent the last two hours driving the back roads of Pulaski, thinking about what Ray Ray had said. About what it all meant.

Bo pushed the buzzer twice more and put his car in reverse. Just as he started to ease the car backward to leave the driveway, a clipped voice blared out of the speaker adjacent to the buzzer. "Who is it?"

"Bo Haynes, ma'am."

Silence for a good five seconds. Then a faint chuckle. "You have a lot of nerve coming over here. What do you want?"

"To talk, ma'am. Just . . . talk."

More silence. Then Bo was startled by another buzzing sound as the gate slowly began to creak open. Feeling a catch in his throat, Bo hesitated, knowing this was probably a bad idea. Regardless, almost without conscious thought he pressed the accelerator down and eased the vehicle forward. The compulsion to follow Ray Ray out the courthouse doors was moving him forward, and he found himself powerless to stop it. *I have to know . . .*

As the Sequoia wound up the hill, Bo's mind filled with images of the day his father was killed. The day that had haunted every hour of his life since. The cross in the yard. The Klansmen surrounding the house. The smell of burning wood mixed with the fear coming from his father as he kneeled next to Bo and made the boy promise to take care of his momma, to make something of himself and to not believe the reasons given for the murder. Forty-five years . . . Bo had gone to law school ultimately so that he could bring the men who killed his father to justice. He'd practiced in Pulaski these past twenty-five years for the same reason. He'd spoken with every living Klansman in the Tennessee chapter. His obsession in life had been to bring Andy Walton to justice. Andy Walton. The monster who had killed his father and made his mother disappear. *"The monster . . ."*

At the top of the hill the house came into view. As with most things you remember being so huge as a child, the Big House really wasn't so big after all. Sure, it was a two-story rancher—a beautiful old relic of a day gone by—but Bo's house in town probably carried more square footage.

Bo had not been invited to be on Walton soil since he was five years old. Two weeks after the murder and a day after his mother had disappeared, he'd moved in with Aunt Mable and Uncle Booker, who lived in the parish next to Bickland Creek Baptist Church. He had never been invited back.

He opened the car door and walked toward the house, his body fueled by adrenaline. Given what he'd been through that day—the trial and then the shooting—Bo should be exhausted. But he felt nothing, his feet propelled forward by a four-decade-long obsession. *I have to know . . .*

As he trotted up the steps of the porch, Bo saw the note. It was a yellow sticky pressed to the front door. He tore it off and brought it close to his eyes.

"At the clearing. Walk, don't drive."

Bo crumpled the note and swept his eyes over the farm, seeing the orange hue of the sun beginning to descend over the western horizon. It was beautiful, he had to admit, and the memory of other sunsets flooded back to him. His mother and father's house had been on the north side of the farm. "House" was really an overstatement. It had been a two-bedroom shack. Less than a thousand square feet. But for Bo it was home. He remembered his father liked to smoke a pipe and sit in a plastic chair under a tree near the front of the house, watching the sun make its slow descent. Sometimes Bo would stand next to him, asking questions that little boys ask. "Daddy, why does the sun rise and fall? Does it go to sleep at night too?"

Bo wiped a tear from his eye and headed north on foot toward the clearing. It had been forty-five years since he'd walked this farm, but he knew the way. He could find it blindfolded.

I have to know, he told himself. *I have to know . . .*

85

The sheriff's office was a madhouse.

Between the shooting of Ray Ray Pickalew, the arrest of JimBone Wheeler, and the suicide of Dr. George Curtis, the parking lot had become ground zero for a plethora of television and print news reporters, all hoping for more information on any of these events.

Tom and Rick had piled into the back of Deputy Springfield's cruiser at the hospital so as to avoid the hassle of trying to park and wade through the cameras. Hank pulled to the front of the building and whisked them all inside. A few minutes later Rick was in an interrogation room being questioned by one of the younger deputies about what he had seen on the square.

Tom waited in the lobby and continued to try to reach Bo, with no luck. Each call went straight to voice mail. He called Jazz and Booker T., and neither had heard a word from him since just after the shooting. Where the hell could he be? It didn't make sense for Bo to disappear. Unless . . .

Tom gave his head a quick jerk and began to limp around the lobby, his thoughts becoming more and more troubled. Andy Walton was dead. Ray Ray Pickalew was dead. George Curtis was dead. Larry Tucker was missing. Bo was missing.

The doors to the interrogation area flew open, and Deputy Springfield ushered Rick through them, his hand on the boy's arm to steady him. Once Rick was seated, Hank turned to Tom, his eyes burning with intensity. "Any word from Bo?"

Tom shook his head. "Nothing. What about Helen? Have you heard—?"

"No," Hank interrupted. "She left right after we told her about Curtis, and no one has seen her since. Not answering her phone, and not replying to texts." Hank paused and wiped his forehead. "She needs to be here. There's no one better in a crisis than the General."

Tom took a deep breath and tried to calm his mind. *Think, old man.*

Think . . .

86

It took less than ten minutes for Bo to get to the clearing. Though the distance was just over a mile, Bo found himself running most of it, a couple of times stumbling on uneven ground and falling on the dirt road. *I have to know*, he kept telling himself. *I have to know.*

By the time he reached the familiar trail that led to the pond, it was almost dark. Two vehicles were parked side by side at the edge of the trail, and Bo squinted his eyes, trying to focus. One of the vehicles was a Chevy Tahoe, probably silver, though the lack of light made it tough to tell. The other one was a two-cab Chevy Silverado truck. Darker. Probably green. As Bo approached, he saw the shadow of a man in the front cab of the pickup truck. He froze, reaching for his pocket and realizing that he had brought no weapon. Usually, he brought his twelve-gauge or his pistol to the clearing, but the state had seized all of his guns.

Slowly, trying to make as little sound as possible, Bo approached the truck. The driver's-side window was down, and the man behind the wheel was slumped against the center console, his head turned away from Bo. *Asleep?* Bo wondered. The adrenaline that had carried Bo this far had now cranked into overdrive.

Something wasn't right about this scene.

"Hey," Bo said, clearing his throat. Nothing. The man, wearing jeans and a plaid flannel shirt with a ball cap on his head, still leaned away, making no movement at all. Though Bo had yet to see his face, there was something familiar about the man's profile. "Hey," Bo repeated, reaching into the truck and shaking the man's arm. When he did, the man slumped toward him, and Bo saw the face framed below the orange UT ball cap.

Larry Tucker, Bo knew, though the gunshot hole just above the man's right temple made it harder to tell. Dried blood caked the right side of what was left of Larry's face, and he gazed at Bo with dead eyes. "Jesus Christ," Bo whispered, dropping Larry's arm and stumbling backward away from the truck.

"Larry was always such an idiot." The harsh voice came from directly behind Bo, and he fell to the ground as he tried to turn toward it. "I think it was a humanitarian gesture to put him out of his misery."

"Ms. Maggie?" Bo asked, rising to his feet as the voice came closer. It was now pitch dark, and Bo could see nothing but the faint outline of the pine trees above him. Even the stars, it seemed, had stayed away on this dreary night. Bo blinked and took a cautious step forward, squinting in the direction of the voice.

The roaring of a shotgun blast sent him to his knees. Heart pounding and ear drums ringing, he ran his hands along his body, searching for a wound and then looking at his palms for blood.

"You're not hit," the harsh voice said. "Not yet. Now get up and open the back door to Larry's truck, or the next shot goes in your ear."

Bo, still unable to see her, stood on shaky legs and did as he was told. The interior light inside the truck came on, and Bo turned back toward the voice.

Maggie Walton was standing three feet in front of him, pointing the barrel of a twelve-gauge shotgun at Bo's head. "Got your bearings?" she asked him, and Bo, unable to speak, nodded.

"Good. Now walk along the path toward the pond."

When Bo's feet hadn't budged, Ms. Maggie spoke again, her voice devoid of emotion. "Go on now, Bocephus. You came out here to talk, didn't you?"

Again, Bo nodded his head.

"Well, we're going to have our talk by the pond."

Bo tried to move his feet, but they seemed to be stuck in the ground. The adrenaline rush that had carried him to this point was gone. He was so tired.

"Go, Bocephus," Maggie said, her voice softer.

"You're going to kill me too, aren't you?" Bo asked, a rhetorical question given the circumstances.

"Yes, Bo. I am," Maggie said. "But not before I tell you."

"Tell me what?" Bo asked.

In the glow from the interior light in Larry Tucker's pickup, Bo saw Maggie Walton's lips curve into a smile. "Everything."

———

The walk to the pond took less than two minutes, but for Bo it seemed to last two lifetimes. Pictures from his past danced across his mind like reels in an old projector-style movie. Was it possible that he had been wrong about so much for so long? He had seen with his own eyes what had happened at this clearing forty-five years ago. He had recognized Andy Walton's voice. Andy had kicked the horse, and Bo's father's neck had snapped. The Ku Klux Klan, led by Andy Walton, had killed Bo's father, and Bo's mother had left because she did not want to suffer a similar fate. Right?

Bo's arms hung limp at his sides as he walked. He made no move to escape. Truth be known, he didn't want to escape. He wanted to know. *I have to know* . . .

Bo walked to within a few feet of where the water met the rocky sand, and stopped.

"Turn around," Maggie said, and Bo did as he was told.

In the darkness, though she was only three feet away, Maggie looked like a shadow.

"Why did you kill Tucker?" Bo finally asked, unable to shake the image of the dead man with the orange cap and flannel shirt from his mind. He had seen two corpses in the past three hours. Ray Ray Pickalew and now Larry Tucker. *And I'll be the third one,* Bo thought.

"Officially," Maggie began, "Larry Tucker dropped by the farm, saying he wanted to talk about what happened at trial today." Though he couldn't see her face, Bo could tell by Maggie's tone that she was smiling. "I buzzed him to come up and meet me at the clearing, as today is my day to inspect the north half of the farm. When he arrived, he was drunk and belligerent. He said, 'George ruined everything,' and that he needed to find him. When I said I didn't know where George was, he said he was going to kill me. He climbed into his truck to grab his weapon, and I shot him through the open window before he could shoot me."

"That sounds pretty good," Bo said, figuring Maggie could probably sell that story. "What's the unofficial version?"

"George called Larry and asked him to meet him at the clearing. When Larry arrived, he saw me and rolled his window down to talk. Once the window was down, I pointed the barrel of this twelve-gauge at him and blew his brains out."

Bo felt a cold chill on the back of his neck that had nothing to do with the temperature. The matter-of-factness with which Maggie spoke was startling.

"Why?" Bo asked. "Why Tucker?"

She shrugged. "Loose ends. Larry knew too much for his own good, and after Pickalew's testimony today he was going to finish his life in jail. I didn't want him cutting any deals for information with the prosecutors."

"What *information* would he have?"

"I really don't know," Maggie said. "Andy's lips had loosened some in the past few years. Since I didn't know what Larry knew, the safer play was to get rid of him."

"Getting rid of people is one of your specialties, isn't it, Ms. Maggie?"

She stepped closer to him, and now he could see her. Her eyes squinted from behind the barrel of the gun. "Don't get sassy with me, Bocephus. Or I'll put an end to this right now."

"What about Sheriff Petrie?" Bo asked, knowing he had to keep her talking. "He's still around."

"Ennis doesn't know anything. He had just joined the Klan when Roosevelt was lynched."

"What about Ray Ray?" Bo asked. "Why did he testify today? Why did he bring it all down?"

Another pause, and faint moonlight began to emerge through the clouds above. For the first time since reaching the pond, Bo could see Maggie's eyes. She was gazing past Bo as if in thought, holding the gun against her hip. He could probably rush her and get the gun if he was quick enough.

"You know how many rabbits and squirrels I've shot in my life with this gun right on my hip like this here?" It was as if she could read his mind. "Don't even think about it, Bo. Or I'll fill you full of lead before you find out what you've waited your whole life to know."

"Why did Ray Ray spill the beans today?"

"You'd have to ask him," Maggie said. "I suspect it was because he didn't care anymore. Maybe Doris died or was already about dead. I guess we'll never know now, will we?" She smiled, and Bo again felt the chill on the back of his neck.

"That was you?" Bo asked.

She nodded. "I hired a man to kill you, but Ray Ray got in the way."

"JimBone Wheeler," Bo said, feeling weak in the knees.

Maggie again nodded. "Mr. Wheeler was fairly easy to recruit for this job. Apparently, you had a bit of a history with him."

Several seconds went by, and the clouds continued to move out. Light from the crescent-shaped moon shone down on the pond, and Orion became visible above. Bo gazed upward at the constellation, blinking his eyes. *Maggie Walton was behind everything. Maggie was the monster my momma was talking about. Not Andy. Maggie . . .*

"Tell me about Andy's murder. I'm assuming your brother and Wheeler were a part it."

Maggie nodded, her eyes twinkling in the moonlight. "Once I hired Wheeler, I had him tail you for several days. He said you went to Kathy's Tavern every night after work and had several drinks, so I asked Andy to take me there for my birthday. I knew you wouldn't be able to resist confronting Andy if you saw him, and I have to say that you went above and beyond with your 'eye for an eye' bit." She licked her lips. "Of course, I also knew that you would eventually come here to the clearing on the anniversary. Every August 18 you come out here to talk with *your father*." She chuckled. "That's what you do, right? You talk to Roosevelt out here."

"How do you know that?" Bo asked.

"I know everything that ever happens on this farm. And I know *everything* about you, Bo."

"Why?"

"Because you've been a constant thorn in my side your whole life. Like a goddamn zit that won't go away. An itch you can't ever seem to scratch enough."

Bo could hear the hate in her voice. "George took my car after I passed out at the office, right?"

"Correct."

"Then he caught Andy coming out of the Sundowners and shot him when he was in his truck, same as how you just shot Larry. Wheeler's role was to make the anonymous phone call."

Maggie had started shaking her head before Bo had finished. "Wrong. George, God love him, has always been a bit of a wimp when it comes to doing the dirty work that is sometimes required. I was never able to make a man out of him." She paused, smiling. "But he sure knew how to touch a woman. I taught my brother how to do that *very well*. Unfortunately . . . after being with me so much as a boy, he . . . wasn't able to move on to other women." She sighed. "A pity."

Bo flinched. *Incest?*

"But you got the anonymous call part right," Maggie continued. "That was Mr. Wheeler. He was driving up and down Highway 64, hanging tight until we sent word that the deed had been done." She paused. "I called him right after I shot Andy. Told him to wait fifteen minutes and then make the call. That would give me and George enough time to hang the body . . . and set it on fire."

"You shot Andy?" Bo asked, astonished, though he knew he shouldn't be surprised anymore. Hadn't Maggie blown Larry Tucker's face off in just the same way?

"Of course," Maggie said. "I shot him with George's shotgun. Then I fired your gun up in the air twice and left one of the shell casings in the grass under Andy's truck.

"George moved the body in your car so Andy's blood and hair would get spread all over the back cargo area. We knew that the back of the Lexus would show up on the club's surveillance tape, and the tinted windows would make it impossible to see who was inside. So George left the Sundowners in your car and drove the quarter mile here, while I followed behind on foot, making sure I avoided the camera lens. Then"—she pointed at the tree where Bo watched his father hang forty-five years before—"we made the decorations." She paused. "Spick and span. In and out. Andy's dead, and for all the world it looks like you did it."

Bo thought it through for several seconds, still not understanding one part of the scheme. "You really hired a killer like JimBone Wheeler just to tail me for a few days and make an anonymous phone call?"

Maggie slowly shook her head. "No. Though that was a necessary part of the plan to kill Andy and frame you." She paused. "The main reason I hired Wheeler was as an insurance policy in case General Lewis wasn't able to convict you." She sighed. "But I guess I'm going to have to do that myself too. You just can't get good help today, Bo."

Bo couldn't bring himself to say anything as Maggie raised her shotgun and pointed it at Bo.

"I don't think so, Mrs. Walton."

The voice came from behind Bo, but he made no move to look. Instead, he focused on the barrel of the shotgun pointed at his chest. If Maggie lowered the gun in any fashion, he would lunge for it.

"Well, now," Maggie said, continuing to point the shotgun at Bo. "General Lewis . . ."

Helen Lewis moved into the clearing, her pistol pointed at Maggie. As she inched closer, Bo could see her out of his peripheral vision. "Drop the gun, Mrs. Walton," Helen said, continuing to approach forward. "Game's up."

"No one tells me what to do," Maggie said, shooting a glare at Helen while still pointing her gun at Bo.

"Put the gun down *now*, Mrs. Walton, or I'll have no choice but to—"

"You'll have no choice but to *what*?" Maggie asked. "Watch me kill this nigger while you try to shoot me. I have the high ground here, and we both know it."

"Even if you shoot Bo, Mrs. Walton, I'm going to kill you. The endgame is a loss for you."

"You don't have the balls, General. You may be a New Age, do-everything-a-man-can-do bitch, but you don't have it in you to take me on. I *am* this town. *Me*. Maggie Curtis Walton. I've survived the past forty-five years and have gotten through dicier situations than this. I'm going to kill Bo. You're going to miss or just wound me with that flare gun you're holding. And then I'm going to kill you." She nodded. "I can see it now. Bo came out here and tried to kill me. General Lewis came out to try to help, but he killed her, and then in self-defense I killed Bo."

"You always have an angle, don't you, Ms. Maggie?" Bo interjected.

"Always," she said, turning her eyes back to him.

"Why do you hate me so bad?" Bo asked. He knew he had to get her talking again if Helen was to have any chance of disarming her. He had to distract her. "The one thing I still don't understand is your stake in all of this. So Andy confesses, and he goes to jail. Yeah, that's bad and all, but is that enough for you to kill everyone? You wouldn't have gone to jail. And you wouldn't have lost your precious farm." Bo paused, seeing that Maggie was gazing directly at him now.

"Why do you hate me so bad?" Bo repeated the question, his voice beginning to tremble. "Why? Andy killed my father. I had a *reason* to hate him. You got no reason to hate me. Why, Ms. Maggie?"

Bo had forgotten about Helen Lewis. He had forgotten about the gun Maggie Walton was pointing at him. *I have to know . . .*

"Roosevelt threatened my family. That is something that you *do not do*."

"How? How could my daddy threaten you? Sitting in your big house on the hill. How could a damn field hand threaten you?"

"He threatened me with *you*, Bocephus," Maggie hissed. Then without hesitation she lowered the barrel of the gun and fired it.

Bo's left kneecap exploded with pain, and he crumpled to the ground. As he did, he saw Helen Lewis fire her pistol. Helen's shot hit Maggie in the shoulder, and she staggered backwards. The next bullet hit Maggie in the stomach, and she lowered the shotgun to her hip, her legs wobbling. She looked like she was about to fall, and Helen lowered her weapon slightly, glancing at Bo. "Are you all—?"

"No, General!" Bo screamed, but he was too late.

Maggie Walton fired the shotgun from her hip, and the district attorney general went down. Helen landed on her back and rolled over on her stomach. Then she stopped moving.

Dead, Bo thought, cradling his destroyed knee in his arms. *Another casualty.*

"I hate to say I told you so," Maggie said, chuckling. "That bitch didn't have it in her to take me out."

Bo stared at her. Maggie's white blouse was now stained red on both collarbones, but she was still alive. And she still had the gun.

Gritting his teeth against the pain and placing all of his weight on his right leg, Bo managed to stand. "How could my daddy threaten you with *me*?" he spat.

Maggie Walton took two steps toward Bo and put the barrel of the gun against Bo's forehead. Hate shone in her eyes as she spat the words out. *"Because he wasn't your daddy."*

Bo blinked, and his right leg buckled. He fell to his knees and looked down at the brown sand, then back up at Maggie Walton. "What?"

"Roosevelt wasn't your father. He married Pearl a few months *after* she got pregnant with you." Maggie paused, lowering her voice to just above a whisper. "Truth is, Bo, you've *hated* your real daddy all your life."

Bo raised his eyes from the sand, the truth finally dawning on him. "No," he whispered.

"*Yes,*" Maggie spat. "*Your daddy was my husband.* Andrew Davis Walton. Imperial Wizard of the Tennessee Knights of the Ku Klux Klan. Andy had an affair with your momma, and *you* were the result. You ask me why I hate you. I've wanted you dead from the moment you breathed air."

Despite the unbearable pain in his kneecap, Bo felt numb all over. His arms hung limp from his sides as he stared up at Maggie Walton. "Why didn't you have me killed as a baby then?"

"*Because your daddy wouldn't let me,*" Maggie said, her teeth clinched together in anger. "Andy owned up to what he had done, but he would not kill his own son." Maggie laughed, but the bitterness in the sound was palpable. "How's that for irony? You have hated Andy Walton your whole life, and he is the only reason you have lived as long as you have. The minute I put Andy out of his misery, I began to plan your death. At first I wanted the state to do it. I would have gotten so much satisfaction out of watching you put to death for the murder of your own father. But Helen couldn't get it done, and Ray Ray stopped my hired gun from doing it, so now I guess I'm just going to have to do it myself."

She took a step back and raised the shotgun at him.

"Why did Andy kill Da—?" Bo paused, closing his eyes. "Roosevelt?" he corrected himself. "Why did Andy kill Roosevelt?"

"Roosevelt came up to the house and said he wanted money for your upbringing. Said it wasn't fair for the son of Andy Walton to be brought up dirt poor, and that everyone was going to know the truth if we didn't start giving them a stipend." She paused. "Greedy meddling nigger. I told Andy that he had to get rid of

Roosevelt, and that he could think of it as a birthday present to me." She shrugged, squinting at Bo. "Truth was Andy was glad to kill Roosevelt. What bothered him was that *you* saw. Can you believe that? He was *worried* about you."

Bo looked up at Maggie Walton. He was beginning to get dizzy, and he blinked his eyes. He was bleeding profusely from his kneecap, and he figured he was about to pass out from blood loss.

"My momma?" Bo asked. "What happened to my momma?"

Maggie squinted at him and lowered her voice to just above a whisper. "She's right behind you, Bocephus."

Bo wrinkled his face in confusion and turned his head toward the pond.

"Andy was so upset when he learned that I killed his nigger whore," Maggie continued, her voice even softer. "I stabbed her with a butcher knife. Then I took her body down to one of Andy's lumber yards and had her corpse incinerated." She paused. "I spread her ashes on the pond behind you."

Bo closed his eyes. His momma hadn't left him. She hadn't disappeared. The monster had killed her too.

He had no further questions.

"You spent your whole life chasing revenge against Andy," Maggie said, raising her voice.

Bo knew he was about to die. He kept his eyes closed and thought about Jazz. And T. J. and Lila. His own upbringing had been a lie, but theirs had not been. They were real. *And they'll be better off without me*, he thought.

"And I've spent my whole life wanting revenge on you," Maggie continued.

Bo forced himself to open his eyes. He turned his head and gazed up at Maggie Walton as she set the shotgun against her shoulder and squinted at Bo.

"I win," she said, pulling the trigger.

Bo's right shoulder erupted in pain as the buckshot entered just above the rotator cuff. As he began to sprawl backward into the pond, three more shots rang out, the last of which was deafening.

Bo closed his eyes, thinking it was only right for him to die here. In the same place where his mother's ashes were spread. Near the tree where the only father he had ever known was lynched.

As his body began to slide into the pond, Bo lifted his head and gazed at the monster who had destroyed his life, expecting that the last thing he would see would be her smiling, satisfied face. But Maggie Walton was no longer standing.

She was lying facedown in the sand. Dead. Her chest was bleeding, and the right side of her face, the side that Bo could see, was all but gone.

Bo dug his hands into the pond's sandy bottom, trying to stop his momentum. His eyes shot to the left, and he saw District Attorney General Helen Lewis crouched on one knee, pointing her pistol at the spot where Maggie Walton had been standing. But Helen's eyes were not on Maggie. They were gazing at a spot behind her at the edge of the clearing. Bo followed her gaze, and his chest heaved when he saw the object of her focus.

Standing under the same tree where Roosevelt Haynes had been lynched in 1966 was an old man holding a Remington .30-06 deer rifle.

"Professor," Bo cried.

Then everything went dark as Bo's head dipped below the surface of the water.

EPILOGUE

Three weeks after the close of the trial of Bocephus Haynes, Rick Drake parked his Saturn on a curb next to the Maplewood Cemetery in Pulaski. Once he had turned the ignition off, Rick turned to his passenger. "We're here, Professor."

Thomas Jackson McMurtrie opened his eyes and rubbed them with the knuckles of his right hand. He had slept for most of the way from Tuscaloosa.

"Sure you're up for this?" Rick asked.

Tom waved him off and opened the door. It was now early November in Pulaski, and the leaves on the trees in the cemetery were an array of yellow, brown, and orange. *Beautiful,* Tom thought as he breathed in the fresh air. The temperature was just over fifty degrees, but the sun was high in the sky, and Tom felt its warmth on the back of his neck. Gazing upward toward the cemetery, Tom was glad they had waited. Having the funeral right after the shooting would have been a circus. His friend deserved a better send-off than that. He had lived a tortured life. Tom would see to it that his burial was as smooth as it could be.

Tom and Rick walked up the hill, both holding small bouquets of flowers. As they passed the rows of headstones, Tom felt the depression that always set in when he went to pay his respects to a departed comrade. He knew it wouldn't be too long before he was underneath one of these blocks of concrete, his bones decaying while his spirit hopefully ascended into heaven.

As they approached the tent under which the small ceremony would be held, it was hard not to think about the people he had loved who were now gone. His mother and father, whose lessons still shaped his life even now. His beautiful Julie, the one true love of his life. Coach Bryant, his teacher and mentor. And his fallen teammate, Pat Trammell, who had died too damn young from cancer. Tom wiped his eyes as he followed Rick into the tent. The mahogany casket had been placed at the far end of the tent, and a man wearing a black smock was standing beside it. Tom approached the coffin and placed the bouquet of flowers at the foot of it. Then, putting his hand on the casket, Tom closed his eyes and said a silent prayer. When he opened them, he noticed that another guest had entered the tent and was heading his way.

Helen Evangeline Lewis had a cast covering her left shoulder, which was black to match her black skirt, black blouse, and black hair. She smiled at Tom and put her own bouquet of flowers on top of those left by Tom and Rick.

"How are you?" Tom asked, kissing her cheek.

"Better," Helen said. "I'd be dead if it wasn't for you."

Helen had been shot in the left shoulder, just above the heart. The shell fired by Maggie Walton had missed killing her by inches. She had fallen over on her stomach and played dead until she sensed that Maggie was about to shoot Bo. Despite her dizziness from blood loss, Helen, using the skills she had learned from her early days as a police officer, had pushed herself up and turned to where her right knee was braced on the ground and her left knee was in a squat. She brought the pistol up and fired just before

Maggie Walton pulled the trigger on her shotgun. Helen's shot caught Maggie in the neck just as Maggie fired her weapon, and the shell intended for Bo's forehead caught him in the right shoulder.

Maggie had wheeled toward Helen, and Helen had fired again, catching the crazed woman in the chest this time. It was her last bullet, and it wouldn't have been enough. Despite her wounds, Maggie was able to point her gun at Helen.

But she never got another shot off. Helen watched in horror as the right side of Maggie Walton's face was ripped off her head with the force from the rifle. The sound of the blast was so loud that Helen could hear nothing for several seconds afterwards. She had turned to her right and stared at Tom, who had started to say something to her when she had passed out.

When her eyes had opened again, she was in a dark hospital room, and Tom was sitting in the corner. They had spoken for several minutes before Deputy Springfield had entered the room to question Helen on the events at the clearing.

They had not seen each other again until now. As they sat down in the plastic seats, Helen elbowed Tom softly under the rib cage. "Why didn't you come back to see me?"

Tom smiled at her. "You needed your rest, and . . ." He paused, sighing and gesturing toward the coffin. "I had some things I had to do."

She nodded and then gave her head a quick jerk. "Such a shame," she said. "Such a damn shame." Then, cocking her head at him, she leaned toward his neck and whispered, "You never told me how you figured it out."

Tom smiled and whispered back into her ear. "When you weren't at the station after Curtis's suicide, I started thinking about where you could be. I remembered what we had been talking about before Ray Ray's death, and I found the visitation log in my briefcase." He paused. "This time I read every word."

She smiled. "You saw?"

Tom nodded. "On August 11, 2011, Andy Walton came to visit Jack Willistone at the St. Clair Correctional Facility. *Mrs.* Andy Walton. We had never paid any attention to the title column, only focusing on the name. Since the signature looked the same as the other times Andy had visited Jack, it didn't even register to check the title column." He paused, shaking his head. "But there it was. On all the prior visits, the title read 'Mr.' This time it read 'Mrs.', though the writing was a bit of a scribble, and the *s* on the end was hard to see because it ran up against the black column line."

"But if you look hard, you can tell," Helen offered.

"You can," Tom said. "I'd say I can't believe I missed it, but actually I can totally believe I missed it. The signature was spot-on. Frankly, I can't believe that you caught it."

Helen smiled again. "You have to remember that I have lived in this town for two decades. Andy Walton hadn't written a personal check in years. Like a lot of wives, Mrs. Walton had learned to forge his signature on things. Hell, she probably could write like him better than he could. And as a woman of the old South, it wasn't entirely unusual for her to call herself 'Mrs. Andy Walton.'"

Tom shook his head. "We spoke with Jack Willistone again, and he confirmed that it was Maggie who came to see him, though he said he *couldn't remember* what they had discussed." He paused. "Jack had told us when we went to see him in prison that the answer we were looking for was right under our nose."

"And he was right," Helen said. "*Mrs.* Andy Walton visited Jack Willistone on August 11, and he gave her JimBone Wheeler's name and contact information. We never got to the specifics, but Maggie admitted that she was the one who hired Wheeler at the clearing. And the visitation log was the tell."

"What's the latest with Wheeler?" Tom asked.

"We're going to keep him here for now, and I think that's where he'll stay. We have him dead-to-rights guilty for the murder of Ray

Ray—there are six eyewitnesses—and with Booher coming forward, we also have him for the attack on you."

"Booher turned herself in?"

Helen nodded. "Two days after Wheeler's arrest, she walked into the sheriff's office. Wheeler had given her an exit strategy if he was caught—she was supposed to go to the Caymans with a fake passport—but she didn't want it. Said she didn't want to run. She gave us enough information to nail Cappy Limbaugh, the hotel owner in Lawrenceburg, on a conspiracy to commit murder charge. She'll do some time—probably two years—but she should be out on parole before she's fifty."

"A good deal," Tom agreed. "What about Sheriff Petrie?"

Helen grimaced. "He's pled guilty and is awaiting sentencing. I suspect he'll spend the rest of his life in prison." She started to say more, but the preacher raised up his hands and spoke in a loud authoritative voice. "Let us pray."

Tom bowed his head.

"We come here today not to mourn a death but to celebrate a life well lived," the minister began, his voice rising so it would reach the back of the tent. "To celebrate the life of a man who lived in this town amongst us almost all of his years on earth. A man who everyone in this tent knew and loved. We come today to celebrate the life of . . ."

Tom closed his eyes, thinking of his tortured friend.

". . . Raymond James Pickalew."

—

". . . and we ask, dear Lord, that you wrap the spirit of Ray Ray into your loving arms so that he may know the eternal life promised through your son, Christ Jesus. Amen."

Tom opened his eyes and glanced to his right. Helen gazed forward at the casket, also lost in thought. To his left, Rick Drake's eyes were moist with tears. Rick had grown fond of Ray Ray during the trial and had watched him die from just two feet away. He was still having frequent nightmares. Behind them in the second row of chairs were a couple of folks from the nursing home where Ray Ray's wife, Doris, was a resident, including Jennifer Eisel, Doris's regular nurse. It had been decided by the nursing staff and Tom that Doris, who was in the last stages of Alzheimer's, should not attend the funeral, as it would only serve to upset her. Also seated, but without showing her customary cleavage, was Ray Ray's red-headed secretary, Bonnie. To Tom's knowledge, Ray Ray had no family who weren't deceased, and Doris's only living relative, a cousin in Maryland, had decided not to come.

Tom started to turn back around when he noticed movement coming from the back of the tent. Two men were walking underneath. One was a lanky teenager whom Tom remembered from the trial. Next to the teen, another man held two crutches and propelled himself forward, his forehead gleaming with sweat from the effort it had taken to climb the hill.

Without thinking, Tom rose and walked toward the man. "You OK?" Tom whispered.

Bocephus Aurulius Haynes gave a weary smile and winked at Tom. "Never better."

"At this time," the preacher bellowed from the front of the tent, "one of Mr. Pickalew's friends would like to say a few words." He paused. "Mr. Haynes . . ."

"Let me past now, Professor," Bo said, and placed the crutches out in front of him, gracefully maneuvering the final ten feet to the front of the tent. T. J. walked with him and took the crutches from Bo, while Tom stayed glued to his spot in the back of the tent. He couldn't believe Bo had made it. His kneecap was basically permanently ruined from the force of the shotgun blast, and the second shot had broken his collarbone. But despite his obvious pain, Bo was here.

"Thank you, Reverend," Bo said. Tom noticed that everyone under the tent was now standing. Bo cleared his throat. "Ray Ray Pickalew was not my friend. He . . . was a flawed man and did some bad things in his life. But . . . I owe this man something, and I wasn't able to tell him before he died, so I'll tell him now." Bo paused. "I spent forty-five years of my life chasing the truth behind something I saw when I was a little boy. Ray Ray, for all his warts, told that truth. If Ray Ray Pickalew hadn't have come forward with the truth when he did, I probably would be in jail. Then if that weren't enough, he took two bullets meant for me. But for Ray Ray Pickalew I'd either be in a jail cell for a crime I didn't commit . . . or I'd be in this coffin." Bo paused and looked at the casket, placing a hand on top of it. T. J. grabbed him under his other arm to keep him from falling.

"Thank you, Ray . . . Ray," Bo said, his voice trembling with emotion. "Thank you."

———

They said their good-byes at the Saturn. Bo gave Rick a bear hug and gripped him around the neck.

"You're still my believer, kid," Bo said. *"My believer."*

"You know it, dog," Rick managed, wiping tears from his eyes as they both laughed.

After shaking Bo's hand, Rick climbed into the car and turned on the ignition.

As the Saturn coughed to life, Bo, using the hood of the car as a prop, walked around the vehicle to Tom. The two men gazed at each other for several seconds before Bo leaned in and gave Tom a hug. "You saved my life, Professor," Bo said.

"You saved mine last year," Tom said, feeling the heat behind his eyes. "I think we're even now."

For a moment neither man spoke. Then Tom put his hand on Bo's forearm. "Are you OK?"

"Yeah, I'm fine. The shoulder is still a little sore, and I'm probably going to be walking with a slight limp the rest of my life. But—"

"That's not what I mean, Bo. Are you . . . *all right?* I mean—"

"I know what you mean," Bo said, gazing off at the cemetery. The sun had begun its descent in the west, framing the graveyard with an orangish-red hue. "Truth?" Bo asked.

Tom nodded. "Truth."

"Truth is I don't know," Bo said. "I'm"—he sighed and shook his head—"a little messed up by it all."

"How are things with Jazz?"

Again, Bo sighed. "Complicated," he said.

"She loves you, Bo. You know that."

Bo nodded. "I know. There's just . . . a lot of water under the bridge."

"What about . . . what you learned about your father? Have you come to grips with that?"

Bo blinked his eyes and looked at the pavement as T. J. pulled the Sequoia to a stop next to them. "Ready, Dad?"

"Yeah, son."

Then, turning to Tom, he shook his head. "I don't know if I'll ever come to grips with that, Professor. It's just . . . impossible to really comprehend. But I'll . . . tell . . . you this." His voice now shook with emotion. "Since I was in law school, there's only been one man in my life that I've looked to as a father." Bo paused, the tears now flowing down his dark cheeks. "I named my boy after him."

Not knowing what to say and feeling his own eyes growing wet, Tom turned his eyes to the young man behind the wheel of the Sequoia and nodded. Thomas Jackson "T. J." Haynes smiled and nodded back.

"You finished it, Bo," Tom said, turning and embracing his friend. *"You finished it."*

Tom opened the door to Rick's Saturn and climbed inside. He rolled the window down and yelled up at Bo, who had grabbed his crutches and taken a few steps backward. "So when are you going back to work?"

Bocephus Haynes smiled. "Tomorrow, dog."

"Tomorrow?" Tom yelled as the Saturn edged forward. Tom saw Bo nod, and then just as the car moved out of earshot Tom heard the familiar words.

"Wide ass open."

ACKNOWLEDGMENTS

I outkicked my coverage when I married the beautiful Dixie Dale Davis fourteen years ago, and I've been counting my lucky stars ever since. Dixie has been my rock along this writing journey, as well as a tremendous sounding board for storylines, characters, and ideas. I am so blessed to be able to share this adventure with her.

Our children—Jimmy, Bobby, and Allie—are my greatest joy. They inspire and teach me every day, and I'm so proud of them.

My parents, Randy and Beth Bailey, have helped in too many ways to count. My dad is a gifted storyteller in his own right, providing valuable feedback, and my mom, a retired schoolteacher, is a meticulous proofreader. Whenever I've needed something along this journey, the answer from Mom and Dad has been a resounding "yes." There aren't enough words to describe how much they mean to me.

My agent, Liza Fleissig, is a force of nature, and her dogged persistence is what every writer wishes for in an agent. I am so grateful for Liza and the entire LRA family.

Thanks to my editors, Kjersti Egerdahl and Clarence Haynes, for their ideas, insights, and expertise. Special thanks also to Alan Turkus, Jacque Ben-Zekry, Tiffany Pokorny, and my entire team at Thomas & Mercer.

A big thank-you to Julie Schoerke, Marissa Curnette, and everyone at JKS Communications for the wonderful publicity they've generated for my work.

A huge shout-out to my friends Bill and Melanie Fowler, Rick Onkey, Mark Wittschen, Steve Shames, and Will Powell for reading a draft of the manuscript and sharing their ideas and encouragement.

My father-in-law, Dr. Jim Davis, provided an early read of the story, and his infectious positive energy has been a blessing. Doc and his wife, Janie, have also done much to promote my books.

My mother-in-law, Beverly Baca, has contributed countless hours to helping me and Dixie during this journey. Bev and her husband, Jerry, have given so much of their time and energy to assist us.

My brother, Bo Bailey, and his wife, Amy, have been great supporters and promoters of my dream.

I am grateful for my sisters-in law, Christi Davis League and Denise Davis Burroughs, who have lent their time and energy to attend and promote numerous book events.

My friend and fellow attorney Tom Castelli provided a tutorial on Tennessee criminal law procedure, which for an Alabama lawyer like me was invaluable.

Pulaski residents Chris McGill and Willa Lamb spoke with me about the town's history and famous landmarks, which was a huge help in the writing of this story.

Joe and Foncie Bullard from Point Clear, Alabama have been amazing friends and supporters of my writing career, and I'm so grateful for them.

Finally, a special thanks to everyone at my law firm, Lanier Ford Shaver & Payne PC.

ABOUT THE AUTHOR

Robert Bailey's bestselling debut novel, *The Professor*, won the 2014 Beverly Hills Book Award for legal thriller of the year. His work in the legal fiction genre was praised—alongside Harper Lee's and Michael Connelly's—in the spring 2015 issue of *Alabama Alumni Magazine*. *Between Black and White* is the sequel to *The Professor* and is the second novel in the McMurtrie and Drake legal thriller series. For the past sixteen years, Bailey has been a civil defense trial lawyer in his hometown of Huntsville, Alabama, where he lives with his wife and three children. For more information, please visit www.robertbaileybooks.com.